Nightrealm
Pathways to Oblivion

I0617868

Alexander Z. Kautz

Ahead of the Press Publishing
St. Louis, Missouri

Library of Congress Cataloguing-in-Publication Data

Nightrealm Pathways to Oblivion Alexander Z. Kautz
ISBN   EPUB   978-1-945594-90-8   (eBook)
ISBN   KINDLE Mobi   978-1-945594-91-5   (eBook)
ISBN   PAPERBACK   978-1-945594-92-2

Manufactured in the United States of America
Ahead of the Press Publishing
St. Louis, Missouri

Table of Contents

ACKNOWLEDGMENTS

First and foremost I would like to personally thank the reader. All art and literature is derived through inspiration but without someone to share that magic it's meaningless. From the very bottom of my heart, I thank you, friend.

I would like to gratefully acknowledge, Scott and Carrie Dayment, Richard Brent MacDonald, James Stewart, Kagome L. Dirksmeyer, James Barrie Benz, and Kenneth John MacDonald.

Honorable mention is also given to the use of, The Ventures, Fear, (Main Title from "One Step Beyond") (1963), The Ventures, "Out of Limits" (1963), Patsy Cline, "Walkin' After Midnight" (1957), Nellie Elizabeth "Irish" McCalla, Sheena Queen of the Jungle (1955), Sir, James George Frazer, Golden Bough (1890), Nicholas Remy, Demonolatry, France (1595), Heinrich Kramer and James Sprenger, Malleus Maleficarum, Speyer, Germany (1487), Francesco Maria Guazzo, Compendium Maleficarum, Milan, Italy (1608), Alexander Jackson Davis and Andrew Jackson Downing, Bram Stoker, Dracula (1897), Mary Shelley, Frankenstein (1818), Edgar Allan Poe, Lord George Gordon Byron, Percy Shelley, Sir Arthur Conan Doyle, Jules Verne.

Few words could ever hope to express my endless gratitude to dear friends and Publishers, S.L. Kotar, J.E. Gessler, and Amy Zimmerman. For whom without, none of this would have been made possible.

Sincerely,
Alexander Z. Kautz

In loving memory of Carrie Francis Dayment, (Nov 29, 1958 – April 12, 2008)

CHAPTER ONE

Thursday October 5, 1972
4:36 p.m.

The winding two lane highway through the *Fraser Canyon* was dangerous at the best of times, but often deadly at night. In less than four years eighteen people had died on that stretch of road, and yet here I was again… It was dark, I was caught in a torrential downpour, and a sudden flash of lightning left me momentarily blinded. I'd picked a bad night to go anywhere. The ascent was steep, a sheer cliff stood at my right, and there was a sudden drop on my left into the raging waters of the Fraser River. The department of highways had placed a cement barrier there, but it was low and almost invisible through the heavy fog. Sometimes I really had to question my sanity…

"Slow and steady, old girl--," Affectionately patting the dash of my triple black, nineteen-seventy-two, Eldorado convertible, I smiled, and said, "We're almost there. Liz. Let's not ruin a perfect relationship—especially out here…"

The car had caught my eye while passing a North Vancouver GM dealership one afternoon. Coincidentally, it also happened to be my birthday and considering it 'kismet' just couldn't resist a deal. It was the last black convertible on the lot and being a sucker for Eldorado's, I just had to have it. Sometimes I missed the old Cougar XR7 convertible that had gone in partial trade, but not tonight… The heavy, front-wheel drive Cadillac was far safer in bad weather and old roads.

Pulling a newspaper article from the glove compartment, I slowed for a sharp turn while reading aloud, "Duff Glenn, McCreary estate to be demolished." Looking at the photograph of the old mansion I couldn't help but smile. It was a Victorian monstrosity in the middle of nowhere, and the thought warmed my dark, little heart. Folding and shoving the page back into the compartment, I was confident that I was on the right trail. In my mind it was the perfect vacation place for a ghost, ghoul, or vampire. In fact, I had even taken the time to look up the translation and meaning of 'Duff Glenn'. It was derived from the *Gaelic dubh* and *gleann* which literally translated as 'dark valley.' It made perfect sense, as according to the article, the manor rested on the dark side of the opposing mountain. This hindsight of the contractors had doomed the McCreary estate to rest within endless shadow. I couldn't help but chuckle with the thought. Not for the misfortune of the family, but my own luck in the matter. Quite honestly, I was worse than any ghost, ghoul, or vampire out there. I was an author of horror and would stop at nothing to find inspiration for a good story.

Single and living alone, my home was a rather large Victorian mansion in North Vancouver. I spent the majority of my time writing, and the rest while chasing things that went 'bump in the night.' The manor, property, and large inheritance had been left to me by a very old and dear friend. It was entirely due to him that I could accommodate this lackadaisical and often unusual lifestyle. Bless his heart, wherever he may be… Officially, I worked for Dave Wolff, the owner and publisher of 'Sinister Dreams' Magazine. It dealt exclusively in subjects of the paranormal, occult, ghosts, and extraterrestrials. This included alien abduction, conspiracy theories, and a fiction column that my stories haunted more often than not. Sadly, Dave had recently decided to give up the ghost where the magazine was concerned. Left without a creative outlet, I was soon adopted by friend and Publisher, Ted Cowan. In fact, he was the sole reason that I was out on that dark highway in the first place… Shooting off my 'big mouth' as always, and upset about poor Dave, Ted had confronted me on the subject of books and publishing. At the time it really hadn't occurred to me. I had it pretty easy writing short stories for 'Sinister Mind.' There was never any pressure, and if I didn't make the deadline, dear old Dave would just smile, and say, "No trouble—there's always the next issue." It began as something I had said as a joke and then Ted had asked if I would consider writing a novel. Once again, and with my mouth preceding my mind, I just spat out the words, "Of course I could do that. There's nothing to it really—just a few extra words."

A few days later a contract was signed and I was panicking to find the inspiration for my first book. The rest as they say was history… It took six weeks to find the story about the House of McCreary. I must have combed through every occult magazine and newspaper article across Canada. Then I found her… Caitlin McCreary was the sole heir to the McCreary estate. She was a descendant from a family of Irish and Scottish merchants who were renowned in the shipping industry. Trafficking in precious stones, linens, and fine furnishing, they had acquired something of a notorious reputation. If experience had taught me anything, it was that every old family had a few skeletons in its closets. Desperate for material, they were bones that I wouldn't mind rattling in the name of a good story.

Contacting her through the Realty Company that had already bought the property, I explained my intentions, and inquired about a short visit. At first, she had openly denied the request. This was mainly because of her concern for my well-being due to the dilapidated condition of the house and property. In the end, I had to agree to sign a waiver just to convince her. This released them from all and any obligation, and bought me a one way ticket into the house of McCreary. In that moment, I couldn't possibly have been happier. Not even the rain and fog on that dark road could keep me away…

The old stretch of highway between the little towns of 'Hope' and 'Ashcroft' had always bothered me. Passing Hope, the Trans-Canada highway entered the wilds and was soon surrounded on either side by a dismal swamp. It was a frightening place even during the day. Utterly silent, the pale and decaying remnants of ancient trees lingered like wraiths in the black and murky waters. The Trans-Canada Highway or 'Number One' as most knew it was an absolutely beautiful and scenic highway on a warm summer afternoon. Yet, given the right conditions, quickly became "Jekyll & Hyde." There were wreathes and white crosses bearing the pictures of the victims for almost sixty miles… I had to look away in most cases as many were hardly even teenagers. The weather conditions and potential for falling rock was bad enough, but there was also the wildlife to consider. It wasn't unusual for a deer to leap from out of nowhere or Moose to suddenly appear. There was a concern about other motorists, hikers, and especially freight trucks. During the day it wasn't too bad, but at night it was a different story altogether. Truck driver's often and carelessly traveled into oncoming lanes while navigating sharp corners at high speeds. I had my fair share of 'hair-raisers' due to these, eighteen-wheeler, Evil Knievel's.'

Needless to say, I had developed a healthy respect for narrow 'two lane' roads through the canyon. The journey continued through the Coastal Mountains and along the Thompson and Fraser Rivers. High in the canyon, I drove through long tunnels bored through the face of the rocky cliffs. Descending from the mountains I was pursued by unrelenting rains, blinding fog, and sudden darkness. Adjusting the intermittent wipers to a higher speed, I squinted while struggling to see out the windshield. It was like looking through the waves of a fast running river...

"So that's what they mean by 'white knuckled' driving?" I took notice of my pale fingers upon the steering wheel, and said, "They must have been driving this road when they coined that term."

Lightning suddenly flashed, blinding me as thunder echoed through the deep canyon. For an instant, I thought to have seen something gazing back from out of the jagged rock face. It was the curse of an over-active imagination. Or at least that's what I kept telling myself...

Without a radio signal in that wild area of the country I was thankful for the factory optional, eight-track, player. I hated clutter and especially when it came to cars. For this reason, I only carried one cassette at a time and it played continuously. In this case it was 'Ventures in Space' and I was listening to the haunting surf beat of 'Fear.' It was the main title from a show called, 'One Step Beyond.' I loved the band and the program, so this album was one of my favorites.

"Now where do I start? At the beginning, of course..." Speaking to myself as I often did in such moments I cleared my throat, and said in a dramatic fashion, "Lightning suddenly flashed, blinding me as thunder echoed through the deep canyon." In a second thought, I waved a hand before me, and said, "For an instant, I thought to have seen something gazing back at me from out of the jagged, rock face. Not bad? I'd better write that down before I forget it..."

Realizing that there weren't any safe places to pull over on that stretch of highway, I decided to wait with the notes. Lightning flashed, and the canyon walls reflected like the faces of stone giants gazing down from the dark peaks. Tap-pity-tap-tap-tap, the rain rapped at the canvas roof, echoing like the bony fingers of the restless dead. Was it just my imagination? Or did it made sense that a place which having claimed so many lives must certainly be haunted? I wondered as to how many of those shadows that I'd seen in peripheral vision, had actually been phantoms along that lonely old highway…

"It shouldn't be too much further now?" Peering through the river that flowed across the windshield I listened to the rain. It was almost deafening, as talking to my-self again, I said, "She said that the gates were just about a mile after passing the directional sign at the top of the hill…"

Lightning flashed again, and my attention was drawn into the fog and steeply ascending, rock face. Through the rain everything was a blurred confusion, and I slowed while making the bend. It was a good thing too… A sharp curve hidden in the fog suddenly brought me all too close to the cement barrier. With my hair standing on end and eyes sticking out of my head, I slowed even more. It would have been smarter to leave earlier, but I was rarely ever awake before the crack of noon…

"You can only blame yourself this this… If you'd gotten out of bed before lunch, you wouldn't be driving in the weather and darkness now…"

In that moment I seriously questioned my own sanity. Being an avid fan of the supernatural, I'd always appreciated the opportunity to dig into something new. Except now I was worried that it might end up being my own grave. I had a knack for getting into trouble or maybe it simply found me? I might have made a better investigative journalist than fiction writer. Excited, I peered over at the antique doctor's bag on the seat beside me. It contained snacks, a few necessities, and a black binder where typed upon the first page was; Nightrealm, Pathways to Oblivion. This would be my first novel, and I wondered whether I could manage the project. Unlike most, my stories weren't entirely fictional, but accounts based from personal experience. Oh sure, I changed the names and disguised locations, but rest assured, a great percentage contained the absolute truth. I managed to gather some fairly extensive material in my travels, experienced a few terrifying things, and it kept the short stories flowing over the years. All the same, the concept of attempting to base an entire novel on a single place or incident now became intimidating…

Reaching the peak and passing the directional sign, I began watching the side of the highway. The rain had finally slowed, but I could hardly see anything beyond the headlights. The fog was a blinding veil, and the forest an impenetrable expanse of looming shadows. During the day every twist and turn of that highway looked the same, but at night navigation was almost impossible. Cursing my lackadaisical lifestyle, I suddenly caught the glint of iron gates in the headlights.

"Ah! I don't believe it!" Patting the dash in a display of affection and victory, I laughed aloud, saying, "Elizabeth, we made it!"

Few would have ever understood that, but I had a habit of naming all of my cars. It made the long journeys seem a little less lonely. I had named her after the notorious, sixteenth century, Hungarian murderess, Countess Erzsébet Báthory. It seemed appropriate. After all, I'd always had a soft spot in my heart for mysterious women and suspected vampires.

"Oh, here we are!" Pulling off and to the side of the road, I looked over to where I had discovered an opening within the dense forest. The entrance stood twenty feet from the road and would have been invisible if I had been coming from the other direction. Pausing to look into the darkness, I nervously tapped a finger on the steering wheel. In the headlights and through the drifting fog I could see the pillars of the gates. Comprised of river rock, they stood approximately ten feet high, and were crowned by stone figures of Irish wolf hounds. Forever guarding those dark gates they appeared wild and even frightening.

"If this is any indication of the type of family they were I can't wait to meet the relatives."

I sensed something very old and hauntingly familiar, but couldn't quite place it? Having never been there before I suspected that it simply reminded of a place I had previously seen. Pulling across the highway and into the drive, I slowly pulled up before the gates. Tall and arched, the black iron gates bore sharp spikes, and slowly swung open and closed in a strong gust. There was a loud squealing as they moved upon rusted hinges and I just stared. Startled as the tracks suddenly switched in the player, I smiled as 'The Ventures' strummed to 'Out of Limits.' It was appropriate…

"It's pitch-black, the road's overgrown and it looks abandoned…

She said that she would be expecting me… It would have been considerate to have left a light on for me, somewhere… Maybe it's a very small light, and the forest is so dense that it can't be seen from the road?"

Passing through the bars of the swaying gates, the headlights cast eerie figures in the dense and rolling fog. I could barely see the road beyond, but knew that it was in very poor condition. I had been warned that it was littered with branches and debris, and large, water-filled, potholes. I could easily imagine how something like that could damage or easily cripple a car. Unwilling to take that chance I was forced to make a quick decision. Simple enough, I would just have to walk…

"Well, it's a good thing that I dressed for the weather…" Switching out the lights and turning off the engine, I slipped the keys into a pocket of my black trench coat. In saying that I had dressed for the weather I was just trying to convince myself of having assumed to have been prepared. In fact, I really wasn't… I wore the same black, three piece suit, black tie, and black leather shoes as always. The only difference in this case, was that I had also worn a black, woolen sweater. This wasn't due to the weather having been that terribly cold, but the dampness that always accompanied the long nights. Still, I knew that it would be a long and muddy walk to the house from where I was parked…

The engine quietly ticked as I sat there contemplating. It was the sound of the hot oil dripping down through the engine block as the car cooled from the long journey. The noise had a soothing effect as I had always attributed this to having returned home. It was an odd feeling to experience in such a dark and dismal place… The old gates swung open ever so slightly in the wind, as squealing upon rusted hinges, clanged together. The resulting ringing resembled an old church bell resounding in the distance. Inspired, I smiled while realizing that the atmosphere in that place was simply perfect. It was already scaring me….

"Alright, we're expected; let's not keep our host waiting." Gathering my belongings, I prepared for the walk to the house. This consisted of a large doctor's bag, suitcase, and compact typewriter. Climbing out and fumbling with my things, I managed to lock the door, and paused to gaze down that dark path. The timing couldn't possibly have been better. Lightning streaked across the blackened heavens, and in that moment I saw the ominous shadow of the mansion in the distance. Guarded by ancient and monstrous Oaks, it stood like a castle caught in a tunnel through time. Vanishing as quickly as it had appeared, I stood in awe as the world fell into utter stillness.

"No sir, nothing is quite as dark as autumn in the country-side... Oh, that's what I forgot..." Hurrying back and opening the car, I rummaged around on the floor in the back seat.

"There you are!" Finding the flashlight, I flicked the switch, rattling it several times before the light suddenly flashed on.

"Old reliable... I'll have to remember to replace you when I get home..." Tucking the small suitcase under my left arm and taking the typewriter in hand, I carried the doctor's bag and flashlight in the other. Resolved, I moved onward and while passing through the gates, heard them clutter and clang shut from behind me. The path was wide, the flashlight dim, and I quickly shuffled along.

"Well, they can't say that this place doesn't have a certain, ambience." Muttering while stumbling along, I looked to where the cold wind whispered among the bare branches. It was a haunting and lonesome sound, which fading into the distance became a faint but distinct howl... Most sounds didn't bother me, but I had an immediate reaction to that one. It caused me to stop along the path, and just stand there for several moments while listening.

"A howling in the woods..." The words were whispered as I shuddered with the memory. Not so long ago, I had gone in search of a story, and discovered an incident involving several 'mysterious deaths' and a pack of wild dogs... In the end, if it wasn't for a quick witted farmer and his son I would have been torn apart ...

The path suddenly seemed darker, the moisture and cold was already seeping through my clothes, and my nose started running. Stumbling onward, it was a struggle to avoid tripping over trailing vines, branches, and decades of heaped, forest debris. Bordering either side of the path stood enormous, ancient, and ivy covered, oaks. With they're gnarled limbs straining ever upward, the bare branches seemed to claw at the dark heavens. Among them were also tall Birch and Maple, which withered in shadow, leaned eerily in the blackness. Tall and yellowed grass lingered at the forests edge, and swaying in every perspective, was whipped about in the cold gusts. Pausing in a small clearing between the trees, I shone the light into an old grove. Caught in the dense foliage, I saw the gnarled and twisted forms of what had once been an apple orchard. Deprived of proper light in the mountains shadow, the trees bore decaying fruit, were sickly, and hideously twisted.

The wind suddenly caught the branches from high above, and rustling the remaining leaves, showered me in a sudden dampness. Spiraling slowly downward, the leaves covered the path and came to rest in great mounds from all about. Glistening in the flashlight's dim beam, the scent of damp earth filled the night with silent decay. Noticing a movement in passing, I paused to look down upon one of those huge and rotting piles. Cursing, I quickly stepped away with the sight of the pale blue and bloated worms. Cold and slippery, they writhed from beneath the piles, squirming in the thick and fetid mud. Disgusted, I remembered having seen the same worms burrowing in the earth of freshly dug graves… Shuddering with the thought, I quickly made my way toward the end of the path. Finding an unseen and water filled pothole with my left foot, I stumbled while narrowly avoiding a nasty tumble.

"That serves me right--," I shook off the wet foot and continuing along, said, "I should have been watching…"

Stepping into an even larger puddle with both feet, I groaned while shining the light down and just staring. It was apparent that I was already off to a good start…

Finally escaping the wet and dark canopy of the old forest, I noticed a small light twinkling in the distance. It flickered, and I saw that it was coming from what appeared to be the main entrance-way.

"It must be a faulty bulb or possibly an oil-lamp? Heck, at this point it could be a candle for all I care."

Squishing along with wet feet, I marched down the gravel path, and soon passed an immense stone fountain in the circular drive. A brief glance in passing revealed that it contained a Greek God, but I decided to have a better look during the day. Moments later and I arrived before the House of McCreary. It was enormous and with exception to that single light burning in the doorway, stood in absolute darkness. Spanning well over one hundred feet, the structure appeared as a central building with a smaller and adjoining one at each side. It boasted three stories including an attic, recessed towers, and stood well over sixty feet in height. With high and arched windows, flying buttresses, parapets, and leering gargoyles, it had all the classic Hallmarks of Gothic architecture.

"Now aren't you an absolute beauty..." Having already forgotten about my wet shoes, I stood in astonishment while staring upon the majestic structure. Historical architecture had always occupied a very special place in my heart. In fact, I owned almost every book containing the crowning achievements of Alexander Jackson Davis and Andrew Jackson Downing. Architects and authors, they were responsible for the Gothic Revival during 1830-1860. Among a long list of others on the subject, I spent countless hours dreaming through the pages of their books.

There was a tall and surrounding Holly hedge, which obscuring view of the main floor windows also concealed the lower portion of the brickwork. Thick Ivy climbed the ancient stone walls, and a brief observation revealed the moss that crept through the cracks of the cobblestone courtyard. Turning to my right, I could just barely make out the coach-house at the end of the drive. Having apparently been abandoned for some time, the doors hung crookedly while creaking in the wind.

"I'd better get going before it gets any later..." Making my way up the stone steps, I halted suddenly as the beam of my light reflected in the face of a large animal... My heart almost stopped, and then suddenly laughing, shook my head. Directing the light upward, the beam fell upon the stone gargoyles. Standing mid-way and on either side of the stairs, they solemnly gazed back from decayed and moss covered faces. Tall and hideously thin, they stood at the ready with partially folded and bat-like wings. With wide and staring eyes and ears drawn back, they snarled ferociously from out long and pointed snouts.

"Talk about atmosphere... I couldn't have hoped for more."

Shivering, I groaned beneath my burden while continuing up the stairs. They were shallow and wide, and I counted twelve before reaching the landing where the gargoyles stood. Moving past, I counted six more until reaching the landing of the main entrance. I was over-heated and sweating after that walk. The damp night was seeping through my clothes, and the wind chilled the dampness that formed upon my brow. I would be lucky if I didn't end up with a nasty cold in the deal. Finally making my way into the dimly lit foyer, it felt as though I had stepping into a wind-tunnel. Icy gusts whipped through the broken glass of tall and arched windows, and it was a miracle that the candles hadn't been blown out. The glow that I had previously seen from the path was coming from a large and rather unusual doorknocker. Comprised of solid brass and standing roughly eighteen inches, it likely weighed close to ten pounds. With the head of a woman, the features blank and staring, her hair was drawn back into a single and long braid. She had the neck of a serpent which elongated, sprouted from the bat-winged body of a lion. The beast was crouched upon an oak-leafed pedestal, and from beneath hung a formidable, spiked ring. A pipe and burning candle protruded from her mouth, and another rested in a bowl from between her front paws.

"It's definitely Gothic revival and looks like some type of Lamia or Sphinx. I'll have to run around with my camera in the daylight and get some good pictures…"

Shivering, I considered the possibility of having been forgotten? To make matters worse, the damp chill now drew attention to a full and aching bladder. Wincing, I grabbed the spiked striker, delivering three brief but firm strokes upon the door. They echoed like thunder and I felt like I was disturbing a sleeping giant… Ghosts may indeed dwell within the long shadows of the house of McCreary, but I had no intention of discovering them alone, and on that dark doorstep…

CHAPTER TWO

Frustrated and reaching again for the spiked ring, I suddenly leapt back as the door was flung open before me. The shadows ran deep in the corridor from behind her, but she was defined in the golden glow of an immense, oil lamp. From beneath a deep green and hooded cloak she wore an emerald and shimmering evening gown. Trailing from behind her, it bore patterns revealed in the faintest of silver, Celtic embroidery. Long and fiery hair drifted past her frail shoulders, as spilling and rolling like honey, rested somewhere within the small of her back. Her eyes were large and the most vibrant color of green that I had ever seen. Brilliantly reflecting the seething jade of a most turbulent sea, she gazed back from a thin, pale, and exotically freckled face. In my mind, she was an even lovelier version of film actress and artist, Nellie Elizabeth "Irish" McCalla. I knew her from a role that she played in a 50's television series, "Sheena Queen of the Jungle." Needless to say, she had stolen my heart as a young man, and that memory now lingered in the vision before me.

"You must be Mr. Michael Schreiber?" She politely inquired, breaking the strange trance and causing me to suddenly realize that I had been rudely staring. Her voice was soft and sweet, but she spoke with undeniable confidence.

"Yes—yes I am--," Awkwardly placing down the cumbersome luggage, I promptly extended a hand in greeting, and said, "And you are--?"

"Caitlin McCreary—," Accepting my hand in a fleeting but firm shake, she promptly stepped aside, and with an inviting nod, said "Welcome to the house of McCreary, won't you come inside?"

Hurriedly gathering my belongings, I fumbled while following her into the corridor. Embarrassed with the squishing sounds of my wet shoes, I shrugged while saying, "I'm afraid that I stepped into a puddle along the path."

"Don't let that concern you." She blew out the candles upon the door, and glancing back at me, said, "We'll see to your comfort, shortly."

The heavy oak doors boomed with certain finality, as drawing long, upper and lower, steel bolts, she firmly fastened the locks. That's when I first noticed it. With exception to a single, oil-burning lamp on a table in the hall, the entire manor was absolutely dark…

"I can see that you're very serious about security out here." Surprised with the darkness I felt obligated to comment, and asked, "Has the power gone out due to a recent storm?"

"The local tribes weren't as accommodating when the estate was first built. So, our methods might seem a little crude or extreme…" She thought briefly while staring into the shadows of the ceiling, and then peering back at me, said, "We don't have power here and never have. The hearths provide central heating, and the family has always used candles and oil lamps. I'm sorry will that be a serious bother?"

"Oh—it isn't any bother at all. In fact, it creates ambience and adds character to the place. I was just wondering…"

Retrieving the large oil lamp from the table, she turned with a subtle smile, and said, "Well then, I'll be your hostess and guide during this visit—please feel free to call me, Caitlin…"

"If it's all the same to you, I prefer to be called, Michael--," Although unnecessary I felt the need to explain myself further, and said, "My mother named me after the arch-angel and my father used to call me Mike when he was angry. So I never really cared for 'nick-names' or abbreviated versions."

"An arch-angel, really--," She nodded, as seeming to find amusement in the thought, said, "She must have very high expectations for you?"

"Not really. Sadly, she suffered a miscarriage two years before I was born. It was a boy that they intended to call Alexander. I suppose that after that, she felt some kind of security with the idea of naming me after an angel?"

"I'm sorry for the loss," She offered a faint smile as she added in thought, saying, "It does make sense, now that you have explained everything in such great detail."

"Sorry, it's a bad habit. I tend to ramble on at times…"

"There's no harm in it. I appreciate open and honest people--," Gesturing with a hand toward the peeling paint and wallpaper, she changed subject, and said, "I'm not certain of how much you know about the estate? But as you can see—the manor is in very poor condition. During your stay, I would advise you to remain in designated areas. The house can be very dangerous due to its decrepit condition and especially at night…"

"I'm sorry to interrupt--," Reminded of a full bladder and squinting with the pressure, I pleaded, saying, "But it was a long trip and--…"

"Oh, of course--," She immediately directed me down the hall and off to the right, saying, "You'll find the facilities a few doors down."

Few words could have politely described the relief of that almost endless moment, or the horror when it refused to flush. Tugging several times upon the chain, I knocked on the raised tank. It was an antique and someone had forgotten to fill the basin so that it would flush… I might have guessed. Closing the toilet seat, I hurried back out with a smile and gesture of thanks.

"I wish that I could offer you something better." She spoke as we continued down the corridor, and said, "But very few things work as they should—and I'm afraid that we'll have to make do with what we have."

"There really isn't any reason to apologize. I'm grateful for the opportunity to be here. Have you lived here for long?"

"All of my life—but it feels far longer…"

Assuming that she was in her mid to late-twenties, I avoided asking her age with the risk of sounding rude. The truth of the matter was that upon the twilight of my forty-third year, I was feeling like an old man in her company. To make matters worse, I was having trouble not noticing the tightly clinging fabric of her sleek fitting dress. I wasn't a stranger to the company of beautiful women, but the attraction seemed simply uncanny.

"Do you travel a lot in your field of work?"

"Yes—I just love visiting old mansions and historic places… I've been writing ghost and fantasy stories for years. I found out early in my career that a little inspiration goes a long way. So, most of what I've written was loosely based on places, people, and stories that I heard or picked up along the way."

"Fascinating--," She peered over at me curiously, and said, "I noticed earlier that you're also a smoker. Please, feel free to smoke. I'd like you to feel comfortable here during your stay."

"Do my clothes smell bad?" I stumbled along behind her with my burden, as sniffing at my coat collar, became self-conscious.

"No—they just smell of cigarette smoke--," Leading me through an immense and exquisitely furnished main hall, she said, "Just be careful, the house is dusty and very old. We wouldn't want to accidentally start a fire now would we?"

It sounded more suggestive than spoken in warning. I had the distinct impressions that she had little care and even less concern for the old place.

"No, we wouldn't want that." I continued after my hostess, as gazing upward and into the high vaulted ceilings, fathomed at the crown moldings. Moving along, the lamps glow caused the shadows to twist and move eerily in the high arches. The light was caught within enormous chandeliers, and the crystals cast golden sparks among the phantoms of the ceilings and walls.

Nearing a set of French doors and peering into the darkness, I could only imagine the beauty of that room through the shapes of its shadows. Eventually the corridor led toward an immense staircase, which parting on either side, ascended to the second floor landings. There was a lavish, red carpet, and angels holding lanterns stood upon either side of the ornately carved bannisters. Passing beneath on the right, we followed an adjoining hallway that carried us toward the eastern side of the building. There was a pervading odor of mold in the corridor separating the two hallways, and I felt the stinging effect at the back of my throat. Of all things I loathed molds, mildews, and fungi the most... Unfortunately, and when it came to old places, it seemed to go with the territory. Looking to the corridor leading into the west wing of the house, I saw that it was closed. I could only imagine as to what stood behind that door, and was more than willing to avoid it.

"I'm afraid that we do have issues with dampness due to improper heating--," She seemed to read my expression, and said, "It causes mold and mildew and cannot be helped..."

"Oh, don't let that concern you. To tell you the truth, these wet shoes are bothering me a lot more than anything else."

"Oh, I'm terribly sorry--," Raising a finger in pause, she vanished into one of the rooms, and reappearing with a pair of shoes similar to my own, said, "Please, try these on for size. They look as though they might suit your needs."

Feeling somewhat awkward, I took a seat on a chair that stood in the hall, and quickly slipped out of my shoes and wet socks.

Accepting and politely thanking her for the shoes, I was surprised when they fit quite comfortably.

"Thank you, so very much." I stood up and walking about, said, 'That sure makes a world of a difference. I feel so dumb. I never thought to bring an extra pair of shoes on the trip."

"If you'll leave yours here for the moment--," She pointed to the chair where I had been sitting, and said, "I'll see to it that they are dried and properly cleaned."

"I really can't thank you enough--," Pointing to my suitcase and taking it from her, I located a pair of socks, and said. "Isn't it amazing how the little things make such a difference in life?"

"Leave the socks as well--," She gestured toward the chair where I placed the shoes, and smiling, said, "What is life, if not for a series of little things, combined?" She took my suitcase and urging me onward, said, "Please follow me."

As I continued after her, I noticed the broken plaster on the ceiling and became immediately concerned. Not due to the clear and present decay, but the hair-line cracks. The fissures began from where the chandeliers were fastened, and ran into opposing corners of the ceiling and walls… I was suddenly worried that one of those massive chandeliers might break loose, and bring a portion of the ceiling down on our heads. Relieved to discover that the cracks vanished and were only present in that area of the corridor, I kept the concern to myself. She was likely more than aware of these faults, and it wouldn't serve any positive means to remind her.

Following close from behind before her, I took notice of our shadows in the lamp-light as they moved across the opposing wall. I wasn't sure if it was just fatigue or a trick of the light, but something didn't feel right… At times they appeared out of place, and when I looked to define their source, just vanished… One in particular, and seeming darker than the others, felt as though it was following us from just beyond sight? I was tired and assuming that it was just my imagination, simply ignored it…

"Was it a long trip?" She glanced back at me and raising an eyebrow in question, said, "I've never been to Vancouver—do you like living there?"

"Yes, it's a beautiful city and I love living there. The trip wasn't terribly long—only a few hours." Suspiciously watching the ceilings and corners for unusual shadows, I said, "But at night and in the pouring rain, the highway through the canyon can get a little, sketchy."

"I can only imagine…"

Ignoring the imagined shadows, I turned my attention upon our surroundings. Even for all of its decay and darkness the house and its many rooms were absolutely amazing. It was enormous and everything was extravagantly decorated. There were marble pedestals with Greek Gods, beautiful tapestries of mythical beasts, and wondrous carvings upon the crown moldings and banisters. It seemed that regardless of where I looked, some strange creature gazed back in proper perspective. Although inanimate, this bizarre menagerie attributed a strange and eerie presence to the house. It lent to a sense of being observed by something, other-worldly.

"They weren't part of the original design--," She spoke without so much as a glance back, and said, "They were additions made after the founding father, and before the birth of the last man to live here."

"He must have had an affinity for myths and old legends."

"Not from what I've read about him." She thought quietly for a moment, and then added in thought, saying, "Unless you consider demons part of that lore?"

"Interesting…" I was beginning to suspect that writing a book based on the history of this house would be far easier than anticipated. Hurrying along as she continued, my attention returned to the large rooms in passing. The furniture was all the finest of European imports, and the family appeared to have an affinity for the Italian 'Rococo' styles in particular. There were several beautiful examples of, James Horner, carved furnishings, and the house was lavishly decorated with some of the most amazing oil lamps and candelabrum I had ever seen. There were tall parlor lamps, hanging lamps with cranberry shades and dangling crystals, and an endless array of large, Hurricane style lamps. For all of their beauty, I saw that the burning oil had blackened ceilings and stained the walls. For admirers and collectors alike, this was the cost of antiquity. Remorsefully, all the dreams and labors of this extravagant estate would soon join their creators, lost and forgotten in time. It always bothered me to see something of such profound beauty simply destroyed.

"This house and its furnishings are absolutely beautiful…"

"Do you really think so?" She halted to examine one of the many adjoining rooms, and placing a finger before her full red lips, said, "That's odd, I've always considered it more of a gilded cage for a distressed bird."

"That's an interesting analogy." I knew that a lifetime spent in the proverbial 'lap of luxury' could easily be taken for granted, and humoring her, said, "I certainly hope that you're not that distressed, little bird?"

"In life, we're all bound by certain limitations." Leading me into an immense dining room, she motioned toward a chair at the head of a long table, and said, "I've arranged for a late supper. We haven't entertained guests here for what seems an eternity. I hope that this will be acceptable?"

"Are you kidding me? This is amazing." Wandering toward the table and looking down at the elegant, silver dinner service, I turned back to her, and, "Knowing that you don't have power here, I would have been excited just to have a pizza and can of soda."

"Please leave your things there." She pointed to the wall behind the table, and I promptly went over, and placed everything down. It was a relief just to have my hands free again.

"I don't think that I can arrange for Pizza and soda…" Entertaining the thought for a moment she laughed, and said, "But there are plenty of others things. We have two fully functional coal stoves and water is drawn from a pump near the kitchen sink. It's all rather archaic but we manage as our ancestors did."

According to proper manners, I insisted upon drawing her chair and seating her first. She took the seat nearest to where I sat and promptly thanked me.

"How quaint—it's not often that one encounters such proper manners anymore. It's a shame—but so much of the etiquette that was once cherished is lost to modern society."

"Spoken like a true Victorian lady." It was uncanny how much her behavior resembled elderly friends of my mother's. She appeared far too young to sound that old. Noticing only a single place setting, I suddenly felt awkward and humbly asked, "Were you going to join me?"

"I dined earlier. I hope that you will forgive me?" She politely motioned for me to begin, saying, "But, I will join you for tea and desert, afterwards."

"Well, you've won me over there!" Amazed at the lovely roasted chicken, potatoes, and corn cobs, I was surprised to find that it was all still warm.

"I kept it in the oven until just before you came--," Noticing my expression, she explained, saying, "I was putting it out when you rang, and that's why I took longer to answer the door."

"As much as I really do appreciate it, you shouldn't have gone through all this trouble over me. Honestly, I'm a man of simple tastes and easily appeased with the little things."

"It was no trouble, really--," She raised a finger in question while asking, "Can I offer you a glass of wine with dinner?"

"I'm not much of a wine connoisseur--," I thought briefly and then said, "But if you have a little brandy and a warm place to share it after dinner, I wouldn't be disagreeable?"

"That can be easily arranged--," She was pleased with the thought and smiling said, "Do you mind if we talk while you eat?" Playfully twirling a finger among the red curls about her shoulders, she raised an eyebrow in question.

"Oh—of course not! What was on your mind?"

"Well--," Observing me rather skeptically, she asked, "Exactly what do you hope to discover here?"

Wiping at my mouth with a napkin while slipping back into the chair, I looked to her, and said, "Quite frankly, an atmosphere of dark mystique, antiquity, and maybe something that goes bump in the night?" Looking into the surrounding and deep shadows, I smiled, saying, "So far, I've got two out of three—no offense."

A strange aura of aversion now reflected within those large and green eyes, as seeming somewhat perturbed, she said, "None taken—please, continue…"

"So, as I had said when we spoke on the telephone--," I buttered and nibbled at a dinner roll, and said, "I'm just trying to find inspiration for my first novel."

"Are you sincere about writing an authentic, ghost story? Or just digging for dirt in the family graveyard, so to speak?"

It was like she had read my mind. Without escape and unwilling to ruin our bond of trust at this point, I simply told her the truth.

"Listen, Caitlin?" Politely coughing into the napkin, I cleared my throat before saying, "I'm not going to lie to you... Yes, I was hoping to find something scandalous and maybe even terrifying enough for a great horror story. But, I'd prefer to write a really dark and romantic, ghost story."

"A really dark and romantic ghost story..." She slowly repeated the words as though savoring the moment, and then glancing back curiously, said, "So, in fact, you're a romantic at heart?"

In an awkward moment I considered graphic and horrendous details described in some of my previous works, and said, "Mostly... although, I have been known to turn a few stomachs at times?"

"Oh, have you?" In some dark and disturbing way she appeared intrigued by this, and smiling devilishly, asked, "How so?"

"Well--," Almost choking on a forkful of roast chicken and gravy, I cleared my throat, and said, "Aside from ghost stories, I also write horror and fantasy. Some of which contains some, to put it lightly, fairly graphic descriptions of monsters, murders, and human remains..."

"Oh, I see--," Crossing her arms over her small but firm breasts, she leaned forward inquisitively, and raising an eyebrow, asked, "But, you don't actually believe in the existence of ghosts, monsters, or the supernatural, do you?"

"Well, we really can't deny the existence of something that hasn't been disproven, can we?"

She laughed, and leaning back without taking her eyes from off me, clapped her hands, saying, "Bravo, you've succeeded within eluding the question."

"Caitlin--," Adopting a serious position in the matter, I looked to her in question, and asked, "Would you enter the home of a complete stranger, which in this case happens to be a young woman. And then, being all alone in an enormous mansion in the middle of nowhere, give her the impression that you were some raving, occult fanatic? What kind of safety and security could anyone find in doing that?"

"You are absolutely right—but in the same turn?" She raised an eyebrow, and grinning rather cruelly, said, "Have you even considered that it might actually be you that's in danger here—and not me?"

"That's silly—how could I possibly be in danger?" Laughing at the thought, I fumbled with the fork while finishing the meal.

"Consider this for a moment—if you will?" Resting her arms on the table, she grinned like a *Cheshire cat*, and said, "It's the same scenario as what you just described... Except... Here you are, all alone in a strange place. We're in the middle of nowhere without a telephone, and cut off from the outside world. What would you do if anything, unexpected, were to happen?"

"Unexpected... What exactly do you mean?"

The once attractive young woman suddenly appeared eerily pale, drawn, and sinister in the dim light. Radiantly beautiful and yet threatening at the same time, she quietly asked, "What makes you so certain that I'm not the very thing that you should be concerned about?"

I suddenly became lost in her penetrating gaze. With all other thoughts departing, I looked to her in all sincerity, and said, "Because, if you were planning to do away with me, we wouldn't be sitting here over dinner, and still talking."

Placing a finger to her lips in thought, she observed me in silent contemplation. Then suddenly burst into a loud and uncontrollable fit of laughter. The entire room echoed to her folly and all that I could do was sit there laughing with her.

Clasping her fingers tightly together, she leaned across the table, looked me straight in the eyes, and said quite sweetly, "You—my dear Michael, could charm the horns off the devil!"

Absolutely delighted, her eyes were glassy and cheeks flushed in a brilliant pink. I suspected that she hadn't laughed that hard in a long time. Sadly, I regretted that it was at my expense.

The moment having passed, I looked to the dinner service, and pointing to my empty plate, asked, "Can I help you with any of this?"

"Oh no, just leave it where it stands--," She assured me with a wave, and said, "My maid, Eva, will be back in the morning. The house is much too cold for her during the winter months. So, she stays in town with a friend."

"Alright then—," The thought occurring in that moment, I peered back in question, asking, "Oh, my presence here won't be disturbing to anyone else, will it? I tend to work late and wouldn't want to be a bother."

"No--," She quietly stared back at me and speaking in little more than a whisper, said, "Not a single living soul…" Her eyes became emerald pools where I thought that I might simply drown. Hauntingly beautiful, it almost felt as though she now looked straight through me. Strangely enough, in that moment I felt unsettled and even vulnerable. It occurred to me at that time, that I might have brought this on myself? Comments of her being alone with a stranger could have possibly caused her to react with a type of psychological, defense mechanism? Of course, it couldn't have been more obvious! She was merely attempting to put me into place with some simple intimidation methods, and it had almost worked…

Given to the moment, I suddenly broke from the hypnotic spell and said, "Wonderful, and with exception to the noisy keys on that old typewriter I shouldn't be too much of a bother."

"No bother—none at all?" She smirked, and peaking in a rather provocative tone, said, "Don't be so disappointing."

"Pardon me?" I played into her little game while allowing her to take the point of advantage. Under the circumstances and being a gentleman it seemed only fair.

"It's been very quiet here—for a very long time." She tapped her long red nails on the table, a coy smile crossing her full lips as she said, "I only meant that I would welcome the company. A little friendly conversation will certainly break the monotony around here."

Given the place of the protagonist she was already becoming far more comfortable. I could hardly blame her, as having been caught in the same position, might likely have done the same thing. Still, she was so beautiful that I could have forgiven almost anything.

"Of course you did--," Caught somewhere between attraction and macabre fascination, I looked around the room while quietly explaining, and said, "I get lost in my work and often lose complete track of time. Not to mention, I've always been a night person. I find it easier to focus while the rest of the world sleeps."

"Me either, but then again, I never could sleep nights. Old places have a soul—sounds of their own as they settle in the night." With a subtle smile reminiscent of Leonardo da Vinci's 'Mona Lisa' she looked back at me, and added, "And as far as getting lost in your work is concerned? I'm sure that I'll find some way to distract you—

from time to time?"

"I'm easily lured away with the promise of tea and pastry—it's my one great weakness." I used a little humor to soften the edge of her well-honed survival instincts.

"Are you always given to revealing your desires to temptation?"

"When it comes to cake, pastry, and donuts? It works every single time."

Sneezing suddenly, I covered my face with a napkin. I suspected that the dust and mildew had been the culprits, but apologizing, said, "Oh, pardon me! I think that I might've picked up a bit of a chill tonight?"

"I certainly hope not!" She appeared sincerely concerned, and said, "I'll give you the room directly beside mine. With both hearths burning the combined effort should offer you additional warmth."

"Thank you, kindly. I would never have even thought of that?"

"You learn many things when put to the test." Running a finger across the delicate and pale flesh about her throat, she said in a second thought, "You'll need more than brandy and a hearth to survive the Duff Glenn…"

My attention drifted to where shadows lingered and long cracks crept across the ceiling and walls. I had to agree…

"If you've finished here--," She moved from her seat and pausing in question, said, "We can share tea and desert in the library."

"Yes—please. Oh, should I leave my luggage here for now?"

"No, I'll be happy to help you with your things." She smiled, and pointing toward the corridor behind us, said, "Our rooms are on the second floor and just down the corridor from the library"

Slipping back into my coat, I grabbed the black doctor's bag and typewriter case, saying, "That suitcase seems a little imposing, but it really weighs nothing. It's just some extra clothes.

"Don't worry, I'm quite capable." Tightly drawing the cloak about her, she retrieved the suitcase and leading the way, said, "It feels much colder this evening than usual?"

"With so much stone and such big rooms it's a wonder that you manage to keep warm at all?" Following closely while looking toward the large windows, I chuckled, saying, "I'd hate to see the heating and electrical bills?"

"What bills?" She glanced back at me with a smile, and shrugging, said, "Our only costs are for oil, coal and firewood…"

"How very Gothic and darkly romantic…"

"All you have to find now is a monster…"

CHAPTER THREE

With the suitcase in one hand and a large candelabrum in the other, Caitlin directed me out of the dining room and into the corridor.

"You'll feel a little better soon. This part of the house always seems warmer than the rest. We can light the hearth in the library while I run down for our tea and desert."

"Did you need me to come back down with you?"

"No—but thank you—I'll be just fine. It'll be quicker if I go alone, anyway."

"If you don't mind my being so forward--," She spoke rather reluctantly, and with a quick glance back, asked, "Are you a married man?"

"No, well, not unless you're counting my publisher and mother?" The comment had caused her to blush ever so slightly, and smiling as we continued along the way, I said, "My specific field of interest takes me into some pretty strange places at times. I couldn't imagine bringing anyone into that world."

"Are you trying to tell me, that an intelligent and attractive man such as your-self doesn't have any attachments?"

"No—not for a very long time now… When I was a young man I was very much in love, once. But she was killed by a drunk driver while crossing the street. Since then, my work has completely occupied my life."

"I'm sorry to hear that--," Though polite, she seemed to have very little interest in my past, and in a second breath, said, "No commitments, whatsoever?" Her eyes flashed as she paused at the foot of the stairway to look back at me.

"If you're asking if anyone will notice if I should happen to go missing, the answer is yes."

"Well, that will complicate things, now won't it?"

She was still playing the game but this time I was enjoying it.

The library was immense and immediately purveyed an unsettling aura of utter stillness. It was a finality that seemed to resonate from within every molecule of the old manor. I was beginning to wonder if it was actually the house itself or the presence of something that now followed me... The room appeared tidy, was well organized and didn't smell of mold or mildew. Still, I couldn't shake that sense of gloom... At first, I just assumed it to have been the weather and poorly insulated house, but it was far more than just that. I began to suspect that the maid had other reasons for not staying after dark.

"Make yourself comfortable." She patted my shoulder, and motioning with a nod toward an oak table and chairs near a large window, said, "Just light the oil lamp—the matches are resting in a tin right beside it. There's an ashtray." She pointed and said, "Feel free to smoke. I'll be back in a few minutes with some nice hot tea and dessert."

Her evil facade was quickly fading as even I knew that the devil never served tea and pastry.

Offering me one of the six candles from her candelabrum, she said, "Something to help you see until you light the lamp, and hearth."

Thanking her, I promptly made my way toward the table, and quickly lit the large hurricane lamp. It was a beautiful antique with an amber shade and floral designs. Casting a warm golden glow, it chased the long shadows away from the table. Retrieving the tin that contained the matches, I hurried over to the far corner of the room. Standing upon the stonework where the hearth would have been was a large Cylinder Pot Belly stove. An iron giant resting upon four legs, it burned wood and coal and was indispensable in the days of the early settlers. Before that moment I had only seen them at auction, and leaning down, smiled while inspecting it.

"It's a Derby stove made by Excelsior Stove and Manufacturing Company in Quincy, Illinois. From the looks of it, this must've been made somewhere between the late eighteen-hundreds to early nineteen-twenties... What a beauty."

Gently patting the old iron beast, I knelt down and striking a match, opened the grate, and tossed it into the chamber. The paper and tinder caught quite quickly, and stepping back, I closed the metal window. In moments it became warmer and the additional light brought an immediate sense of comfort to the room. I loved antique stoves and sighing deeply, stood there while rubbing my hands together before the flames.

"Now that would take the edge from off any cold night..."I turned with a smile and went back to the table. Lighting a cigarette, my attention was drawn to the interesting design of the room. Octagonal in shape, five of the eight walls were built in book cases, one housed the stove, and two contained windows. These windows were separated by one of the massive shelves, and the table had been placed against it. Beyond the faded purple and gold-trimmed draperies, I could see that the shutters had been tightly drawn. This seemed to be the case throughout the mansion, or at least appeared that way while passing in the dark. The walls were oak paneled, the shelves reached to the crown molding of the ceiling, and were absolutely filled with books.

In the center of the room stood four, oak bookcases. Rather than being splayed in the usual fashion, they stood against one another while forming a cross. This allowed for simple access, and provided the reader with ample space to draw a wheeled cart in a circular fashion from about the room. The floors wood were polished, and the central book cases rested upon a circular and red, Persian carpet.

Strangely enough, and unlike the rest of the house, the library appeared relatively untouched by time or the elements. I could only assume that rising heat from lower levels, and direct sunlight had prevented mold and mildew. It was like a diamond ring that still glittered long after the bride had withered in the grave...

Pulling a pen and pad from the doctor's bag, I swiftly scribbled down the thoughts. Excited, I looked around while detailing some of the more interesting aspects of the room. Old libraries were like the heart and mind of the family that had once owned them. In many cases, they reflected generations of interest, career, passion, and even their worst fears. Locating a smaller lamp resting on a near-bye shelf, I lit the wick, and adjusting the flame, began exploring the book cases. The subject material was neatly written on wooden plaques that were fastened to individual shelves in each book case. The subjects varied and the books must have ranged into the thousands. Slowly wandering between the book cases with the lamp, I read the titles aloud while looking, "Art, architecture, history, science, medicine, music, and poetry. Oh my, first edition copies of Lord George Gordon Byron, Percy Shelley, and Edgar Allan Poe. Oh, I don't believe it, the complete works of Sir Arthur Conan Doyle, the books of Jules Verne, and original copies of Bram

Stoker's Dracula, eighteen-ninety-seven, and Mary Shelley's, Frankenstein, eighteen-eighteen."

Fascinated, I fingered through a section containing esoteric and occult literature. Among these were, Demonolatry by famed witch-hunter, Nicholas Remy, published in France 1595. The notorious judicial book of the Inquisition, 'Malleus Maleficarum' or 'Witch's Hammer' of Heinrich Kramer and James Sprenger, first published in the German city of Speyer, 1487. This was accompanied by 'Compendium Maleficarum' which documented the crimes of witch's against the people, and was written by Francesco Maria Guazzo and published in Milan, Italy, 1608. During the time of the Inquisition few would have dared being in possession of such a collection.

"Oh, a collection of world mythology and a shelf dedicated to the great philosophers--," I searched through the numerous volumes while reading aloud, and said, "The dialogues of Plato, Socrates, Herodotus, Aristotle... Oh, and what do we have here? Oh, my... The original eighteen-ninety, first edition, two volume set of Sir James George Frazer's, 'Golden Bough', a study in religion and magic. This entire collection is absolutely, outstanding..."

I had spent countless hours pondering the wisdom and terrors of those brilliant scholars and theologians. It was an amazing collection and being awestruck, deeply desired to possess them all.

"So you have a penchant for old books?" Returning with a silver tray containing a small lamp, tea, and assorted biscuits, placed them down upon the table.

"I'm something of an amateur collector, mainly works on the occult, supernatural, old myths, legends and folklore." Making my way to the table and taking a seat across from her, I said, "I also love art, old world architecture, and illuminated manuscripts."

"It sounds as though you keep very busy with your hobbies and interests?" She slowly nodded while serving our tea and then grinning mischievously, asked, "What do you do when you're not nose-deep in books or chasing the boogeyman?"

A moment of silence passed between us, and then sipping at my tea I looked up quite seriously, and said, "I've never really stopped looking..."

"Personally--," She offered the small platter of biscuits and pastry, and said, "I prefer to experience life, rather than dwelling in the dusty pages of old books, filled with other people's delusions, dreams, and theories."

"Sometimes, I find that a little push in the right direction goes a long way. Which in my case, often comes from between the dusty pages of old books." I couldn't help but smiling with the thought, and said, "As you know, wisdom is derived through experience and being shared in books, can unlock the door to understanding. In the end, wisdom being that key might very well save your life."

"Have you ever been accused of being melodramatic?"

"All of the time… It comes with the territory of being a writer and artist." Returning her smile I winked, and said, "I'll have to warn you in advance, I also possess an over-active imagination. So, if you should happen to hear whimpering in the night, or notice me cringing fearfully at the hearth, just ignore it."

"How very quaint…" She was amused, and placing a finger to her lips in thought, said, "You say that you've never stopped looking for the unknown?" A strange light of dark fascination now shone in her eyes, and she asked, "Have you ever wondered what might happen if you ever found that proverbial, boogeyman?"

In that moment the shadows seemed to grow deeper and gather closer from all about us. It almost felt like something in that house was listening from the darkness, and waiting for the lights to go out.

"That's the strange thing about pursuing anything. It's all about the chase and most people never consider that possibility."

Presently the room grew brighter, my spirit lifted, and she seemed satisfied with the answer. Still, I could see that something was troubling her.

"What would you do, Michael, if you were confronted with your worst fear?"

"How could anyone anticipate their actions when confronted with the unknown?"

"Or be aware of it—even if it were right before them." She moved from the seat and toward a small wheeled cart that stood off to the side, saying, "I have something to show… But, I have to ask for complete and absolute discretion where this is concerned…"

"I understand—absolute discretion—," I swallowed hard while sensing that she now dared expose some mystery or dark family secret, and said, "You have my word."

The old stove had warmed the large room far more than expected, and noticing this, Caitlin removed her cloak. Folding and placing it upon a chair beside her, she put a book on the table, and went back to the cart for something else.

"Wait for me before you touch that book, please...." She spoke while I reached across the table for the book and had her back turned to me. I felt like the boy caught with his hand in the proverbial cookie jar.

"Of course—sorry..." Settling back into the chair, I watched her quietly fingering through the books and scrolls on the cart.

The glimmer of her clinging gown had immediately caught my attention. Leaning to look into a lower shelf of the cart, the gown became all too revealing... She noticed my absent-minded stare but continued what she was doing.

Looking to where the light of the stove shone in the far corner of the room, I fought to stay focused. It was a losing battle as my gaze returned to that emerald gown...

Returning with a large leather tube that obviously contained a scroll of some type, she placed it down on the table before her.

"Are you alright?" She hesitated, and said, "You look pale as a sheet..."

"I'm pretty sure that I've managed to catch a chill. But it's nothing to worry about—really." Trembling with a sudden fever, I wiped a palm across my sweat beaded forehead, and said, "All I need is a little rest and I'll be right as rain."

"Did you want to call it a night--," She patted a hand upon the book, saying, "We can have a look at this in the morning?"

"No—really, I can manage." The curiosity being almost too much to bear, I squirmed in the seat and pointing to the scroll and book, asked, "Exactly what are those?"

"It's something that's never been revealed to anyone outside of the family." She carefully laid the ancient book before me, saying, "And I would like it to remain that way..."

"I won't breathe a word to anyone—but--," There was hesitation as looking between her and the items on the table, I said, "If there's something that I can alter for a fictional story, would you mind me using it?"

There was a moment where we both held opposite ends of the book. Resisting briefly, I wasn't sure if she'd changed her mind? Then there was some strange type of connection. It felt what could only be described as a flow of static energy, which passing through the fabric of the leather somehow connected us. It wasn't enough to cause a spark, but I felt it in my fingertips and almost dropped the book.

Her eyes flashed eerily in the lamp-light and dropping the book into my hands, she said, "At your own discretion, but please consider my family reputation when doing so..."

Running my fingers across the cold leather surface I felt a strange numbing sensation. I was tired, nauseated, and suddenly feeling weak as a lamb. Without a doubt, the cold walk and draft in that old house had given me a nasty chill. Clearing my throat, I leaned closer to examine the title while reading it aloud, and said, "A history of Duff Glenn and the House of McCreary: A narrative of leading events by Sir Reginald Andrew McCreary, including family genealogies, seventy-eight-six to nineteen-fifteen. This looks like it's in terrific condition for something written so long ago."

"Yes, I know." She became strangely distant as drifting into thoughts of despair, whispered, "Isn't it amazing how the things that we least desire seem to linger longest?"

The fire crackled, the shadows danced in the flames, and once more I gazed upon her form within that tightly fitting gown. It happened without any thought. Peeking into places where none would dare by day I was suddenly caught within her wide-eyed stare.

"Oh, pardon me! I was just drifting off for a second. I didn't mean to be rude."

"I have to admit that it takes two to stare—one to look and the other to notice." She blushed while covering her mouth with a hand, and looking away.

She was making this far too easy. Michael, be responsible and act your age! She's a young, lonely, and beautiful girl. Even if it was just a game it wouldn't be right to play into this.

"Have you actually read this?" I brought her attention back to the book while changing subject, and said, "It looks like a concise family history."

"I read them a long time ago." Moving closer, she leaned to look over my shoulder, and said, "It's an interesting play on paranoid delusion and illnesses affecting the mind." She frowned and staring at me, quietly said, "Poor old Reginald died from complications of Syphilis."

"He died of Syphilis?" Swallowing hard as while horrified with the thought, I said, "I wasn't aware that something like that would kill a person."

"It affects the heart and the brain--," She winced with the thought, and said, "And, it causes a painful, hideous, fungal type of growth on the reproductive--."

"Yes, yes, I was aware of the physical aspects of the illness." Interrupting while unable to listen any longer, I nodded, saying, "So Sir Reginald was very sick, and likely not functioning with all faculties at the time of these diaries."

"Yes, he was very sick, indeed." Pouring more tea, she shuddered in revulsion and nodding at the book, said, "You'll see what I mean when you read the diaries."

Rubbing at my eyes, I attempted to drive the grotesque images of Reginald's illness from my thoughts.

"Oh—one moment--," She remembered something, and moving from her seat, retrieved a long scroll from a near-bye shelf, saying, "You'll need this as well. It's the genealogical chart mentioned in the diaries. They work together."

Watching as she carefully unrolled the large and hand drawn chart, I marveled at the beautiful illustrations, saying, "That's amazing and should have been framed."

Moving closer, she gestured at the dates beneath the persons nearest the bottom of the symbolic oak, and said, "It paints a rather bleak picture—don't you think?"

It wasn't until after I had looked at the lowest branches that I noticed the birth and death dates of the last two generations.

"I see what you mean--," I looked up at her and licking at dry lips, said, "Apparently, there were a lot of tragedies in the early years?"

She simply rolled up the scroll and placing it on the table near the book, said, "The family history is all very dark—as you'll likely soon discover for yourself..."

Flipping through the pages of Sir Reginald's narrative, I was speechless, and glancing back at her, said, "I really appreciate you doing this for me. I can't even begin to thank you enough, for everything."

"Once I'm gone it's all over for the house of McCreary--," There was no sadness but a sense of relief in her tone, as looking back at me, she said, "Maybe some good can still come of this—for you at least..."

Putting a hand to my face I suddenly felt unsteady and wavering barely caught my balance."

"I don't mean to mother you?" Brushing the hair from out of my eyes with a hand, she pressed a palm to my forehead, saying, "But you have a fever, and should really get some rest?"

A quick glance at my wrist watch and I nodded, as tapping a finger upon the book, wearily said, "I didn't realize that it was already half past eleven? Um—would it be alright if I took the back and scroll back to my room?"

"Be my guest. But Michael, I wouldn't suggest reading that before bed..."

"Oh, don't worry. Not much bothers me anymore." Tucking the book under my arm and collecting my things from the table, I said, "I must've read every M.R. James and Sheridan Le Fanu ghost story ever written before I was fourteen years old. I doubt this old stuff will keep me awake."

"Our rooms are at the far end of this corridor, I'll see to your luggage."

"Ordinarily, I wouldn't expect a lady to carry my luggage, but can't argue at the moment..."

"Regardless, you'll soon find that arguing wouldn't get you the least bit further where I'm concerned." She smiled as though offering the terms of a dare. It was a game of which I had no intention of pursuing. Gathering my coat and doctor's bag, I bowed politely before following as she took my suitcase and typewriter.

11:47 p.m.

"I noticed a lot of portraits on the walls of the stairways--," I pointed out the pictures on either side of the corridor, and said, "Are these also members of the family?"

"They are the lords and ladies of the house of McCreary." She casually nodded toward them in passing, and said, "Or at least, all that remains of them now."

Staring at the ornately framed paintings I failed to see any distinct family resemblance? In actuality, I had always found a certain profound and even macabre significance to portraits. It was the work of masters, which casting an image, remained long after both model and the artist were dead. Centuries later, all that remained were the ghosts in silent repose, gazing back from out of the canvas.

"I don't see any family resemblance. Do you mind if I ask how you were related?"

"I'm related through distant family." She mumbled without as much as a backward glance, and said, "And was adopted—so you won't find any record or resemblance…"

"So, are you from Scotland then?"

"No, I'm from the Irish side." Her eyes glinted eerily in the deep shadows, and she said, "My adopted parents died some time ago in a boating accident. Neither of them could swim and the boat tipped in turbulent waters. Their bodies were never found…"

"I'm terribly sorry to hear that."

"Don't be—we were never really close… Eva has always been the one true mother in my life. I don't know what I would have done without her…" There was a sudden silence between us within that final thought she seemed an eternity away. The moment having passed, she glanced back at me, and said, "Stay close—it's almost impossible to see here at night. Not to worry though, I know each passage and room of this place like the back of my hand…"

I followed without question. The corridor was pitch-black, and even by the light of the lamp I felt increasingly unnerved by the pursuing shadows. They came in progressive waves, as with each step we traveled the darkness surged, becoming deeper from behind. There was a draft coming from a broken window somewhere, or a gust creeping in through the open flue of a forgotten chimney. It chilled me to the bone, as with every footstep through the blackness I heard whispers echoing in return. The short hairs stood from all over my body, and I felt the flesh of my arms begin to crawl. There was a cold spot on my neck which felt as though a wet finger was pressed against it, and I suddenly turned to look. Nothing, only complete and utter blackness, but I knew that something was there… It was taunting me, daring me to fall behind and wait for it in the growing darkness…

"Our rooms are just around this corner." She broke the stillness and startling me, said, "If you wait in the corridor I'll light the hearth so that you can see where you are walking."

"If it's all the same to you, I'll come along and just wait."

"Is something wrong?"

"I'm not feeling very well, to be honest. Having wet feet and being out in that cold has given me a slight chill. Also, I'm beginning to suspect that the fever might be causing me to imagine things…"

"Oh dear-," She hurried me onward, saying, "I wouldn't be too concerned… It's just late, and the darkness in this house can become a little, disorienting. Most old, dark, and drafty places do…" Pausing before an open doorway and raising the lantern to look into my face, she said, "If you'll take the lantern I'll manage your luggage and see to the fire. Please, just trust in me, it won't take more than a few moments."

Nodding, I took the lantern from her hand and quietly watched as she quickly gathered my belongings, and hurried into the room. I could hear moving about in the room, but was unable to catch even the slightest indication of movement. A chilling draft sent shudders coursing the length of my spine, and I turned back to look down the blackened corridor. I couldn't see anything, but felt that something was lurking in that darkness, and lingering from just beyond sight… There was a sudden flash and I saw Caitlin putting a flame to paper, and then casting it into the hearth. The room brightened, I breathed easier, and she hurried over to where I stood.

"The hearth is stoked. Be sure to keep the flue open and the screen tightly closed." She pointed, and assisting me toward a large roll top desk, took the book and bag from my hand, and said, "Just a moment, I'll light the oil-lamp for you."

I watched as placing the book and bag on the desk, she struck a match and lit the large old lamp. My face felt hot, and although the light brought comfort, I blinked while having become sensitive with the growing fever.

"You need rest--," Moving back toward the open doorway she turned to look back, and said, "I'll be in the room right beside you--," Motioning in the direction of her room with a hand, she said, "If for any reason you should need anything in the night, please, don't hesitate to knock."

"I should be fine now—but thank you."

Appearing reluctant to leave, she slowly began pulling the door closed from behind her, and said, "A parting word from the wise in warning... In the night and in the darkness, always keep doors, tightly closed..."

Her words echoed in my thoughts as her emerald eyes eerily reflected the dancing flames of the hearth. With the deep shadows of the closing door casting sinister lines within her pale features, I halted her while raising a finger in question.

"Just so that we're both completely clear on this... Exactly why do we need to keep those doors, tightly closed?"

Poised within the deep shadows she quietly looked back, and said without much thought, "On occasion, raccoons have been known to enter the premises and wander these halls in the night. They're harmless for the most part, but when cornered, can become quite dangerous... "

"Surrounded in such antiquity, I forgot that we were in the country-side... Thank you for the warning and pleasant dreams..."

"Good night, Michael..."

I watched as smiling, she pulled the door closed, and giving it an extra tug just to be certain, was gone.

"Well, so much for any late night bathroom trips... I might as well get as comfortable here as possible..." Looking around the room and noticing a large bureau, I took my suitcase and began unpacking. In moments I had everything neatly sorted, and changed into my favorite blue flannel pajamas, slippers, and black robe.

"Oh, who am I kidding? Fever or not, there's just no way that I'll be getting to sleep this early." Looking at my wrist-watch I scoffed at the thought, saying, "I'll just get settled in a little bit more before calling it a night."

Retrieving and opening the protective case, I lifted out and placed the 'Smith Corona' typewriter on the desk. It was smaller than some of the older models and perfect for these occasions. Slumping into the chair and locating my lighter and cigarettes, I lit one while looking around the room. I felt terrible but the curiosity was killing me. I had to know the secret of what had bothered Caitlin so much about that diary... So, barely able to see and suffering with a high fever, I reached over and grabbed the book. Opening the cover with the intention of just examining the first few pages, I paused while hearing a faint but distinct sound from behind me. It came in low tones and was a type of muffled, gasping. It reminded me of the sound of rushing air flowing from between damp and severely cramped spaces. There wasn't any central heating or ventilation, so it couldn't have been a furnace. It came again, except a little louder and more defined... Raspy and gasping it gurgled hideously. The noises sounding like the pus-filled lungs of someone drowning in their own phlegm with pneumonia...

"You're just tired—there's nothing there... It's just a gust from some broken window and the resulting draft in the corridor... Of course, that has to be it... Just a wind, whispering through the dark halls of a very, very old house..."

CHAPTER FOUR

The cigarette almost fell from between my trembling fingers. This time I had seen it… It was the distinct shade of a shape, that being deeper than all others, vanished beneath the door when I had turned to look.

"That wasn't real—it couldn't have been…" The words were uttered in something beneath a whisper. Swiftly turning to look back to the hearth, I stuttered in thought while saying, "It must have been my own shadow reflected by the firelight. Of course, that had to have been what happened…"

Realizing that the hearth stood behind me and that I was out of the direct line of its light, my blood ran cold. Moving from the chair and tossing the cigarette into the hearth, I stood and stared between the desk and fireplace. My own shadow, cast by the lantern on the desk and growing smaller in approach, lingered upon the wall near the hearth… It was impossible. In order for my shadow to have been anywhere near that doorway, I would have had to have stood directly beside the hearth… When clearly, I was sitting ten feet away and against the opposite wall…Moving about to test that theory I suddenly stopped and just stood there staring.

"Oh, but that still wouldn't have worked… The doorway is rear center, and the hearth and light from the lamp on the desk only cast shadows on the walls beside it… Someone would have had to stood between the hearth and the desk--," Moving into position and observing my shadow upon the floor and bottom of the door, my heart skipped, and I said, "And even so, it could never have slipped out from under that door the way it did…"

Slowly crossing the room I paused before the door while stopping to listen. All was utterly silent with exception to the sound of my own, shallow breathing. Then I heard it. A faint pounding… It was the echo of my own heart as the coursing blood raced through the arteries and thundered within my head. Reaching for the door handle with trembling hands, I felt the touch of its cold steel as my fingers slowly closed about it. Then ever so cautiously, I turned it while cringing to the deafening click of the inner mechanism. Squealing upon rusted hinges, I winced while opening the door just far enough to peek out and into the corridor. A cold and moldering gust entered through that sliver of an opening, and I recoiled from its vile breath. The corridor stood in absolute blackness and though I couldn't see it—I knew that it was there… I could feel its presence from out of the darkness. It was a tangible force that penetrating the body and mind, subsequently chilled the soul… Noticing my own shadow caught in the firelight and cast into the corridor, I stood frozen with the realization. It had given me away…That tiny sliver of light which escaped from beneath the partially open door. Whatever was out there in the darkness had surely noticed… The fever sent my thoughts running wild, and I imagined horrible things in that blackness. The shadows becoming twisted masses of unrecognizable things, swarming, writhing in the blackness. They were the pale worms that slithered in the foul mud beneath those decaying mounds… Far worse, they were graveyard worms and seeking human flesh from which to feed… My flesh… They're moving. The shadows are alive in this place, watching, waiting for what? The light—yes, that was it… They were waiting for me to turn down the lights… Then in darkness and while utterly alone, the worms would come creeping to feast upon my living flesh...

With my heart racing wildly I peered down and into the long and endless dark. Somewhere and very near, lost within that blackness was the door to Caitlin's room. Not a single sound… Shouldn't I have been able to see a light, or heard the noises of her preparing for bed? Maybe even just a little squeak from an old bed spring as she climbed beneath the covers. Why was everything so bitterly cold, endlessly dark and deathly silent? I was sure of it. It was the shadows in that place… They drowned all sight and sound… and stole the life of all and any that came into their path…

"In the night and in the darkness, always keep doors, tightly closed…." I whispered through cold and trembling lips, and said, "Yes, that's it… just close and lock the door…"

Ever so slowly, painfully, I closed and quietly locked the door. In a second thought, and carefully pulling it free of the lock, I slipped the skeleton key into the pocket of my robe. With the boards creaking beneath my weight, I crept back to the hearth while adding several logs to the fire. Cautious while fitting the screen back into place, I stood back while watching the flames. With a face heated by fever and brow dampened with sweat, I was utterly exhausted but too frightened to sleep. I needed to find some form of escape and a way to clear my thoughts before bed.

"The diaries—I'll just look through a few pages.... That should ease my mind enough to finally get some sleep."

Turning to go back to the desk, I caught a strange glimmer in the corner of my eye. Shimmering and pale, I soon realized that it was the moon peering in from between the parted draperies of my window.

"That's strange--," I went to the window and drawing the draperies aside to peer out, said, "The shutters on all the other windows are fastened, except this one. Maybe Caitlin opened them? No, she didn't have time—it was a last minute decision to take the room, and we came here together..."

Leaning closer, I watched as the faintest of crystalline formations frosted the edges of the glass, and the internal warmth struggled against the night's icy breath. It was almost magical as from out of a starless night, the moon cast a pale twilight into the room. The darkness of the heavens seemed to expand from all about me and I suddenly felt very tiny, insignificant, and utterly alone. It was during that moment, and when the moon had slipped free of the clouds, that I noticed a pale structure in the distance.

"That's not a building at all--," My eyes grew large as whispering, I said, "Those are mausoleums..."

Revealed beneath the moon's glow, and rising high above the western hills were the pale and distinct shapes of three marble structures. Spellbound, I wondered what lurked among the graves, and wandered those lonely fields by night. Lost in thought, the clouds swallowed the moon and the houses of the dead faded into shadow. There was no longer any doubt in my mind. It was happening... The foundations of my book were rising from the fevered delusions of a terrified mind.

"I wonder what evils lurk in the ancient halls of the House of McCreary..." Making my way back to the desk with a sudden determination, I dropped into the chair and cursing, said, "Alright, let's see if we can't find a few skeletons in the family closet..." Carefully unrolling the large genealogical chart, I located several candles from around the room, and placed one on each corner for weight. Satisfied that the scroll was safely fastened, I retrieved a pen and pad and began scribbling notes.

"Okay Michael--," I spoke purely for the sake of hearing a human voice, and said, "Let's start at the bottom while listing accidental deaths, suicides, or anyone that had passed away due to illness. And, from the looks of things, this family's had a colorful past in the old, morgue department…"

I began making notes, cautious of the names, places, and properly dating everything. Although I had no intention of betraying Caitlin's trust, I always kept certain details accurate for the sake of consistency. I was known to have a few grammar issues at times, but few things bothered me more than stories filled with mistakes and contradictions…

"Oh geez, I can see why she was so concerned. I would be too if one of my relatives was hanged for grave-robbing. No wonder she didn't want any of this to get out…"

Within minutes I had compiled a small list of names and important dates. Double-checking the details in lieu of my somewhat, compromising condition, I paused in thought.

"Okay, we've got a list of names, deaths, and the details of their crimes and specific disorders."

Removing the candles and carefully rolling the scroll back into its appropriate, leather tube, I placed it between the wall and desk for safe keeping.

"Alright then, it's time to crack open the proverbial vault and see what crawls out?"

Gently brushing a hand over the cold leather surface, I felt for the cover's edge. Carefully drawing the old book open, I quietly began reading aloud, "A history of the House of McCreary and Duff Glenn, a narrative of leading events by Sir Reginald Andrew McCreary, including family genealogies, seventeen-eighty-six to nineteen-fifteen. That's interesting, why isn't there any current family records for the past fifty-five years? Oh well, we'll just work with what we have for now…"

Looking through the seemingly endless pages and archaic terminologies, I decided to cut to the chase. Scribbling notes, I quietly began reading, and said, "The estate of the *Clan McCreary* began construction in the year of our lord, seventeen-hundred and eighty-six, under the rule of Sir Jonathan Stephen McCreary. A man of honor and integrity, his livelihood was derived entirely of the import and export of precious stones and metals. The manor was completed in seventeen-ninety-one, the same year that his wife, Maria Marguerite gave birth to Henry Augustus."

Flicking an ash, I read down several paragraphs through Sir Reginald's accounts of business, the shipping industry, and hazards of bad weather

"Blah-blah-blah, second son, Thomas was born in seventeen-ninety-three—and hey, a third son, Peter, born in seventeen-ninety-five. No one could ever accuse them of not being productive. In October of eighteen hundred and one, ten year old Henry disappears… His body is found in the pond by servants the following morning. It was established that after having fallen into the deep and muddy water, that the boy had been tangled in willow roots and hence was drowned. Oh, God… The poor kid drowned in the mud—what a nasty way to die..."

Scribbling the details of little Henry's death I felt bad with the thought of including the material for a book. I had to talk myself back into it. Truth being told, it wouldn't matter when the manuscript was completed as the names, dates, and places would all be changed.

"In the wake of little Henry's death, Jonathon begins construction of the mausoleums. Located in the south western region of the grounds, the mausoleums would be accessible by passing through an adjacent gated, stone memorial garden and cobblestone path."

Passing through several more pages of details outlining construction features of the house itself, I found another point of interest. It concerned a business partner who just happened to be a relative living in Ireland. Could this possibly be Caitlin's family connection?

"Glenn Doyle, a distant cousin managing a ship-yard on the Emerald Isle. Not bad—they even covered distribution costs by using their own shipping fleet."

Briefly searching through the pages I found another unfortunate accident. This time it was Thomas, the second eldest of the three sons. In this, Sir Reginald accounted for the incident through Parish records.

"April sixteenth, year of our lord 1809."

Reading the account several times while attempting to properly record the incident, I shivered. The fever was catching up to me due to fatigue and it was becoming harder to concentrate. Still, I continued while reading aloud, saying, "While attending the site of the newly constructed McCreary mausoleums, Thomas McCreary, sixteen years of age and the eldest of two remaining sons, became the victim of a terrible accident. It was as while over-seeing the completion of the third and final structure that Thomas, accidentally dislodging a structural support beam, was caught between and subsequently crushed to death by the collapsing marble wall."

Flipping the page, I scanned down from where Sir Reginald discussed Jonathon's grief and subsequent alcohol abuse.

"In June, eighteen-fourteen, Peter, aged nineteen, marries a local girl by the name of Elaine Marie Crofton. Might not be important, but I'd better keep this in perspective, just in case…"

Butting the cigarette in a large crystal ashtray, I continued scanning through the pages, "Blah-blah-blah, in a drunken stupor Jonathon beats a man-servant half to death. I see drunks haven't changed much over the years? Oh here we are! Elaine becomes pregnant and gives birth to twin girls in May of eighteen-sixteen. Names--," I reached for another pen as the ink ran out, and said, "Amelia and Vanessa. Eighteen-seventeen, Peter travels to Germany with his family and takes up a degree in medicine at the University of Krakow. The addition of the West Wing chapel and family crypts, the renovations were finally completed in eighteen-twenty. Peter returns home and to the ailing Jonathon's delight, proudly introduces his two year old son, Michael Augustus."

Hurriedly taking down the details I read through the monotonous accounts of numerous business exploits. This included company expansions, and the introduction of fine furniture, antiques, and works of art.

"Okay, so Elaine gets pregnant again and in October of eighteen-twenty-six, gives birth to a son, Alistair. Good grief, how could anyone keep all of these details in perspective? And for that matter, how did Sir Reginald, who was supposedly suffering from an incapacitating disease? There's no possible way that he would have been coherent enough to write this… Maybe he wasn't as far gone as some would like us to believe?"

For several minutes I just sat there, scratching at my head, and drifting into that dark place where dreams and imagination collide with common sense.

"But then again--," Reaching for another cigarette, I paused while shaking the lighter and said, "Diseases are progressive. He might have started the writing before he was too far gone?"

A sudden crash sent me backward and to where falling from the chair, I stared up from where I sprawled on the floor. Swinging while caught in a sudden and strong gust, I watched as the shutters slammed against the framework of the window.

"Great, well that explains why they keep the shutters locked in place." Crawling from the floor and moving to the window, I opened the glass panes and reached out while attempting to draw the shutters back. Yelping, I leapt away as the wind tossed the heavy shutters back against my hands. Frustrated and more than just a little angered, I managed to catch them on the second attempt, but was almost pulled out the window in the process. It was a cold night, and shivering in the dampness, I leaned out while trying again. Swiftly drawing the shutters back, I had barely latched them when the wind whipped up, and blew all the papers from the desk. Closing and fastening the latch on the window, I cursed under my breath while shutting the draperies.

"I just don't have the strength or patience for this right now..." Wandering back to the desk and gathering the fallen notes, I rescued several pages that had gotten far to near the hearth. Slipping out of my smoking jacket, I dropped it on a bed-side chair, and pausing to look around the room, thought aloud.

"I'll finish with the notes tonight. They aren't going anywhere and I still have the whole weekend... Okay, old man, it's officially bed-time..."

The bed was a classic four-poster style with canopy, wine colored draperies, and white sheers. The bedding and pillows were luxurious, and being made of the finest linens, bore a burgundy and golden, Damask pattern. Aside from their obvious quality, I couldn't help but notice their condition. In that moment, I wondered if anything had been washed in the past, half-century... Patting down the covers and pulling the blankets aside, I immediately began sneezing in the resulting dust-storm.

"Nope, nothing has been dusted for the past few decades… But, I don't even care. The room is warm, the bed is soft, and I'm absolutely beat… Nothing is going to keep me from getting some sleep…"

Carefully drawing back the top cover I suddenly froze while catching a swift movement in the corner of my eye.

"Except maybe for that…"

Leaping back as an enormous wolf-spider dashed out from under the covers, I grabbed a poker from the fireplace and began smashing at the scrambling insect.

"Die you ugly, furry, little bastard!"

Pursuing it across the bed and whacking at the ghastly thing, I gasped as it dashed across the blankets, dropped onto the floor, and then vanished beneath the bed.

"Oh no—it's—under the bed…"

In the silence I could easily imagine what the little monster was doing. It was lurking somewhere in the dusty shadows around the hanging edges of those old blankets. It would be watching with those eight, beady little black eyes… and waiting for me to go to bed… Yes, it would wait for the lights to go out and then it would come in the darkness… Silently, it would come creeping upon those eight, long and hairy legs. Ever so cautiously, it would crawl, those razor sharp fangs twitching with venom as it crept beneath the covers… and then…

"Oh, God I hate spiders!" I leapt back and dropping the poker, indulged a ridiculous 'shudder and shake' dance about the bed. Rubbing at the creeping flesh of my forearms I stared into the shadows beneath the bed. I hated spiders… They were one of the few creatures on earth that truly unnerved me… Just the thought of that hideous thing crawling anywhere near my body was enough to cause uncontrollable shudders of revulsion.

"I'll just wait around until he comes out. Then I'll squash the furry little bugger…" Pulling off a slipper, I went back to my chair at the desk and waited…

Friday October 6, 1972.

4:26 a.m.

Sitting and waiting at the desk for what seemed over an hour, I scanned the floors from all around me. It hadn't come out from under the bed, but I just couldn't wait a moment longer. After drifting off several times and almost falling I finally gave up the ghost. Turning the flame down and extinguishing the lamp, I grumbled while uttering in an almost incomprehensible slur of gibberish.

"That's it." Moving unsteadily from the chair and stumbling toward the bed, I dropped onto the edge, and said, "It's just a little, disgusting, filthy, hairy, buggy thing... By now it's long gone and there's absolutely nothing to worry about..."

Turning and dusting off the pillow, I took one last look under the covers before slipping into bed. The sheets were cool to the touch, and while crawling beneath the blankets, I fought back a violent sneeze. Any previous concern about the dust had soon vanished with thoughts of that spider.

"Please God—don't let it get me..."

Basking in the gentle twilight and unable to keep my eyes open any longer, consciousness finally slipped away. There was a sensation of utter weightlessness, a sudden absence of mind, and then something cold touched me in the blackness... What was happening? Standing, yes, I was now standing in some kind of long and dark corridor... I couldn't see anything, but somehow knew that it wasn't the house of McCreary.... Remaining absolutely still, I gazed into the blackness at the far end of the corridor. There was a strange twilight, which slowly growing grew made me aware of a shape in that darkness. I was barely able to make out the pale form. Crouching, it huddled with its face pressed tightly into a corner of a near-by wall. Shuddering, it glistened in the dim light. It's bony frame dripping with some kind of luminescent and primordial ooze...

Terrified, I wondered whether it was aware of my presence in the deep shadows of that place. I wasn't sure, but the growing fear now forced a desperate need to escape. I thought to run? Yet, for some reason, knew that it would be hopeless. In that moment I noticed that the thing had begun to rise from where it had been crouching. Moving ever slowly but with a distinct sense of purpose, it began turning toward where I stood. Although horrified and unwilling to even look upon the thing, I forced my gaze to where it now silently stared from across the corridor. From the shadows of a drawn and leathery face, more animal than human, were two tiny and luminous, green eyes... They were cold, devoid of soul, and hungry... The blood froze in my veins, as raising long and clawed fingers it began coming toward me... Its movements were sluggish and appeared hindered, as though it were traveling through deep water. Horrified, I realized that I couldn't move a single muscle to run or raise a hand in defense...All that I could do was watch helplessly as the fiend approached... Razor sharp claws clicked from upon blackened fingers, and I now heard the fleshy slap of its feet against the cold stone as it moved faster, and ever faster. Desperate, I tried to look away before the hideous thing fell upon me, but was helpless to even do that.

All at once it began to tremble, and shudder violently as its body started to change. Dropping to the floor, it crawled and slid upon its belly as it became repulsively swollen and began lengthening. With its flesh blackening, long and hideous roots sprouted, erupting from beneath and thrashing wildly. From all around its sides sprang tendrils and thrashing tentacles, limbs of which it used to drag that ghastly body through a trail of thick and putrid slime. Ever closer it came as growing huge, the head rose upward, and the thing stared with black and soulless eyes. A long seam parted from the bottom of that face, and splitting wide, revealed bleeding and blackened gums. Steaming decay spilled forth and hung from that gaping wound that mocked anything resembling a mouth. The tiny and glowing eyes erupted from upon long stalks as it approached, and a slithering tongue oozing with blackened filth, lolled from out of its mouth. There was an overwhelming stench of decay, as struggling to avoid the flailing roots and oozing tendrils I cried out, "God, oh, God! Someone, anyone, please help me!"

A sudden and thunderous echo caused me to leap upward abruptly, as awakening from the nightmare, stared in utter horror. There was a violent hammering, and I turned toward the sound of Caitlin's desperate pounding on the bedroom door.

"Michael, please answer me--," Beating furiously upon the door, she called out, "Are you alright in there? Michael, please unlock this door!"

Fumbling blindly through the darkness, I searched the pocket of my robe for the key, and said, "I'm alright—everything's fine! Just a moment, please!"

"Michael—what's going on?" She was terrified.

"I'm having a little trouble with this lock? It seems to be jammed or something?" The truth was that my hands were shaking so badly that I could barely hold the key. Finally managing to unlock the door, I flung it open while stepping aside.

"I heard you screaming! What happened—are you okay?" She appeared from out of the darkness, and wrapping her arms tightly about my neck, wept as she said, "You scared me half to death!"

"I'm so very sorry… it was just a really bad, nightmare." Covering my face with a trembling hand, I suddenly noticed that my night-clothes were damp with an icy sweat.

"You look awful. Are you sure that you're going to be alright?" Brushing the clinging hair out of my face, she gazed deeply into my eyes, asking, "Can I get you anything or do anything at all?"

"Oh, no I'm fine now, honestly. I think that I was just too warm under all those blankets? I must've kicked them off in my sleep and gotten cold? That would explain the nightmares--," I raised a finger in thought, saying, "Cold feet have always given me bad dreams. That started when I was a kid."

"You poor thing—you're completely soaked." She frowned while picking at my damp and clinging pajamas, and said, "I could stay with you for a little while? We could talk about your nightmare? Sometimes that helps?"

"That's really very sweet of you--," I already felt like a fool for having put my hostess through this as reassuring her, I said, "But, I'll be fine now—really."

"Are you sure? I really don't mind?" Concern deeply creased her brow as gesturing toward the desk with a nod she said, "I could bring some nice hot tea?"

"I've already caused enough of a racket around here. I'll be lucky if you don't just toss me out on my butt, tomorrow…"

"Oh don't you be silly--," She frowned as tapping her nails on the door-frame, glanced back, and said in a thoughtful manner, "For future reference, it might be a good idea to leave the door unlocked…"

Pulling the skeleton key from my pocket, I moved to where she stood and dropping it into her open hand, said, "I'm used to locking doors wherever I am... you better keep it."

"You seem to have an affinity for keys and locked doors..." She looked into her open hand and then back at me, and said, "If I was the superstitious type, I might find that somewhat, concerning."

"Like I said—it's best that you keep it..."

"If you expect to accomplish anything you better get to sleep. The light arrives later in the colder months, but morning still comes early... I'll just leave this open for tonight..." Glancing up and down the corridor from behind her, she added in thought, saying, "We don't seem to have any visitors tonight..."

"Thanks again—and I'll see you in the morning.... Good night, Caitlin..."

"Pleasant dreams to you, Michael..." Slipping away she vanished into the darkness beyond the doorway.

She was only gone for several moments when I became uncomfortable with the thought of that open doorway. If not locked, it should at least be closed...

"On second thought, maybe it would be best that we keep this closed--," She appeared from out of nowhere and observing me rather curiously, said, "If you should happen to wander out of this room for any reason, please avoid going too far..."

"Thank you, but all the same, I won't be leaving the room again tonight..." I watched as nodding, she turned away and quietly closed the door. In that moment some part of me had desperately wished that she hadn't gone. At first the emotion left me feeling awkward and confused, but then the truth came. It was simple enough, but was something that had eluded me for many years. Until meeting her, I never realized just how truly lonely I was...

.

CHAPTER FIVE

Utterly exhausted, I was too frustrated to fall asleep. After tossing and turning among those dust-covered blankets, I finally abandoned all hope of getting any rest, and climbed back out of the bed. One thing that struck me as being entirely odd was the fact that as tired as I was feeling, the fever seemed to have faded. Maybe it was just a matter of getting nice and warm in that bed before I could shake the chill? Regardless, slipping into my robe and wandering back to the desk, I was feeling a lot better than earlier.

Slumping into the chair and lighting a cigarette, I looked at the old book and grumbling, said, "Obviously, regardless of how lousy I'm feeling, there won't be any sleep today... Well, it's not like this will be the first time, so I might as well do a little more reading..."

Lighting the old lamp, I rubbed the sleep from my eyes and returned to the page where I had last left off.

"Okay—now where were we? Ah, yes, the month of August, year of our Lord eighteen-thirty-four. Amelia turns eighteen and takes a suitor named, Charles Raymond Devonshire."

Skipping through a lot endless dates and non-pertinent information, I ran a finger across the page while reading. "Although infuriated with the supposition of marriage, Jonathan, having been attentive of Charles' notorious repute, fails to dissuade the young woman. As might be expected, news of Charles' infidelity with Carolyn Ellesmere, a local Inn keeper's daughter, soon reaches Jonathan. Rumor speaks of Jonathan having traveled into the village, visited the Inn and spirited the Ellesmere girl into the night."

Reading further, I began recording the dates and events carefully while seeing the story unfold.

"Charles vanished about the same time, and its weeks later before the estranged Amelia, approaches local authorities. She learns of Charles and Carolyn's affair, and is informed that their disappearance was likely a romantic interlude, rather than a probable misdemeanor. It would be a fort-night before Michael would discover the corpse of the Ellesmere girl in the pond. Submerged among the willow roots, she was secured by rope and stone anchor, and bound to Charles, her unfaithful lover..."

Inspired by the heinous and horrifying nature of these developments, I looked to the typewriter while contemplating a beginning for the novel. The only thing stopping me at that point was consideration... I knew that pounding at those keys would sound like I was riveting bolts into the wall between our rooms. It was something that I had experienced as a child, and while listening to my mother work through the nights. Having already disturbed the peace and serenity of Caitlin's home, I decided to keep it simple. Besides, I had brought more than enough paper and pens to manage whatever notes I might need.

"So now we have a double murder--," I puffed at the cigarette while returning to the book, and, saying, "But what's this? It doesn't get reported to the authorities... Jonathan reveals the truth to Amelia, enlisting her allegiance by threat of being an accomplice to a crime, punishable by death. Blackmail—this just keeps getting juicier... Amelia, stricken with grief and unwilling to accept the blame or share the guilt, fled from Jonathan.... During a struggle with him, she accidentally falls, and dies after striking her head upon the mausoleum steps.... Bereaved but unwilling to disclose the unfortunate accident, he hides her corpse in the mausoleum. The bodies of Charles and Carolyn vanish, and Jonathan blames the estranged and now missing Amelia for the murders... Good Lord, how very cold and cruel..."

Butting the cigarette, I reached down and opening the doctor's bag, retrieved a bottle of soda. In seconds I had the top off, and drank deeply while attempting to soothe a parched throat. If an endless thirst was a curse among the sleepless, I was forever damned... Finishing the bottle, I dropped it into a trash can beside the desk and clearing my throat, returned to reading aloud.

"Okay—so Peter sends Michael, age seventeen, to University in Geneva in eighteen-forty. Shortly after, it's said that Peter is seen in the company of reputed heretic's, occultists, and other characters of equally sinister constitution. There is talk of black magic. Imagine that now... It would be the spring of eighteen-forty-three, when Peter would find Jonathan, who after having written a detailed testimonial and relinquishing all evidence of his crimes, to have hanged himself in the west-wing crypt."

Tapping a finger on the book I shook my head, saying, "Imagine that? The man lives well into his eighties and then hangs himself? Well—that explains how Sir Reginald had all the gory details on the murders.... The news of Jonathan's death traveled fast, reaching Elaine who subsequently returns to Peter with young Vanessa. Over the next ten years Peter would continue his occult studies, often consulting with known practitioners of the black arts and gypsy spiritualists. In May of the year eighteen-fifty-three, Vanessa would marry Arnold Humphries, the village physician. Arnold was a brilliant doctor, admired by his associates and reputedly a man of virtuous character. That would make Vanessa thirty-seven years old and a granny by the standards of that time. Oh well—spinsters, every family has one... It would be these qualities that inspired Peter to request that he take permanent residence within the estate. Arnold accepted immediately, drawing his practice and enlisting the aid of Michael who had recently returned from Geneva. It would be young Alistair who in the late fall of eighteen-fifty-four, would discover Amelia's corpse while surveying the mausoleums. Holy-smokes, if these aren't reason enough for a haunting than I don't know what is? Vanessa bore twin girls in December of that year, Elizabeth Ann and Lenora Marie, whereupon due to complications during birthing, she takes ill for several months. It was during the following months that Peter withdrew, and subsequently dissolved all previous association with Jonathan's prior business relations."

Writing the events down in proper sequence and underlining the dates, I sat back to review what I had written before continuing. Yawning and rubbing the sleep from my eyes, I turned the page while reading aloud, and said, "The decision both abrupt and entirely unwarranted, exasperated his colleagues, many of them suffering hardship while having become entirely dependent upon his financial support. All business repute and integrity established by Jonathan falls into absolute ruin within those final months. Peter establishes Arnold's office in the medical profession, catering to military outposts, employees of The Hudson's Bay Company, and Native tribes. He incorporates the McCreary fortune in the already industrious, fur trade. Good move and great business connections, but now he's never home... On the fifth day of the month of February, eighteen-fifty-six, Alistair takes, Kathleen Meyer, the daughter of a local shoe-maker as his wife. Disappointed with

Alistair's choice of a common wife and the predominating illness of both Elaine and Vanessa, Peter becomes reclusive, spending endless hours locked in his study. The year eighteen-fifty-eight, Kathleen gives birth to Sarah Lynn, the child immediately falls ill, and merely weeks later, succumbs to the night chills. Regardless of pernicious rumor concerning the moral constitution of the McCreary family, Arnold's reputable skills as a physician escalate and his practice flourishes. April of the year eighteen-fifty-nine, Arnold Humphries and Michael McCreary are discovered to have participated in the practice of grave robbing, and other heinous crimes against the people. They are tried and found guilty, and are promptly hanged in March. Peter inters them within the family crypt, and having lost all professional credibility, abandons his practice, sojourning to the privacy of the estate. It would be during the month of July that several of the female servants would seemingly abandon their responsibilities and altogether vanish... In the year eighteen-sixty-one, mid-February, an inexplicable fire breaks out in the west wing where Kathleen and little Elizabeth are overcome by smoke, and hence perish in the ensuing flames. Peter inters them within the crypt, and enlisting several artisans, begins restoration of the west wing and chapel. No wonder Caitlin keeps that west-wing door closed... That side of the house was nothing but an endless source of suffering and death..."

Pulling a candy bar from my bag, I opened the wrapper and chewed at it while continuing.

"The spring of eighteen-sixty-three marks the completion of the Glenn Doyle manor. November, eighteen-sixty-five, Peter McCreary passes unexpectedly in the night. The grief-stricken Alistair remains alone to contend with business and estate. Under extreme duress, Alistair immediately enlists regulatory management. The Glenn Doyle Mercantile and Affiliates swiftly re-establishes and maintains its prior conduct under the administration of Edward Allan Thomas. Reassured of continued success, Alistair concentrates all efforts upon the Humphries Funeral Parlor. With the proprietorship in capable hands, he takes the opportunity to regain proper management of the Duff Glenn estate. It would be during these following months that he would discover the occult literature hidden within his late father's private study. These were black pages, which providing evidence of witchcraft and ritualistic murder, would cast Alistair beneath the shadow of madness that prevailed over his father. The estranged Alistair would soon become driven by silent madness. Often found within drunken stupor, he pursues matters best left to darkness and devil-lore… Now why doesn't this surprise me?" Tapping the pen at the pad, I said, "This family has so many skeletons there isn't a closet in the world big enough to hold them all… Trouble finds Alistair once again, as several of the servants make claims of having witnessed strange lights among the mausoleums during the night. With the previous unsolved disappearances, the authorities quickly investigate the claims. September sixteenth, eighteen-sixty-five, Alistair is arrested while caught exhuming remains from the mausoleums. Richard Charles Terence, an attorney at law, spoke in Alistair's defense during a lengthy Court trial. He established that the transference of human remains from a mausoleum to a crypt upon private property, be it by day or night, is not a criminal offense. Alistair was pardoned of all charges, but never released him from legal scrutiny. Alistair would become more secretive and deranged over time. It would not be until the sudden and unexplained disappearance of his dark research material that he would return to life and society. Although vague and never proven, suspicion implicated Alistair's niece, Lenora.

November, eighteen-seventy, Alistair is subjected to public ridicule after Lenora, aged sixteen, is discovered to have become heavy with his child. It would be within the late December of that year that Alistair, overwhelmed with guilt for his father's unspeakable atrocities, ends his life when leaping from the west-wing parapet. Destitute, young Lenora would remain in isolation, a moral prisoner of the estate and unborn child… Pictures, I'll definitely have to take some pictures of that west-wing parapet…"

The numbing glow of the distant dawn ached painfully in the back of my mind. Closing the book and sluggishly wandering over to the bed, I slumped onto the heaped mass of blankets. Closing my eyes, I covered my face with a pillow while attempting to avoid the growing light.

"Hello and good morning to you, sir." Eva spoke softly and with a heavy Scottish drawl, as gently though persistently knocking on the door, called again, "Mr. Schreiber, the breakfast is ready and waiting, sir."

Rolling over with a groan, I instinctively shielded my eyes with a hand. Blinded in the dull glare of a clouded morning, I coughed on the dust while calling back in reply, and said, "Yes, thank you kindly. I'll be there in just a moment! Oh, God, it's going to be a very, very long day…"

Saturday October 7, 1972.
9:18 a.m.
It was an effort to even move as half-dazed, I stumbled at the foot of the stairs.

"Holy smokes!" I caught the railing with both hands in the last second, sparing a headlong tumble into certain death. Clinging to the old banister, I just stared down at the cold marble floor some twenty feet below. It was a sobering moment to say the least… I counted thirty steps before finally making it to the bottom of those stairs. They squeaked and gave way far too easily for my liking, and I didn't trust the brass rails that fastened the red carpeting to each step. Along with the ceiling cracks and shadows the list was steadily growing… It was a miracle that I even found my way back into the dining area. The place looked so different during the day that I almost thought I had wandered into the wrong house.

"Good morning, you must be Eva?" Extending a hand in greeting, I couldn't help but smile when seeing the woman. She was singing an old Scottish folk-song when I had first entered, and her voice and accent were immediately endearing. Short and pleasantly plump, she wore a pretty pink and white, polka-dot dress, full apron, and white shoes. With her white hair fastened into a bun, rosy cheeks and big blue eyes, she was a picture of health and happiness.

"Good heavens, Mr. Schreiber?" She gasped, as placing a hand before her mouth, said, "With all due respect, sir. You look like you haven't slept a wink in days?"

"No—I was up late reading and lost track of the time. In fact, I hardly slept at all." Jabbing a thumb in the direction of the staircase, I scoffed at the thought, saying, "Not to mention, I almost took a nasty spill down the stairs this morning."

"Oh my--," She gently grasped my wrist and stroking it like a favored pet, asked, "You didn't hurt yourself—did you, dear?"

"No—I caught the banister in the last moment--," Feeling rather silly, the embarrassment caused me to smirk in a boyish manner, and thinking for a moment, I said, "But I did manage to scare the Dickens out of myself."

"Well then, you just set yourself down, laddie--," She pulled me toward a chair and seating me before the table, said, "Help yourself to some nice hot tea and I'll fetch your breakfast."

Suddenly becoming aware of Caitlin's absence I looked around the room, and then asked, "Are we alone this morning?"

Glancing back from where she served breakfast from a silver dining cart, she said, "I'm afraid so, sir." She grinned mischievously and said, "It seems that the both of you were up quite late? Not that I'd be hinting at anything, improper, you know?"

"No, no—it wasn't anything like that!" Blurting defensively and spooning far too much sugar into my tea, I felt obliged to explain and stuttering, said, "There were some strange things going on late last night, and she came into my room.... To check in on me, and make sure that everything was alright..." Attempting to correct myself she just laughed while waving off the thought.

"There's no need to explain anything to me, sir--," She chuckled, saying, "It's not my business to be prying into the lady's affairs, anyway."

"The truth is a little embarrassing--," I decided to be completely honest, and said, "I had a nasty nightmare and for the first time in my life, well, I guess I woke up shouting? So, as you can imagine, and being in the room beside her, I woke Caitlin and she came running. I've never felt more ridiculous in all my life..."

"I doubt that anyone's ever slept very well in this place?" She appeared vaguely disturbed but not entirely surprised, and said, "It's just too big, old and drafty." She stared around the room and rubbing her hands together, said, "I won't stay here in the night. It's far too noisy and much too chilly for these old bones."

"After spending the night, I can imagine why you might feel that way... Caitlin mentioned that you were staying in town with a friend?" I sipped at the tea and coughing due to all the sugar, asked, "Have you been employed here for long? I mean—if you don't mind me asking?"

"Oh no, I don't mind at all." She shrugged as running a hand across her tightly bound, white hair, fidgeted with the pins and said, "It seems like forever, really? I've been with Caitlin since she was a wee baby. I've been in other places previously, but none were a finer home than what we've shared here."

"That's a lovely accent--," I nibbled at toast and said, "It's a wonder that it's lasted through the years? You are from Scotland, right?"

"I certainly am, dear, and quite proud of my heritage too. I was born in Aberdeen Scotland, astride the rivers Dee and Don." She proudly announced, saying, "That's on Scotland's North Sea coast. It's a busy port town to this day. It's how my family first came into the service of the McCreary's."

"Oh, of course, so you knew Caitlin's parents."

"You'll pardon me for saying, sir?" She became visibly uncomfortable with the conversation, and said, "But, I would prefer not to discuss such things."

"Of course... This breakfast is absolutely wonderful." Respectfully, I directed her attention from the previous topic, saying, "I feel badly that you went through all of this trouble, just for me?"

Her features brightened as refilling my tea cup, she said, "Oh goodness, that's what I am here for, dear. Can I get you anything else?"

"No, thank you. I'll be lucky if I can even finish what I have?" Utilizing a rasher of crisp bacon to shovel eggs onto a piece of toast, I suddenly realized my poor etiquette. Cringing, I looked up rather shamefully, and said, "Oh, pardon me."

"Oh, don't you be bothered, dear--," She waved a dish towel, and chuckling, said, "You just enjoy your breakfast in whatever fashion pleases you most."

"Thank you, but—believe it or not, I actually do use cutlery in most cases." Attempting to explain, I spilled again, and wiping egg from my chin with a napkin, said, "Although it does seem like I'm having a little trouble with it this morning?"

Adjusting the frilly white apron about her waist and offering another napkin from the tray, she said, "Mr. Schreiber... do you mind if I ask you something?"

"Not at all—and please—call me Michael." Accepting the napkin I looked up as she seated herself across the table, from me, and thoughtfully said, "Caitlin tells me that you write ghost stories. Do you really enjoy prowling about in the dark, and chasing spooks and nasties?"

"I've been fascinated with the supernatural since childhood, and am thrilled the possibly of encountering a real ghost at some point. But, what exactly do you mean by, nasties?"

"Well, you know--," Gesturing with her hands as though they were claws, she looked to me and said, "The nasty little things that linger about graves, lurk under beds and hide in closets."

"So far—I haven't encountered anything like that?" Grinning, I pulled the cigarette package out of my pocket and waving them, asked, "Do you mind if I smoke?"

"Certainly not, you go right ahead, dear." She poured herself tea and dropping a slice of lemon into the cup, asked, "Have you been too very many of these supposed, haunted houses? And, do you always go running off alone on these spooky adventures? Not that I intend to pry, you understand?" She nodded her head politely while speaking in a reserved manner.

"Oh—on the contrary! I'm happy to talk about it!" Sipping at my tea and clasping my hands together, I said, "I have traveled across Canada and visited several, assumedly, haunted locations. Most of them just have noisy old plumbing, unusual drafts due to lack of insulation, and their owners are the ones with bats in their belfry. As for your second questions, yes, I live and work alone. It's just easier that way…"

"Oh, now that's such a shame." She frowned and clicking her tongue, said, "It's just not good for a young man to spend all that time alone."

"Well, as you already know my interests can be a little unnerving to some, and down-right dangerous at times."

"Pardon me for a moment." She excused herself while gently patting my shoulder, and hurried off into the service area.

"I'm a very private person and to be honest, enjoy the personal freedom. I can come and go as I please without worrying or having to explain myself to anyone."

"With all due respect, it sounds like girls scare you far more than ghosts?" She grinned while returning with a tray containing a glass of orange juice, and a small platter of assorted fruit.

"A writer's world is a lonely place. It's a passion that demands one's full attention while slowly stealing the years, one page at a time."

"There is always a price to pay for anything worthy of having or doing in life." She stood with a blank stare while looking down at me, and said, "For every blessing granted by the angels--," She whispered in thought, saying, "The devil waits for his pound of flesh in payment..."

"Well, that's rather dark--," I thought for a moment, and shoving a piece of bacon into my mouth, said, "And all the more reason to avoid girls."

"Oh—so now you admit it, do you?" She laughed and leaning closer and whispering, said, "Well if the ghosts and Ghoulies don't get you first? Eventually the girlies will?"

The heavy lilt made it hard to diversify between Ghoulies and Girlies. Over the past few years, and with my experience with them, there hadn't been much difference at all. The Girlies, more often than not, were 'gold-diggers' and those whose lives ended at the bottom of a wine bottle every night. As everyone knows, Ghouls are 'grave diggers' that end up at the bottom of a coffin each night... I just laughed with the thought. She must have sensed this because she changed the subject.

"Have you ever encountered an 'honest to goodness', ghost?"

"You know, it's funny that you should ask that? I just discovered a story about an unfortunate local woman who recently disappeared..."

"You don't say?" Her eyes became huge, and she almost whispered, leaning closer, and saying, "Local was she?"

"Oh yes, very local in fact. The truth is--," I leaned across the table and quietly said with a smile, "She never arrived for breakfast..."

"Ach, you ought to be ashamed, young man! Putting me on like that..." Pointing an accusing finger and chuckling, she said, "You really had me going there for a moment."

"My apologies—but I couldn't resist."

"Aye, I can just imagine. Excuse me for a moment—I have some things to tend to in the kitchen."

"Well, I'm all done here—thank you for a lovely breakfast, and delightful company."

"Oh, well aren't you the charmer." Laughing, she gathered the plates and cutlery, and loading everything onto the serving cart, moved toward the kitchen,

Butting the cigarette, I casually followed her into the kitchen and to where placing the platters on a long white marble counter, she turned to face me.

"Michael, might I ask you something more of a personal nature?"

"Of course, please feel free."

Her bright blue eyes narrowed in thought, and speaking somewhat reluctantly, she quietly asked, "Michael, what terrible thing happened in your life that now has you chasing death, instead of living it?"

I knew the answer but it hurt too much to admit. I shrugged and looked away.

She turned back to the counter and began cranking on a pump to fill a pail with water. Then pouring it into the double stainless steel sink, began washing the dishes, quietly saying, "The estate is very old and can be quite dangerous… what remains of the place is filled with broken hearts and bad dreams. If pain is what you came looking for--," She glanced back at me in warning, and said, "Then you're in for a world of hurt in this place, my lad…"

12:15 p.m.

It was a cold and overcast afternoon, and my ears and face were already numb with the damp chill. In Caitlin's absence I had decided to leave Eva to her business, and wander around the property to take a few pictures. Feeling exhausted, it was the only thing that I could still manage without much thought. Or at least that's what I had assumed… I soon found myself wandering further than intended. Pulling the camera from the brown leather case that hung from my shoulder, I slowly turned for a panoramic view.

Having traveled several hundred feet from behind the mansion I now stood in an immense, stone walled, octagonal garden. Like the pillars to the main gates, the masonry was comprised of river rock, and overgrown with long and trailing blackberry vines. Barely visible from beneath the dense bush, I could see a marble statue in each adjoining corner of the wall. These were likely figures of Dryad's from Greek mythology, as clinging to Oak branches and facing inward, focused upon an immense, marble fountain.

In the center of the octagon was a huge marble fountain where a figure of Poseidon stood within a chariot drawn by sea horses. With trident held high, the statue stared upward in defiance, challenging the heavens and yes—even the Gods themselves.

Remembering the description from the newspaper article that I had previously read, I sat down and tried to imagine what it might have once been like? In thought, the sky cleared as turning toward the immense marble centerpiece, I looked upon the surging waters of the fountain. Time had suddenly stood still as captured in the moment, I smiled in admiration. Standing in a living dream, I gazed upon the brilliantly colored and sweet smelling flowers. There were bushes of roses, pink and white carnations, gardens filled with tulips, daisies, China asters, bleeding hearts, freesias, dahlias, and baby's breath. Lilac bushes bordered the wall from behind, and from wherever the sweet smelling flowers hung over, was a bench for lovers to share.

"Paradise--," The word offered strange comfort as I whispered in thought, "It must have been a complete paradise."

The splendor of the moment was suddenly shattered by the call of a raven. Fluttering among the branches of an old and massive oak, the enormous black bird croaked, and peered down at me.

Snapping a series of pictures without the flash, I waved at the bird, and said, "I'll frame one of those! And use it for a dart board…"

Looking back, the house of McCreary loomed ominously from beneath the cloud-filled heavens. It rivalled the 'Lyndhurst Mansion' in splendor and easily matched the 'Margam Castle' in sheer size. Yet for all of its Gothic and dark majesty, time and the wrecking ball would soon bring it all down.

Snapping several more pictures I paused to just look at the place. Peering out from behind the twisted and dark limbs of old Oaks it certainly was a haunting sight. The wind whistled, branches swayed, and I sensed that something was gazing back from those dark and empty windows. Startled again by the ravens call I turned angrily, and shaking a fist, shouted, "Hey—beat it you boneyard buzzard! Don't you have a date with some road-kill somewhere?"

Looking into the tall trees of the Southern forest I stopped to think.

"We know where this goes—now don't we? It passes the old pond where poor little Henry drowned and ends at the mausoleums…"

The wind tossed the leaves and I watched as they spiraled down from all around me. The huge fields appeared as an emerald sea, and from where pastel shades of autumn painted the wind-swept waves.

There was a wide expanse of open land before the path vanished into the wilds of the distant forest. It was a place virtually untouched through the better part of a century and there would be animals there...

"It couldn't be more than a thirty minute hike? If I'm quick and make noise I shouldn't startle anything or get surprised by something? I hope..."

The decision made, I flung the long scarf over my shoulder, pulled my collar up, and marched down the trail. The scarf has been a Christmas gift and always reminded me of my dear friend, Bill Kaba and his wife. He was a retired merchant and jeweler from Lebanon who worked at a local flea market with his wife and two sons. They had a kiosk and dealt exclusively in gems and assorted minerals. For obvious reasons we quickly became good friends, and spent countless hours discussing minerals and mysticism. In essence, he truly was a 'mystic-man.' It was the winter of 1970 and during one of our lengthy conversations that his wife had overheard my mentioning being in need of a good scarf. Being the wonderful people that they both always were, it came to me as a gift not a month later. It was heavy woolen knit, black and gray striped, had black tassels, and was five feet in length. It went everywhere with me in the colder months and so did their memory. Sadly, Bill and his family relocated, but soon owned a flourishing rock and mineral business in Toronto. We still spoke on the telephone, but distance and time have a way of drawing people apart.

"God bless you and your family, wherever you are, Bill." The cold wind had a way of making me sentimental while hiding behind that scarf. Some people just had a way of leaving their mark on your heart, and I felt blessed for knowing them.

Although the grass was still green in the field it had already grown tall and yellowed at the forests edge. The leaves crunched beneath my feet, and I was startled as a rabbit raced off into the dense thicket. Chilling gusts whispered in the branches of the Birch, Aspen, and Oak, and I hurried along as the forest grew ever closer from all around me.

"There you are!" Caitlin laughed as I stumbled backward in shock, and she promptly apologized, saying, |Sorry, I thought that you had noticed me coming after you?"

"I would have waited if I had." Gasping and with a hand to my breast, I looked back and across the open field, and asked, "Where did you come from?"

"I took a short-cut through the woods."

She wore a fox fur vest over a dark green turtleneck sweater, brown slacks, and knee-high leather boots. A long scarf of autumn shades blew in the wind from about her, and I could imagine how she might easily blend with the forest.

"I was just out looking for a Gingerbread house. Have you seen one in your travels through the woods today?"

"No, but you might encounter the big bad wolf if you're not careful." She winked as thoughts of animals on that path bothered me even the more.

"I was just out taking some pictures--," Grabbing the camera from around my neck, I tugged at the straps and said, "I'm on something of a time limit here, so thought that I would get this done while you were, well, preoccupied?"

"Sorry--," Blushing ever so slightly, she said, "I warned you that I'm not an early riser at the best of times." In a second thought, she looked ahead on the path, and then asked, "What possible interest could have brought you so far from the house?"

"It was the diary and mausoleums—to be completely honest. I hope that it isn't an issue?"

"No, not at all--," She walked with me down the path and raising an eyebrow in question, asked, "Exactly how much of that story have you read?"

"I read about Johnathan and Amelia and what happened at the mausoleums. Oddly enough, they caught my eye when I was looking out from my window last night."

"I'll have to see to the shutters in that room." The thought visibly bothered her as apologizing, she said, "The wind is terrible and they keep coming open for some reason…"

"Oh, not to worry--," I smiled and shrugging said, "There's just something about a window overlooking a cemetery that adds to the ambience and mystique of it all."

"All the murder, grave-robbing, suicides, witchcraft and demonology aren't enough already?"

Wiping the cold sweat from my brow while admiring the tightly clinging fabric of her slacks, I said, "That was another thing that had me wondering? If Sir Reginald was truly that sick, how in the heck did he manage to keep all those details, names, and dates straight? To be honest, I even had a hard time just following it."

Stopping suddenly, she turned to look back and appearing strangely amused, smiled as she said, "Oh, come now. Don't tell me that you're actually beginning to believe any of that nonsense?"

"Believe? No—not exactly. But you have to admit that it does make for an interesting read."

"If you think that's interesting--," She laughed while leading the way and saying, "Just wait until you get to his personal notes. But Michael--," She pointed a finger in warning, and said, "I really wouldn't suggest reading that before bed."

"That has honestly never happened to me before." Still embarrassed for crying out in the night, I said, "I don't know what came over me?"

"Look around you, Michael!" She gestured into the looming and ancient forest, and said, "How could you possibly avoid nightmares, when according to Sir Reginald, you're standing in the middle of one?"

"He does paint a very bleak picture. But then again, I've never felt this alive or more inspired anywhere else. It's uncanny, really..."

"Tell me something if you don't mind?" Her eyes suddenly flashed with mischief and something that I couldn't quite describe, and she quietly asked, "Above all other things, what scares you the most?"

The answer arrived all too easily, "The death of loved ones... that overwhelming sense of helplessness that it leaves, and then being alone."

"That's a good answer." She brushed the long red locks from her eyes, and said, "But not the complete truth."

"I'm not sure that I understand what you mean?"

"I think that your real fear isn't the loss of loved ones, but the possibility of death truly being the end. And that all of this--," She waved a hand above her head while looking back at me, and said, "Is all there ever was or will ever be..."

She was right... Nothing terrified me more than the thought of a big black nothing waiting at the end of life's door.

"I prefer to believe that there might be something more. But, you're absolutely right. That does scare the living daylights out of me. We hardly know each other. Can I ask how you might've just guessed at something like that?"

"It was obvious enough. Most people do not go poking about in dark places in the night… Those who do have good reason and some are deeply rooted, psychological issues. So, if a person who seeks out mysteries to the afterlife is merely trying to establish its existence--," She hurried along and glancing over her shoulder and smiling, said, "Imagine their horror at finding nothing at the end of their dark little rainbow?"

"You know, for someone so intelligent and attractive, you have a distinctly morbid sense of humor."

"Oh, but my dear, Michael--," She acted shocked, and then smiling as she playfully skipped along, said, "Isn't that part of the initial attraction?"

She pranced playfully while laughing and I knew that she was absolutely right…

CHAPTER SIX

The path was overgrown and gradually becoming more narrow. In lieu of this, we were forced to walk in single file to avoid from being caught in the trailing vines and stray branches. It wasn't long before the path widened again, and ascending a hill, opened into a vast clearing. The trees were far larger and much older, as covered in moss and lichen, circled wide into the distance. The grass faded into gravel, and large rocks jutted from sparse patches of grass along the forests edge. Ascending a hill, I stopped to catch my breath as the pond came into view.

One hundred feet in circumference and surrounded by a three foot wall of river rock, two enormous Willows stood upon its Northern edge. Old and gnarled, their enormous roots spilled over the sides and vanished into the murky waters. From all about that immense pool rested benches, large urns where flowers had once grown, and statues of marble angels in silent repose. It had once been a very lovely place, but that had been a very long time ago...

"Little Henry drowned among those roots." She pointed and frowning said, "They also became the final resting place of Amelia's estranged husband, and his mistress..;"

"Charles Raymond Devonshire and Carolyn Ellesmere..."

"Yes, I believe those were their names."

"Aren't you coming along?" I noticed that she hesitated and now stood behind me.

"No—you go ahead." She gestured with a little wave of her fingers and fleeting glance, and said, "I've never felt comfortable going anywhere near that filthy water or nasty old trees...."

"I can't imagine why?" Smiling sarcastically as while turning away from her, I was speaking more to myself than within reply. Pulling the camera from its case, I strolled casually toward the pond.

Located a short distance from the mausoleums, this was obviously a place where mourners had once gathered. There were eight angels in total for every ten feet of wall. In between them stood moss covered, stone planters from where only the withered remnants of weeds still lingered. Blackened and stained by moss that clung to its Northern regions, and angel stood sadly from behind me. The marble had yellowed, its eyes ran as though with tears, and I took several pictures for posterity's sake. The pond was obviously man-made and quite deep, and the water replenished by rain and winter over the passing years. Looking into my reflection upon the murky waters, I shuddered with thoughts of the dead. It wasn't just the knowledge of what had happened there, but an unnerving sense that someone or something was still down there…and watching... Leaves and rotting vegetation slowly drifted as though eerily suspended between this world and the next. Unable to permit my reflection and soul to remain part of that foul mess, I quickly stepped away and snapped several shots of the pond and trees.

It was hard not to imagine poor little Henry as all alone, he laughed while playing among those horrible old tree roots. Tripping and falling into that foul water, struggling while entangled, and then mercilessly drawn down. In the darkness, helpless, as screaming, his lungs filling with that filthy water and mud. With eyes wide open and becoming suddenly still, the last few bubbles of air vanish among those horrid old roots…

I could only imagine as to what vile sustenance those roots had drawn from the rotting dead. The evidence was likely revealed within their hideously twisted trunks, gnarled limbs and sickly appearance of the roots…

"Michael, are you just about done? The weather is turning! If we don't hurry we'll be soaked, and possibly be caught in the dark before we're done."

"Oh, yes, I'm done with this place!" Glancing back at the murky waters one last time, I saw the wind create a ripple, and the wave pass into the enormous old roots across the pond. It almost looked like they were still holding and hiding something from just beneath the surface…

"Are you going to be okay?" Grasping at my sleeve and shoving her face close to mine, she examined closely before saying, "You look pale as a sheet. Are you sure that we shouldn't just go back to the house?"

"What, are you serious? No, not when we're this close!" Anxious, I motioned past the pond with a hand, and said, "Let's just go over for a quick peek and a few pictures. I promise, after that we can go straight back. Okay?"

I felt like a kid again and begging my mother to stay up to watch the Late show in a school night. She looked at me with serious concern, and after a moment's deliberation nodded.

"Alright, we go straight there, take a few pictures, and then straight back to the house." She was either testing me or already knew me too well.

"Cross my heart." I made the motions with a finger across my chest and while giving her my best 'puppy-eyed' look. It had never worked on my mother but I was hopeful. She didn't appear impressed, but after a moment's thought, nodded.

"The mausoleums are on the hill, and hidden from just behind that grove of trees--," She pointed while leading me toward them, and frowning, said, "If we hurry—we might still beat the rain…"

An icy gust whispered through the withered trees of the ancient groves. Having climbed the hill, we now stood and looked toward the pale buildings. Surrounded by an eight foot, spiked, iron fence, the mausoleums stood centrally and to the rear of a memorial garden. It spanned a distance of roughly one hundred feet in circumference and was octagonal in shape. The entire property was overgrown with blackberry vines, and vast bushes filled corners while spilling over from the tops of the buildings. There was a gateway with a marble walkway, and stone angels stood guard at the doors.

"Alright then--," She looked to me as we approached the gate, and appearing paler than usual, said, "Let's be quick about it. The weather is against us and I despise this place even more than the pond…" From the look in her eyes it seemed obvious enough…

"I won't be long…" I promised while peering from between the black and rusted, iron bars, and saying, "It's unsettling the way that nature reclaims things over time… Just look at the way those old tree roots crawl under the marble, creeping ever deeper, and until reaching those who lay rotting, in silent repose…"

"Has anyone ever told you that you're quite creepy at times?" She fumbled with the keys and smirking, said, "But I suppose that you would find that flattering—now wouldn't you?"

"Yes, and I'll accept that as a compliment. Now, can I be of any assistance?" I pointed to where she fought with the key and padlock.

"Of course, please and thank you." She stepped away to observe.

I stood there like a fool for several minutes while wriggling at the chains and tugging at the rusted barrel. We looked at each other several times during the course of my struggle, and she quietly stood there while appearing greatly amused. Finally, I stepped back in utter defeat and sighing deeply, said, "This thing must be rusted beyond repair. It's simply impossible…"

Clicking her tongue and moving forward, she tightly grasped the padlock, and shoved the key into the slot. After a brief attempt, and to my utter chock, it suddenly fell open in her hand.

Smiling victoriously, she nodded while waving at the open gate, and said, "A gentle hand and a little patience go a long way."

"Well—that saves me from having to climb over, now doesn't it?"

"Oh, really now--," Directing my attention to the long and pointed spikes, she grinned devilishly, and said, "Even if you did manage to climb up—you might be less of a man before you reached the other side."

Nervously peering upward, I could easily imagine having become impaled on the jutting and rusted spears. They were far longer than what I might have expected and had several rows of pronged barbs.

"So, off you go then." She pulled open the tall double gates and speaking in a ghoulish tone, said, "And do try to be quiet—we wouldn't want you waking anyone, now would we?"

"Am I going alone?" The thought hadn't occurred to me even after her previous comment about despising the place.

"I'd rather not go in there--," Crossing her arms over her breast she shrugged, saying, "I'm sure that you understand." Diverting her attention from me and nervously fidgeting with the collar of her coat, she wiggled her fingers in a mock wave, saying, "Just, don't be too long… You know how fragile women are. I might get startled by something and run away screaming at any given moment."

"Oh, sure, that's real funny…" Swinging the scarf over my shoulder with a laugh, I wandered in through the gates, and said, "There's nothing dangerous in here whatsoever…"

"And it's a good thing too!" She called after me, and said, "Because if something should happen to go wrong in there? You know that there's absolutely no way that I would come in there looking for you!"

She smiled cruelly when I paused to look back at her, and waving me onward, said, "Hurry along now! Places to go—dead people to meet!"

Pulling the camera from its case and turning suddenly, I began snapping several images of Caitlin. I had the flashbulb covered with a tissue and elastic band to cut glare, and against the dismal background she was absolutely radiant.

Crossing her arms and casually leaning a hip against the gates, she wiggled her fingers at me and smiling, said, "Okay, off you go now—bye-bye!"

She was so cute… Realizing that it was getting darker and might likely rain at any given moment, I hurried along without another word.

"It's a good thing that I brought lots of film. This place is far bigger than I'd expected?"

Standing on the plateau and gazing back down the path, I noticed the memorial grounds to be slightly sloping and of a triangular dimension. The point having been formed by the entrance, I turned to examine the two immense stone pillars near the fence. That's when I noticed it… The property was octagonal in shape, but there were four angels placed in strategic points. All faced inward, and their eyes were focused upon a marble fountain that stood before the doors of the mausoleums. A tall angel stood at the foot of the fountain. With wings spread wide and its head thrown back, it pleadingly motioned into the heavens with outstretched arms. Bowing beneath the angel were the forms of three cherubs with closed eyes, and hands clasped in silent prayer.

"The builder's used octagonal shapes throughout the estate—and triangles here—I wonder?"

Hurrying to the far corner of the mausoleums and struggling through the thorny blackberry vines. I peeked around the building. It was almost invisible from beneath the blackberry thicket, but I could barely make out the pale and raised arm of an angel.

"Now why in the heck would anybody put a statue behind the building like that? No one would ever see it?"

Pulling the pad and pen from an inner pocket, I quickly drew the angles and dimension of the gardens, and then added the angels in proper perspective.

Drawing lines from between each point from where the angels stood, I stared in amazement, "A perfect pentagram."

The Victorians were well known for their interest in the occult, but had the designers intentionally created this symbol of protection? It was fairly common to see sphinx, mystic symbols of the Masonic order, and even animals in the graveyards of the Victorian era. There were even figures of death himself in the cemeteries of Florence, but never anything like this... Not so cleverly concealed anyway?

Spinning to the sound of a sudden movement in the brambles behind me, I stared intently. The wind whistled through the vines while rustling long dead leaves, and nothing moved in the shadows from beneath.

"I must have spooked a rabbit or something? With all the blackberry bushes this place is probably full of the little stinkers."

Focusing upon the Mausoleums, I made notes while thinking aloud, and saying, "Resting upon a raised stone plateau comprised of river rock, stand three marble, mausoleums. The largest is central, slightly receding, and stands higher than the others with the addition of several steps." I thought for a moment and squinting suspiciously, said, "That is obviously where Amelia," I quoted; "dashed her brains out upon the marble stairs."

It was a ghastly thought and even worse while standing there in the actual place where it happened.

"All three mausoleums are gated, appear to be locked, and have ornately carved reliefs of angels above their entranceways--," I spoke while continuing with the notes, and said, "They are overgrown from the rear and sides by blackberry bushes, and time has stained them in ashes and amber shades. That should do it for the notes."

Slipping the pad and pen back into my coat pocket, I shoved the scarf aside and took several pictures. Regardless of the pictures I always took notes due to the fact that a photo could not explain a mood or sense. In the same turn, notes and senses easily missed things that the clever eye of a camera always caught. They were both indispensable in my specific field of interest.

"That's strange—I thought that they were locked?" Drawing open the iron gates of the smaller and nearest building to the right, I peeked into the shadows.

A large sarcophagus stood centrally, as lit from a portal above, cast light upon the beautiful figures upon its lid. The moment caused me to sigh mournfully just with the sight of it.

The figures of three Cherubs leaned from the sides of a pool, as reaching downward, gently drew the body of a child from the water.

"Poor little Henry..." The thought chilled me to the bone.

Adjusting the tissue and elastic on my flash bulb, I took several pictures from outside the gates. Usually I would have gone inside for better angles, but something caused me to reconsider. The place had and boy had been left in peace this long and I was willing to disturb either of them. Leaving the central mausoleum for last, I hurried along and made a quick inspection of the other. The gates were locked, I had no interest in causing any damage, so simply snapped a few shots from outside. Somewhat disappointed, I made my way to the largest of the three, and paused to take pictures of those notorious stairs. Time and weather had stained them with iron and the deep amber reminded me of dried blood. I had my doubts...

"Oh, it looks like our luck is about to run out?"

The clouds moved faster, the afternoon grew darker, and I could feel the moisture in the wind. It was going to rain very soon and I had to hurry. Climbing the steps I was feeling hopeful as I didn't see any locks on the gates. Reaching for them, I was suddenly set back with a shock. Looking between my hands and the gates in surprise I could not image what might have happened for the life of me?

"What the heck was that all about?" Rubbing at my wrists I suddenly stopped, "Now what is that?"

Moving forward and looking between the black iron gates I was surprised to see a small gold chain and pendant? It was bound around them and appeared to be the only thing holding them closed?

Usually I would have left it exactly where I found it, but had to have a look inside that mausoleum.

"I'll just have a quick peek around and put it back before I leave..." Slipping the pendant into a pants pocket, I cautiously reached for the gates. I had read stories about static energy remaining in places that were not properly grounded for many years. Maybe lighting had struck the building at some point and some infinitesimal portion of that energy had remained in the iron of the gates?

Tapping at them with a finger I soon found the strange charge to have completely vanished. A moment later I swung them wide, and with hardly any light, crept into the chamber.

Unlike Henry's tomb, this one remained in almost complete darkness. I didn't wander inside very far, and looking up, assumed that whatever portal might have permitted light must have somehow been covered? It was too dark to see anything and I didn't have time for a length examination of the place.

In the light that entered through the gates from behind me I could see that the crypt was literally barren. Although larger and more impressive, it didn't have any of the beautiful figures or carvings displayed in the others. There was a table against the wall far wall and from where a tall candelabrum stood. It held ten candles, an old leather-bound bible sat on one side and a tall silver chalice upon the other. Taking several pictures, in the light of the flash I became aware of an antechamber leading downward from the rear of the tomb. It was pitch-black, a draft issued from out of the darkness, and the hair on my arms and back of my neck stood on end.

"No—I definitely don't need to look down there—or stay here for another second longer." My instinct for survival was stronger than my curiosity in that moment and I turned to leave.

In that moment the wind howled through the vault, and stepping back I noticed a sudden, though dim light. Looking upward, I saw that the strong gusts had blown off part of the obstruction.

The tomb was illuminated by a central stained glass window which was located in the ceiling. Barred from beneath, it was ornately crafted into the form of a huge diamond that shone down upon a sarcophagus located directly below.

"Now that—is absolutely gorgeous." Admiring the stained glass diamond I pondered briefly, and said, "I wonder if there's some way that we could save that? And do I really want to? No, I'd better just leave the treasures of the dead in the grave where they belong…"

In the dim glow I could now see details that I couldn't before. The sarcophagus was carved from solid white marble, and although faint, there were delicate etchings along the sides and upon the lid. These consisted mainly of delicate and intertwining Calla Lilies, and the form of a girl resting among them.

She was young, beautiful and appeared to simply be sleeping among the surrounding flowers. The Victorian era brought a distinctly beautiful mysticism to the mystery of death. Where people ended in the modern age, they only dreamed while awaiting discovery into realms beyond. It was an age and presence of art and mind to be revered and cherished.

"What a nasty shame to just demolish it all." Snapping pictures of the stained-glass and intricate carving upon the vault I slowly turned to leave.

"Oh, now what happened here?" Pausing to closer examine the lid of the sarcophagus, I ran a finger the length of an ugly crack that threatened of eminent collapse. It was invisible from the angle that I was previously standing, but clear from the toe end. Someone had obviously forced that sarcophagus open at some point, and damaging it in the process, slid it back into place.

"It might have been thieves looking for jewelry? There's still grave-robbing going on in some countries, even today. Everyone knows that they used to bury wealthy people with their gold wedding bands, pearls, and diamond necklaces."

A sound caused me to turn and listen. At first I thought it as just the wind and then remembered leaving poor Caitlin outside and waiting.

"She won't be too happy with me—I better get back out there."

A shrill scream sent me tumbling against the far wall and to where I fell hard against it with my back. Realizing that it must have been Caitlin, I moved to rush out but was suddenly halted by movement from the entranceway. The room brightened as though some unseen light now shone from all around, and through the amber glow, shadows moved. They were the shapes of people that stretched while twisted in sunlight coming from beyond the door. I knew this was impossible because an early evening shower was only moments away, and moved to look out. I was just a step away from escaping the vault when I looked out and froze in absolute fear.

"Amelia! Halt girl! Millie you must listen to me!" The pale and translucent form of an old man pursued a young woman across the steps before me.

"Murderer, beast—do not touch me!" Weeping hysterically, the specter of Amelia attempted to evade the swiftly pursuing shadow of Jonathon McCreary. They were the shapes of people colored in the shades of their surroundings, and their voices sounded strangely hollow. It came in the same way that sound might carry in a wind tunnel and be heard through an old microphone. It was an echo without depth or base.

"You must listen to me, child! Millie—you get back here this instant!" His speech slurred with obvious drunkenness, as pursuing the fleeing girl toward where I now watched, grabbed at her while shouting, "Cease this foolishness, now!"

Unaware or simply unconcerned with my presence, they fought and argued as I stood staring in utter disbelief. Either I had fallen and knocked myself unconscious due to fatigue, or I was witnessing an actual preternatural event... Pinching my arm, I winced with the pain of it, my eyes widening as they came within several feet of where I stood in the doorway.

"Millie, halt—I demand it!"

In that moment he grasped at her wrist and she ripped free of him while spinning out of control and losing her balance. I watched in horror as she fell backward and smashing her head upon the step, died before my eyes...

"Millie, oh Millie what have I done? No!" The apparition of Jonathon bowed over his granddaughter's still form, covering his face and crying out, "Forgive me child, I beg of you!"

My heart thundered as reaching down and gently lifting the girl's body from the steps, he carried her into the mausoleum. My whole body suddenly tingled as they passed and I could feel an icy static energy, shuddering uncontrollably.

"What have I done, dear God in heaven--," Placing her down upon the tomb he bowed and wept bitterly over the body, saying, "Millie, please, it was an accident and nothing more. Awaken from this damnable sleep. Do not leave me. All that I have done was done for you... Charles and that harlot...that filthy wench! Can you not see that I've done all these things out of love? Love for you dear child. Please Millie, come back..."

Unable to move or barely even breathe I stood there watching. It was like standing in a dream that was long lost in time and being played over, and over again...

"You must--," He insisted, taking her hand and gently stroking her wrist, pleaded, and said, "Awaken from this. Millie, I will never let you go... Do you hear me? Never..."

Lifting her from off the tomb, he turned toward where I stood and blindly approached. Stepping aside as he passed, I turned to watch as he carried the girl's body across the vault, and vanished into the wall. The strange light fading in his passing, I suddenly stood alone in the cold dark.

"It had to have been a hallucination... that couldn't have just happened..." "Raising a trembling hand before my eyes, I looked toward the dismal shadows beyond the doorway, a cold gust hitting my face.

The wind and scent of rain in the air were real, and I was wide awake in my own nightmare. Stumbling out the door I almost slipped on the steps, and looking back saw that the iron stains had vanished...

Without another thought, I ran across the plateau and jumping down, raced down the pathway toward the front gate.

"I was beginning to wonder if you fell asleep in there--," Caitlin locked the gate as I stepped out and suddenly staring, asked, "What on earth happened to you..."

"Nothing—," Gasping for breath, I grabbed her by the hand and towing her along, said, "Sorry, I lost track of the time—we better hurry before the rain comes!"

"Are you absolutely sure that you are okay?"

"Yes—just very tired and I could really use something to eat."

"Well, we've already missed lunch." She shrugged, her eyes attempting to reach into mine as we slowed, and she said, "Eva never stays late. But, I'm sure that we can find something?"

Feeling the first tiny droplets of rain on my face, I cursed under my breath and apologizing, said, "I'm sorry about taking so long. We'll likely get soaked now, because of me..."

"We aren't that far from the house--," She didn't seem very concerned at all, but asked, "Did you manage to get the pictures that you wanted so badly?"

Waving the camera and finally breathing normally again, I smiled and said, "I sure hope so, I ended up using the entire roll of film."

"Oh no, you didn't? Not on that horrible old place." Obviously disappointed, she slapped my shoulder, and said, "It seems like such a waste of perfectly good film?"

"I've got many more rolls in the bag." I waved it before her widening eyes and said, "I learned a long time ago to always be prepared."

"You know?" She slowed on the path, grinning mischievously as she glanced back at me, and said, "You could always take some pictures of me? I mean, if you really wanted too?"

It took little convincing as enticed with the prospect, quickly switched the film in the camera, and aiming the lens toward her shouted, "Say cheese!"

The frightful experience of the tomb fading in the moment, I chased her with the camera. Laughing like children we raced about, as posing before old stumps and massive boulders, I caught her in every pose and perspective. It went fast, and before I knew it, I had snapped thirty four images and only had one left.

Looking through the lens that one last time, I noticed the grim willows and pond in the picture behind her. I took the photo anyway, and waving, motioned for her to follow.

"Is that it already?" Obviously disappointed, she gracefully leapt down from a large and twisted stump and walking toward me, said, "We don't have to stop? The house is huge and we'll have it all to ourselves for the weekend."

"All to ourselves for the whole weekend--," I repeated the words almost fearfully while remembering the incident in the tomb, and asked, "Doesn't Eva usually work on the weekends?"

"Of course she does—but I gave her this one off so that you could work, unbothered…" Her eyes shone with all the enthusiasm and passion of youth, and fire that kindled the furnace of my deepest desire.

It's pointless Michael. Don't get caught in a daydream that can never happen. We would be forever separated by the cruel hand of time… And besides, I would be leaving soon…

"Oh, no, here it comes!" Changing the subject and pointing into the dark skies, I laughed as the rains came in a blinding torrent. Grabbing at my hand and pulling me along, she laughed as taking shelter near the forests edge, she said, "Let's wait here for a few moments to escape the worst of it. It never lasts long."

We stood close and beneath the branches of an old Maple, sheltered from the wind and rain, and neither caring if it ever stopped.

CHAPTER SEVEN

Soaking wet and chilled to the bone we burst through the French double doors of the rear patio. Shivering and laughing like children, we leapt back while being unexpectedly surprised by Eva.

"You'll both catch your death of cold fooling about like that!" She shouted, tossing towels at us, and saying, "I could hear you coming from a mile away!"

"It's—it's you!" Completely startled with her appearance, I stepped back.

"The two of you shouldn't be creeping about out there. The Duff Glenn isn't the safest of places and the old burial grounds are not meant for the living—they're just not safe…"

I was beginning to wonder exactly how much she really knew. It was obvious why she refused to remain in the house but why was she so concerned about an old cemetery… She was obviously frightened by something, it was apparent by her wide eyes and the scolding tone in her voice,

"Oh Eva, don't fuss so much." Caitlin laughed, drying her face and looking at me while binding the towel around her hair, she said, "We need to get out of these wet clothes." Her attention fell upon Eva as she asked, "Would you mind bringing some lunch up to the library?"

"That's why I stayed later—waiting on the two of you. I only fuss because I care, dear." She stared into Caitlin's face, reaching up and gently stroking the woman's face, she said, "I couldn't bear the thought of anything ever happening to you."

"I know, Eva--," Hugging the kindly old woman and kissing her cheek, she said, "And I love you for it. But right now we could really use some dry clothes and hot food."

"Some nice hot soup will do you both a world of good." Eva nodded, her entire demeanor suddenly changing as she looked to me, and said, "I found some nice things that might suit you? I took the liberty of leaving them in your room. I hope that you don't mind?"

"That's really very kind of you. I only brought a few things from home." I pulled the soaked cigarette package from a coat pocket, and looking between the two women, said quite sadly, "I suppose that's the end of my smoking for now?"

"Oh?" Eva reached into her apron and retrieving several packages of cigarettes, promptly extended them toward me, and said, "I picked them up when my friend took me into town this morning. I wasn't sure if you might need them, but it's always better to be safe than sorry, I always say."

The endearment I already felt for the old woman now blossomed, as surprising her with a gentle embrace and kisses on the cheek, I said, "You're a perfect angel and simply amazing. Thank you ever so much!"

"Oh my goodness, you're very welcome!" She grinned, as pressing a hand to her cheek in the reddening onslaught of a blush, she said, "I wonder what might've happened if I'd bought you an entire carton?"

"I might just have to go shopping with you next time?" Caitlin winked as pausing in the hallway and glancing back at me, said, "Go get into some dry clothes. I'll meet you in the library for lunch."

"Eva—one moment, I owe you for the--." Reaching into my coat and producing the dripping wet wallet, she halted me with a hand,

"I won't hear anything of the sort." She smiled as patting her cheek quite bashfully, said "They're already paid for, my lad."

Wandering out and pausing in the doorway, I looked back at her, and said, "Don't spoil me too much. I might not want to leave."

"Who ever said that you had a choice in the matter?" She winked as something dark glistened in her eyes.

It shouldn't have, but something bothered me when she said that. I just smiled and with a wave, hurried off to get changed.

6:15 p.m.

When I entered my room I was pleased to find a neatly folded stack of clothing on the foot end of the bed. It only took a few moments to change, and standing before the mirror, admired the suit. It was a 40's style, gray, three piece suit, white shirt, and black tie. It was just a little loose in places and the sleeves were a bit long, but it was clean and dry. In place of my smoking jacket she had left one that was purple velveteen with a black silken collar and sleeves. The design appeared far older than the suit but it was in immaculate condition. If I hadn't known better, I might have suspected that it had been recently purchased. Searching through my coat pockets and those of my wet suit and pants I placed all personal belongings on the desk. Eva had insisted upon taking my laundry with the promise of returning with everything on Monday. It was hardly an offer that I could refuse, all things considered.

"Oh—now what do we have here?" Putting my wet pants into a plastic bag I curiously peered down and into the palm of my hand. In my rush to escape the mausoleums I suddenly realized to have accidentally taken the golden locket from the tombs…

"Are you decent in there, my lad?" Eva knocked at the door before entering.

"Oh, yes, of course." Slipping the pendent into my pocket while turning to greet her, I said, "Thank you for the clothes. They fit wonderfully, and I really love this smoking jacket."

"Oh, you are quite welcome." Swiftly entering and gathering the bag with the coat, wet clothing and other things requiring washing, she looked to me thoughtfully, and said, "The smoking jacket and clothing are yours for the taking if you really like them. It's not as though anyone here will ever be wearing them again."

"Bless your heart and thank you for everything that you've done." Moving to where she stood in the open doorway and kissing her cheek, I said, "I'll keep this beautiful smoking jacket and think of you whenever I wear it."

Blushing while putting a hand to the place where I kissed her, she smiled and said, "It's been a true pleasure having you here with us." Sighing deeply and noticing my shoeless feet, she pointed and scolding me, said, "What are you thinking? You can't be running around on these cold stone floors like that! You'll catch your death of cold!"

"My shoes are still wet from the rain" Hurrying to the bed-side and getting into my slippers, I said, "I'll just wear these for now."

"That's much better." She was visibly pleased, and said, "Now you get yourself over to the library." She winked and petting my shoulder in passing, said, "You don't want to keep the lady waiting, now do you?"

"No ma'am, I certainly don't."

When I arrived in the library the room was already warmed by a lovely fire. The oil lamps were burning, shutters were opened, but there wasn't any sign of Caitlin, Deciding that she was likely helping Eva with bringing the food upstairs, I soon was soon occupied in that amazing book collection.

Fascinated with the collected works of French artist and illustrator, Gustave Dore' I fingered through the volumes. He lived during the mid-eighteenth century and was famed for his beautiful ink illustrations. Known for his work on Edgar Allan Poe's, The Raven, Miguel de Cervantes, Don Quixote', and illustration for the Bible, he was responsible for a host of other amazing works. I smiled with the memory of the children's fables that his talent had brought to life.

It was nothing short of pure nostalgic bliss to discover those very same books in that complete collection.

"Oh, you must be joking!" Pulling the book of children's stories from the shelf, I stared in awe while flipping through the pages.

"Fables of Aesop and La Fontaine, my mother used to read these to me as a boy... I lost it years ago... Fontaine's fable, the Shephard Wolf..." I looked at the illustration of a cloaked wolf that eerily peered out at the observer. It had always frightened me as a child.

Pulling the notepad from my coat pocket I began making a list of favorites. This included renaissance masters such as Michelangelo, Rembrandt, Albrecht Durer, Leonardo da Vinci, and Hieronymus Bosch. There were far too many to list, and I humbly stayed within the boundaries of my absolute favorites. It wasn't easy to do...

Moving slowly along with the lantern in the fading afternoon light, I stumbled upon something of specific interest.

"The Life and Doctrines of Paracelsus..."

The book was first published in Germany, 1887 and was the work of author and translator, Franz Hartmann. I knew it from an old University library but had never seen a copy anywhere else.

The subject, Phillippus Aureolus Theophrastus Bombastus von Hohenheim, was born between 1491 and 1492, no one was ever really sure, and died in September of 1541. The reason that I remembered was because his sudden death, according to Hartmann, wasn't by natural causes... For obvious reasons, he later simplified his title and was known by the name, Paracelsus. A Swiss physician and alchemist, he was accredited as 'the father of toxicology' and possessed an uncanny fascination with the supernatural. Flipping through the pages, I spoke while reading aloud, and said, "Lilith, the

Hebrew demon mother of the Incubi and Succubae. According to Hebrew tradition she was Adam's first wife and was cast out for consorting with demons. That's funny, I once knew a cocktail waitress who was very much like that... Spiritual vampires, they seduce and drain the life from the living as they sleep..."

It was a very old legend and one that author, Montague Summers had revived in his 1928 publishing, The Vampire: His Kith and Kin. In fact, he actually believed and through extensive research, tried to prove their existence. The Greek philosopher, Plato, had even spoken of them while referring to them as, Larvae. He described them as ghost-like entities, that attaching to the living, would drain the life energy until the host died. Between the three authors, they would almost have you believing that the world was over-run with these things... and who knows, maybe they were right?

"I'd be willing to bet that none of these guys ever got a decent night's rest..." Chuckling while heaping the books into neat little piles from all around me, I searched through the next shelf.

"I'll just sort the ones I want into piles, write the list, and put back everything I can't take now. It'll be faster that way..."

Starting in the art and history I worked my way through the numerous wall shelves and large bookcases. It went fairly fast as selecting only favorites, built neat little piles before their appropriate shelving. The entire venture taking roughly thirty minutes, I was surprised when there still wasn't any sign of Caitlin or Eva?

Finishing with the written list and placing it down on the nearest book pile, I paused to look toward the doorway.

"Maybe they had something else to do before they came back?"

Wandering across the room and standing before the huge window, I leaned forward and looked out. It was pouring again, and the dusk became an ashen blur through the waves that ran down the window.

My thoughts began drifting, intermingling with every shapeless and shifting shadow in the fading heavens. Caught in the lamps golden glow, my reflection was a ghost in the darkening waves of the window glass. For a moment, I suddenly felt like I was staring into that foul pond again...

"I'm sorry that we took so long." Eva apologized, appearing in the doorway with a large platter, and saying, "We had a nasty spill at the foot of those evil old stairs, and I had to fix you something else."

"There's no need for apologies--," I turned and quickly clearing the books from the table, assisted her with the tray while saying, "I'm just grateful that someone's feeding me."

"It's no trouble at all dear." She winked, "Caitlin will be right along. She's just fetching the tea."

"What happened in here?" Caitlin arrived with a tray and noticing the heaped books, laughed while saying, "It looks like a hurricane went through here?"

"My guess would be a book worm." Eva looked to me with a smirk, and said, "And a very large one at that."

"Oh boy, I'm so sorry about that! I might've gotten a little carried away?"

"A little carried away?" Caitlin stared, and said, "That's the most attention those old books have had in almost a century."

"Well, if there's nothing else? I'll be off for the evening now." Politely excusing herself, Eva looked to the mountain of heaped books in passing, and chuckling, said, "Oh my, but wasn't someone a busy little bee?"

"I'll have this cleaned up before you come back on Monday." Embarrassed, I peered about the library, and shrugging, said, "Or at least within the week?"

"Don't you bother yourself with a thing, lad. I can see to them after all is said and done. Good night my dear's—be good while I'm away." She winked and with a wave at the doorway, and said, "My friend is waiting out on the road. I 'd best be off if I expect a ride."

"Can I ask which town you're speaking of? I wasn't aware that we were close to anything."

"Ashcroft--," Eva looked to Caitlin before saying, "I stay with my dear and eldest friend, Lorna."

"That's a long drive…"

"Not the way that she drives." Eva giggled.

"Did you want me to walk you out to the road? I can carry the laundry down for you." I moved to get up and she halted me with a wave.

"You'll do nothing of the kind—you just sit down." She patted my arm and smiling, said, "Thank you kindly, anyway, Michael. I have been walking that path for ages and know it well. I'll be just fine my dear, laddie."

"But it's raining and--," I looked to the window in explanation and she laughed while cutting me off before I could say another word.

"And it'll be snowing soon enough, and be far worse than any of this. I'm a wee bit tougher than I may seem." Pointing to Caitlin with a sudden thought, she said, "I've prepared some chicken stew for tonight's supper. There's a ham for Saturday, a nice beef roast in the ice box, and all you have to do is heat it up." She seemed a little concerned as looking between us and focusing upon Caitlin, asked, "Are you certain, that you won't have me come in for the weekend?"

"Thank you, but I'm sure that we'll manage just fine on our own." Caitlin lovingly embraced the old woman and affectionately kissing her cheek, said, "You just have a nice weekend and enjoy your time in town."

"I will and you both as well." She politely nodded between us, and with a wave, went out the door.

Taking a seat at the table, Caitlin looked to me, and smiling sadly, said, "I see that you have taken a shine to Eva?"

"She's a wonderful lady—and reminds me a little of my own mother."

"I can see that she already thinks the world of you as well," She paused in thought, and peering about at the clutter of heaped books, laughed, saying, "You know I had a feeling that something like this would happen if I left you alone in here too long?"

"Sorry, when it comes to sweet and old books I've got that proverbial 'weasel in the henhouse' syndrome."

"It doesn't matter, and it's like I had said before? What you don't take will stay behind anyway." She offered ham and cheese sandwiches and pouring tea, added in thought, "They can rot for all that I care."

"You can't be serious? Most of these books are extremely rare and have collector's value. At the very least, you should have them appraised and sell them to collectors before they're lost to the world."

"Rare is just another word to describe unpopular or undesirable things." Ladling tomato soup from an urn, she served me, and said, "If you have the means to move them and storage space, by all means, take everything."

The comment had left me choking on the soup, and grabbing at a napkin, wiped at my mouth and chin, while saying, "Of course, I would love to have them—but like I said—some are very valuable. I would have to get them appraised before I could even offer you anything."

"You can take the whole 'kit and caboodle' for all I care. I'm not interest in selling them—consider them a gift, from the house of McCreary." She leaned forward, curiously looking to the nearest stack and observing my notes, said, "It appears as though you've already written a list?"

Moving from her seat she retrieved the pages from the heaped books and smiling, pointed a finger at the list, asking, "Are these the only ones that you wanted?"

"My dear, Caitlin—that list contains over one hundred titles." Almost gagging on the sandwich and politely placing a hand before my mouth, I cleared my throat, and said, "And most of them are complete, first edition, unabridged sets. Some of them are very rare and really expensive."

Apparently unimpressed, she dropped the list onto the pile, and returning to the table, sat and looked at me. Feeling somewhat awkward, I put down the sandwich and spoon, and leaned back to return the stare.

"You know what?" She raised her hands as though framing me into a picture and peeking through, said with a smile, "I see a lot of heavy work at great expense and a book store in your future."

"I wouldn't be opposed to the idea. Is there also a business partner?"

"No--," Watching through her imaginary window and grinning mischievously, she said, "Not yet—but possibility in the near future?"

"Anything worthy of having is worth waiting for..."

"Oh look--," She pointed to the window and smiling, said, "The rain has finally stopped! That is a good omen."

"Why would you assume that?" Smiling, I went back to my sandwich and soup.

"Because, now we can begin loading the books into your car--," Smirking, she spoke the words in the semblance of a dare, and said,

"Only the ones on your immediate list—and only if you feel well enough to manage?"

"Of course I do! Are you kidding?" Waving a hand without the slightest concern, I said, "I'm a lot stronger than I might look."

"I'll just see to the dishes and then we can get started." Returning to her meal, she peered up curiously, and asked, "Will there be room in your car for the books?"

"Sure there will, I have a Cadillac Eldorado--," Scoffing at the question, I said in a rather smug tone, "That car could likely carry twice that amount without the slightest problem."

"That is fantastic--," Looking between the books and table, she said, "Then we'll do exactly that! I'm sure that modesty forced you to limit the titles on your list. Would it be much trouble to choose a few more?"

"I could almost do it blind-folded." Gesturing toward the heaped books that surrounded us, I laughed and said, "They're the bottom half of the books in those piles."

Caitlin argued when I tried helping her with the dishes. So I just sat there quietly while smoking and waiting for her to finish. Being a gentleman, I made a point of never arguing with a woman. It was a good thing, because in her case, anything they ever said about the tempers of redheads paled in comparison.

Doing everything by the glow of an oil-lamp had its advantages if you wanted a certain 'romantic' ambience, but made everything else that much harder. We spent the better part of an hour digging for boxes in an old storage room adjoining the kitchen. We found antique doors, window glass, additional shelving, and enough spiders to populate every house in Vancouver. Eventually we did find a large pallet full of folded boxes, and with packing tape in hand, carried them all up the stairs. I had forgotten about them and was already regretting it. The actual sorting and packing of the books took less than an hour. We used a wheeled cart to move them to the stairs, brought the cart to the bottom, and then carried down the books. I tried to explain that she didn't have to do any heavy lifting but once again, refrained from arguing. Wheeling the books into the main entrance, we set the boxes off to one side, and went back for the next load. It was almost ten when we finished with the last few boxes, and I was completely beat. That's when she reminded me that we still had to bring them out to the car...

Finding a wheelbarrow in the coach-house, she carried a lantern and accompanied me as we weaved around the pot-holes along the path. Granted, the path was much shorter with company and additional light, but the weight was taking its toll. I managed eight medium sized boxes with each trip, and there were one hundred and eighty boxes. Greed had never been more painful... We took turns which made things a little less terrible, but I was amazed at her strength and stamina. For such a frail looking waif she was stronger than any woman, and most men that I knew. In the end I was absolutely right about the freight capacity of the car, I just hadn't considered the impact on my body. So, while we made the last trip back to the house and she laughed while pushing the wheelbarrow, I almost wished that I was riding in it.

"I know that you were relieved to see that your car was alright out on the road--," She left the wheelbarrow in the coach-house, and closing the gates, said, "It's a beautiful machine."

"I call her Elizabeth." Sweating and still gasping for breath, I said, "I always name my cars."

"That's lovely..."

The wind whipped at the collar of my coat and something caused me to look up into the blackness. The high arched windows seemed to stare back as I gazed into the dizzying heights of a tower, and stumbled backward.

"Oh, are you alright?" She caught my arm as we stood before the stairs, and leaning to look into my face, she said, "I think that you might have overdone yourself a little this evening?"

The wind called as something howled in the distance, and the forest didn't seem so pleasant anymore. Looking to Caitlin in the lamp-light's glow, I feigned a smiled and urging her onward, said, "You might be right? I haven't done any real work in ages now. It's the curse of a lackadaisical lifestyle..."

"Watch your step--," She laughed, as walking arm-in-arm while climbing the stairs, paused to where I leaned upon a Gargoyle to catch my breath.

"Until now, I never realized how out of shape I really was--," Coughing while lighting a cigarette, I shook my head while saying through a cloud of smoke, "I really need to start thinking more about my health."

When she finally slid the heavy locking bolts into place I felt a whole lot better. It was almost as though she had blocked something that now stood in the darkness, and from just behind the door.

Placing the lantern on the little hall table, she gestured with a hand, and went off to hang her coat. The shadows moved in the flicker of the flame and something caused my skin to crawl. The wind blew through the cracks beneath the door, and shivering in the chill, I nervously looked down.

There's nothing out there it's just the wind, darkness, and your imagination…

"Are you ready for some nice hot tea?" She startled me while returning and surprised with my anxious reaction, asked, "Is something wrong?"

"No, I'm just really tired and you were right." Throwing a hand to my lower back with a groan, I chuckled while admittedly saying, "I did push things just a little with all those books."

"You poor, dear…" She thought for a moment and then said, "Let's go into the kitchen for a cold drink. You can freshen up a little, and then maybe you would like to join me for a little breath of fresh air? It might help you to sleep?"

"Well?" On the verge of calling it an early night due to the pain that now throbbed in my lower back, I looked to her in question.

"I thought that it might also be a point of interest for you?" Taking the lamp and slowly leading me down the corridor, she glanced back, and said, "The upper halls aren't quite as bad as the lower, but if you would be interested, I can show you the west wing tower?"

The offer was just too enticing to turn down, and given its notorious history I accepted without a second thought.

"You know what? Maybe a splash of cold water and fresh air might do me a world of good?"

CHAPTER EIGHT

After freshening up a little and accepting a glass of orange juice, which she insisted that I drink before doing anything else, we were off and running again. The second floor doorway leading into the west-wing had been sealed for many years. It had that same lingering odor of mold and mildew, but wasn't quite as bad as it was downstairs. Struggling with the lock for a few minutes, she pulled several times until finally getting the door open. It wasn't really a surprise, as over time and with the dampness, the heat and cold would have caused the door to expand in the frame.

When she swung it open it sounded like the house had breathed in after suffocating for many years. When it exhaled, I was almost blinded in the stink of a house long overdue for its own funeral. There was a thin layer of mildew over everything and it glistened in the lamp-light as we walked. The furniture was far older in that section of the house, and there was a lingering smell of smoke. It wasn't from cigars, cigarettes, or the flue of a hearth accidentally left closed, but the smell of a house-fire. With a wave and holding the lantern before her, she swiftly led the way. It was dark and there was an immediate sense of dampness in the chill. She moved quickly, but with a strange hesitation that showed when she passed open doorways. If I didn't know better, I would have assumed that she was almost expecting to see something waiting in the darkness.

The west-wing felt very different from the rest of the house and the shadows seemed far deeper. I realized why when finally noticing that all the windows were tightly shuttered, or simply boarded up. The place was absolutely stifling with mold and mildew and without any air-flow, kept me coughing.

"Here--," Reaching for French doors leading onto a balcony, she shoved them outward, and said, "The corridor was awful, but the view from here should be well-worth the trouble."

Passing through the doors I was immediately captivated by the sheer beauty. In the night it seemed far higher than two stories, and as though walking out of a nightmare and into a fantastic dream. Tales of valiant knights, dragons, and damsel's in distress filled my thoughts. It felt as though I stood upon a castle tower in a realm of dreams.

The moon was full and seemed huge as it fought its way out from behind the dark and ominous clouds. The cold wind whistled from somewhere high above and I breathed deeply in the night air. It was nice to escape that dismal and moldy hallway…

"What do you think?" Moving close to where I stood, she leaned a hip against a support pillar and smiled.

"It's absolutely enchanting…" My thoughts were suddenly lost into the blackness at the edge of the balcony.

There were four wooden pillars, one upon each side, and two toward the front. They were spaced several feet apart, and from between was fastened the ornate, iron railing. Though weathered, the pillars were beautifully carved, and the rusted railing incorporated a spiral design of which I now stared, almost mesmerized. It wasn't old-world craftsmanship that caught my attention, but the recollection of Alistair McCreary having leapt to his death from that very same balcony. Curiosity being my curse, I was tempted to discuss the matter with her, but she seemed so tranquil in the moment. Instead, I decided to keep quiet and just enjoy the moment with her.

Gazing into the moon, she whispered from somewhere deep in thought, and said, "Sometimes it's so beautiful here…that it can make a person forget everything else."

Turning toward where the moon shone upon the distant mausoleums, I couldn't help but stare. Cold and pale, they stood as a dismal reminder of those who lay in silent repose…

The wind suddenly whistled from somewhere in the heights, and turning, I saw that she was quietly watching me. With a gust playing among her fiery locks and eyes reflecting in the moonlight, she was a pale and ethereal beauty. I saw her as a queen among the 'Tuatha Dé Danann' and fairies that ruled over the night.

With all other thoughts fading I whispered, and said, "So beautiful… It's like sharing the magic of a moment—that only existed in dreams before..."

"Do you believe in the power of dreams?" Looking high into the night sky she searched through the stars while awaiting an answer.

"Sometimes, dreams are all that we have. So yes—I do believe in dreams—because I need to…"

The moon seemed suddenly huge, but all I saw in that moment was her hip touching the edge of the railing. It was barely noticeable, but the squeak became an echoing thunder in my head. She moved ever so slightly, and the resulting impact became painful while resounding through my thoughts. I knew that it couldn't have been an actual sound as she never reacted, but it now terrified me beyond words. With my eyes flitting from between her speaking and to where that hip pressed against the rail, I couldn't hold back.

"Caitlin, do you think…do you really think that you should be standing so close to that old railing?"

Cautiously testing it with a hand and looking between the pillars, she glanced back at me, and said, "It seems to be fine?"

An icy gust suddenly whipped that brilliant and red hair about her pale and delicate features. Drawing it back with a hand she peered down into the darkness and then back at me. She appeared confident about the railing and shrugged while looking back at me. The moon was so bright in her eyes that they shone like twin emeralds, glistening in the darkness. Captivated in the moment I just stood and stared at he. Then she changed… Her entire demeanor seemed different, as appearing confused, looked nervously into the night. There was a moment of utter and complete stillness and then a movement from beneath my feet. Unsettled by this, I looked to Caitlin who appeared unaware. Having already having heard strange things, I questioned as to whether I was just so fatigued that I was becoming hyper-sensitive? The wind moaned and whistling from between the railings caused me to look down. In that moment I suddenly felt a deep rumbling at my feet…

Without so much as a second thought I suddenly leapt forward. Clutching at her wrist, I desperately held on to the screeching woman. It all happened so fast. The squeal of twisting metal, and then the sudden roar of splintering wood as the ancient and rusted balcony tore free. Twisting as it leaned, the supports snapped like twigs as the beams broke outward from beneath. With the structure failing under our weight, it ripped away from the building and was sent crashing downward. There was an instant of deathly silence and then a thunderous explosion as everything burst into rubble in the darkness far below. A moment later and there was only the sounds of the wind whistling through the darkness, and I slowly looked down…

"Michael! Don't let fall!" She shrieked, desperately grasping at my right arm with both hands.

Somehow, during the ensuing chaos I managed to pull her back, and to where I now lay in the open doorway on my stomach. With my left hand holding us back from the edge, I clung to her with my right as she was suspended over certain death.

"Hold on! I'll pull you up!" It would have been a simple effort a few years ago as she weighed very little, but time and a slack lifestyle had taken its toll. Managing to raise her almost to the point of reaching the edge, she slipped down again.

"Reach up! Try to wrap your arms around my neck!"

"I can't!" Too terrified to even try she was hysterical and in tears.

"You have to try! Please!"

In a state of sheer panic she simply couldn't, and I knew that we were almost out of time. Our hands becoming slippery with sweat, in mere moments it would be over…

Oh God! Somehow I just had to save her! There was no other choice! After what happened to Leigh I couldn't live with another loss, not like this! Either I pulled her up or we would go down together…

In a desperate attempt I pulled her upward! In that same moment and flinging her arms tightly about my neck, she hung between certain death and one last chance!

Oh God in heaven—give me the strength, just this once…please…

"I'm slipping! Michael, I'm going to fall!" Her arms began slipping from around my neck as losing her hold, cried out, "Please don't let me fall!"

With tears in my eyes, we both slipped ever forward, the inevitable only moments away! Then it happened… Whether by sheer adrenaline or due to inexplicable terror, a sudden strength surged from deep within me! Grasping her tightly with both hands, I gazed down into her terrified eyes, shouting, "I won't let you fall! I won't let you die!"

In one last effort, straining and crying out in desperation, I pulled with every remaining ounce of strength! The sheer force of the effort drew her out and from over the breach, and to where landing upon me, I grabbed her and rolled away from the edge.

We clung desperately to one another with our backs pressed firmly against the far wall of the corridor. Trembling violently, she buried her face in my chest and my shirt became wet with the heated tears.

All that I could do was thank God, and look in horror toward that dark opening where the moon solemnly gazed back. Caught in the wind, the French doors squeaked while swinging slowly outward and into eternity.

"Michael--," She whispered, her features torn between terror and confusion, she asked, "How could you have known that was going to happen?"

"I didn't..." I lied without rational explanation and simply holding her close, said, "We're safe now—and that's all that matters."

For reasons beyond explanation, something had warned me against the imposing threat. It was almost as though the house itself was trying to kill us and some unseen force was working against it...what was going on here?

"You're hurt!" Directing my attention to a tear and blood-soaked wound on my left elbow, she said, "We need to get you cleaned up and have a better look at that."

"I must've caught it on a nail? I had a tetanus shot a little while ago so it should be fine." Offering her a hand while climbing from the floor, I thought for a moment, and said, "All things considered, I wouldn't mind that brandy if the offer was still open?"

"Of course--," Retrieving the lantern from off the cabinet and taking a firm hold of my hand, she said, "Let's get out of here..."

"One moment--," I went to the French doors and carefully swinging them back, closed and locked them, saying, "Better safe than sorry..."

"You might have been killed while trying to help me..." She took my hand while drawing me along, and said, "You hardly know who I am... You don't know--..."

"I know enough to say that I couldn't have lived with myself if you'd fallen..."

Saturday October 7, 1972.
12:15 a.m.

After a quick stop in the kitchen for water and a cloth she attended to my wound. It was deep and looked horrible, but I was more disappointed about ruining the suit and shirt. On a lighter note, it would have been far worse to have torn that wonderful smoking jacket. I was grateful for having left it in my room. Still wearing the torn and bloodied clothes, I went into the living room and tended the hearth. In minutes we shared a comfortable place on a couch, sipped brandy, and enjoyed the warmth of the roaring flames. Sinking into the thick padding, I watched the fires reflection in the diamond cuts of a crystal ship's decanter. There were so many beautiful things. No matter where you looked, something shone or sparkled from somewhere.

"That is a beautiful old decanter." Pointing to where it rested on a silver tray on the table before me, I asked, "Is it Waterford?"

"I'm not really sure?" Retrieving the bottle and looking for some type of identifying mark, shook her head, and said, "I can't find a maker's mark.... but if you like this? I have something to show you."

Moving from the couch she gestured with a wave for me to follow. It didn't take much effort on her part. I had already been eyeing the liquor cabinet from across the room.

It was an Italian made, Walnut case, and had beautiful carvings of cherubs, grapes, and birds among vine leaves. It stood the height of a man, the handles were brass, and it was polished to a glassy sheen.

Pausing before the cabinet she pulled keys from a lower drawer, and quickly unlocked the upper doors. Then smiling, opened the doors wide and stepped away to reveal the display case within.

It was literally filled with old liquor bottles, expensive crystal of all sorts, and shone like a treasure trove in the fire-light. There was a mirrored backing, glass shelves, and everything else was brass and silver. Afraid to touch anything, I pointed into the case for permission before retrieving a very old bottle of French Cognac.

"Remy Louis XIII, individually, hand fashioned, Baccarat crystal. Just an empty decanter would be worth more than I could ever afford."

"You're more than welcome to help yourself to anything that you like in this cabinet. Or just take the whole thing." Shrugging, she said without much thought, "Neither Eva or I really care for spirits. I can't be bothered trying to sell it. So, either you take it or it goes with the estate—it's your choice."

"Wouldn't that make me a thief? I mean, the Realty people already bought the property, right?"

"They bought the property but I still own everything inside of it."

"I'm very tempted…" Returning the bottle to its proper place and carefully closing the cabinet doors, I smiled and said, "This place is filled so many wonderful things. You should really consider saving something for yourself?"

"They're just old things." She appeared saddened with the thought and turning away, said, "Bad memories…that are best left far behind."

Putting an arm around her shoulders and leading her back to the couch, I seated her, and said, "You should never allow the bad memories of others to ruin your happiness."

Slipping off the couch, she picked up the poker and kneeling before the hearth, began absent-mindedly jabbing at the coals. There were other things occupying her thoughts and the sly backward glances gave it away immediately.

"You must meet many people in your travels--," She peered over her shoulder, and said, "And likely, most are pretty girls?"

"No, it's usually older couples or the dried up, other kind. You're the first young lady, to be honest."

"The dried up other kind--," She burst into a fit of laughter, her eyes glistening between the brandy and firelight, as she said, "You have a very dark sense of humor—it's so wonderfully, refreshing."

"Thanks, it comes with the territory. Speaking of being refreshed? Would it be possible to take a bath?"

"Of course, but we'll have to boil the water, and then take it upstairs to the tub. There are other bathrooms in the house, but sadly, that is the only one suitable for use."

"Well, I'm sure that I can carry a little water—if it's not too much trouble?"

"Oh, it's no trouble at all. If we work together it will go quickly."

"That sounds fabulous." I knew better than to try arguing.

"I was wondering?" She was reluctant to speak and swirling her brandy glass, nervously asked, "When it comes time to leave here…have you already made plans to go elsewhere?"

"No, I'll be going straight home. At best, my life has become nothing more than an endless pursuit of finding, and writing a really good, ghost story..."

"If you did happen to find that ghost story and wrote it, what then?"

"I'm not really sure? I suppose that I'll find the answer at the end of that haunted, rainbow."

There was a subtle smile and an eerie glint in her eye. If I didn't know better, I would have suspected that she was up to something.

Using several large pots and four metal pails we began the process of boiling water, and filling the tub. The second floor bathroom was just down the hall from our rooms and thankfully, close to the stairs. Amazingly enough, by the time that it was half-filled the water was still scalding hot. This was due to Caitlin having also carried two pails while leading me up those accursed stairs.

Still wearing that evening gown, she laughed playfully while racing ahead of me. Aside from being startled with her strength and agility, I was noticing the curves flowing beneath the gown. In fact, it was due to a careless eye that I stumbled on the stairs, and almost fell on the final trip to the tub. She was concerned, but grinning foolishly, I just nodded for her to continue. In my mind it was the price for peeking, and I was more than willing to pay.

She had provided a towel and wash cloth, soap, and a robe that she had found in one of the closets. Lighting a large oil lantern that stood on a table near the sink, she wished me luck and went on her way. All said and done, I could not have been happier.

The rising steam was nothing short of bliss. Wearily undressing until wearing nothing but briefs, I sat down on a small stool near the tub's edge.

"This must have really been something in its day? It's hard to believe that this Latrine' is almost two hundred years old..."

The room was at least ten feet wide, approximately fifteen feet in length, and had a high ceiling. It was wall-papered in a white and dark blue Damask pattern. Stained and peeling it was bordered by a gold leaf, crown molding, which formed a boundary between the paper and white ceiling paint.

The sink, toilet, enormous claw-footed tub, and vanity were all white with brass fixtures. The towel rack was brass and so was the frame of an immense mirror which hung above the long marble counter.

"Now that's something that you don't see every day? Why would anyone need two mirrors in a bathroom? Maybe they didn't—but when you can afford it, why not?"

It wasn't the presence of the mirror that had caught my interest, but the design of the framework. It stood the height of an average man, was oval and covered in an old sheet. The frame peeked out from beneath the sheet on either sides, and I could see that it was something fancy. The water was still much too hot and with the curiosity killing me, I just had to look.

Making my way across the room, I paused like a burglar at a window before leaning down, and tugging upon the sheet. Firmly fastened by a string from all sides and through the middle, it barely moved...

The long and ovular glass was beveled, and encircled by an ornately carved, dark stained, oak framework. The heavy figural base was also covered and tightly bound, and I couldn't make out the nature of the forms beneath. Judging by the shape, they were either winged dogs or possibly even Griffins.

It was tempting, but rather than start unraveling everything for a closer look, I decided to focus on the frame.

Carefully pulling the linen away from the top right corner I stepped back in astonishment. The framework that I had assumed to have been a Victorian leaf pattern was actually the sprawling forms of nude women! Embracing and posed in vulgar positions, they committed acts considered atrocities in most circles. Putting a finger to my lip in thought I couldn't help but smile and laugh.

"This has to be French--and a private commission. Not even the old perverts of Florence would've gotten away with creating something like this. Maybe it belonged in a bordello?"

Compelled by a certain deviant curiosity, I drew back the veil in order to closer examine the fine details.

"Oh, what happened here?"

Surprised while noticing that the mirror cast no visible reflection, I peeked into the blackness. I knew that the protective coating wore off over time and that the silver nitrate and copper sulfate would oxidize, turning black. This was known as 'mirror rot' and usually never went any further than two inches from the edge. Strangely enough, pulling the sheet away and peeking underneath, I saw that it had affected the whole surface.

Even worse, I was somehow unable to blink and mesmerized, felt drawn into the shadows of the mirror. Something suddenly fell from behind me, as awakened from the spell, spun toward the sound. It came from somewhere near the sink… dropping the sheet back into place, I went over to investigate.

"Now that doesn't make any sense?" Leaning down to retrieve the heavy brush from where it had fallen to the floor from the counter, I stared at it. Cast in the form of a seashell and with a seahorse handle, it was silver plated, and the bristles were full of long, red hairs. It was funny really as I considered that she was even keeping a watchful eye in here. Suddenly feeling awkward, I put the brush back on the counter and looked the mirror.

Although I didn't want to admit it, that shameful allure wasn't just with the mirror, but my fascination with Caitlin as well. Within imagination I saw that frame again, as every face and form changed and became Caitlin… Writhing, moaning with pleasure as the entire frame shuddered with carnal desire.

"What wrong with me? Is this one of those demoralizing, mid-life crisis situations that I've heard about? Or is something in this place affecting my mind?"

Wandering back to the tub and testing the water with a hand, I nodded, slipped out of my briefs, and climbed into the bath.

"Sure that's it!" I tapped a finger to my forehead in thought, and said, "I'll blame the house for my dirty little mind."

Sighing deeply, I settled down as the hot water gently washed away the pain and bitter chill. The calming steam and sweet scent of soap soon caused my thoughts to drift. Allowing my eyes to slip closed for just a moment, I felt light as a feather while transcending all care and concerns of the day.

It seemed like it was just a moment, but I soon coughed, spitting water and leaping upward. I had fallen asleep in the bath!

"Oops, I better not do that again. I don't want to be the next ghost here!" Abruptly raising myself in the huge basin, I firmly grasped the sides, saying, "I just need to stay focused on something—let's see? Not that!" I looked away from the mirror and noticing a large window, said, "That will do the trick!"

Gazing at the beautiful and brilliantly colored peacocks, I kept my attention fixed on the stained glass window at the far end of the room. The window itself was similar to a fancy archway. The picture represented a Victorian fantasy garden. It incorporated exotic flowers, a majestic waterfall in the background, and the fantastic birds. The rising steam created an illusion of surreal beauty as the images, extending beyond the window, now drifted in thought. The shadows moved ever so slightly in the lamp-light, and my eyes grew heavier with each passing moment.

"I'm going to stay awake. I'm awake, yes. Wide awake now…Okay eyes stay open!"

I was no stranger to the risks of exhaustion, but there was no way that I was giving up this wonderful, hot bath. Raising myself in the water, I reached for the heaped clothing pile beside the tub, and grabbed my cigarettes. Lighting one, I tossed the lighter and pack onto the pile before slipping down and into the tub.

"Now that's nasty looking?" I favored the bruised and bloody gash where the nail had caught my left elbow. Still shaken by the near death experience, I slipped the arm into the soothing water while refusing to look at it. What bothered me even more was the fact that I had entirely anticipated and even expected it to happen?

There was an immediate fear, a tension that kept me on edge from the first moment that we had stepped out and onto that landing. At first, I had blamed my own discomfort with heights, excusing the feeling as nothing more than paranoia. Yet, when she'd leaned against that railing, in thought, I had already witnessed her death.

It's a gathered opinion among parapsychologists that events tend to reoccur in places where people have suffered either extreme trauma or sudden death. The common belief being that due to an immense discharge of preternatural energy, the area or place where the incident occurred often becomes thus charged. Presumably, this affects receptive individuals who feel this force in much the same way as a frequency is picked up by a radio.

Then again, it could also have been a matter of common sense. If a parent watches a child fall near the edge of a table, they'll always be cautious of that table whenever the child is near. Being aware of Alistair's fate, it stands to reason that my attention and suspicions were already roused concerning the balcony. Regardless, whether precognitive or by some 'unknown' presence in warning, I knew that something supernatural was happening here…

"This place has to be haunted…" Puffing at the cigarette I searched for an ashtray and without one, used a soap dish on the counter behind me.

"Someone or something tried to warn me on that balcony tonight. This is either some kind of a real ghost story, or I'm starting to lose my mind…"

The slowly rising steam created a warm and sweet scented fog while ebbing away all sense of will and strength. The shadows crept ever closer as the golden glow of the lamp became a dulled blur, and I fought to keep my eyes open. With only the swirling vapors of steam for company, the world soon faded into a haze of shadows… I'll just close them for a moment. Only a few seconds and then I'll get out of the tub." A moment of absolute stillness, and then a shadow passed from between the lamp and my closed eyes.

What was that? Was someone in the room with me? No, the door was locked… And even if it hadn't been, I would have heard the squeaking of those old hinges. My eyes, why couldn't I open my eyes? To make matters worse I suddenly discovered that I was totally incapable of moving a single muscle! Paralyzed and blind, all that I could do was lie there and listen. What was that? It sounded like a sack of wet laundry being dropped onto the tiled floor? Then slowly but steadily there came a noise similar to open palms, being slapped into wet mud… No… it was the sound of wet feet that awkwardly moving across the floor, now came toward the bath…

Overwhelmed by an icy presence, I sensed something near the tub's edge and was numbed to the bone. Breathing became almost impossible, painful as the stench became ammonia, burning in my nostrils and lungs. Helpless, whatever was happening, I was utterly helpless to prevent it! Oh God—what is that?

The room fell into sudden darkness again, and there was a sound of a slippery thing, sliding as it crept across the floor. Moving along the tub's edge, I sensed that it now leaned inward and came close to my face… My heart pounded, thoughts raced, and something cold and greasy dripped, oozing down the side of my right cheek… The gelatinous mass ran ever so slowly, a line that spreading, hung suspended from my chin before dripping, and pooling on my chest. That smell, that hideous and unbearable stench. I had known something like it before—but where? Of course, it was summer camp as a boy... There had been a mentally challenged teen there that had refused to remove his boots, even after they became soaked... I was there when no longer able to walk, he screamed as the councilors had pulled those boots off... Without socks, great clumps of skin and dead flesh peeled from off the bottoms and between the toes of his rotting feet... That ammonia smell was the result of wet and putrid, human decay...

Helpless and gripped in unspeakable horror, I felt my heart skip as the shadow began slowly leaning over the tub's edge. There was a sudden splash as something moved into the bath, and I knew without doubt that I was no longer alone... The water became deathly cold, and an icy wave rolled over my chest as the water rose with the things advance.

Dear God, it's crawling into the tub... I felt something thin creeping into the water from either side of my knees... It touched me in the process, but was so cold that I hardly noticed the pressure against my trembling flesh. A shudder of revulsion tore through my entire being as petrified beyond rational thought, I desperately attempted to shriek. But nothing came, not even a single, solitary sound. The water began rising again as the thing came closer and a wave crested my neck. Like a mindless and terrified animal, all logic failed as I fought to move or make a sound.

Why can't I move? Get out, scream—do something.

Then I heard it. The faint and rasping breath of something that gurgling, spewed decaying filth as it hissed, saying, "You took what was once mine... now I shall take what is yours..."

It spoke, oh dear God in heaven, it spoke.

Ever so slowly the shadow grew deeper as I felt the cold, slippery and oozing form settling against my flesh. Sliding, covering me from foot to chest in that vile and oozing sludge. It seemed to grow in the process, and its immense weight bore me down and ever deeper into the cold and rising water. Barren of all rational thought beyond escape, my heart raced as the thing began melting against my flesh. I could feel it dissolving, becoming like glue, sticking... It was slowly but surely enveloping and absorbing me... The tub was filling with the horrid mucus, and being encased, I began to feel my body slipping away…

"Mine…" It whispered, sliding its hideous, slimy head against my cheek, and trailing with cold and oozing decay, said, "Your life—is forfeit. Thief—you are mine…"

What was it talking about? Thief! What the hell does it mean by, thief? I've never stolen anything in my--… Oh no, the pendant that I took from the mausoleum… It couldn't be…

Gurgling horribly, I felt thick and oozing mucus running down the flesh of my cheek and throat, and it whispered again, "Mine…"

No! No, this isn't happening, it can't be! In moments I'll be drawn inside the thing and dissolve like a fly inside some carnivorous plant! I can't let it take me—I won't let it.

Fighting for my life and very soul, it took everything just to snap my eyes wide open. What I saw made me wish that I was still blind…

Black, porous and oozing with slime, its greenish underbelly was resting upon mine. With writhing tendrils that sprang from out its upper torso, the horrendous slug looked down upon me.

Its face hideously human in shape, black and soulless eyes swayed from upon four long stalks. Its mouth ran wide and without lips, a hideous and black tongue slipped from side to side. It writhed while holding me helpless, the tendrils brushing against me, static sparks dispersing with every pass.

I could feel the life draining from out of me, a battery being slowly bled dry… It was changing, the eyes flashed as though lighting reflected in them. The form trembling as its skin becoming pale and silken, now bordered some horrid transcendence from the grave into the living world! I was dying and knew that I had to escape before it was too late. God above, please help me.

The tendrils began withdrawing into its sides as the mass shriveled and shrank. In horror, I watched as arms and legs formed, lengthening as fingers and toes began reaching and stretching.

The oozing flesh became a sickly, pinkish-white as the horrendous slug took on human characteristics. Shrinking, writhing as it transformed and looking upon me once more, I saw those ghastly eyes slink back into sockets, and then blink.

In that moment the monstrous thing crushed me against the bottom of the tub and I began slipping down. Staring wildly, I felt the rising water pass over my chin and then cover my face. Submerging beneath the fouled waters, I choked while desperately gasping for air! In a final attempt, I screamed through streaming bubbles and oozing filth.

"Help--," In one soul-rending shriek I finally managed to utter a sound, and cried out at the top of my lungs, "Help! Someone— help!"

The world suddenly exploded in a brilliant and blinding flash as spitting water, I suddenly awoke. Leaping up and out of the ice cold bath water, I wailed in horror. Staring wildly about the empty room, I gasped for breath while realizing that I'd fallen asleep.

"Michael! Are you alright in there?" Caitlin shouted, pounding heavily upon the bathroom door, "Answer me—or I'm coming in there!"

"It's okay!" I shouted, as still gasping for air, managed to say, "I must have fallen asleep and had another nightmare? I'm, okay though, sorry about that… again."

Coughing violently, I struggled to get out of the tub and balancing on the edge, turned as she called out again.

"I'll wait here until you come out—are you sure that you're okay?"

My mind swam in a dizzying haze as leaning down and reaching for a towel, I called back to her, saying, "It's okay, I'm out of the bath now—and I'm just drying off. I'll be out in a minute!"

Looking at my watch I rolled my eyes in shame, and calling out to her, said, "After one in the morning… I didn't wake you up again— did I?"

"No, I couldn't sleep anyway." She stood close while speaking through the door, and said, "Should I make some tea? I'm not really that tired. Would you like to sit up together for a little while longer?"

"Sorry, I feel awful—but would love to take a rain-check." Hurriedly drying off, I stood closer to the door to keep from shouting, and said, "I'll be lucky if I don't pass out trying to make it back to my room."

"Of course--," She sounded reluctant and very concerned, and leaning her head to the door, she said, "If you need anything, anything at all—just call for me... I'll leave my door open for you tonight…"

"I really appreciate that--," Drying my hair and face I leaned close to the door, and resting a hand upon it, said, "Pleasant dreams, my dear friend…"

Leaning her head against the door from the other side she gently stroked at it with a hand, and sighing deeply, said, "I'll be here for you Michael, pleasant dreams, sweet friend…"

It was almost as though I felt her from behind the door and my heart ached in that moment. The sound of her voice carried a sadness that my soul truly understood. For our own reasons, we were both so very alone in this world…

Unsteadily moving toward the clothing pile near the tub, I slipped into the robe and looked around the room. Noticing a sudden draft, I turned to look back while suspicious of the space beneath the bottom of the bathroom door. Leaning down and running my fingers the length of the space, I could feel a draft issuing in from underneath.

"It's nothing… Just another cold night in a very big and very old house…"

Moving to where my pants lay crumpled in a heap on the floor, I retrieved the pendant from a pocket, and sitting on the stool by the tub, silently stared at the odd little charm.

Round and golden with ornate trim, it shone brightly in the lamp-light. Without thought, I began stroking the ruby jeweled points with a thumb and suddenly recognized the design.

"Now isn't that a big surprise?" Holding the pendant upward and closer to the light, I tried to make out the intricate details, muttering to myself, "Another pentagram…" Running a finger across its face while remembering the formation, I said, "There are five points, earth, air, wind, fire, and the fifth element being the spirit. The circle of eternity brings unity while binding them all."

It was originally a Christian symbol of protection and represented the sufferings of Christ, but Satanists inverted the symbol to create the Pentacle. Abandoned by Christianity, Pagans adopted the Pentagram as protection against evil. Its original purpose had never changed, though it had passed into different hands through time.

"I'll put you back on that gate, first thing tomorrow…"

Moving from the stool with the intention of slipping it into the pants pocket again, I suddenly became dizzy. Losing balance, I tripped and falling, the pendant flew out of my hand! Barely missing the edge of the tub with my head, I dropped heavily to the floor.

Searching the floor, I leaned down to look beneath the tub. In the darkness I couldn't see anything, but then caught a glimmer on the edge of an old heating grate... The pendant had somehow been caught upon the lip and was on the verge of falling.

"Oh no—please, don't fall in there!"

Reaching under the tub I carefully felt around for the end of the chain. Pressing my shoulder tightly against the tub while reaching ever further, my finger-tips touched the cold metal. Desperately grabbing at the locket as it now dropped into the vent, I caught the pendant just before it passed through the grate.

"That was far too close..." Clutching the locket and chain to my breast and sighing deeply, I nervously looked to the place where I had fallen. There wasn't an article of clothing, curled carpet, or anything that could have caused me to trip.

Looking down as the locket suddenly popped open in my hand, I gazed upon the tiny image revealed from within. Squinting to better see the face, I looked upon a petite blonde girl, and reading the inscription aloud, said, "For my dearest Amelia, always and ever—Jonathan... Amelia, but what the heck is her pendant doing on a mausoleum gate?"

Looking closely at her picture, I was surprised to discover that there was something strangely familiar about the general features, and especially eyes. At first this had bothered me, but realizing to have seen paintings of her relatives, it made perfect sense.

Closing the locket and slipping it into a pants pocket, I turned with the intention of draining the bath water. Faltering, I stepped back from the tub and stared in shock and disbelief.

Floating above the soap clouded surface was my cigarette, and a thin film of decaying filth such as one might expect to find in a stagnant pond...

"Okay—this is easy enough to explain. That mess must have backed up through the plumbing while I was asleep? Of course, and being so old, naturally it would be foul and--..." I suddenly remembered that there wasn't any plumbing to the faucets or spigot...

Walking around to the other side of the tub, I noticed a drainage pipe that slightly angled, ran from the tub and out through the wall.

Going to the window and sliding it open, I leaned out while peering into the darkness. In the pale glow of the moon I could see where that pipe emptied into a larger one that directly ran down from the side of the house. There was absolutely no possible way that water could have come up from out of that pipe…

Closing the window and returning to the tub. I leaned down to examine the faucets. They had never been connected to pipes and there wasn't even the plumbing to attempt it.

Looking to the ceiling while observing for cracks or any possible place where water might have spilled down, I soon realized to have been wasting my time. There was simply no rational explanation for what had happened…

Reaching for the chain and pulling the plug, I stood there watching as the murky water began draining from the fouled tub. Shivering and reaching with the intent of pulling the robe closed, I accidentally brushed a hand against the bare flesh of my thigh. Something just didn't feel right and turning, I paused to look down.

"What's this? Oh, God—it can't be?"

A thick film of gelatinous ooze coated my fingers as fearfully opening the robe, my eyes widened in horror! Dark bruises appeared on my chest, thighs, hips, and lower abdomen. Terrified, I saw that my skin was glistening with the very same putrid decay that had coated the nightmarish thing in the dream!

Without water and panicking, I used the towel while wiping the filth from my body. It caught in the fiber of the towel and becoming like glue was even harder to remove from my skin. Scrubbing at the sticky filth and looking into the tub I suddenly noticed that it had vanished from the sides and bottom.

Shocked, I went to the edge of the tub and looking down, saw that nothing remained but a little residue from the soapy water. Stunned, I could only shake my head as looking upon my bare chest, realized the bruising to have vanished as well…

Curiously raising the towel I was surprised to find that it was also clean. It was the same for my thigh… Only the reddened results of my cleaning attempts remained where the filth had once been.

"What's happening here…and what's happening to me?" Gathering my belongings and taking the lamp, I hurried out of the bathroom.

The trip down the hall and into my room went fast, as quickly and quietly closing the door, I listened before doing anything else. Exhausted, sore, and finally finished, I stoked the hearth and slipped into bed.

Without a care about the dust or concern for spiders, I shivered while unable to shake off the chill. It was a bitter cold that still burned in my chest, lower abdomen, and thighs. I could only blame myself for falling asleep in that freezing water. It was no wonder that I had nightmares about hideous and cold things…

Slipping deeper beneath the blankets I watched the shadows dance about the hearth, and slowly closed my eyes. The room became silent with exception to the crackling embers and popping of the damp wood. The wind whispered from beyond the window, the moon drifted behind the clouds, and the night carried me away…

CHAPTER NINE

Saturday, October 7, 1972.
12:25 p.m.

Blinded by the dull afternoon glare I was awakened from a dreamless slumber. I didn't feel much better but at least the chill was gone. Rolling over, I looked at my watch.

What day was it? Saturday—that's right. The late night had run into the following day.

"Writing this is going to be tough enough... but nobody's going to be able to figure out what day or time it is? I'd better make sure to date and time the stories, just to keep things in proper perspective."

Retrieving a note pad from the night-table, I scribbled down my thoughts. The fire had become embers but the chamber was still quite warm. There was a sense of safety and comfort in the moment and I enjoyed it for all that it was worth.

Writing out the dreams and events of the previous day, something caught my attention from the corner of an eye. Looking down at the floor beside the bed, I noticed an oily reflection on the dark wood.

"What on earth is that?"

Climbing out of the bed and shoving my feet into slippers, I moved to investigate. Like the impressions that one might make when walking barefooted through gelatin, the strange prints traveled from the partially open door to the side of my bed.

Leaning down, I touched a finger against the irrefutable outline of a very thin, small, and naked foot... Without a doubt it was the same kind of slime that I had experienced the night before...

Following the prints to where they disappeared beneath the foot end of my bed, I leaned down and raising the blankets, peered into the darkness beneath.

Barely able to see anything between the blackness and accumulated dust, I hadn't noticed the huge spider that sat close. Suddenly racing out, it ran over my hand, and when I jumped up, went scrambling across the room.

"Oh crap—for crying out loud! What's with all the damn spiders around here?" Leaping back and shaking the hand as though it were on fire, cursed, saying, "And they're bloody huge! Is someone raising them to ride?"

Noticing the beast near my bag, ever so slowly I reached for something to toss at it. No sooner had my fingers touched a book than did it suddenly disappear under the bureau. Unwilling to be bothered with the horrid little thing, I grabbed my robe and cigarettes, and hurried out of the room.

Pleasantly surprised to find Caitlin already waiting with breakfast in the dining room, I quickly took a seat. It was modest fare but I thanked her anyway, and we talked over tea and pastry.

"I'm not nearly as good in the kitchen as Eva--," She smirked as while pouring tea, and saying, "But I expect that you should survive until Monday morning?"

"Well, I think that you're just fine!" I sniffed at the delightful selection of Pastry, and rubbing sleep out of my eyes, said, "This is like being on vacation—only far better!"

Smiling, she took a seat close beside me, and offering napkins, said, "Let's talk about that on Monday. Well, that's if you're still here? You might just get bored of me and this old place, and run off to find some real adventure?"

I wondered if she had seen or suspected anything, but didn't say anything. There wasn't any reason to frighten her without substantial evidence.

"I don't think that you should have any concerns about that ever happening. This place is an endless source of inspiration, no matter where I look. Oh, and speaking of looking? I noticed that old mirror while taking my bath. You wouldn't happen to be willing to sell it, would you?"

"Believe it or not, that's the only piece of furniture in this house that I actually like--," She picked at an apple Danish and raising an eyebrow, grinned while saying; "It caught your fancy, did it?"

Feeling a little awkward I blushed and looking away, said, "Well, you do have to admit that it would definitely make one heck of a conversational piece."

She looked away, her features torn within some distant reflection as she said, quite sadly, "I'm afraid that it's something of a keepsake. I just couldn't part with it. I'm sure that you understand?"

"Of course--," I nodded, and sipping at my coffee, said, "But in that case—would you at least tell me who the artist was?"

"It's a late seventeenth century piece and as you might have already guessed, one of a kind." She frowned as though having tasted something bitter, and offering another pastry, said, "It was a private commission. As you already know, my family was in the antiques trade and had plenty of opportunity to acquire—interesting things. It was imported from somewhere in Germany, and has been in our family all these years. It once stood in your room but I had it moved. No offence--," She gestured with a polite nod, and said, "But, I just couldn't bear the thought of seeing it accidentally damaged or broken."

"Oh, no need to apologize—I can relate. My house is full of breakables and I'm the same way. Who was the artist?"

"From what little I remember, he was basically an unknown talent and died very young…"

"That's very sad." The thought of his short life and lost talent troubled me deeply. I had always held a special place in my heart for art and artists, and said, "Do you know his name?"

"I did—once?" She put a hand before her mouth in a gesture of passing thought and slowly shaking her head, said, "But that was some time ago and I have long forgotten…"

"It's not really that important." I could see that the topic deeply disturbed her and preferring to avoid the issue, said, "Would it be alright to un-wrap the mirror for a few pictures?"

"I would prefer that you didn't—it's rather private…"

"I understand…how about some pictures of the rest of the house, and family crypts?"

"With exception of the main floor and parts of the east side--," She shrugged apologetically, and said, "Most of the house is sealed off. It's old—and can be very dangerous. You saw what happened last night…"

"I was just hoping for a photo's to remember the place for when it's gone?"

"Alright then—you'll get your photos. But speaking of pictures--," She pointed an accusing finger and grinning mischievously, said, "You promised that we would take more together. So, I had something special planned… I'll just be a moment—wait here!"

Before I could even respond she was up and gone. Whatever happened now, I knew that I would have to cater to her whims to get those pictures. What difference did it make, I liked her and it might even be fun?

Searching my pockets for extra film, I cursed while suddenly remembering that I had left them in the bag. Hurrying out of the kitchen and back up to my room, I retrieved the film from the doctor's bag. There were still eight rolls and shoving them into a coat pocket, a sound caused me to suddenly turn and look?

"So—what do you think?" She appeared in the doorway as posing playfully, caught me by complete surprise.

She stood there wearing nothing but a sheer and pale green gown with matching veil. The gown was cut low between her breasts, hung in fronds just below her knees, and had wide and flowing sleeves. The veil was a lighter shade, fastened at her shoulders, and flowing long and loosely, drifted like a dream from all about her.

Dancing barefoot, she spiraled and sprang like a deer while running across the room. Caught in the rays of the sun her hair flowed like fire as with the grace of a ballerina, posed before the window. With the light shimmering through her costume and her waif-like figure revealed ever so slightly from beneath, my heart almost stopped…

Oh, good Lord, she isn't wearing anything under that…

"I thought that for the sake of art—this costume would be the most flattering." She hurried across the room and sitting cross-legged on the bed, leaned forward while asking, "Do you like it?"

I was speechless… She looked like a pale and fiery fairy resting upon a flower on a bright summer morning. Without question, I much preferred her fairy to Nellie's "Jungle Queen."

"Of course, yes—it's amazing and you look absolutely radiant." I stuttered, as caught completely speechless, asked, "But, will that be warm enough to take pictures?" I gestured downward with a finger and said, "In the crypts?"

"Silly." She leapt off the bed and rushing past me, stood before the window in the sun-light, and said, "I'll get changed before we go down there. This is just for pictures while we're up here. You do have enough film—don't you?"

"We have more than enough…" My eyes were fixed as the sun shone through the gown. Her pale and exotically freckled skin glowing as she was revealed in all of her most intimate beauty. She was a ghostly, leopard fairy with sheer and shimmering, emerald wings.

Once more the thought of being along with such a young woman suddenly bothered me, especially in that moment. Without giving it much thought, I just blurted out the words.

"Do you have any interest in astrology? I mean, when was your birthday?"

"Don't you know that its poor etiquette to ask a lady her age?" She apparently guessed the motive and moving from the window, said, "If you must know—I'm thirty two. My birthday is on October the twentieth, and I'm a Scorpio."

"I'm sorry—that just came out of center-field..." Laughing with the embarrassment, I suddenly felt relieved. It wasn't such a big sin being ten years her senior. Waving a finger in thought, I said, "I wouldn't have guessed you were any more than early twenties, at the very most?"

"That's very sweet—and what about you--," She raised an eyebrow and then said, "Oh wait—let me guess?" She paused in the doorway and curiously looking back at me, smiled as she said, "Thirty five?"

"Well, my birthday is the fourteenth of May--," I chuckled, still feeling a little old and saying, "I'm forty two and a Taurus. But, I'm a horse in the Chinese horoscope! Either way, I'm still stuck in a barn."

"In Egypt--," Spreading her arms, the sun shone through the long folds of her draping sleeves, and she said, "You are the Eagle."

In that instant the sun appeared as an immense ball of fire that she had caught between her arms. With the gown flowing like wings she was like the Egyptian goddess Isis offering worship unto the great sun god, Ra. It was a once in a lifetime opportunity. Snapping several sets of pictures I stood back as the sun faded behind, and the moment was forever lost. I was grateful to have caught it on film.

"Did you know that according to the horoscope--," She returned to the bed and sitting on the edge, peered up thoughtfully while saying, "That Taurus and Scorpio supposedly make the perfect match?"

"No—as a matter of fact I didn't?" Grinning foolishly, I shrugged and jokingly said, "But then again, you can't really believe everything that you read on a fortune cookie."

Laughing, she slapped at my shoulder as I sat down on the bed beside her.

"You see this?" Rolling up the long and flowing sleeve of the gown, she pressed a finger into the taught muscle of her arm, saying, "I may be thin? But I'm as tight as a steel cord."

"Oh yeah—do you see this?" Drawing up the shirt and gently patting the slightly bulging stomach beneath, I said, "I'm as firm as—a marshmallow…"

"Oh that's just adorable." She grinned and poking at my stomach, said sweetly, "A man is permitted to be comfortable."

"We should really get going if we plan on getting more pictures." My thoughts returned to the book and photographs.

Vibrating with obvious enthusiasm she jumped up, and tossing her hair aside, asked, "Okay—so where do we start? And what do you want me to do?" Her eyes burned with a sudden excitement.

"Well, I was just thinking…" I knew that I was about to spoil the party and was praying that she would forgive me. Then again, I wasn't known for having the best timing…

There was disappointment in the decision but it made the most sense at the time. Tugging on the cuffs of her knee-high, leather boots, she sighed deeply while saying, "I guess that it was a better idea to start with the crypts? I really don't like the idea of being down there at night."

"Isn't it dark down there all of the time?" Shaking the flashlight as a bad connection caused it to flicker again, I said, "I mean—the crypts are below ground, right?"

Tugging upon her tightly fitting slacks, she pulled at the green turtleneck, sweater, and said, "Yes—but everything always seems worse at night."

Raising the camera as we stood before the door to the west-wing, I smiled as she immediately posed. With an arm flung above her head in the archway and the other at her thigh, she peered back from out heavy-lidded eyes.

The tight brown corduroy pants and knee-high boots making her legs appear even longer; her hair flowed like fire against the emerald sweater. In that dismal doorway she was nothing short of stunning.

When we entered through that main-floor doorway I was sickened with the smell, once again… We moved at a quick pace, it was dark due to the shuttered windows, and I felt like we were lost in some horrible old maze. Strangely enough, that wasn't far from the truth.

At first there was a sense of excitement, but that soon changed as we wandered into the lower west wing corridor. According to Sir Reginald there had been renovations done in this part of the house after the fire. From what I saw you would never have known it. The walls were stained with a blackening rot, and unlike the rest of the house, the furnishings were covered in a fine, white mildew.

The faded wine and gold colored carpet was so thick with the pale and ghastly mildew, that soaking with dampness, it caused me to slip several times. It was a good thing that she had brought the lantern because my faulty flashlight was an endless source of grief. She obviously saw my disgust while glancing back, and felt obligated to comment.

"If you think that this part of the house is unpleasant?" She recoiled while avoiding an immense cobweb that hung low in a doorway, and said, "Then the crypts will really thrill you…"

"Oh, goody—I just can't wait…" What had I gotten myself into this time…?"

The mildew became increasingly worse as we traveled further down the corridor, but it wasn't the worst… What really got to me were the spreading clumps of black and festering fungi. It clung in the corners of the ceilings and floors, crept through the cracks, and lined the walls. A black filth ran from wherever it gathered, and in the darkness it was alive in every shadow.

"That's some really horrible looking fungus." I snapped several pictures while asking, "I didn't notice it upstairs or in our rooms?"

"It's only in this part of the house—," She scratched at her arms with a shudder and looking back at me, said, "It's like this part of the house died and is slowly rotting away…"

Sickened with the sight, I turned my attention toward a set of oak, double-doors on our immediate right.

"Those lead into the chapel. Its open—but I'm not going in there. It gives me the creeps…"

"Now that's odd—the doors haven't been touched by mildew or fungus?" I took several pictures of the ornately carved doors and scoffing, said, "It seems that the mold doesn't care too much for the chapel either?"

The comment had visibly bothered her as slapping at my shoulder, she groaned, and said, "Don't be too long. I don't think that I can take much more of this?"

"I'll be quick as a bunny—I promise…"

Grasping the handles, I looked back at her before pulling them open. They parted with a deep and echoing groan. There was a strange and lonesome stillness here, but it was different than anywhere else in the house. It felt safe and prompted a certain calm and peaceful feeling. Oddly, I couldn't explain the absence of decay on the doors, or lack of odor inside the chapel.

"You should really take a look in here?" I called back to her, and said, "Except for the dust this place is as clean as a whistle!"

"That's terrifjc--," She called back, saying, "Just get your pictures and let's get out of here, please."

"Well—she did say please." I mumbled to myself while slowly making my way into the large and shadow filled room.

Six rows of pews lined either side of the aisle. There was a wine colored carpet, and red and gold tapestries hung on either side of the hall. Statues of the Saints stood against the walls in every corner, angels guarded the pulpit, and cherubs were carved into the surrounding, crown molding.

Tall candelabrum stood on either side of the main doors, before the gated entrance to the altar, and likewise beside the pulpit. Amazingly, it all appeared as though it were caught and frozen in time.

Passing through the alter gate and moving toward the pulpit, I stood in awe beneath the enormous stained glass window. Approximately ten feet in height and six feet wide, the colorful glass was so dirty that I couldn't clearly identify a single image? The light being poor I snapped several shots with the flash, halting as I noticed something looming in the shadows behind the pulpit.

"Now that's an impressive piece of old world art."

It stood seven feet in height while spanning four feet in width at its widest points, Fashioned from dark oak with silver inlay, it was one of the most beautiful *Celtic* crosses that I had ever seen.

"That must have taken forever to carve?" Halting to examine the intricate *Celtic* weave and silver-craft, I moved around the pulpit while taking several angled photos of the cross.

"Are you just about done poking around in there?" Caitlin called as waving from the open doorway, said, "Because I'm ready to go whenever you are?"

"I just want a few more pictures and we're on our way!" I shouted back while saying, "You should see the Celtic cross in here… it's absolutely fantastic."

"I know…" She didn't sound impressed.

Hurrying out and to where she stood in the dark hallway, I motioned with a nod, and said, "Okay, what next?"

"The entrance to the crypts is at the end of this hall." She curiously watching as reloading the camera with film, I shoved the spent roll into a pocket and she asked, "How much film did you bring with you? Will you have enough for us?"

"I usually carry ten rolls—just in case?" I noticed the strange apprehension in her gaze as pointing, she asked, "And how many rolls do you have left now?"

"Six--," I checked twice while saying, "I have six rolls left."

She seemed relieved as grasping at my arm and pulling me along through the hallway, said, "Alright then, let's get this over-with. The night's still young and we have a lot of other rooms to see!"

Following her to the end of the corridor I slowed within approach, and paused to take several pictures. Obviously the oldest part of the house it was a Gothic nightmare. The stone entrance yawned before us and I shuddered while caught in a chill.

Built from huge cinder blocks, the arched entrance stood eight feet high and was barred by spiked, iron gates. There were lanterns mounted upon either side of the wall, and it smelled worse than anywhere else in the house.

Noticing my apprehension, she raised the lantern to look at me in the blackness, and asked, "Are you still sure that you want to do this?"

Dreading the thought of coming into contact with the hideous fungi, I wasn't so sure? I wondered as to how deep it had crept or dense it might have become in the darkness? I now feared what may have been waiting for us down there…

"Has this stuff?" I pointed at the gruesome curtains of dangling decay, and asked, "Always been here?"

"It thrives in the shadows…" She groaned as pulling at my hand, began towing me along, and said, "It just keeps getting worse and worse. When I first came here it used to scare me. It wasn't so bad in the beginning. Not until my father had told me that the stuff was actually alive. At first, they tried to get rid of it, but it just kept coming back. So eventually, they just gave up and sealed off this section of the house."

"That would have given me nightmares as a boy." I swallowed hard and looking around the corridor said, "And, it still might?"

"I use to sit in bed at night and was afraid to go to sleep. I'd be hiding under the covers." She paused as waving a hand into the deepening shadows, said, "And wondering if after they turned out the lights, whether it would be waiting under the bed…"

My heart leapt into my throat as my imagination began running wild. I envisioned her as a child, enveloped within that ghastly fungus while being consumed in her own bed.

"You can probably imagine how terrible that was for a little girl?" The horror of the memory caused her to falter and then stuttering, she said, "I just couldn't stomach the way that it got all over things. Grew on them, and then slowly devoured them while covering everything…"

"Of course, it must have been terrifying for you as a little girl?" My attention focused to where the decay thickened in a glistening and bulging mass.

"Still, it's perfectly harmless--," I choked on my own words while pointing and saying, "They're just disgusting, and festering, mushrooms."

"Maybe so--," She slowly paused before the gates with me and glancing back, quietly said, "But the fungus also grows on the bodies of the dead. So in the end—it eats us too…."

I knew that she was right and in the same turn, pondered as to what nourishment the fungi had derived in the tombs below… To my surprise the gates were not locked, and she swung them open while leading me inside. It was far colder than the corridor and the stone chamber left me feeling claustrophobic. The stairs spiraled ever downward as moving deeper and into the endless night, we soon arrived before another pair of black iron gates.

"Oh—we'll need this!" She reached for a large brass key that hung from a hook near the gate, saying, "You might have noticed that everything around here is locked up tight?"

"Yes—it does seem a little odd in some cases, doesn't it?"

Fidgeting with the camera bag, I watched while she struggled with the enormous padlock. Dreading another experience like the one at the mausoleum gates, I refrained from offering assistance.

"How long has it been since anyone was down here?"

"The Realty people were here a month ago." She pulled the padlock free and placing it on a ledge, swung the gates open, and said, "But being as they're planning on demolishing the place, didn't bother looking down there."

She lifted the catch, and then carefully latched the gates on metal hooks that were firmly fastened on either side the stone wall. Looking back, she directed my attention to the lock, and said, "These gates have a self-locking, internal latch mechanism. One closed, they can only be released from the outside. So, when they close? Nobody gets in—and nothing gets out without this key." She held the old and rusted skeleton key before my eyes, and shoving it into my hand, said, "No matter what happens—do not lose this."

"That seems a little drastic?" I looked down at the key in my hand and shivering, slipped it into a breast pocket of my coat.

"People always have their reasons for doing things--," She swallowed hard and peering into the deep shadows, said, "And sometimes, it`s better not knowing them."

"Is it just me? Or has the temperature dropped a good fifteen degrees, just since we came down the stairs?" I pointed and said, "There's some kind of cold draft—coming from down there?"

"We're surrounded in solid granite walls and thirty feet below the surface." Motioning with the lantern as she led me down-ward, she said, "The crypts are sealed and there is only one way out. The darkness just has a way of deceiving your mind and senses..."

Having been lost in an old mine as a boy I had some idea of how subterranean chambers affected the sight and senses. Still, everything about this place felt wrong... By now, the stifling odor had become so bad that I was coughing and could literally feel the dampness through my clothes. Even uglier, was the thought that the moisture was actually spores from the mold, seeping into the pores of my skin.

I felt sickened by the large and glistening tumors of fungus which clung to the walls, and hung from the vaulted ceiling. In passing, I took notice of several antique oil lanterns resting upon a little table. They were both smothered in a hideous mass of filth that ran from the walls, and I veered wide to avoid coming anywhere near it.

There was a sound from somewhere in the black tunnel ahead, and we both stopped. It was a muffled thump, and reminded me of a large mass dropping onto damp earth.

"What's wrong?" She whispered as moving closer, peered fearfully into the long shadows.

"It was nothing--," I shook it off, and ignoring the cold greasy lump that now formed in the pit of my stomach, said, "I just thought that I saw or heard something move up there?"

"Oh—well it does tend do that--," Her features twisting with an utter loathing, she swallowed hard, and said, "As it grows it becomes too heavy. At some point, it slides and drops from the ceiling and walls…"

Unnerved, I slowly looked to the ceiling directly above us. Something moved in the darkness and without hesitation, I grabbed and pulled her aside! Not a moment too soon, as a huge clump of filth splattered to the stone floor before us! Erupting like a blackened and long rotting melon, it oozed with brown and yellowed mucous. The stench was unbearable, and we both threw our hands before our mouths in disgust.

I could see in her wide-eyed and almost tearful gaze that she was truly terrified. We looked at each other for what seemed far too long for such a simple and obvious decision. In all truth, I had already long regretted having brought her down there.

"I feel perfectly awful for insisting that we come down here. You were right--," I peered nervously about and looking deeply into her eyes, said, "It's like crawling into the rotting bowels of some long dead monster. But you have to admit—it does make for some terrific and really ghastly pictures…"

"Sir Reginald's tomb is just down there." Directing my attention into the blackness at the end of the passageway, she shrugged, saying, "We've come this far—why not just finish what we started?"

"I won't be long—you can wait here."

"Not on your life. There's no way that you're leaving me alone down here for even a single moment…" She was adamant.

"Okay--," Gesturing for her to wait for a moment, I said, "Just so that I'm completely clear with the details? Little Henry, his older brother Reinhardt, and Johnathan were all interred at the mausoleums, right?"

"So was Amelia." She reminded me, saying, "All the elders and other members of the family were entombed down here."

"I thought that Amelia was brought here as well?"

"No—Johnathan was brought back here, and her body was laid to rest in the mausoleum." She raised a finger in thought, and said, "It's an interesting story. You'll read about that when you get to Sir Reginald's personal notes. It's the final entry in the diaries and roughly six pages long."

"Okay then." With a nod down the corridor, I asked, "So who's the closet right now?"

"Johnathan, he's in there." She pointed down the corridor and pondering briefly, quietly said, "On the right side, and directly across from his wife, Maria. I'm not sure why—but they were interred in their own chambers rather than buried together…"

"Alright then—are you ready?"

"I'll walk with you." She waved the lantern toward the end of the crypt and shaking her head, said, "But, I told you before, I have always been afraid of what might be waiting for me down there. So, there's no way that I'll enter those crypts…"

"I'll make this as quick and painless as possible…"

With that thought, we began the final trek to the end of that damp, dark, and miserable hell. The floors, walls, and vaulted ceiling were so thick with that vile filth that every step felt hideously cushioned. Our shoes crushing the horrendous sacks, which bursting, leaked with what looked and smelled like thick and congealing puss.

There was sudden warmth in the depths of the corridor. A heat that felt more like a fever than an actual temperature. Rubbing at my arms, I pulled back the sleeves and noticed the reddened patches in the dim light.

Was it an imitation caused by some type of parasite attributed to the decay and filth? Or was it the mold, festering, and feeding upon my living flesh… Quickly drawing the sleeves down, I fought while attempting to focus on taking the last few pictures.

It was a short distance but done painfully slow. The floor became so thick with the stuff, that it was a fight to avoid from slipping and falling. My shoes were covered and I feared the slime that now soaked my feet and lower pant legs.

"Watch it!" She caught my arm as saving me from a nasty spill, shone the lantern upon the gates, and said, "You'll need the key to open it… It's almost as though they were worried that someone might go poking around in there for some reason?"

Smashing the fungus away from the padlock with the butt end of the flashlight, I gagged while saying, "Doctors used to pay good money for bodies during a time when work and money was short. In those days, the dead weren't safe in their own graves."

Producing a large skeleton key from a coat pocket, she motioned with a nod at the lock, saying, "This key will give us access to all the vaults in the family crypts. Here, take it--," Slipping the key into my hand and stepping away, she said, "I'll be waiting right here…"

Thanking her, I turned and began fidgeting with the key in the lock. With fingers that quickly because sticky with the foul mucous I worked ever harder. Suddenly releasing, the lock slipped out of my slimy hands, and fell heavily onto my right foot.

"Are you okay?" She looked down at my shoe.

"Yes, it just startled me." Swinging open the gates with a reassuring nod, I shone my light inside, and said, "This will only take a moment."

"Be careful…" She spoke in a whisper while raising the lantern and peering in from behind me.

It all happened so fast that there wasn't even time to shout. The floor was so thick and slippery with those seething tumors that I went down in the third step.

"Oh no—Michael, are you alright?" She cried out as the glow of the lantern shone into the blackness of the crypt.

"Yes, I'm perfectly fine! Just a little surprised, that's all." Briefly blinded, I fumbled around and finding the flashlight, attempted to climb back to my feet.

Directing her light around the room and upon me, she suddenly gasped, and said, "Michael? You might want to brush off a little…"

"I'll just be a second--," Finally managing to get to my feet and balancing precariously, I raised the light and slowly looked around.

Enormous masses bulged from off the walls and ceilings, filling well over a third of the chamber. The floors three feet thick with the stuff in places, and then I noticed my legs... In that same moment, I was frantically swiping at the masses that clung to my right thigh and leg with the flashlight. It was thick and with a leathery skin was almost impossible to scrape off. Worst of all, was the sickly green and oozing puss that ran from the broken and leaking pieces!

"Michael! Are you going to be okay?"

"Yes, I'm just covered in this nasty crap!" Smearing a hand on my pants, I wiped the yellow sludge from my palm, and said, "I'll just be a moment. I just want a few shots of this before we go."

Pulling the camera out of the bag, I carefully stepped around the heaping mounds of fungus. My eyes having adjusted to the gloom, I noticed what looked like the shape of a sarcophagus to the rear of the chamber. On closer inspection, all I found was disappointment.

"Oh no—that filth covered Johnathan's coffin..." What little remained visible from beneath that mess wouldn't have been worth the film or the effort. Still, I snapped several pictures, horrified by the nightmarish scene revealed in the flash.

Caitlin suddenly screamed from behind me. The shock sending me tumbling and straight back into that hideous fungus! Utterly disgusted, I scrambled to my feet while shielding my face with a sleeve against the asphyxiating clouds of spores.

Once more, I used the flashlight to batter the clinging filth from off my body. The light flickered and went out, but I shook it back to life! Then turning, looked back to where Caitlin stood staring in the entranceway. At first, I was upset with her screaming, but then realized that she had seen something that I hadn't...

Casting the beam of the light toward the head of the sarcophagus, I moved very slowly. I had no intention of slipping into that nightmare again. Cautiously approaching a large and ghastly mound, I leaned while examining the unusual shape. Caught briefly in the trembling beam of my light, was the fungus covered remains of what had once been a human being...

My stomach heaved with the sight! Lurching away, I cast a hand before my mouth while fighting back the bitter and heated bile.

"Oh, dear God--," I gasped, as spinning toward Caitlin, choked out the words, "They buried Jonathan alive!"

"No—they couldn't have. He hanged himself." She wept in horror, as leaning in through the entrance, said, "No Michael, that's someone else. Oh, God—what's that?" She pointed to a parchment that was sticking out from beneath the edge of the mound of filth, and said, "There's something there—partially covered by that fungus…"

In the dim glow of our lights I could see the yellowed edge of the parchment. Reluctantly, I crept back through the heaped membranes, and reaching down, gently pulled while trying to loosen it from the filth. Almost indistinguishable from the mass, I realized that I now wrestled with the leathery and mummified fingers of a corpse…

"You're right—," Wincing, I glanced back as the dead fingers seemingly refused to release the page, and said, "It looks like a letter of some kind?"

Cautious but determined, I gently pressed with a shoe against the fungus. Using the end of the flashlight, I gently raised the hand of the corpse while drawing out the note. Although yellowed and stained, the page was complete and though slightly smeared, the hand writing was still discernible.

"The letter was dated, August fifteenth, 1921." I read aloud, saying, "My name is Giles Thomas Ellington, and being of sound mind and body. Oh God—it's a last will and testament. He must have somehow become trapped down here. But how and why wasn't he noticed missing or discovered by the family?"

Horrified with the thought I stared wildly into the surrounding and ghastly mounds. Giles had been left to face a horrible death by starvation, alone and driven mad in the silent darkness…

"I'll have to keep this for when we notify the authorities." I looked to the fungus covered remains, and quietly said, "I'm sure that even after so long, that somebody must still be wondering whatever became of this poor soul?"

"Notify the authorities?" Her eyes glistened with the onslaught of tears as shaking her head, she whispered, saying, "Please, I don't want to be involved with this too…" She moved forward, her hands gently resting upon the gates, and she asked again, quietly, "You're not really going to call the police—are you?"

She looked absolutely terrified with the thought. Looking into her eyes, for a brief moment I suddenly feared that those doors might slam closed. Blackness, the loud click of the closing padlock, fading footsteps as forgotten and alone, I would face the endless dark…

Indeed Michael, how does one become entombed alive within such a place, unless by the willful hands of another?

"No—there's no real need--," I choked on the words as looking back at the corpse, quietly said, "If this was a crime scene it's an old case now. It doesn't really have to involve either of us." Slipping the parchment into a coat pocket and moving back toward the entrance, I said, "In the end you're right—as sad as it may seem? It really doesn't concern us." I gazed deeply into her wide and staring eyes and whispered, "It's our secret—I promise."

"This place has already taken so much from me. I don't want to share in any more of its evils, sins, or secrets--," Her features became strangely cold as she looked to me and pleading, said, "Michael—you do understand?"

"Yes—I believe that I really do…"

Slowly moving around from beside her, I slipped out and into the corridor. My heart was racing, there was an immediate paranoia, and the thought of being the only witness left me feeling terribly vulnerable. For the first time since we had met I suddenly didn't trust her…

CHAPTER TEN

Sunday October 8, 1972.
12:10 a.m.
The incident in the crypts had created a bitter estrangement between us. It was due to this awkward feeling that after washing, we shared a quiet dinner, and then parted company early. Our evening of pictures spoiled, we retired to our rooms before ten that night. The house had become utterly still. After having heard her quietly close her door, for some reason, I had listened against the wall. In that utter silence my heart had broken as she had cried herself to sleep... This wasn't the behavior of a monster or murderess, but a woman at the very end of her wits

Why couldn't I have just left it alone instead of going down to those crypts? It could have been a truly wonderful day—but this is what I had made of it all. In truth, I was not only a writer of death and darkness but the unwilling author of the sad ruin that now grew between us...

Tempted as I might have been, I refrained from knocking on her bedroom door. It was late and would be an invasion of privacy.

It was almost twenty years now since the death of my fiancé. She was killed by a drunk driver one winter's night while crossing the street. She was the great love of my life and though I had known other women, never dated another one since.

People will always tell you that we all have to move on, but that's because they could never truly understand. They change lovers like socks and mortality plays for keeps. In a world filled with costume jewelry few ever find a diamond.

Leigh was beautiful, intelligent, charismatic, and had a heart of pure gold. They just don't make women like that anymore. At least that's what I believed until meeting Caitlin.

Unable to concentrate, I quietly sat before the desk while lethargically gazing into the hearth. She had looked so disappointed when I had suggested that we call it a night. I felt her pain and shared the disappointment, but was at a complete loss.

It was during a meal of that wonderful chicken stew that Eva had prepared, that frustrated with the awkward silence, I had asked if we should call it a night. I was hoping that it would break the ice. Instead, she had sadly glanced up and then slowly nodding, politely excused herself. Taking her untouched meal and placing it into the kitchen sink, she quietly disappeared into the shadows of the corridor. I felt like even more of a monster than before...

In that moment I had suffered for the sadness and that I had caused. There was simply no excuse for such cruelty! She had done nothing wrong, and couldn't have possibly known about the corpse. Why had I become her self-appointed judge, jury, and executioner?

"The right thing to do--," I spoke quietly while tapping a pen against the pad, and saying, "Is to walk down that hallway, knock on her door, and apologize for everything. Then we can enjoy the rest of the weekend together. No one will ever have to know the difference? No—I can't do that... But why not—there isn't any evidence that would substantiate murder? And besides—as sad as it was the guy was trapped down there for over fifty years. Who would even still be alive to remember him? What's wrong with me? I hardly know this girl and I'm willing to cover up a possible murder for her? Am I losing my mind? No—maybe it's just the first time since... Don't think about that. Just leave it alone..."

Lighting a cigarette, I rubbed at my face. I felt like hell and needed something else to occupy my thoughts. Reaching for Sir Reginald's history of Duff Glenn, I began flipping through his personal notes.

"First, I'll finish what I came here to do. And then—I'll work this out with Caitlin. And if it's not possible to redeem this situation— I'll leave first thing in the morning... Because that's what I'm good at—running away from the real world and people I love..."

Raising the flame in the lamp for more light, I grabbed my pen and began reading aloud.

"October fifteenth, year of our lord eighteen-ninety-eight. The days grow short, the nights seemingly endless, and the sickness will soon bring an ending to all. Such is my legacy, that with the passing of my dear mother, Lenora, I now speak without hesitation of that which none other has dared. I am the bastard offspring of the union of kin! The sins of which flowing within my veins, have become an evil termed syphilis. It is a vile disease which growing upon and devouring the flesh, destroys the mind and spirit."

Taking the time to write the text in its true form, I decided to keep my own copy of the final few pages. It wasn't like I didn't have the time, and it helped to keep my thoughts occupied.

"Though I spoke of being alone, I share this darkness with something else. Veiled in deaths white shroud, she watches from out blackened eyes and from where no mortal soul dwells. She is the devil's concubine, and one who by means of seduction derives life from carnal desire. Fiend, ghoul, she steals the breath of life and I fear for my very soul dare I sleep! This madness, for I can call it nothing less, transcends the foulest symptom of even my own disease! Had I only the courage of my father, I would prefer to share his fate than exist within this torment of living death! I am haunted, stalked by these abysmal shadows, how they creep and slither among corner and crook. Flocking like sheep before she who comes through fevered dreams in the night."

Startled by a sound I turned in the chair to look behind me. It was just a movement in the corner of my eye, and then I saw it. In the far corner, a tiny grey mouse scurried frantically across the room and disappeared beneath a large bureau.

"A visitor, I wonder what the little stinker got into." Shaking my head, I wandered across the room and to where my luggage rested at the foot of the bed. A brief search of the bag turned up a bottle of soda, candy bar, and small pack of black licorice. Relieved, I sighed while saying, "Thank goodness—still safe!"

Sitting on the edge of the bed, I indulged the soda and snacks while watching for any sign of the mouse. Several minutes passed without any more excitement and finishing off the treats, I went back the desk. The sugar had me flying in high gear again. It was a passion for sweets that I knew would eventually come back to bite me. Soda and candy bars had become a staple of my diet, especially on road trips and late nights.

"Maybe the mouse will eat that spider? Or then again, maybe the spider will eat—I don't even want to think about it…"

Sliding the diaries aside and deciding to leave the typing for another night, I began flipping through my previous notes. I knew that the information was pertinent to the story, but feared that it might come across in a slightly 'text-book' fashion. Frustrated, I wrote everything down, and completed the written account of the McCreary genealogies. Circling the important names, events, and dates, I double-checked everything for consistency before being finally satisfied.

"Okay, I wonder how well this will read." Taking my hand-written page, I read the content aloud, saying, "It was utterly astounding that Sir Reginald, of all people, should have become the narrator of the family history. The unfortunate and ailing bastard child of a strange union formed of loneliness, he had valiantly stood alone in the face of an unwarranted guilt. A crime of which he'd shared no part. It's been said that the son should never bare the sins of the father, but in this case it couldn't have been further from the truth. I'd better write this as something I said, rather than a narrative. There are already so many other narratives to deal with… Poor old Reginald, he really didn't deserve what happened to him…"

In the same turn, what right did I have to involve Caitlin with that thing in the crypt? Being the adopted daughter of a distant relation, she was even less to blame than the unfortunate, Sir Reginald…

Tossing down the pen in utter frustration, I covered my face with a hand, and grumbling, said, "I've got to fix this mess with Caitlin before it drives me out of my mind—but how?"

Reaching into the desk drawer and pulling out the parchment that we found in the crypt, I quietly read through the details.

"So you had one living relative? An aunt that was twice your age in nineteen twenty one. I doubt that she's still alive, not that she would even remember you if she was?"

Moving from the chair to the hearth, I looked down at the stained page as it moved ever so slightly in a cold draft. It was terrifying to think that something so fragile could become so utterly devastating.

"I'm sorry friend, but I can't let your death ruin her life. I'll find some way to make things right for you. But for now, somehow and wherever you may be? I can only hope and pray that you'll understand—and forgive me…"

With that final thought I cast the page into the flame, silently watching as the fire devoured the evidence of Giles Thomas Ellington's lonely death.

My guilt for the act was by no means justified, but only served to delay the inevitable. I would write the details on a new page and when the authorities discovered the remains, discretely provide the information. This would release her of all responsibility and still provide the necessary venues for authorities. In the end, and suffering from serious conscience, it was the only way that I could live with myself.

Returning to the desk and slumping into the chair, I went back to Sir Reginald's personal notes.

"Alright, so we know that you're sick and suffering from sleep deprivation due to nightmares… Aren't we all…?"

Was I becoming paranoid too or was there some kind of inexplicable connection? Was there an unexplained force, or some kind of ancient evil lurking in the dark halls of the Duff Glenn? Whether or not it bore any semblance of truth I planned on writing it that way. In my line of work it was simply referred to as 'artist's liberty' and I would stretch it to its full extent on this one.

Shivering and rubbing at my arms, I went to the hearth and added several logs to the fire. The stone was warm, and I knelt there for several moments while huddled before the flames. I knew that I would miss the House of McCreary when it was gone. Even for all of its dust, fungus, mildew, spiders and mice, it was a Gothic treasure trove. I had never felt a greater inspiration, been more terrified, or know anyone quite like Caitlin.

Forcing the thought from my mind, I went back to the desk and settling into the chair, returned to the reading.

"So where were we? Oh yes—here we go! The nights are exhausting as I preoccupy much of the time delving into the accumulated works of occult scholars. I am certain that by distinguishing the origin of this monster, there shall be a means of either destroying or dispelling the abomination. She stalks all manner of shadow, dwells within the ether and haunts the mind. Even during the few quiet moments that I attempt to take during the day, she relents to discover me upon that narrow path between waking and dreaming. I now fear that there is little hope. I can only pray that my one true friend, Dr. Edward John MacDonald, arrives before exhaustion forces me to succumb. October twenty-third, year of our Lord Eighteen-ninety. Edward has arrived with his trusted manservant, Clyde Ferrell. With concern for their health and safety, I have relieved all other staff from their responsibilities here. My health is quickly failing… I pray that we shall soon arrive upon a conclusion to this entire, ghastly affair. October twenty-fifth…

Truly, a great peril exists within the deep and gathering shadows. Once indiscernible, the evil now manifests as forms that lurk in nook and cranny by day, and haunt the corridors through the night. These fiendish apparitions, by means of night terrors, have also afflicted Edward and the elder Clyde. I fear this cumulative hysteria and suspect that by due process, mortal expenditures of energy only serve to revitalize the fiend. Although vigilant, our persistence begins to fail against such insurmountable odds. We suffer wakeful days, while throughout the dark of night, enduring terror and utter fatigue. Edward insisted upon summoning occult scholar and confidant, Thomas Phillip Jorgenson. The message having been couriered, our efforts continue as while anxiously awaiting his response. October thirty-first.... Both Edward and Clyde perilously border physical exhaustion. Wearied beyond capacity to facilitate the simplest of tasks they persevere by sheer will alone. Madness abounds within the shadow haunted halls of the house of McCreary. Death and damnation surely follow within our footsteps... I think that I see what Caitlin meant now? It's like he's slowly losing his mind? It must have been the final stages of mental illness due to the syphilis? So—he goes on about the summoning of a demon, resurrection of the dead, and something about—human sacrifice..."

The wind moaned in the chimney from behind me and a shudder ran the length of my spine. It felt like the icy fingers of something long dead, making its presence known. Avoiding several paragraphs that appeared as little more than the rantings of a lunatic mind, I continued reading.

"It is by no delusion of a fevered mind that I have concluded these things. Take note, that only by delving deeply into the realms of the occult, have I discovered the truth of this evil. It was by the hand of Johnathan himself that this devilry began. Invoking spirits of darkness in hopes of reviving his dearest Amelia, he brought death and disaster upon the house of McCreary. Many have since followed in his path, and by unspeakable atrocities, earned this abominable persecution. These walls have become a prison of the damned and a roost to the devil."

Picking up the pen, I hurriedly scribbled out the paragraph and thinking aloud, said, "I'm sure that it won't matter if I quote a few things? It'll sound better anyway."

"November twelfth, year of-- blah—blah we know that. Oh, here we go! Mid-day announced the arrival of, Thomas Phillip Jorgenson and his good wife, Anna. Being heavy with child and of resolute constitution, she insisted upon accompanying her husband. In regards to this, I must state my immediate concern for the woman and unborn child."

Running a finger down the page and through descriptions of fears for his guests, I found another point of interest.

"We have discovered several scrolls containing black spells, unspeakable rituals, and rites of exorcism. These were concealed in a hidden panel of Johnathan's chambers in the west-wing. The room having been sealed long ago, still contained all evidence of his sorceries. Among his things was also found a Grimoire, of which pages concerning, 'resurrection of the dead' and 'protective spells' were duly noted. The scrolls have been burned, the book hidden, and only the rites of exorcism remain in our keeping. Thomas alone retains the authority to perform these rituals, being an indoctrinated minister of the Lutheran order. November nineteenth. Thomas and Edward conducted a ceremony of purification within the chapel. Through means defying rational explanation, I perceived a storm to suddenly rage within the holy chamber. Thomas read from biblical transcript as Edward following closely, repeated certain text in passing. The maelstrom being expelled from the chapel, a great howling could be heard, and the sound shook the very foundations.

The terror inducing Anna into labor, all efforts were directed upon the woman. It is within solemn reflection that I look down upon the newborn child. With hair as white as snow, eyes bluer and by far brighter than the clearest of summer skies, they named her Catherine. She is the first child to have been born of the house of McCreary in over thirty-seven years. Now that's interesting, the name Caitlin is a variant of the original *Gaelic*, for Catherine." I remembered having seen the name when I was looking up the literal meaning of Duff Glenn."

The wind whistled beyond the window and interrupting the thought, I moved from the chair to peer out and into the night. The clouds raged against the black heavens as the moon fought through the churning shadows. The Oak branches swayed in the strong gusts, leaves flew, and the mausoleums were hidden from view. The shutters clattered, an icy draft crept in from an unseen crack, and I became lost in thought.

"I wonder—could Caitlin be the adopted grand-daughter of this Catherine person? Aw heck—I'll just ask her in the morning. If she'll even talk to me anymore after what happened today?"

Drawing the curtains tightly closed, I paused before the hearth in passing to poke at the coals. With the warmth in my face there were thoughts of sleep, but I fought them back. The weekend was almost over and I still had so much to do. I could only hope that there was still time...

Everything was happening so fast. So many things had occurred in such a short span that days felt like weeks. To make matters worse, I was exhausted and still had a slight fever. So, with all the events becoming a blur it was getting harder to stay focused.

Moving back to the desk, I smiled while gently petting the old roll-top. It was far larger but reminded me of the one I had at home. To some people these were just pieces of furniture. In my life they were finely crafted and very dear, old friends.

Slumping into the chair, I resolved to complete the reading of the diaries before bed that night. With only a few pages, I read only the relevant information.

"November twenty fifth. The child bodes well though Anna has taken ill. She struggles through a delusional fever and fearing the worst, Thomas has requested that Clyde take her and the child away. Clyde has abandoned the carriage in favor of a horse and sled. They depart with great haste and through bitter weather conditions.

Rubbing the sleep from my eyes and looking around the room I couldn't believe what I was reading. I now understood why Caitlin was so concerned about the diaries becoming public. The only thing worse than a lunatic in the family was one that made sense...

December fourth. We have discovered the bodies of poor Edward and Clyde in the lower west-wing corridor. They were both in a state of complete dehydration, and Thomas could find no evidence of blood within or anywhere about the bodies. Edward and Clyde have been given last rites and laid to rest in the crypts. I pray that they shall remain there... Now why would he say something like that? The men were both dead. It's not as though they would just get back up… Or would they? That might explain why all the gates have locks… December ninth. I am deteriorating. The blessed chapel has provided shelter but my own illness worsens by the day. I fear the arrival of the inevitable…

December twelfth. Thomas has established the origin of the fiend through Johnathan's notes, of which were hidden within the Grimoire. Due to fatigue, hunger, and the sickness I am no longer able to properly narrate the series of events. I had torn the aforementioned pages from the Grimoire, burned the book, and include them here…Pages—what pages?" Flipping through the manuscript and looking around in case they had accidentally fallen, I scratched at my head, saying, "Maybe they fell out while Caitlin was reading it? Either that or they must still be in the library? I'll have to look around in the morning… December fourteenth. Snowbound, winter has consigned our fates to this tomb of wood and stone. We are weak with hunger and the cold, but a hope still remains. Without doubt, the unfortunate Amelia plays host to this vile and maleficent spirit. With the coming light we shall venture forth and attempt to dispel this evil. May the good Lord guide and have mercy upon our souls. December fifteenth. It was as though by divine intervention that the storm has ceased before the dawn. We make haste now through deep snow, bitter cold and great distance to where Amelia lies within the mausoleum. The horror is complete! To our utter dismay, the corpse lay within a state of complete preservation! Yet once exposed to the light of day, did quite rapidly and visibly dishevel! Through rites of exorcism, Thomas has restored the earthly remains of Amelia McCreary to final rest. With the expulsion of the demon complete, a symbol of protection was crafted into Amelia's pendant. The charm was then bound upon her mausoleum gates, wherein Thomas recited a sacred spell of binding.

From this day forward the mausoleum entrance and all tombs shall remain barred. These records remain in testimony and warning to all who should enter into this domain. I pray that God now grant the house of McCreary, final peace…"

Closing the diaries I just sat there staring for several moments before saying or doing anything else.

"So, Amelia McCreary was possessed by whatever Johnathan summoned up while trying to restore her to life. She became some kind of demonic vampire, and Sir Reginald set the record straight… The place was locked up tighter than Fort Knox, he left a written account in warning, and everything should have been just fine. Until I came along…"

Drawing the pendant from the breast pocket of my smoking jacket, I held the chain between my fingers. Suspended between my fingers it swung ever so gently. Gleaming in the lamp\s glow, the ruby's reflected like fire from the pentagram. When I had first seen the pendant I had questioned the origins of that unusual design. That alone should have been warning enough to leave it exactly where I had found it…

"Maybe, those weren't just nightmares? Is it possible that I haven't just been seeing things around here? What if by removing this pendant, I opened the door to Amelia's tomb and allowed the demon back into her body?"

Placing the pendant down upon the diaries I could only question my sanity in that moment. What began as the pursuit of a ghost story was becoming so much more. It now involved murder, sorcery, possession, and demonic influences…

Were the shadows that Sir Reginald spoke of the same shades that I saw in the corridors? Did those ghastly footprints in my bedroom belong to the demon, Amelia? What was that hideous thing that tried drowning me in the bath?

"It's finally happening—I'm so tired that I'm falling for everything and losing control… I need some sleep."

Slipping the pendant back into the breast pocket of the smoking jacket, I moved the chair. I was finished with the diaries and satisfied with the notes, placed the pen and pad back into my doctor's bag.

Returning to the desk for the camera and carefully removing the film, I slipped it into a canister. I still had five rolls left but would likely not use them now. Winding the leather strap around the camera case, I slipped the parcel into the bag as well.

"You've likely out-stayed your welcome at this point--," I began packing my things away, and said, "I might as well tidy up and be ready to roll in the morning."

Placing the bag, suitcase and typewriter on top of the bureau across the room, I watched for the mouse. It became obvious after a moment that it was likely long gone or living in one of the drawers.

Neither of these things posed any real problem at that point, so I went back to the desk. Turning down the lamp, I went to the hearth to check that the screen was fitted tightly, and went to bed.

The moon peeked out from behind the clouds, and looking into my room, caught my eye. The hearth cast a gentle golden glow as the moons pale light crossed my bed in parting. It felt as though we were bidding farewell for the last time in the house of McCreary, and it broke my heart.

Slipping under the covers I rolled onto my side while watching the window. The moon slipped behind the clouds, the wind moaned in the heights, and the embers crackled.

"It's time to stop dreaming while you're awake--," Whispering into the pillow while watching the night beyond the window, I said, "If there ever was anything between you and Caitlin its gone now... you've ruined that. There are no ghosts, creeping shadows, or boogeymen in this place. Only the ones that you'll imagine while writing that book... so close your eyes, sleep and forget you were ever here... and ever met her..."

The wind moaned, the moon faded and the fire burned low. Somewhere in the night I heard a call, and knew that it was only the lonesome whispers of my empty heart...

CHAPTER ELEVEN

A blood-curdling scream sent me reeling from off the bed and falling to the floor. Half-asleep, I leapt up and stood as though having imagined the sound. The shrieking continued as panic stricken, I rushed frantically to the door, and throwing it open, ran out into the pitch-black corridor.

"Caitlin, I'm here!" Faltering blindly through the blackness, I followed the sounds until finally reaching the door of her room. Pounding madly, I began shouting, "Caitlin—I'm here—Open the door!"

There wasn't any reply, only that mindless and hysterical screaming.

"Caitlin! Answer me!" I cried out, hammering a fist against the door and shouting in warning, said, "Alright then! I'm coming in there!"

Shoving down on the handle I cursed while realizing that the door had been locked! After everything, she had locked the damn door! Faced with no other choice, I pounded furiously upon the door and calling out, "I'm going to break down the door! Hang on!"

Bracing a shoulder, I leaned back and with an immense effort, threw myself against the door with incredible force! A sudden pain seared and rocked through my entire frame. Having failed to have even budged the solid oak barrier, I tried again while calling out to her, "Hang on! I'm here Caitlin!"

Whether it had been some weakness caused by decay in the ancient framework or sheer desperation, I suddenly crashed through the door! Flung forward, I fell inward and tumbling to the floor, raced to get back to my feet!

"Caitlin!" I leapt up and rushing toward the bed, reached out to her, saying, "I'm here, say something! Speak to me—please!"

Flailing wildly and thrashing about, the hysterical woman screamed through sheer terror. The only words escaping her mouth were shrieked at the top of her lungs, as she said, "No—no—no!"

Obviously caught in some horrendous nightmare and unaware of my presence, she fought desperately against an invisible assailant!

All the more horrible was the way that she stared into wide-eyed oblivion! Grabbing at her wrists, I fell back as she exerted an unearthly strength in her terrified state. Attempting to restrain her from causing any self-inflicted injury, I shouted, "Wake up! Caitlin, wake up damn-it! Wake up!"

We struggled on the bed as tightly grasping her shoulders I shoved her downward with all of my weight. She fought against me as shouting, I pleaded with her, "Please—for pity's sake! Wake up woman!"

Her mouth suddenly gaped, every muscle tensing and straining as her eyes bulged hideously. In a moment of deathly silence, she looked straight at me. The fear hideously twisting those beautiful features beyond anything that I have ever imagined! Leaning forward and holding her in a firm embrace, I desperately pleaded, "Caitlin, please, wake up—wake the hell up!"

She suddenly became silent and to my absolute horror, her face became flushed and ran a pale blue! Those wide green eyes bulging as though they might just explode from out of their sockets! Her tongue suddenly protruded, longer than I had ever thought humanly possible! She was suffocating and now fought desperately for her life.

"Caitlin, please—wake up!" The thought of assaulting a woman was absolutely intolerable by my standards, but I was left without any other choice! This I did abruptly and several times while shrieking in terror, as slapping her face, cried out, "Caitlin—wake up! For the love of God, Caitlin, please come back to me!"

Suddenly all sound and struggle ceased as collapsing to the bed in convulsions, she fought to draw breath. A second later and her eyes opened, as leaping forward, desperately clung onto me.

"It's okay now, everything is alright—I've got you." Holding her tightly and slowly rocking her in my arms, I whispered, "It's all over now—you're safe, I'm here—I'm here..."

"Michael--," She wept, as gasping and coughing while attempting to explain, stared wide-eyed as she looked up at me, and said, "It was horrible. It was trying to kill me!"

"It was just a nightmare." Looking deeply into her wild and terrified eyes, I held her firmly while speaking in a calm voice, and said. "It was just a bad dream. It's over—and I'm here now."

"But it wasn't just a dream." Placing a trembling hand upon her throat, she drew my attention to the dark and deepening bruises, and said, "Something attacked me and it tried to choke me to death."

"No." I swiftly formulated an explanation, and said, "I've heard of these sorts of things happening during nightmares. People are capable of doing some of the most unimaginable things."

"Are you trying to say that I did this to myself?" The terror in her face was suddenly replaced by a confusion, and then seething rage as she shrieked, "I didn't do this to myself—and if you're trying to say different?"

"Please--," Brushing the tears from her eyes I spoke calmly, saying, "All that I was saying is that you've had a nightmare. It happens and has even happened to me here, several times…"

Slipping free of my embrace she leaned over to light a small lamp near the bed's edge, and sniffling, said, "I'm so sorry—Michael—nothing like this has ever happened to me before…"

"And I'm sure that I didn't do anything to make things better either…" Feeling sudden shame, I looked over at her and holding back the emotions, said, "I'm really sorry for what happened today—and what happened in the crypt. It was really none of my damn business in the first place, and--."

She pressed a finger to my lips, her features softening as she quietly said, "That's okay—this place seems to turn everyone's life into a nightmare?" She hesitated while noticing something on her right arm, and turning to hold it into the light, asked, "What's this?"

I watched in horror as the trailing and glistening mass ran down her wrist. Dropping from her arm, it slid across the bed and gathered into a pool among the blankets. Pulsating, the black and leathery fungi absolutely oozed with filth.

Shrieking, she leapt off the bed while frantically wiping her at arm with the bed-sheet. Suddenly looking down at her legs she screamed, saying, "Michael—oh no! Get it off of me! Oh no—it's all over me!"

Horrified, our worst fears were realized in that moment. The fungus had come for her as it had in her childhood nightmares… Grabbing her robe from where it lay on a bed-side chair, I dropped to my knees. Struggling, I fought to wipe the ghastly mess from off her legs! In a moment of hysterics, she slipped out of her evening gown and tossing it aside, used a pillow case to wipe the horrid mess from her upper body.

Leathery, foul and clinging, it was a struggle to tear the hideous and oozing masses from her body. It was almost as though they were more animal than plant, and resisted our efforts. This was very different from what I had seen in the crypts. It was alive... Frantic, I managed to remove the last few clumps and toss them into a pile in the middle of the bed. Slithering, the gelatinous masses slowly pooled while coming together.

Scrubbing the foul mucus from Caitlin's body with the robe, I removed my jacket and slipped it around her shoulders. In a moment of complete and utter terror she seemed unaware of my presence or her own vulnerability.

Throwing a trembling hand before her mouth, she gawked while pointing toward the bed, and whimpering, said, "It came out of those old crypts—and came after me... Like I always knew it would..."

Looking to where she was pointing I suddenly noticed that the fungus withdrew from the light. Ever so slowly, its slippery tendrils dragged the leathery and quivering sacks deeper into the sheets, and beneath the blankets.

"That isn't what we saw in the crypts..." Taking the lamp from her hand, I moved to the bed and reaching for the blankets, peered back at her. The room was dark and with only the light of the lamp between us, she stared in absolute horror.

Gripping the blankets and sheets, I leapt back while ripping the covers from the bed! There was nothing among the sheets and covers, but Caitlin's scream brought my attention back to the bed.

In the very place where she had been only moments earlier, a large and slug-like thing struggled to avoid the light! With tendrils flailing and uttering a horrendous squeal, it convulsed and smoked.

"What is that thing?" She wailed, as throwing her back against the wall, cringed in terror.

"It wasn't that fungus—or isn't anymore," I stood before her defensively with the lamp, and shouting, said, "It's something else... But look—it's trying to escape the light!"

I rushed forward, and shoving the light merely inches away from the creature, threw a hand before my face. Shrieking, it burned in the light's glare, cowering as it began shrinking and shriveling before our eyes! Choking, I stepped back as a putrid smoke began pouring from off its dissolving, and pooling mass. The nightmare began liquefying as within only moments, all that remained was an unrecognizable, pale and chalky sludge...

Rushing into my arms she held me tightly, as burying her face in my chest, whimpered, and said, "What's happening here? This can't be real! How could something have possibly come to life from out of a nightmare? Michael—that was the thing that was in my dream and trying to kill me..."

"I don't know? But whatever it was—it's dead now..." I could only stare down in disbelief. Watching as the horror was rendered into a smoldering heap of powdery residue beneath the light.

"It's turned to dust..." Caitlin looked closer as still wary of going anywhere near the bed, glanced at me, and asked, "But what is that powder? Is it still dangerous?"

"I'm not sure--," Moving to the hearth and tossing several logs onto the hot coals, I said, "Let's not take any chances, we need more light in here."

She went to where two tall parlor lamps stood against the far wall, and in moments had them lit. The room became far brighter, and taking the poker from the hearth, slowly approached the thing on the bed.

Cautious not to get to close, I began jabbing at the thick and pasty mess. It was lifeless. In fact, it was nothing more than a heap of something that resembled talcum powder. Drawing the bottom sheet from off the bed, I tossed it down and examined it closely.

"That's strange--," She pointed to the bed and appearing confused, said, "It never affected the mattress at all? Shouldn't it have soaked through?"

"I don't have any answers at the moment..." It bothered me as before this I could have explained almost anything away.

"What about that mess on the bed?"

"Parapsychologists might refer to that as ectoplasm. It's a kind of spiritual residue that occurs when mediums communicate with spirits of the dead. From what I've read on the subject, it's supposed be a similar consistency as chalk. But I've never actually seen it before..."

"Are you insinuating that I might have psychic ability—and drawn that thing out of the nightmare?"

"It's a possibility, but I'm not sure of anything at the moment. All I know for sure is that we've got something nasty going on here." Nodding toward the bed and staring back at her, I said, "And the evidence is real and right there on the bed..."

"If ectoplasm is the residue of spirits—how can this possibly have been the same thing?" Crossing her arms before her, she said, "This was not a ghost—it was some horrid combination of a slug and that horrid fungus. What's to stop it from coming back? Oh, Michael, we simply mustn't sleep!"

"Listen to me, please!" Embracing the hysterical woman I held her close, and pleading, said, "Panicking is the worst possible thing that we could do right now. So please, let's try to remain calm and deal with this one step at a time."

The horror that shone in those wide and bright green eyes broke my heart. I knew that to some degree, and possibly more than I would be willing to admit, that the nightmare had been my fault...

Gathering up the sheet that contained the horrid mass, I carefully folded it into a small parcel. Cautious not to spill or come into contact with any of it, I hurried over to the hearth. Removing the screen and shoving it into the flames, I stood back while holding Caitlin close, and watching as it burned.

Sunday October 8, 1972.
12:28 a.m.

Piling the wood high in the living-room hearth, I looked to where Caitlin, lay buried beneath blankets upon the facing couch. Sipping at a glass of brandy, she wore that same sheer green gown that she had danced in earlier. Still using my smoking jacket to cover herself, she appeared so small, frail and lost. I felt bad for not having retrieved her robe, but we had left the room in such a hurry. Truth be told, neither of us wanted to go back in there. In a last thought, and being the only thing close at hand, she had snatched up the gown on the way out.

"Are you feeling any better?" I asked, suddenly leaping back while being startled with the chiming of the grandfather clock.

"I'm better—but it seems that we're both a little shook up." She rubbed sleep out of her eyes, and looking to me, asked, "Do you think that what happened upstairs, might have had something to do with you taking that pendant?"

"Not unless you believe in ghosts?" For some reason I really didn't like the sound of my own words. It was like admitting guilt. Then I realized what she had said, and shocked, said, "I never told you about the pendent?"

"You didn't answer the question?" She sipped at the brandy, and raising an eyebrow, stared back at me.

"If what Sir Reginald wrote in his diaries is true—there's a distinct possibility." I shrugged, as standing before the hearth and gazing into the flames, said, "Regardless, I'll make sure that it's returned to its rightful place—first thing in the morning." Turning to look back at her in apology, I added, "I really didn't have any intention of keeping it. I just wanted to have a better look, and it seemed like such a waste to just leave it there... I would have given it to you before leaving here."

"Michael--," She swallowed hard, and sitting up while pulling the robe closed, said, "What if simply putting it back—isn't enough?"

There was a brief stillness, and then, a low and drawn out deep moan. It was a sound that seemed to resonate from the very bowels of the ancient structure. An echoing boom, that resounding within the walls and beneath the floors had filled every single room, corridor, and dark corner of the place.

"It's just old plumbing—and built up water pressure." The explanation had worked before. Nervously peering about and listening for several moments, I quietly said "It happens a lot in these older places, and especially during the colder months."

"I've never heard anything like that before?" She whispered while looking around the room and frightened, said, "And I've lived here all of my life. Michael—I'm really scared..."

Moving to where she sat, I slipped down beside her, and retrieving my brandy from the coffee table, said, "Seriously, don't let it bother you." I smiled somewhat nervously, and attempting to comfort her, said, "I'm sure that it's nothing. Most things can be explained—it just takes a little time and common sense."

Unwilling to admit it, but unsettled by the sounds as well, I looked to the large windows at the far side of the room. Just beyond the reflection of the firelight, I could make out the forms of the oaks as their branches, swaying in the wind, tapped and scratched at the window pane.

"Well, there you have it?" Patting her shoulder reassuringly, and pointing to the window, I said, "There's a virtual tornado going on out there. Obviously, there must be an open or broken window somewhere? Believe me; the wind can create some very surprising sounds in a big old place like this." Peering to the high ceilings and around the enormous room, I added in thought, saying, "I've heard and experienced some crazy things over the years, and in places like these. The acoustics are amazing…"

Suspiciously looking into the direction that I was pointing, she said, "So if it was a broken window? And we can both still clearly see the wind in the trees out there--," Her eyes darted through the deep shadows of the room, and she turned to whisper, asking, "Then why has the sound stopped when the wind, clearly hasn't?"

A deafening roar sent us sprawling together as the wind erupted in the hearth! Casting sparks and embers in a blinding, ashen cloud, it howled, roaring down the chimney!

"There—that was the sound!" Hurrying from the couch, I began stomping at the smoldering embers, and saying, "I told you! It was just the wind--," I pointed into the hearth and astonished, said, "Can you imagine how this might have sounded if all the flues in the house had been opened?"

She didn't appear the least bit satisfied with the answer. Snatching up the brandy glass, she drank deeply before saying, "I'll just be glad when this place is sold, demolished, and long gone."

"You know, just a few days ago—I would have disagreed with you." I felt unnerved as the fire-light caused shadows to dance demonically upon the ceiling, walls and floor, and shrugging, admitted, "But now—I'm not so sure?"

"Not so sure?" She scoffed, as raising her glass in a toast and speaking loudly, called out in defiance, saying "To the house of McCreary and all of its ghosts, devils, and nightmares! May they crumble and sink into the flames of hell, where they belong!"

There was a strange apprehension stopping me from sharing that particular toast, as pondering briefly, I sighed, and raising my glass, said, "How about—to forgiving and forgetting, and to new friends and memories?"

"Alright then--," She raised her glass, her voice barely above a whisper as she said, "To new friends and memories."

With a gentle tinkle of good crystal we toasted, as taking a sip, she added, "And a well-earned death—to the damned house of McCreary."

The glasses suddenly shattered within our hands. There was a brilliant eruption of bright blue flame, which exploding from the hearth, came with such incredible force that it pressed us deeply into the cushioned couch. An icy gale howled through the room as sending furniture crashing over, we cowered, huddling close and covering our faces to the sound of breaking glass. A moment later, and with the fire having been extinguished by an icy wind, we held each other close within the blackness. I could still hear the hissing of the dying coals, the temperature having dropped so much that I could see the breath before my face.

"Oh, dear God in heaven--," Trembling uncontrollably, I looked into the shadows, and whispering, said, "What have I done..."

"Michael—we can't stay here." There was an urgency and desperation in her wide and staring eyes, as she said, "We can't stay here—in the dark. Something will come for us... We need to find a safe place."

"The chapel--," I thought aloud, as horrified and shaking her head, she gasped, pleading, "No. Not that horrible place! It's at the far end of the house and too near the crypts, and that hideous fungus... I don't want to go there—I just can't, please!"

"The hearth is still burning in my room—it's a lot closer. We can stay there until morning." Fumbling for my Zippo lighter, I felt around on the floor, and finding a candle that had fallen from the table, lit it while saying, "We'll be safe as long as we have light. Stay close. Everything will be just fine."

"I'm so scared—I don't think that I can do this?"" Embracing me so tightly that I could hardly breathe, she looked to the little flame on the candle, and said, "If the spirits of this place are powerful enough to extinguish a blazing hearth—what good will that candle be?"

"It's going to be alright--," Attempting to appear as reassuring as possible, I gently brushed the hair from her face, and said, "It seems to be gone for the moment? In any event—like you said, we can't stay here—in the dark…"

We moved ever so slowly as rising from out of the chaos, paused to look around. The floor was littered with strewn debris as broken lamps, tables, and heavy shelving had been tossed about like children's toys.

Amidst the mess I caught the glint of broken glass, and was dismayed to see the shards of that lovely crystal decanter. Realizing that Caitlin wasn't wearing any shoes, I lowered the candle to closer observe the floor.

It was in that moment, and as the room had grown darker that I noticed something move in the corner of my eye? It was a shadow which passing near the edge of the hearth, and just beyond view of the candle-light, now held absolutely still...

Unwilling to scare Caitlin any worse, I refrained from saying anything. Instead, raising the candle, I began searching the room for a candelabrum. In doing this, I gained a better view while suddenly noticing the shape move again. Hideously malformed and no larger than a child, it crept into the darkness behind an overturned table, and crouching down, hid from the candles glow.

It wasn't just a shadow. No—you saw what it was and now you're just too damn terrified to admit it! So what was it then? This strange thing that now silently hid in the blackness, near the far end of the couch? You knew—you saw it this time. It was the hideously bloated, and fungus covered corpse of a child. Yes Michael—that's right! It was the shadow of a young boy who had drowned in the pond, and been dead for the better part of a century…

The thought had barely passed when I became aware of the fact that the shadow had not been the only one… I had just failed to take notice of the others as they too now came closer. They were the shapes of the dead, which covered in that ghastly, clinging, and all-consuming fungus now crept and crawled from all about us…

"Michael—," Tightly gripping my free arm and shivering uncontrollably, she leaned closer as whispering, said, "I just heard something—and I think that it's coming from behind the couch?"

I hadn't said anything, but I'd heard it too. It was the sound of something that slithering, crept stealthily up from the other side of the couch. Swiftly reaching for a nearby candelabrum, I hurriedly used my candle to light the six stems, and trying to appear calm, said, "There's broken glass all over the floor—so I'm going to give you my slippers."

"What about you?"

"Don't worry about that right now." Forcing her to accept them, I whispered, saying, "Just get ready to make a run for the stairs when I tell you too."

Reluctantly raising the candelabrum above my head, I peered into the long shadows. At first there had been immediate relief to have not seen anything, but I knew they were there, waiting...

Looking from side to side, I motioned for Caitlin to follow. She took my hand and holding it tightly was close at my side. Faltering in mid-step; I suspected to have seen something? Leaning down and picking up the broken decanter top, I tossed it into the darkness beyond the couch. No sooner had it struck than was there an angered hissing, and my heart leapt into my throat.

Caitlin tugged upon my hand, as holding back her terror, gasped while saying, "Michael—it's either now or never. We need to go, now!"

Racing out from behind the couch, we dashed madly across the living-room and into the corridor! It was nothing short of a miracle that I hadn't stepped on broken glass, or hadn't noticed during the surge of fear and adrenaline. Struggling to avoid dropping the candles, I shot a glance backward as we ran, and looked into the darkness behind us. The night was alive and moving from behind and all around us. They were coming, following, and almost on our heels. Stay calm. They can't enter the light—I must not drop the candles. Oh God, please don't let me drop them.

"Michael, look there!" Caitlin screamed, as pointing a trembling hand toward the ceiling and walls, shrieked, "The fungus from the crypt! It's alive and it's coming after us!"

The corridor was smeared with pulsating masses of blackened filth! Glistening, it crept across the ceilings, sliding down the walls and to where accumulating, soaked the carpet beneath our feet. Holding the candelabrum higher, I cried out as the hideous fungus drew away from the light, and gathering, rapidly swelled from all around us. There was no choice.

"Come on, run—run for the stairs!" The steady pounding of my heart increased into a deafening thunder as watching the mass grow in pursuit, we raced hysterically through the house!

It couldn't be happening—but it was. It was coming after us. Faster and faster as it filled the hallways behind us, absorbing and covering everything in its path.

Bursting through the corridor and fleeing toward the stairs, we suddenly slipped, shrieking and stumbling through the seething mass. Almost losing the candelabrum I cried out. Dropping a single candle, and watching as the light and flame were extinguished in a sickly vapor that now caused the vile mass to withdraw.

"Oh no—it's all over me!" She screamed, as thrashing wildly at her bare arms and legs, she cried out, "I can't get it off! It's spreading—growing all over me! It burns!"

Holding the candelabra high in the air, I grabbed at her flailing arms, and catching a hold of her wrist, shouted, saying, "Caitlin—listen to me!" I pulled the hysterical woman along as we rushed toward the pulsating, glistening mass on the stairs, and said, "It'll be okay, just keep going, we're almost there!"

Dreading the touch of anything on that foul and slippery path, I dragged the screaming woman along. Our feet sucked down into the foul mire, and still we fought our way ever upward.

"We should never have gone down there! It's biting, stinging--it burns!" She burst into hysterical tears, as raking at her legs, she shrieked, "It's all over me—it's eating me alive!"

Looking down, I choked in horror while noticing the gruesome filth as pulsating, it expanded, small root-like tendrils swelling and creeping the length of her legs. Breathless, I fought harder as instinct and fear driven adrenaline now created one final, mind-shattering effort. Reaching the top of the stairs, I shoved her forward. Choking as the corridor behind us filled with the sickening, seething ocean of death, and cried out, "Go—run, run for your damn life!"

Adrenaline burning in every vein I pushed her onward, wailing as the surging wall of putrefying decay now exploded through the hall like a tidal wave. Every nerve screamed as mindless panic drove me, throwing the shrieking woman forward and into the room, I barely had the time to close and bar the door. I could hear it like thunder, forcing against the door, and pushing its great mass against the walls. A dim glow still emanated from the hearth. Turning, I rushed toward the fire and hurriedly heaping the wood high, shouted, saying, "Get over here—and into the light! You're safe as long as you're in the light!"

Caught in a state of utter panic and shock, she was deathly pale and had fallen suddenly silent. Without having even acknowledged a single word that I said, she stared without emotion of any kind. In that moment, the straps of her gown slipped from off her shoulders, and it dropped to the floor. In the fires light, I saw the hideous fungus that now clung and crept from all over her naked flesh.

"Oh God—Caitlin, don't move!" I cried out, as grabbing my pajama pants from where they were hung on a nearby chair, rushed forward. Kneeling, I desperately attempted to scrape the swiftly spreading fungus from off her legs. It won't come off. The harder I scrape, the worse it gets. It's like some kind of horrible plant, spreading roots all over her body and growing. Looking down at my hands and shoes I noticed that the mold had faded, and pausing in thought, suddenly realized the reason why. Cologne, I had accidentally spilled cologne all over myself earlier!

"Of course, Cologne, why didn't I think of that earlier?" Snapping my fingers I cursed, shouting as I said, "The alcohol, of course!"

Hurriedly returning to the bureau, I grabbed the Brandy bottle and rushing back, began frivolously splashing at her arms and legs. "Come on, damn you—die you rotten filth!"

A moment passed as turning her into the fire-light, I watched as the fungus began shriveling, bursting like infected pustules, and running like yellowed and bloody mucus from her legs.

"Yes—thank God! Come on sweetheart—work with me here!"

The flames burned high in the hearth, as working feverishly I sprinkled her down, wiping and washing the festering mess from her flesh. It was almost impossible, as surging beneath her gown I was forced to rip it from her body to draw out the hideous mass.

"I'm so sorry—I had to do it," I looked up at her, as ashamed, suddenly saw a spark or recognition burning within those eyes, and asked, "How do you feel?"

"Much better—but you'd better see to yourself as well." Suddenly becoming aware of her vulnerability and shielding her-self with an arm and hand, she looked nervously about, and said, "Please, could you find me something?"

"Of course—sorry…"

Hurriedly pulling my trench coat from off a nearby chair, I threw it over her shoulders. Then gently seating her upon the sill before the hearth, said, "Just stay there for a moment while I clean up."

Moving into the privacy of the far corner and removing my pants, I gasped as the mold suddenly surged, spreading up the length of my left calf and thigh. Fumbling and dropping the brandy bottle, I fought against the flailing roots and spreading tendrils.

"Here—hold still!" Panicking, she rushed over as half-blinded by tears, grabbed the bottle from where it had fallen. Barely able to hold the brandy within trembling hands, she began desperately splashing at the fungus. Gritting my teeth I fought the urge to cry out. I felt the tendrils burrowing deeper into my skin, gripping as they tried to take root in my flesh! In that moment I wondered whether Sir Reginald was truly afflicted by Syphilis, or some pre-existing variation of this hideous, fungal nightmare?

"Just a little bit more--," She wept hysterically, and fighting against the grotesque and pulsating growths, gasped, saying, "Hold still—I've almost got it!"

It took everything to just stand there. My flesh felt as though it was burning as the filth dissolved in the alcohol, and ran like a hot and putrid river down my legs. I felt sickened by the very touch of it, and trembling, glanced down as she fought to wipe it away.

In a moment of sheer terror I saw the filth slip beneath the last article of clothing I wore! Without hesitation, she tore the shorts from where they now clung to my body with the moldering and foul mucus. Vigorously splashing at my lower extremities, she shrieked as the tendrils and leathery, blackened mass moved toward the worst place imaginable. My heart leapt into my throat and the breath froze in my lungs! Fearing to share Sir Reginald's fate, I was speechless and caught in a state of absolute horror, and suspended disbelief.

Forced to literally use the alcohol soaked material to tear the thing loose from my inner thigh, she leapt back. Desperately scrambling upon hands and knees, and extending it before her, tossed the vile thing into the hearth! There was a ghastly popping and cracking sound as it burst upon the hot coals. Then a putrid, black smoke as flailing, it was utterly consumed in the flames.

With eyes still filled and running with tears, she flung her head over a shoulder and looking back at me from where she still sat upon the floor, whimpered, "Are you alright?"

"Yes, thanks to you." With thoughts of Sir Reginald and that oozing filth affecting my most intimate regions, I shuddered, saying, "And I think that you might've just spared me a fate worse than death…"

"Worse than death…"

CHAPTER TWELVE

With the pain subsiding and politely covering myself, I rushed over to my luggage. Slipping into fresh shorts, shirt, socks, and trousers, I returned to where she sat waiting.

"I'm beginning to suspect that the source of that rotting filth began with Sir Reginald. Whatever evil he encountered, somehow manifested in the form of his sickness. Then, festering and eventually killing him over time, transferred from his body to this house… Like he wrote in his diaries, an invisible fiend that feeds on the living to sustain itself…"

"But, how and why would it begin as a sexual disease?"

"In those days, many still believed that Syphilis was a curse caused by sin."

"And, the house of McCreary thrives on the evils that men do…"

Nodding in agreement, I said, "As crazy as it all sounds, it does make some kind of twisted and horrible sense."

"I'm sorry about earlier this evening--," She gazed tearfully while slipping into my night shirt, and saying, "And you were right. We should report the body that we found down there, in the crypts. In some terrible way, I feel responsible for that poor man's death…"

"I'm sorry as well, for everything." Taking a seat beside her and sighing deeply, I moved closer, and admittedly, said, "I burned that parchment that we found… I've written down the name, and once you're long gone from this place, I'll send an anonymous letter to the proper authorities. They can figure things out from there…"

"You didn't have to do that for me…."

"I've had a talent for finding trouble all of my life. So, it was just a matter of time before something really bad caught up to me."

"In the days of old, knights once sought out dragons in defense of kingdoms and fair lady's--," She gazed thoughtlessly into the flames, and speaking out of thought, whispered, "Perhaps, there might be a little dragon slayer in you?"

"I doubt that it's anything quite so honorable." Looking down at my wrist-watch, I realized that we wouldn't have enough firewood to last through the night. It was still hours before the dawn.

She seemed to almost read my mind, as looking between the few logs that remained and to where I sat beside her, said, "We'd be lucky if this wood lasted us two hours."

"It's only a little after one... maybe if we burn the furniture?"

"Even if we do manage to make it until morning--," Desperation tore through her pale features, as pulling me close and gazing deeply into my eyes, she said, "Then what? We can't go back out into that dark hall. And there's no other way out of here..."

"There's always a way—we just have to find it."

"Well, if we can't fight this evil--," Scoffing at the idea, she mumbled, saying, "With all the books on witchcraft in that old library, maybe we can get some brooms and just fly out of here?"

"Books and black magic—maybe we can fight it?" Quickly retrieving Sir Reginald's diaries from the desk, I came back, knelt down before her, and said, "Caitlin, I need to know something? Sir Reginald mentioned some pages that were torn from a book. He claimed to have left them between the pages of his diaries—but they seem to have been lost?"

"No, they weren't lost." Remorsefully shaking her head, she frowned, and almost whispering, said, "I burned them."

"Burned them—but why would you do something like that?"

She had no answers and simply looked away. I tried to conceal my own fear, and speaking calmly, said, "Alright then, the reasons don't matter. What's done is done and can't be changed. But do you remember, or have any idea of what might have been written on them?"

"I don't really remember anything, clearly?" Her voice faded into a whisper as she looked away, and said, "It was written in a different language, possibly Hebrew or some middle-eastern origin. It was very old, and contained symbols and illustrations of abominable things committing vile acts... She spun toward me, and pleading, said, "You do understand why I had to destroy it, don't you?"

There hadn't even been a moment to think or consider, as hearing the subtle, yet distinct sound of a handle turning, I looked toward the door. There was the faint click of a latch, as though someone or something now attempted to release the catch. Ever so slowly, it turned as squeaking loudly, the handle was caught and would turn no further. Locked, oh thank God… I'd locked the door…

"Resurrection—the pages had something to do with bringing back the dead." Her face became deathly pale as she whispered as though fearing to be overheard, and said, "The drawing depicted a ritual—and something about human sacrifice. The pictures were progressive, and the second image was the figure of a demon." She thought briefly, and terrified, gazed at me with wide eyes, saying, "The third showed a type of portal, and a demon flying out—and into the body of a person that lay on a kind of ceremonial altar."

"Of course—it's the invocation of a demon and possession of a willing sacrifice… or maybe not?" Staring wild-eyed, it all suddenly made horrible sense, and muttering, I spoke the thought aloud, saying, "Oh dear God, Johnathan must have tried to bring Amelia back that way…"

She hadn't responded, but covering her mouth with a hand and suddenly gawking, pointed a trembling finger toward the door. There was a sudden sound of splintering wood as the door, being forced beneath incredible pressure, started cracking while bending ever inward. The hinges bent, the screws began ripping free and popping out, dropped to the floor.

Ripping the poker from where it still lay among the hot coals, I took a firm hold of Caitlin. Poised defensively, I swung the still smoldering poker high, and prepared to face whatever nightmare broke through that door.

The entire room shook, thundering deafeningly as Caitlin suddenly tore at my sleeve. Frantic, she pointed to where a pale and sickly mucous surged, and flowed in from beneath the door. I fought the urge to cry out as the gelatinous tendrils thrashed and flailed, as forcing inward from all around, crept from beneath the cracking framework. Although the flames of the hearth had provided a dim glow closest to the bed, I now realized that the opposite side leading to the doorway was in deep shadow.

"Oh no—light, we need more light in here right now!"

Racing toward the far end of the room, I desperately tore at the covers, and rushing back, cast them into the hearth. The old cloth burst into flame as wailing, I dragged the blazing linens across the room. Then throwing the burning fragments against the door, I began batting them against the hideous mass. Thick black smoke billowed upward as a horrendous hissing resounded from behind the doorway.

It was working! Dear God in heaven—the fire was working! The eruption of a shattering window caused me to turn suddenly, as looking to where Caitlin threw herself backward, I cried out as she fell before a shower of crystalline shards! Rushing to her side, I dropped to the glass covered floor beside her, and lifted her from the chaos. Gently holding her in my arms, I gasped, "What happened—are you alright?"

"It just exploded—I don't know"" Still stunned, she plucked broken shards from her hair, and looking around, suddenly panicked.

"Oh, no—the flames—we have to stop the fire before this whole place goes up!"

Ripping the remaining sheet from the bed, she rushed toward the door, desperately battering at the flames. The heated and choking fumes caused me turn away, as a movement in the darkness suddenly caught my attention. Forcing my gaze into the frozen darkness beyond the broken window, I pondered?

Was it just some trick of the fire-light in the trailing smoke, or had something moved out there? Peering into that jagged portal once bordered by glass, it stared back at me from out of the blackness! Like two pale and shimmering moons which ran with blood, unblinking, the luminescent eyes focused upon me. Paralyzed with terror, I watched as they flashed and then vanished back into the night. It had happened so fast that doubting my own vision, only the shock and blood-curdling fear of what I had seen remained. Unaware of the sinister presence, Caitlin screamed in frustration, desperately swatting the blanket against the burning floor and wall.

"It's not working! I can't stop the flames!"

"Hang on!" Grabbing a wash basin from a near-by bureau, I rushed ahead and dumping the soapy water against the door, leapt back as the flames hissed, smoldered, and went out.

Pointing in warning and shouting, I wailed, "Look out! It's coming back!"

The vile and oozing fungus bulged from beneath the ashen ruins of the door, bursting with filth while forcing itself into the room. Pulling Caitlin from the doorway, I directed her attention to the bed while shouting, "Help me with this! We need to drag it to the doorway!"

Struggling with the massive oak bed, we managed to shove it across the room. It moved painfully slow, but in a desperate effort, we pushed the heavy headboard firmly against the splintering door! With the bed no longer blocking the glow of the hearth and reinforcing the door, we hurried clear. The thing in the hall crashed heavily against the door, as with flailing tendrils, withdrew as the barrier held fast! It was a small victory, but offered hope where none had existed before. Our efforts had been rewarded as the glow from the hearth now filled the chamber. Rendered helpless, the gruesome fungi, unable to escape from the darkness, writhed in the shadows beneath the bed. I felt her hands tightly encircling my arm, as looking down our eyes met, and desperate, she asked, "What are we going to do?"

"It can't come any closer now—not with the light. Still, I've got a gut feeling that it we don't try to do something, that we might not make it through the night--," Gesturing toward the windows, I said, "Help me pull down the draperies, I've got an idea…"

"What are you talking about?" She seemed utterly confused, as pointing toward the hearth, said, "We can just stay here—near the fire, and wait until morning."

"I' don't think so--," Drawing the pendant from my pocket, I held it before her wide eyes, and said, "We both know that until I return this to the gates of Amelia's mausoleum, that this might never end…"

"You can't seriously be considering going out there?" Her attention traveled to the window and then back to me, as she said, "It's a thirty foot drop and it's pitch-black out there. Even if we manage to survive the fall, we'd never make it all the way out to the mausoleums in the dark…"

"Please, just help me…"

Pulling down the draperies, we knotted them end to end while creating a makeshift rope. Securing one end around the heavy old desk, we proceeded to shove it across the room and against the wall beneath the window. With adrenaline rushing through my entire being my face was flushed with a heated fear. Nauseated and fatigued, it took everything just to stay focused.

"That should do the trick" She tested the line, and looking back at me, said, "It should be fine as long as we go down one at a time."

"Not we--" Testing the strength of the knots I looked back at her, and said, "You just stay here and keep that fire burning bright. We have no idea of what might be waiting for us out there."

"Well we definitely know what's waiting out in that hallway. You can't seriously mean to leave me here alone?" She put her hands to her face, the tears filling her eyes as she said, "I think that it would be best if we stayed together—no matter what happens."

Dropping the linen rope and tightly embracing her, I pleaded, saying, "You'll be okay, trust me. Just keep the hearth stoked and stay close to the fire. I promise that I'll be back as soon as I can..."

We both knew that there was no protection in the darkness and very little chance of making it out there, much less ever returning...

The determination fading from her eyes, she tightly embraced and kissing me, said, "That was for luck."

Before I could say anything else she went to my bag and drawing a t-shirt from within, cast off my coat, saying, "You're going to need this more than I am. It's bitterly cold out there."

Slipping into the shirt and finding a pair of boxers in my luggage, she took whatever modesty remained to her in the moment.

Breaking a leg from off a night table, I bound a piece of torn linen around the end and soaked it with brandy. Checking my coat pocket for the old Zippo, I nodded, saying, "I suppose I'm as ready as I'll ever be."

She followed me to the window and with one last glance, tightly held the fastened end of the line. Leaving her alone was almost as terrifying as climbing out and onto that wet, moss covered ledge. It was pitch-dark, slippery, and the icy wind bit into my eyes, face, and hands. Struggling to keep my balance as while kneeling and clinging to the linen rope, I reached out for a drain pipe.

The thoughts raced through my mind in that moment, and none of them were reassuring. Michael, don't look down—you know what will happen if you do... You'll get the shakes, lose your grip, and most assuredly fall to your death... Those stones are so cold and there's hardly anything to hold onto, Oh God, please don't let this old drain pipe break...

Holding the makeshift rope in one hand and using the rusting and squeaking old pipe for balance, I managed to get down to the lower sill just as the rope broke loose from above. Desperately fighting for a grip on the old stone-work, I pressed myself tightly against a window pane.

"It's okay!" A wild-eyed Caitlin stared down as tightly gripping the remainder of the linen rope, said, "Grab the rope—I've got it!"

With a wave, I reached out and tried grabbing at the dangling line! Frustrated and terrified as the wind kept tossing and pulling it just out of reach. Just a little further—come on old man, you can do it. Just reach out, a little bit more. Just then, I became aware of a sudden flurry of movement in the darkness of the window behind me. I knew what it might be and terrified beyond thought, began panicking. Losing balance I cried out, as suddenly falling backward, was cast out and into the night.

The distance was only a few yards but the fall had seemed to last forever. Spinning out of control and utterly helpless, I flew outward and into the darkness. It was only by pure luck that the fall had been broken by the garden hedge, and that I hadn't landed on the stone pathway. Instead, having been caught and repelled from off the tall hedge, I lay sprawled and winded within the tall and wet grass.

"Michael, are you alright?" She cried out, pleading as she said, "Answer me—please!"

"Yes—I'm okay!" I shouted back, coughing and groaning as the pain of being winded now hindered my efforts, and I called back, saying, "I was caught by the hedge and the lawn broke my fall. I'll be alright—just go inside and stay near the hearth!"

Taking a moment, I leaned against the brick-work of the stone garden while trying to catch my breath. It was so dark that I could hardly make out the little path. The moon passed from behind the clouds while casting pale phantoms in the long and trailing fog. Tightly gripping the make-shift torch, I looked at it several times, but knew better than to light it. I would need it for the mausoleums, and could not afford to have it fail somewhere in between.

"Did something just move out there?" Terrified and whispering to myself I peered into the darkness, and said, "Or was it just the moon-light causing shadows in the mist? Nerves Michael, it's just your nerves…"

There was a sound of something that slowly moving through the dense and surrounding forest, now hesitated. Was it just a deer that had taken notice of me and become wary, or was something else following? Terrified, desperation suddenly overwhelmed all sense of conscience and turning back, I hurriedly began making my way toward the road.

"The car, that's it! Get to the car and drive as fast and far away from this place as you can!" Staring blindly upon the wide and clear path leading out and away, my heart raced. The moonlight shone brightest there and it would be the safest and fastest route out. Stumbling, I fell into the open arms of a marble angel that broke my fall. Turning to look back, the house of McCreary ascended like a nightmare from out of the drifting fog. Against the blackened heavens it was dark with exception to a single and tiny light. A window from where a lone figure waited while lost within the surrounding and endless night.

"Caitlin." The thought of leaving her tore through my heart. Looking between the open roads and to where she stood in that distant window, hope found me in the darkness. Taking a firm hold of the stone angel's wing, I pulled myself up, and cursing under my breath, said, "I'll not leave you behind. No matter what happens. Better a hero in heaven than a coward in hell…"

The sound of breaking twigs and branches caused me to move even faster. I knew that it was a race for life now and losing was not an option. I ran blindly along the path, my legs working furiously as I dashed across the field. The wind whipped through the tall grass as the dark heavens became huge against the blackened plain. Escaping from behind the clouds for an instant, the moon gazed down and the fields became bright. I could see the trees growing in the distance and knew the path was close. My lungs burned, heart thundered, and still I ran as fast and hard as my legs would carry me. The clouds covered the moon, the world fell into blackness and I ran blindly. The sounds of something huge moving through the dense foliage echoed through the night, and I knew that I was being followed.

It's back there. Oh God, I can hear it following. It must be huge… It sounds like an elephant breaking through the trees. No, don't look back—don't stop. Run, damn you—run.

The moon breached the clouds, lighting the way as the twilight fields narrowed and the path through the woods came into view. Slowing, as my heart and lungs couldn't take any more, I was forced to stop at the mouth of the forest. Fighting for breath, I looked into the blackness all around me. That's when I noticed it… The sounds of being followed had entirely vanished... Had it stopped? No... It was silently waiting on that dark and narrow path through the woods... I could feel it... There was no choice...

The wind rustled through the tall grass as the moon cast an eerie glow upon the forest. In that moment, I ran for everything that I was worth! Charging into the forest and along that path, I could see the open field beyond in the moonlight. It was only several hundred feet. The distance closed rapidly, and I was nearing the three quarter mark when a movement at the forests edge stopped me suddenly. Something was there and lingering in the blackness near the paths end... I was so close... There was still a chance...

Faltering briefly, I made a conscious decision and bursting forward, raced madly toward the end of the path. Seconds away the moon suddenly vanished, the night becoming utterly black. Blindly, I ran for all that I was worth. With lungs bursting and heart thundering, I ran madly through the brush as the moon reappeared, and I broke free of the forest. If anything had been waiting there, I was certain that the light must have caused it to retreat in that last second. Racing out and into the clearing, I could see the reflection of moon's face upon the wind-swept ripples on that horrible pond.

The howl of the wind startled me, as with every nerve tingling and trembling uncontrollably, I forced ever onward. In the pale glow I could now see the looming forms of the mausoleums from over the forests blackened edge.

"Just—a little—further now... you can—make it!"

Gasping, I desperately clambered up the moss covered stairs, every step becoming more painful than the last. The groves appeared from either side and terrified, I crawled while climbing the last few steps. Stumbling across the grounds I fell to my knees before the gates, gripping the cold iron bars for support. That's when I realized that after emptying my pockets for Eva to take the laundry I had left the key behind...

"Oh no, no—this just couldn't be happening! How the hell could I have forgotten about the damned key?"

With no other choice I tossed the torch up and over the spiked barrier. Gritting my teeth I gazed up at the blackened spears of the gates in the moonlight and began climbing. Scaling one of the stone pillars adjoining the gates, I struggled to avoid from becoming caught on the various hooks and ornamentation along the way. The stones were bitterly cold, slippery, and offered little opportunity for a firm grasp. Making my way upward and reaching the top, I felt the sudden sting of cold steel and cried out.

"Damn it—I should have known better!" Warm and slippery, the blood ran freely from a deep gash where I'd caught a rusted spike with the palm of my right hand.

"Just keep going—almost there..."

Finally reaching the top of the pillar, I was balanced between the stone and speared gates. I couldn't stop from shaking, and the wind forced against my body just as I balanced before the spikes. Ever so carefully, I swung a leg over the spears, tightening my grip while precariously positioned directly above the sharp points.

"Stop shaking, damn you... you can do this—just hang on a little longer."

I fought to keep my balance as between fatigue, fear, and the icy wind, teetered dangerously. The bloodied hand slipping from its hold upon the icy spear, I lost balance and suddenly went down. Twisting while trying to avoid those deadly spears, I cried out, helplessly plummeting over the edge. With the icy wind in my face, I squeezed my eyes tightly shut, terrified and waiting for the inevitable. It seemed to take forever, as narrowly clearing those points and dropping ten feet from off the pillar, crashed heavily to the earth. With my head missing a large marble pedestal by mere inches, I lay wide-eyed, winded, and gasping from the fall.

The moon crested the clouds and looking upward, my eyes caught the silhouetted spears against the heavens. Long, cold, and cruel. I imagined myself impaled upon those barbed spikes, bleeding and dying in the shadows ...

I shook the image from my thoughts as struggling to climb back to my feet, gasped, "Okay—you made it this far. All that you have to do now—is make it to the mausoleums..."

The moon cast an eerie twilight over the midnight gardens of the dead. It was a haunting blue haze which creeping from behind the clouds, made the mausoleums appear as though they were rising from out of the fog. An icy gust chilled my sweat-soaked brow, and I caught a sudden movement in the corner of my eye. At first I assumed it to have been a person, but soon realized I was mistaken… The shape or shadow leapt over the gates in a single bound, and landing on the marble plateau, crept silently past the tall support pillars. Disappearing somewhere into the shadows, I could have sworn that I saw two burning eyes staring back at me.

Pulling out the strange locket, I looked down while whispering, and said, "If there is any power of protection in you—please, please work now…"

The pentagram shone pale in the dim light, as attributing an unearthly life to the little charm, I swallowed hard, saying "Alright then—let's do this…"

It wasn't the dead that I feared. It was that hideous fungus and the demon possessed thing that Sir Reginald had once called, Amelia.

"That's just not possible." I stopped and staring at the trailing mist, whispered, saying, "The fog is moving against the wind. Covering the ground almost as though it were trying—to hide something…"

Holding the amulet before me, I hurriedly climbed the ancient marble stairs. Though desperately desiring to light the torch, I knew that it would be a final hope in the last moment. Reaching the end of the path and passing between the angels that guarded the stairs, I hurried toward the mausoleums. There was a faint shuffling in the darkness and it caused me to glance back. What I saw there turned my blood to ice. The night seemed to move from all around me as squinting, I soon realized that I was almost completely surrounded by that ghastly fungus.

The mass bulged and spewed, as creeping from behind the old crypts, flooded and seemed to flow like a blackened ocean, Covering and devouring all within its path, sightless, it seemed to sense my presence. Moving quicker and with obvious anticipation, it rapidly spread like a festering disease, and swiftly came from across the grounds.

Good God I'm done for! But wait—what's it doing now? Why is it lurking in corners when it could easily come straight at me? And then it struck me, as muttering, I said, "The moonlight…"

Shooting a quick glance into the heavens my heart leapt into my throat. Dark and heavy clouds crept ever outward as strong winds carried them ever closer to the moon. In moments the world would fall into blackness and the fungus would come for me… Reaching into a coat pocket for the lighter, I was horrified to discover that I'd lost it in the fall from the gate. Panicking, I looked back and forth between the advancing fungus and slowly clouding moon. The wind became stronger as the shadows grew longer, and I floundered in the failing light. The mausoleums became blackened with the filth as it crept from all around, and hung in great clumps while suspended from doorways. The clouds began drifting across the moon as the light faded, and darkness slowly settled from all about. It would all be over very soon…

Fumbling for my cigarettes, I struggled with the package while discovering the lighter inside. In that instant, and as the Zippo ignited, the seething mass reared back as a shrill hissing ripped through the night. It was almost upon me when the light had forced it back. Casting a flame to the torch and raising it before me, the fire became a beacon of hope in the blackness.

Scrambling onto the marble plateau with the torch held before me, the vile filth swiftly withdrew from the light. Slithering into cracks and crevices, it moved inside the blackness of the mausoleum gates. The victory was short-lived though, as the wind, dampness, and chill were quickly working away at the fading flames. Catching sight of an oil lamp that hung from a nearby pillar, I raced toward it and struggled to free it from its mounting. I knew that I couldn't get near those gates without the light.

"Damn you—come off of there!" Pounding with a fist against the metal bracket, the blood ran from the torn flesh of my hand. Desperate, I fought ever harder and through the searing pain until the lamp suddenly broke free, crashing to the cold stone floor. Kicking at the old lamp and stepping back, I gasped as it began leaking dark fluid from a cracked base. Grabbing the lamp and splashing the oil all over the grass before the steps, I ignited it with the torch. The flames spread rapidly through the dry blackberry vines, dead underbrush and tall grass. The night erupting in a sudden brilliance that forced me back while shielding my eyes.

Swiftly becoming a wall of flame, the heat warmed my body as the light restored hope. With the pendant clutched tightly in my bloody hand, I stumbled through the blazing chaos. The filth had completely vanished before the flames, and slipping and falling to my knees, I crawled toward Amelia's tomb. Reaching the stairs, I grabbed at the iron gates and pulling myself up, turned to a sound from behind me.

Standing on the plateau behind me and caught between the light of the flames, the fog and the full moon, was an abomination. Little more than a rotting carcass, it swayed as though caught within the winds of hell. Throwing myself forward against the gates, I fumbled while attempting to bind the little chain around the rails. It seemed that no sooner did I have it wrapped, than did it suddenly fly off again. It was like trying to force opposing magnets together.

Reeling with a sudden and intense pain, I was pulled backward as something ripped through my shoulder. Falling to my knees and gasping, I looked up. It had come for me... Twitching hideously and glistening with decay, the corpse of Amelia McCreary leaned downward. The long and filthy blonde hair streaming in the icy wind, she paused mere inches from my face. Choking with the stench of death, I stared straight into those black and empty eyes. I had seen them before... In dreams and hanging from upon the stalks of a monstrous slug...

Gripping me tightly with razor sharp and bony fingers, I felt the flesh of my shoulder tear with the searing heat of flowing blood. Before I could even react she pulled me away from the gates, and with incredible force, flung me aside. The world spun as my body twisted through the air before crashing down near the edge of the stairs. The wind having been knocked out of me, I heaved while fighting for breath, and struggling to one side. Blood suddenly filled my eyes, and passing a trembling hand before my brow, found the terrible gash above my left eye. A shadow passed before me and I froze, as partially blinded through the blood, slowly looked upward. Retching as a putrid and trailing stream of filth dripped down, I cast a hand before me as it ran the length of my face...

"Destroy it..." The sound was all too familiar but somehow different. The hissing and gurgling was gone as she now whispered with a voice that she might have once spoken within life. Demanding, cold and cruel, she repeated, saying, "Destroy—it.... Destroy the pendant..."

I knew that the charm was my only hope, and resisting, forced my eyes away from the fiend. Crying out as she clawed at my shoulder, I defiantly looked up and spitting blood, said, "If you're so powerful—do it yourself, Amelia!"

A sudden rage shone within those blackened eyes, as dropping to her knees before me, a cold claw clamped tightly about my throat. "You—will—destroy—the—amulet…" The words came as though she spoke each as its own sentence. I knew that the transcendence into our world wasn't complete. She would need to take a life… A life that would inevitably be my own…

I could only watch as leaning closer, its leathery features twisted horrendously, the mouth gaped, and I saw it's blackened and rotting teeth. I could feel that I was becoming weaker to her touch. In doing so, she altered and changed. The black eyes faded into gray and like a pebble dropping into a pool, she blinked several times before staring down through white and shining pupils. The once disheveled flesh and leathery skin began softening, the muscles twitching as life was seemingly returning to the corpse.

Helpless and struggling for breath within her vice-like grip, I managed to choke out the words, "I'll see you in hell, first…"

Enraged, she flung an arm and clawed hand high into the night, as intending a fatal blow, uttered a mind-shattering shriek.

"Michael—Michael where are you?" Caitlin screamed from somewhere beyond the blinding light of the flames.

Panicking as while unable to utter even a single sound in warning, wild-eyed, I gazed up at the monster. In that moment she knew and her features twisted into a cruel semblance of a smile. Her intentions becoming obvious, I flew into a sudden and complete panic. Hysterical and ripping free, I desperately grappled with the demon, wailing as I cried out, "Run Caitlin! Run for your life!"

With Amelia's claw once more fastened tightly about my throat, she began crushing my wind-pipe, and the world begun spinning from all around me. With the severe blood loss draining whatever consciousness that remained, broken of spirit and drained of strength, I suddenly collapsed.

Caitlin screamed as crumpled upon the cold marble, I made a feeble attempt in turning toward the sound of her voice. Through the ensuing smoke and flames I saw her wrestling with Amelia before the mausoleum gates. With the pendant clutched tightly in the fingers of her right hand, both of Caitlin's wrists were caught in the demon's grasp. They stood upon the brink of utter madness, as lashing out, the demon shrieked in fury. Releasing Caitlin's left wrist, it lashed out, knocking her to her knees, and grasped the fallen woman by the throat.

"No—no!" Tears of anger burned in my eyes as fighting for the strength to move, made one last effort. Clambering to my feet and stumbling across the plateau, with sudden force and violence, I threw myself upon the unsuspecting Amelia. Enraged, she ripped at my arms and chest as toppling over, we fell together, rolling several yards distance from where Caitlin lay in a crumpled and bloody heap. With the taste of my own blood in my mouth and half blinded, all remaining strength now failed. Knowing that it might be my last effort in life, I rolled onto my back while staring up and into death's pale face. She stood out against the raging flames and beneath a full, blood red moon. In the moment that she drew back her claw with intention of finally taking my life, I could do little more than tightly close my eyes…

From somewhere behind us Caitlin shrieked at the top of her lungs. It wasn't the sound of terror, but a woman's rage that now filled the night and drew the demon's attention.

"You go back to hell, Amelia!" Tightly gripping the gates, Caitlin swiftly bound the pendant about one of the iron spikes.

Amelia suddenly released me as seething with an unearthly rage, raced toward Caitlin with outstretched claws. Battered and bleeding, I dropped to my knees and toppled forward. It took everything just to roll my head and look toward the mausoleum gates.

Pulling a large marble vase from the sill of the mausoleum and raising it above her head, Caitlin flung it against the approaching monster. Swatting it aside, Amelia sent it rocketing against the mausoleum wall, and to where it exploded into tiny fragments.

There was a sudden and deafening, sonic boom. It was like worlds colliding and dimensions being forced into each other. The earth quaked beneath us as sending Caitlin backwards, brought her down to her knees. A shrill wailing shattered the night, and from out of the blackness of those gates, burst forth a stream of absolutely horrendous apparitions. Shrieking, they created a spinning vortex as the mouth of an immense portal yawned from before us. There was turbulence and an icy gale that escaping from Amelia's tomb, extended while growing stronger and expanding ever outward. It was a frozen vacuum that escaping from hell began drawing everything within its gaping maw. Reaching out and grabbing onto the gates of Henry's tomb, Caitlin narrowly escaped being dragged into the void.

Deafened by the unearthly shrieking my eyes became fixed upon the loathsome figure of Amelia in the moonlight. Falling to her knees before the stairs, she began clawing at her smoldering flesh. Her body began liquefying into a steaming puddle of absolutely putrid filth beneath her quaking form. She fell forward, clutching and clawing at the cold marble. Amidst the chaos, those horrid and shining eyes suddenly focused upon me. I stared aghast, as clawing her way across the plateau and through a trail of wet and smoldering decay, she came at me…

Weak from loss of blood I tried desperately to crawl away from the approaching nightmare. It was hopeless, I could hardly move much less do anything to defend myself. Turning to face the thing, I stared in wide-eyed horror as she approached. Blackened and disheveled, her flesh shrank like leather against the bone. The muscles bursting and running with blood and puss as she slid through the oozing putrefaction. Helpless, all I could do was watch as rotting before my very eyes, she clawed ever forward, inching her way across the cold and slippery stone. The souls of the wailing damned flowed faster and ever faster, spiraling into a blinding maelstrom. The force began drawing us both across the plateau and into the raging portal. The thing was almost upon me. Kicking and thrashing to avoid her clutching fingers, I cried out as she took a firm hold upon my right ankle. Sliding across the cold marble surface, I managed to reach out and catch hold of a stone angel in passing. Wrapping my arms tightly about the base, I clung for dear life as my body spun. Unable to catch hold of anything else, Amelia slid past while still gripping my ankle, and hung suspended before the void.

"Oh, dear God…" I looked back at Amelia.

Hanging suspended in mid-air by her grip upon my ankle, her eyes burned like white fire. Having abandoned all hope of escaping that void, I knew that she intended to drag me with her. Convulsing, her body bulged, limbs twisted and lengthened, and she began to change. The claw that had been holding my left ankle began melting away, and was replaced by a long and blackened tendril. Slithering upward, it painfully tightened around my lower calf. Tentacles burst from her thighs and legs as her feet began stretching. The legs and toes growing into long and trailing tree roots that whipped from behind her. The body began swelling and elongating as the flesh blackened, oozing with slime as it became an enormous slug. In that moment she gazed up at me and I saw death as empty sockets now gazed back… Her mouth fell open as within a silent scream, and widening to impossible proportions, her face erupted into a mass of seething tendrils. Any semblance of humanity having been stripped from the hideous thing, I cried out while seeing its true form. With coiling and flailing roots and tentacles it became a blasphemous union of wood, animal, and vile decay. Undoubtedly, the demon was a manifestation of all the sins and evils ever accrued to the house of McCreary. It was the sickness that became Sir Reginald's, ghastly affliction. The Syphilis, which acting like a flesh eating fungus had slowly devoured both his body and mind. It was the ancient and monstrous roots of the old willow, that embracing the victims of a double murder, had also taken the life of little Henry. I knew that this embodiment of sin and evil was the demon that summoned by Johnathan, possessed and had become Amelia. The same nightmare that now gripped my leg as we hung suspended before the pathways to oblivion.

Flailing and thrashing wildly before the growing portal, the tentacles began streaming upward. Creeping, they traveled the length of my calf as intending to ensnare me further, fought against the immense gravity of the void. Weakened and fading quickly, at any moment I would be dragged into that gaping abyss by the horrendous thing. That's when the unthinkable happened. My grip failing, the marble angel had suddenly toppled from its base. Narrowly missing where I lay from just beneath, the figure fell forward as being drawn by the storm, soared into the void. With the ensuing chaos it struck the fiend and broke its hold upon my leg. Slipping away the nightmare and angel were cast backward and swiftly lost within the raging abyss.

Utterly overwhelmed, I couldn't keep my hold upon the marble base. The strength finally failing, I felt my arms begin to slip away from the cold stone. In the final moment, a hand suddenly reached from out of nowhere and took a firm hold of my wrist

"Don't give up! Michael—," Caitlin shrieked as still gripping the gates of little Henry's tomb, cried out, "Take my hand! Fight damn you—fight!"

Eternity seemed to tremble from all around me. Struggling against the deafening echoes of damnation, I fought to escape the vacuum of that horrendous pit. There was another sonic boom and the night became deathly still.

"It's over." A tearful Caitlin leapt forward and throwing her arms tightly about my neck, clung desperately while saying, "We did it Michael—we did it..."

"I don't understand? I asked you to stay at the house, safe, and near the fire. Why—what made you come out here?"

"Because--," Extending a hand and opening her fingers, she said, "You forgot this?"

In her trembling palm and caught beneath the moon's glow was the key to the cemetery gates...

"Remember what you said to me in the library—about books and keys?" She whispered in the darkness, her eyes huge as a single tear ran down her pale cheek, and she said, "Sometimes—a key can save your life."

CHAPTER THIRTEEN

Tuesday October 31, 1972.

   When Eva had returned on Monday morning she had found an absolute disaster. Without any rational explanation, our only saving grace was the fact that the house was scheduled for demolition. Gathering my belongings, I had arranged to return for the books within the week. I had kept that promise, but when I came with the truck and movers Caitlin had already gone… Eva didn't say much, I felt terrible for everything, and in parting she had given me a parcel left by Caitlin. Along with a few personal items was a note. It was a simple request. All that she had wanted was an autographed copy of the book when it was published… After that weekend with her I was hoping for so much more…

   While the movers loaded the last few boxes of books I took a moment to search the contents of the parcel. Inside were the diaries and genealogical chart, a ghastly doorknocker and a single, skeleton key… There were tears in my eyes when I turned to look away from where I stood between the gargoyles on the steps. The cold wind whipped the hair into my eyes, and something sinister whispered from out of those ancient oaks. In that moment I realized that I had found the beginning to my book, and lost something far more precious in the process. In the end I got my ghost story, the gift of an unusual doorknocker and an enormous book collection…

   The house of McCreary still stands in all of her dark majesty. Empty, decaying, and ruled by shadows it awaits demolition. A place filled with bad dreams and broken hearts…

   Typing out the last few words I sat back while reading what I had written. It would have made an acceptable epilogue but wasn't the end of the story.

   "What am I going to do? I've only got one hundred and seventy four pages…" Tapping my fingers at the desk while glancing toward the window, I slowly nodded while smiling.

   "There's no need to panic, old bean. We've still got time, and I'm sure that something will come up…"

Monday January 1, 1973.

2:27 p.m.

"Honestly Mike—this stuff is something else!" Ted's laughter echoed through the phone, and he said, "Are you sure that you're not smoking any of that wacky tobacco?"

Just ignore him—he's your friend and more importantly, he's also your publisher.

"Does that mean that it's okay?" I'd been dreading his reaction since dropping off the partial manuscript just before Christmas.

"Its fine—but what I'd really like to know--," He paused before asking, "Is when you're planning on finishing it?"

"I'm working on some new material already--," Tapping a finger upon my typewriter I stared upon the empty page, and said, "You know these things take time."

"Oh, I know alright--," His voice wavered, and he asked, "You're not still moping around over that girl? What was her name? Caitlin?"

"What me?" That familiar shadow crossed my heart as chuckling, I said, "Oh heck no--, I'd almost forgotten about her until you brought it up."

It was obvious that he knew that I was lying, but as usual, he just dropped the subject.

"Well the holidays are over now, son." He chuckled, and pausing in thought, said, "It's time to get back to work. You know—I told your mother how important this project was to your future. You don't want to worry and disappoint both of us now, do you?"

"Um—you really didn't have to say anything to her. You know what she gets like."

"Oh come on, I was just kidding you Mike. But seriously, you need to get motivated."

It wasn't that he was being pushy. After all, this was his business. In all truth, he had a big heart and I owed him more than money could ever repay. He was taking a big chance on me with this project and I was truly grateful for the opportunity.

"I'll get busy with it right away--," Fidgeting with a pen and glancing out through the office window, my attention was drawn to the distant and mist-covered mountains, and I said, "I suppose that you may be right, Ted? Caitlin has been on my mind a lot."

"Oh—don't I know it?" He laughed, sipping at his coffee and

saying, "You haven't stopped crying about it for months! Frankly, I just wish that you would piss or get off the pot."

Turning from the window and sighing deeply, I said, "Gee, you always make everything sound so easy."

"Listen—I do have a heart and understand these things better than you might think--," He sounded frustrated, and clearing his throat, said, "But, the next time that I hear from you? I'd like to hear some good news in the progress department. And Mike—the sooner you complete the book and we get it published. The faster you can bring your girlie that autographed copy and get things sorted out between you. Am I right?"

"Sure, and I know. I guess that I've just been slacking a little?" I tossed down the pen and rubbing at my eyes, said, "But come rain or shine—you know that I'll deliver, no matter what."

"I know that and I'm counting on you--," There was a compassion in his voice that bordering sympathy caused him to fall short, as he said, "I want to see you happy and successful too, my friend. Let's put this together and make some magic happen. Oh—and by the way, happy new year!"

"Same to you Ted. And thanks again. I'll talk to you soon." Hanging up the phone and wandering toward the window, I drew the heavy purple draperies, and peered out.

With a foot of snow at the door and more on the way, I simply couldn't imagine wandering around out there? The short trip to my mother's for Christmas dinner had been a chore. Even with the snow tires and powerful front-wheel drive I'd barely managed. I'd always hated the winter months. With no desire to venture beyond the comfort of home, there hadn't been any new source material for another story. At this rate, the book would not be finished until the summer. I had to do something….

The written account of the haunting of the McCreary estate had left me feeling utterly empty. The days were far too long and the nights endless. Needless to say, they were also spent occupied within a single thought…

"Caitlin, I wonder if she ever thought about me? And if so, would it even make any difference now? It's been two months, twenty four days and--?"

Looking down at my wrist-watch I mumbled, and said, "Eleven

and a half hours."

I had abandoned counting the minutes as they drew attention to the seconds, each moment taking us further into the future and even farther apart.

"Oh what's the point? She's never going to call. Why do I keep punishing myself like this?"

Turning my attention back to the completed story on my desk and reconsidering the epilogue, I picked up the pen and tapping it to my brow, said, "I've already thought it all over, many times, and typed it all out. That's all there is to say—just leave it."

Dropping the pen amongst the clutter surrounding the old typewriter, I wandered aimlessly around the desk. Pausing before a small glass cabinet that stood next to the window, I stared and said, "Well, my sweet monster, I guess that you're all that I have left now?"

The gruesome old doorknocker shone eerily from inside the oak display case. The cabinet had been specially made to accommodate the heavy old brass knocker. Caitlin had even been kind enough to provide an antique door of which the backing was made, and the knocker mounted. With a golden light shining from a hidden lamp above, it was like gazing back in time... I vividly remembered seeing it for the first time on that doorstep, and in the flickering candle light.

Gently stroking the glass with a finger, I stared into the eyes of the demon, and whispered, "What I would give to have seen all that you have through the centuries…"

In my life, all that now remained of Caitlin McCreary were the books, nightmares, and that ancient doorknocker. I had returned to the house of McCreary with a cube van in the following week. The driveway had been cleared, there was easy access to the main doors, and between us it had been loaded in under two hours. She had remained reserved, and respecting this, I had not attempted to revive anything that we might have previously shared. This was extremely awkward to say the least, and I felt defeated in every aspect of the matter.

In parting, she had given me the doorknocker and striker as a memento of the Duff Glenn. In a thoughtless moment, I had made a joke in saying that I would also need a door of which to hang it. In one of the few clean and dry storage rooms, we had discovered exactly that. A door of which having been long forgotten, she promptly presented to me and assisted within loading. With the promise of returning with an autographed copy of my published book, we bade farewell, and parted ways...

So, I ended up with an office and storage room filled with boxes of books. There were seventy four small boxes in total. Piled between the office and main floor, they still sat exactly where they had been left. Usually the clutter would have bothered me and demanded immediate attention, but for some reason I just didn't care...

Returning to the desk, I slumped into the old high-back chair. It was one of those heavily padded, maroon, leather classics that lawyers and judges preferred. It rolled upon steel casters, swiveled, and often squeaked when it disapproved. I'd spent countless hours and many years at the old roll-top desk, and practically lived in that old chair. A Smith Corona typewriter rested in the center of the desk, as surrounded in books and papers, was cluttered with objects of numerous types. I had favorite pieces of Smoky quartz, Amethyst, Ammonite, and fossil shark teeth. There was a lovely Trilobite specimen from the Burgess shales, and a display with a large, Atlas Chalcosoma beetle with spread wings. I had wooden carvings of West Coast Indian deities, stone gargoyles, and an exceedingly large, antique, magnifying glass. Needless to say, the most important thing now was to finish the book. At a complete loss and without nearly enough pages to justify the manuscript, I had no idea of where to take the project now...

Before the thought had entirely escaped my mind the telephone rang. Fumbling with the receiver, I answered in my usual calm and polite manner, saying, "Good afternoon, Schreiber residence, Michael Schreiber speaking."

"Mike—hi there it's me, Harry." The familiar voice echoed through a field of static, as reluctantly, he asked, "Did I get you at a bad time?"

"Harry—I was beginning to wonder if you'd fallen off the planet, how are you!"

Harry O'Donnell was a childhood friend who now served as sole justice officer of Hedley B.C. It was the little Okanogan town where I had spent most of my youth.

"I'm fine, and I know that the weather has gone for a crap. But is there any chance that you might consider coming into town?"

There was an unmistakable tension in his voice. Being completely uncharacteristic of my old friend's usually boisterous manner, I felt obligated to ask, "Harry, are you alright?"

"Yeah, I'm fine, but there's something a little strange going on out here... I can't really explain it." There was a reluctance in his voice and something distinctly unsettling, as he said, "Listen, Mike, I know that it's a huge hassle, but I'd really rather see you in person, than speak over the phone."

"For crying out loud--," Leaning back into the chair and uttering a nervous chuckle, I grinned, saying, "What's wrong Harry? Did you discover Bigfoot out there and all alone one night?"

There was a sudden silence on the other end of the line and after a moment's thought, he quietly said, "Mike, I don't know what's going on. I just know that I could sure use your help out here, right now..."

This being completely uncharacteristic of my dear old friend, I became immediately concerned. I had never heard him sounding afraid of anything, and something certainly had him rattled. The decision came without a second thought.

"Listen, Harry." Looking out and into the winter-wonderland beyond my window, I swallowed hard, and said, "I'll tell you what? I haven't seen you in ages, and to be completely honest, I'm going a little stir crazy sitting around here anyway. I'll pack a few things and head out your way first thing in the morning, if that's okay?"

"You have no idea of how much I appreciate this, buddy." There was a sound of immediate relief in his voice, as pausing for a moment, he said, "Oh, and bring that thing that I have you a while back okay?"

He was speaking of the old thirty-eight revolver that he'd insisted upon giving me. It had already saved my life once and his concern now had me very worried.

"Of course—I'll see you soon, old buddy..."

"Mike, make sure that it's loaded..."

"Alright..."

"See you soon--." His voice began fading into a field of static, as he said, "Godspeed, my friend..."

The phone went dead in my hand, and sitting there and just staring toward the window I felt my heart sink. I had known old Harry since high-school, and after working homicide for many years he was tough as nails. In his entire life he had never called upon anyone for anything, or ever needed it for that matter. Yet, after that phone-call and hearing the hesitation in his voice I knew that something was terribly wrong...

Tuesday January 2, 1973.
4:38 p.m.
The windshield wipers thumped loudly while forcing back a blinding veil of sleet. Having departed early that morning in anticipation of avoiding the worst of the forecasted weather, I soon found myself cursing out the weatherman.

"Well it's a darn good thing that I listened to the weather report and left early this morning. Who are these people? Are they sitting somewhere on a hill with binoculars and laughing? Hey look, the dummy went for it!"

Reaching for a cigarette and lighting it with my Zippo, I grumbled, saying, "Well at least we're almost there..."

The journey started in North Vancouver and to where I followed the Trans-Canada highway east through Hope. From there I continued onto the old Crowsnest Highway. It was commonly known as the "Number 3 Highway' and traveling eastward I'd managed to slip in behind a snow plow. It wasn't fast, but it certainly made the last part of the two hundred mile journey a lot safer. Due to treacherous weather and road conditions the usual three and a half hour drive had become a six hour game of follow the leader. All things considered, it was better slow and steady than not arriving at all. I knew this country and had a healthy respect for the old highways.

Turning on the radio, I leapt back as the stereo blasted a steady stream of static, and cursing, said, "Well, that was stupid! I'm in the mountains, there's never any reception around here. Why would I have expected anything different?"

The sound of sand and salt assaulting the under carriage caused me to cringe, saying, "Sorry Lilly, I'll get you cleaned up when we get home."

Lilly was the name that I had given to the black 1972 Cadillac Superior Hearse. The name had come from a character on the television series, "The Munster's" and given the car a sense of identity. I bought the coach at a terrific discount. To avoid excessive repair bills, I had a habit of trading my old vehicles when purchasing new ones. In this case, Lilly had replaced Boris, my 1970 Superior Cadillac Hearse. The fascination with funeral coaches had started for me as a boy and I'd owned quite a few over the years. Unlike some individuals, I didn't buy them because I considered myself unique and unusual. I simply hated trucks and needed something to use when shopping for larger antiques. Considering the poor weather it might have been better to use the front wheel drive, Eldorado, but I just couldn't bring myself to drag her out in this weather. The coach had a wide wheel base, was heavy, and provided an opportunity to bring back treasures along the way. It was unlikely that I would be making any stops, but I rarely turned down an opportunity.

Shocked as an immense wall of slush suddenly came from out of nowhere and covered the windshield, I cursed aloud. Blinded and grumbling, I shook a fist at the freight truck that raced past from beside us. Traveling close from behind the plow there hadn't even been any warning. It was surprising as most truck drivers were courteous, considerate, and conscientious. Unfortunately and usually in mountain passes and other dangerous places, I always seemed to encounter the daredevil's of the freight industry.

"So what do we have in here?" Fumbling in the glove compartment I frowned while discovering several eight track tapes, and mumbling, said, "Oh goody—Country oldies."

Tossing the first tape out of the partially open window I glanced at the second, and retching, said, "Western hits. No wonder the dealership left these in here?" It followed the first as peering nervously at the third and final tape I gasped and smiling, said, "Oh, God bless you, to whoever left this behind…"

Shoving the cassette into the deck I beamed joyously to the haunting sounds of 'The Ventures' playing 'Out of Limits'. I had a passion for the instrumental 'twang' of the California surf beat and they were one of my favorite bands. It sure brightened the mood. The weather was absolutely horrible, and the plow painfully slow but this would certainly help pass the time. Reaching for a soda and bag of donuts on the front seat, I sat back to enjoy the snacks and music.

5:47 p.m.

There was certain relief when I finally saw the friendly lights of town from over the snow-capped trees. With the day fading fast and snow coming down I had no intention of being out on that highway any longer than necessary.

"There you are you old devil…" Peering up at the icy peaks of the Hedley Nickel mine I felt my stomach drop. For several reasons that place held a special place of horror in my heart. It was just after my eleventh birthday, when alone and quite courageously, I had begun investigating beyond the safety of home. After searching the forests and abandoned cottages of the little town, it wasn't long before I yearned for greater adventure. So, while preoccupied with thoughts of hidden treasure, I had wandered into the dark tunnels of the old nickel mine. Of course, it hadn't taken long before I'd become hopelessly lost. Then panicking, dropped the flashlight and stumbling in the pitch blackness, soon lost all hope.

I began attributing nightmarish presence to many things as only a child can do. Alone and in the pitch-dark everything became utterly still. It's a silence that few have ever known and even fewer would care to experience. Time suddenly stops and as all senses fail, you're confronted with the silence of your own death. It was as while blindly feeling my way along the cavern wall that it happened. I stumbled, and then felt something cold and slippery brushing against the bare flesh of my left calf.

Don't scream… It might just be some small animal. If you scare it—it might bite… Be very, very still... maybe it'll go away?

The moments passed like hours as I stood in the blackness with my heart pounding furiously. Without even the slightest sound or sight of anything, I waited for what seemed an eternity. Terrified to the point of utter desperation, I decided to attempt an escape rather than waiting for the inevitable. Ever so slowly I knelt down, and then crawling on my hands and knees, began creeping along the cavern floor. Tearful and shivering I had imagined unspeakable horrors. Ghastly things with large pale eyes and razor sharp claws, that reaching, groped at me from out of the blackness.

Wait—what was that... a sound?

Holding absolutely still and straining to listen, I heard it again. It was like the low moan of an autumn wind in the trees. At first it came as a whisper, a rustling sound that grew louder in approach. Unmoving, unwilling to even breathe I listened in the blackness. It grew louder and ever louder as the sound went from a whisper to a wailing shriek.

What was it? You know what that is Mikey—you're just too chicken to say it. But we know what it is—don't we? It's them isn't it? The dark things that wait in closets and under beds until the lights go out. The ones that eat children....

I couldn't take any more... Scrambling upon hands and knees, I began racing down the dark tunnel. I was out of my mind with fear, and then suddenly something touched me in the darkness. Terrified and throwing myself backward I collided against the cavern wall. I cried out, lashing blindly at an invisible assailant, but there was nothing there... Ever so cautiously, I reached outward for the cavern floor and my fingers passed into emptiness. Losing balance, I wailed, as twisting bodily, narrowly caught the edge of a rocky precipice. There had been an opening in the cavern floor... Not huge, but just large enough for someone of my size to have easily slipped forward and fallen through... Rolling away from the edge, I barely escaped a drop into oblivion. Clinging to the cold rock face and too terrified to even move, I desperately cried out for help.

The distant echo of the shrieking grew ever louder, as becoming almost deafening, forced me backward. With my ears burning and mind swimming in the blackness, I was driven to turn back on the path. Realizing that I couldn't stay there a single moment longer, frantic, I began crawling in the opposite direction. Within moments, bruised, battered, and bleeding from the perilous trek, I had discovered the old rail tracks. With the wailing voices in the tunnel behind me and within close pursuit, I hurried onward. Suddenly, a tiny light appeared in the distance. I'd never been more terrified than in those final moments, and as I'd desperately raced against the fading dusk.

Closer, oh no, they're catching up! I'm not going to make it! Oh, God—someone help me! Don't let them get me! Don't let them eat me!

Adrenaline burned in every vein and artery as within one last and blinding effort, screaming in horror, I burst from out of the cave entrance. I distinctly remember having fallen to my knees several yards from the mine entrance. Gasping for breath and shaking uncontrollably, I had slowly turned to gaze back into the dark mouth of the cave. From somewhere deep within the shadows of that old mine something moaned. It seemed to linger as though watching, waiting from just beyond the light of the setting sun. I knew why it was still there… It was waiting for night-fall. Then it would come out of there and drag me back down into those dark and endless tunnels… Turning, I ran screaming from that place and never went back. The incident remained a secret but the fear had never faded. My mother had never inquired as to why I'd insisted on sleeping beneath the glow of a night-light, but I suspected that she'd known… She was just like that.

Flicking the cigarette out the window, I turned my attention toward the comforting lights of town. Not a moment too soon. I was almost out of gas and really needed a bathroom.

Hedley was a small community which was nestled within a valley bordering the highway on either side. It consisted mainly of farms, a diner, several small businesses, and a few tourist attractions resting within the shadow of the looming, nickel mines. It had been many years since my last visit, but took only a few minutes to locate the 'Western Star Motel'. It was an old, two story place which being located just off the highway, rested upon the very edge of town. It was bitterly cold, the wind was brutal, and I slipped all over while carrying my bags inside. The clerk was an elderly fellow and within minutes I was booked into room number five. It was kismet really. I couldn't help but smile with memories of having brought an old girlfriend to this very same room on the weekends.

Closing and locking the door, I dropped my luggage, kicked off my boots and rushed into the bathroom. A few moments later and with a renewed enthusiasm, I wandered out with a smile. Sitting on the edge of the double bed, I took immediate notice of the stained and yellowed wallpaper, and sighing, said, "Well, it really hasn't changed that much over the years."

Switching on a small bed-side lamp I reached for the telephone, and dialing out, anxiously waited for a response.

"Hedley police department--," The familiar voice replied, saying, "Sergeant Harry O' Donnell speaking, how can I be of assistance?"

"Harry, I just got into town--," Fumbling with my cigarettes and lighting one, I coughed, and said, "It took longer than I was expecting. I followed a plow most of the way out here."

"Mike—where are you?" He sounded immediately concerned.

"I'm in room five at the Western Star." Unable to locate an ashtray, I stretched the telephone cord to full length and flicked an ash into the toilet, saying, "Did you want to get together, tonight?"

"I haven't slept much over the past two weeks." He admitted and sounding terrible, said, "It might be better if we both get some rest. Trust me... we're going to need it... Listen, I'll be there to get you first thing in the morning. I'll take you out for breakfast."

"Sure thing, Harry, That'll be just fine." Peering out from between the curtains and into the frozen night, I pondered briefly before asking, "Is the old diner still open late?"

"No—not for some time now--," There was a pause and then speaking in a solemn tone, he said, "And if it's all the same to you? I'd rather that you didn't go anywhere—until morning."

The comment caused my skin to crawl, as feeling unsettled by my friend's strange and even distant behavior, I said, "It's too cold tonight anyway."

"Oh—and by the way? Did you remember to bring that little keep-sake that I gave you a few years back?"

Turning to look to where the black doctor's bag sat upon the bed, I nodded and said, "Yes—and I've carried it ever since that incident with the dogs..."

"Just keep it loaded—and keep it close." Clearing his throat and speaking quietly, he said, "You might never need it. But all the same—I feel better knowing that you have it."

"Harry, are you sure that you're alright?"

"I'm not really sure? But Mike, please, promise me that you won't go wandering around out there, in the dark."

"You've got my word..."

There was a click and the phone went dead in my hand. I suddenly felt very alone and vulnerable. Hanging up the receiver, I tossed the cigarette into the toilet and turned my attention back to the bed and bag. The black leather medical bag had been a gift from a retired physician. We had become friends during my college years, and knowing my passion for antiques he had given it to me shortly after retiring. His name still shone from off the little brass tag that read; James Barrie Benz. Although he had passed away some time ago, his memory still traveled with me everywhere.

No longer used for medical practice, it now contained my camera, batteries and extra film. There was a small first aid kit, assorted candy bars, several bottles of Root Beer, hygienic items, and other personal necessities. Aside from a bible and large crucifix, it also concealed a .38 caliber revolver. It was registered to Harry, but after a near-death experience he'd insisted that I keep it.

Removing the weapon from the bag I closely examined the chamber. I had always regarded weapons as entirely unnecessary in my particular field of interest, but that had soon changed. There were far worse things than ghosts out there…

Placing the revolver on the little night-table beside the bed, I rummaged through the suitcase. Swiftly changing into my favorite blue flannel pajamas, I switched off the light, and slipped beneath the covers. It was still far too early for bed by my own standards, but it was a long and very cold day.

"I wonder if Karen still lives here." She was the girlfriend of my youth and the one who had once shared this room and bed. It was an amusing thought but I knew better. We'd parted on bad terms… Besides, it was best to leave some things in the past and sadly, she was one of them. It felt strange being back in a town that was filled with the ghosts of my childhood. They still lingered in familiar places and haunted the dark corners of my mind. Switching off the little lamp I lay staring into the darkness of the room. A lamp in the parking lot cast a golden glow from between the drapes. It wasn't enough to be disturbing, but caught the shadows of the snow which now came in a steady stream. The wind moaned beyond the window, and I thought to have voices from out of the past.

"They're just the whispers of the lost upon the winter wind and nothing more…"

With that final thought I rolled over, and shoving my face deep into the pillow, closed my eyes. The shadows lingered in the window, the snow drifted in the wind, and the night became utterly silent…

CHAPTER FOURTEEN

Wednesday January 3, 1973.
9:22 a.m.
Continually awakened by bad dreams I felt as though I hadn't slept a wink. When the loud knock bearing Harry's familiar "shave and a haircut' had finally arrived I was still feeling totally exhausted.

"It can't be morning already?" Rubbing at my eyes, I shoved my face back into the pillow.

The knock came again, as drowsily; I struggled to make an effort to move. I had always hated mornings and still did.

"One minute." Crawling out of the warm bed, I shivered and rubbed at my arms. I'd forgotten just how cold it could get.

Grabbing my robe from where it had fallen on the floor, I groaned while rubbing at a stiff neck. The bed had seen better years and judging by the way that I was feeling, so had I.

Unlocking the door, I threw it open, blocking my eyes with a hand as the morning glare blinded me. A brutal and frozen gust forced me back, as shielding my body with the door, I peeked out.

"Sergeant Harry O'Donnell, Royal Canadian Mounted Police—it's good to see you again, Mike." He saluted, and removing the black, round brimmed, regulation hat, tucked it under his arm while.

"Good to see you too, Harry! Now, get in here before I'm frozen solid!"

Hurrying into the room, I closed the door behind him and patting at my arms for warmth, whined while saying, "Oh geez, I forgot what it was like up here during the winter months."

"Yeah, it's cold enough to freeze the balls off a brass monkey." He nodded, and said, "Now you know why I didn't feel right about you wandering around out there, and especially at night." It was almost as if he was trying to cover for some other concern, and only used the weather as an excuse. Watching as he took off his long black overcoat I marveled at his uniform. He wore a bright red, black belted tunic, black and single yellow striped pants, and highly polished, black boots. Although we had stayed in contact over the telephone for many years, I hardly recognized him. This certainly wasn't the reckless teenager that I had once known. Standing at six feet tall and weighing well over two hundred pounds, he was a formidable figure. His face was rounded, clean-shaven, and though bearing a few extra pounds, he carried it well. His military cut was graying without sign of balding, and he sported a neatly trimmed mustache. From behind large horn-rimmed glasses his deep gray eyes were still as piercing and sharp as youth. We extended hands in greeting, and then both laughing, embraced as old friends do, heartily slapping one another on the back.

"I see that you've put on a few pounds." He duly noted, and pointing at my large sideburns and somewhat unruly hair, said, "And you could sure use a shave and a haircut."

"I don't know, I kind of like it. Just the other day a waitress told me that I looked like, Robert Redford." Slipping into my aviator sunglasses and crossing my arms over my chest, I offered a profile.

Peering at me from side to side, he shrugged, saying, "Maybe a slightly fatter version of Redford. All the same, you still need a shave and a haircut."

"You know, you're starting to sound like my mother." Slapping his shoulder, I dropped the glasses on the little table near the window, and said, "She still thinks that I'm a kid and need supervision."

"I wouldn't argue with her about that." He chuckled, and pulling a chair up to the table and producing a cigar from a breast pocket, asked, "You um—mind if I smoke?"

"Sure, the way this room smells it might be an improvement." Retrieving my cigarettes from the night-stand I smiled, joining him at the table, and saying, "I'm still smoking two packs a day. I need to think about cutting back."

"I quit smoking cigarettes almost three years ago. It's just cigars for me now." Glancing at the smoldering cigar between his fingers, he sighed, and said, "I only have two a day—so it's not nearly as bad as my old habit. I was going through almost three packs of cigarettes a day by the time that I quit."

"Stress will do that..." Rubbing the sleep from out of my eyes, I lit the cigarette, and speaking through a cloud of smoke, said, "You know, you had me a little concerned when you called last night. I've known you for a long time and never heard you sound like that..."

His eyes narrowed as he paused in thought. I could see that he was having trouble with whatever was bothering him.

Looking toward the window, he pulled the cigar from his mouth and quietly said, "You're right—we've known each other for a very long time. So, you know that I'm not the type to get jumpy, or make something out of nothing."

Why was he having such a hard time discussing this? For crying out loud—he couldn't even look me in the eye!

"So, I'll just tell it the way it is…" Puffing at the cigar, his attention remained focused beyond the window as he said, "It started about two months ago. It was the strangest thing? People were calling me about their pets going missing. At first, it was just a few cats here and there. And then dogs. Now, you know that we get a lot of coyotes and the odd cougar out here. So, I didn't take it too seriously—at first." Nervously rolling the cigar between his fingers he grimaced, and looking over at me, said, "Do you remember old Barry Thompson?"

"Of course I do. How could I forget? He had that hog farm, the big green barns about a mile out of town." A smile swiftly grew within the memory, and I said, "I don't think that I could even count how many times he must've chased us out of his apple orchard?"

"Yeah, that's him." Slowly nodding, he tapped his fingers on the table, and said, "Well, about a month ago he calls me up—all hysterical! He tells me that I had to get out to his place, right away. Naturally, I didn't waste any time. If you'd heard his voice, you would've thought that the Russians were invading. Anyway, when I got there, he took me out to the barn." Harry looked pale, adjusting his glasses and swallowing hard, he said, "The first thing that I noticed were the gates to the hog pen. They were all smashed in. The boards were splintered like twigs—and everything was just covered in blood. Sweet Jesus, if I didn't know better? I would've figured a bomb had gone off in there."

"So a grizzly broke into the pen and--." The answer seemed feasible until Harry's wide-eyed expression caused me to falter in mid-sentence.

"Mike, this wasn't a damn bear... Barry had a prize boar, a four hundred pound monster that he kept for breeding. Whatever got to those hogs? Grabbed that boar, and smashed it against those boards so hard—that there were big chunks of meat and bone caught in the busted planks."

"So if it wasn't a bear? What the hell could've done something like that?" Butting the cigarette, I nervously lit another, and snapping my fingers, said, "Prints—those pens are all filled with mud and straw. You must've found something?"

"Not a damn thing that shouldn't have been there. And before you ask? I couldn't even do an examination on the boar—there wasn't enough left of him. It seems that the other pigs ate most of the evidence."

"Is it possible, that for some reason, the other pigs just went crazy and killed the boar?"

"I honestly wanted to believe that... but even Barry said that there was no possible way that they could've done that much damage to the pen. Not without hurting themselves or each other in the process. We looked at every single pig in there. None of them had a single mark on them. But that wasn't the reason that I called you."

He'd gotten my full attention now. I just knew that it was about to get a whole lot uglier.

"It was a little over three weeks ago, when I got the call that little Connie Shepherd didn't make it home after work. She was a part-time waitress over at the diner. I can't even tell you how many times she served me coffee? Seventeen years old, cutest little thing—blonde with these big, bright blue eyes, oh God--," He looked away, and sadly shaking his head, almost choked on the words, saying, "She was such a sweet kid..."

Instinctively retrieving my tape recorder, note pad and pen, I waited for a nod of approval before recording the details.

"She'd just finished an afternoon shift, and left the diner shortly after five. It was a clear day and she was walking the three quarter mile trek home. Even with the snow? That shouldn't have taken any longer than half an hour. But she never made it...."

"And when was she reported missing?" I asked, making notes of the more significant details.

Harry climbed from the chair and rubbing at his eyes, promptly began pacing back and forth, saying, "It was just after dark. Oh yeah--," He remembered, "It was somewhere after six. Her mom had figured that she might've gone to visit with a friend? So, she didn't get worried until after she'd started calling around. After the situation at old Barry's place I didn't take any chances. I got Gene

Doherty and his hounds out there."

"Did Connie live anywhere near the Thompson farm?"

"A little over a quarter of a mile, and believe me, the possibility of that connection never left my mind."

Was the excitement I now felt caused by morbid fascination, sincere concern, or the fact that I'd possibly stumbled across material for a new story? Putting the guilt aside, what difference would it make in the end? I was here for Harry. The rest was speculation and whatever the case may be? This could work out in everyone's better interest.

"Okay then, so you had Gene out with the dogs." I moved the recorder as to better catch his voice, and asked, "Where did you find her?"

"We didn't." He halted in mid-step and turned to look back at me. His face became blank as he stared in utter disbelief, and said, "Not a single trace or shred of evidence. And trust me. We searched every lousy inch of that damn road. Not even a foot-print. It was snowing that afternoon, and if there'd been anything, it was long covered by the time that we got out there."

"So—what happened?"

"A couple of locals were walking their dog, and found what was left of her in a ditch, the next morning."

"How is that possible? Why didn't Gene's dogs find her?"

"Because the body was found seven miles down the highway…" Slowly shaking his head, he muttered, saying, "And we both know that she couldn't have walked that far in such a short time…"

"So obviously, someone must have picked her up?"

"No—not someone…"

"Harry, I'm sorry, but you're not making any sense. You said that she disappeared between five and six. It was snowing that day; she was walking down the highway, and lived close. The logical assumption would have to be that someone saw her, likely someone she knew, and that she got into a vehicle with that person."

"It wasn't a person--," He was adamant, his eyes filled with sheer horror, as he whispered, "If you'd seen what we dragged out of the ditch that morning—you wouldn't have believed your own eyes. Mike, I've seen a lot of things, but no human being is capable of doing that…"

I was speechless. Harry was a hardened detective with years of homicide experience. I'd been with him at the scene of a Grizzly attack on campers. Together, we bore witness as game wardens pulled the remains of a ten year old boy from out of the animal's stomach... I remembered seeing the chewed parts and clothing spill out of its steaming entrails, and still, Harry hadn't even flinched... More than most, he had the experience, and knew exactly what he was saying.

"Alright, then what do you think happened out there?"

"I don't have any idea..."

"Oh God..." Thinking for a moment, I butted the cigarette, and said, "All that we can do now is hope that we can keep this, isolated incident, quiet until we can figure something out."

"It's not an isolated incident, Mike--," The true impact of his horror and confusion left him pale and drawn, as staring, he said, "They found poor old Shirley Conrad's body down at the cemetery, last week. She was frozen solid, and her brains had been smashed out on her husband's tombstone..."

"Shirley Conrad?" I knew that name and frowning, asked, "Not that nice little old lady that used to run the local grocery?"

"Yes—the same one that used to always give us those huge scoops of ice cream." Harry's features twisted with grief and he said, "Her husband, Clark, passed away a few years back. She used to visit his grave every Sunday. That's where they found her, last Tuesday."

"What happened?" I asked, quietly listening as something now caused my skin to crawl.

Removing his glasses and rubbing at his eyes, he said, "Oh, it was just another freak accident. Apparently, she'd been hurrying for some reason or another, slipped on the icy path, and hit her head when she fell. She died almost instantly from what Lou Watkins said. He's the coroner in Penticton, and the same guy who wrote Connie's death off as a hit and run."

"A hit and run?" Now I was truly shocked, as leaning back into my seat and staring, said, "But, you were at the scene. And, from what you've told me, you can clearly see that it wasn't just some case of, hit and run. Or you certainly wouldn't have called me."

"We both know that. But, someone had to fill out a report." Harry sat down again, and tapping his cigar in the ashtray, grumbled as he said, "So, the official cause of death was established as blunt trauma, and it's an open case of vehicular homicide."

"Alright then, and what did our friend Lou have to say about Shirley?" I could not believe what I was hearing....

"Like I told you--," He frowned, puffing at the cigar and through a cloud of smoke, said, "It was considered a freak accident. One of those things that just happens and never gets properly explained."

"So tell me something?" Staring deeply into my friends wide eyes I spoke softly, asking, "What do you believe—is really going on around here?"

"I really don't know? All that I can say—is that for the first time in my life. Mike—I'm honestly scared. Not just for myself. But for everyone in this town."

"Okay, what can we do about this and where do we start?"

"You can start by getting dressed. Then we'll take a run down to the funeral home. The weather's been bad, so they've postponed the services for a while. I'd like you to see the bodies for yourself. Maybe that'll help you understand why I don't believe that a human being had anything to do with these deaths..."

"The Versailles funeral parlor--," It left a bad taste in my mouth as I asked, "Is Tim still running the place?"

"Yeah—," Harry butted his cigar, "His dad passed away two years ago. My guess is that he'll likely spend the rest of his days there too."

The mere mention of his name revived irreconcilable resentment. Our first encounter had been during the seventh grade. For some reason, there had been an almost immediate animosity between us. It was something that had soon grown into pure and competitive hostility. He was an only child, the son of the local mortician, unpopular, and subsequently avoided by most of the other children. He was a shadow in the halls at best, and ate his lunch alone. I had the impression that he was just use to being rejected, so had simply given up trying to make friends.

It might have for that exact reason that I'd intervened while "Big Bill Jenkins" and his pals were bullying him in the hallway one afternoon.

The odds were five against two. If it hadn't been for Harry suddenly appearing from out of nowhere things might've been far worse. It was a brutal fight to say the least, but victorious, bruised and bloodied, we emerged as friends.

Over time, the three of us had become virtually inseparable. In fact, it wasn't until the summer after graduation that Tim had done the unthinkable...

I was on route to the service station, intending to pick up a carburetor gasket for my old Chevrolet, when I'd noticed him alone in the park with Karen Gearing. Ordinarily, that wouldn't have bothered me, but she was my current girlfriend, and they were holding hands.

In passing they had noticed me, and then laughed at my surprise. It was a small town and people thrived on gossip. I couldn't bear the thought of what would happen next. So, without a second thought, I returned home, informed my mother, packed my things and left for the Coast. Within days I had a job, rented a room, and was looking into college.

That very same August Harry had informed me that Tim and Karen had been married...

"He's changed a lot, you won't even recognize him." Harry slipped into his coat, and said, "Karen left him, it must've been over ten years now? She moved somewhere up north."

"She left him?" I couldn't help but smile, "What a shame..."

CHAPTER FIFTEEN

10:35 a.m.

Harry drove a gold and cream, 1969, Chrysler Newport, Custom sedan. It was a four hundred and forty cubic inch engine and he had a lead foot. This wouldn't have been so bad, but even the chained snow-tires couldn't keep us from sliding all over the old back road.

"Um—Harry." I gestured with a nod while gripping the dash with both hands, and nervously saying, "Maybe we should slow down a little?"

"Nah, it's only a couple of feet deep. As long as we don't make any quick moves and keep an even pace we should be just fine." He grinned, obviously amused with my concern as he chuckled, saying, "It sounds like you've gotten spoiled living on the coast?"

"Oh we get snow on the coast too. But the roads are better maintained."

"If bad weather and road conditions were my biggest concern--," He scoffed and turning his attention toward the steadily growing flurries, said, "I'd consider myself a lucky man."

"Hey?" I slunk down in the seat as we slid, and asked, "Whatever happened to that lady friend of yours?"

"Who—do you mean, Maureen?" He replied as though having forgotten the woman and smiling, said, "I still see her. But she's got a cozy little place in Penticton and neither one of us wants to sell or move. So, we see each other every weekend. I was there for Christmas, but you know me. I've lived in this town for so long that I couldn't just pack it in and move away."

"Why don't you just give in? I mean—really Harry? We're not getting any younger and let's face it? You could drive into town in the morning, it's not that far."

"No, I need to be here. It may not be much—but its home. Who knows, maybe if she gets lonely enough she'll change her mind about moving here?"

"Same old, Harry, you'll never change."

"Me? At least I'm trying." Peering over suspiciously, he raised an eyebrow in question, asking, "Whatever happened between you and that, what was her name—Caitlin?"

"Nothing's changed since the last time that I talked to you on the phone." Lighting a cigarette and rolling down the window, I squinted in the icy gust, saying, "But you know me. I'm not really the settling down sort anyway."

That's right Mike, just keep telling your-self that. In time who knows? You might even start believing it?

"Here we are." Harry pointed, carefully maneuvering the vehicle down the slight grade and into the parking area.

Staring the length of the drive-way my eyes followed to where the road swerved, and then disappeared behind the old building. I knew that path all too well. Swallowing hard, I remembered the hearse as it had slowly made that turn while carrying my father's casket from the chapel. It rained during the graveyard service, but I could still see the tears that my mother tried to conceal from me. She had always tried to be strong, and support me before ever considering her own needs or feelings. Even then, I remember feeling bad about that...

The Versailles Funeral Home had all the appeal of an old horror film. In fact, it wouldn't have been surprised me in the least if Vincent Price had answered the door. Under different circumstances I might have found this rather appealing, but not at the moment.

Built in 1909 by Tim's grandfather, Irving Versailles, the parlor resembled a two story Southern style manor house. With pillars and a beautiful surrounding veranda, it was an eloquent reminder of old world architecture. Sadly, and due to neglect, it was a dream that was swiftly fading. The once majestic stained glass windows were hazed with filth, and the Victorian gas-light sconces were dulled and pitted. Even the recent coat of white paint, for all its many layers, could not conceal the decaying boards beneath. The wooden sign squeaked loudly upon rusting chains, and the white Gothic lettering which had once proudly read; Versailles Funeral Parlor had all but disappeared. The parlor occupied an almost barren stretch of land, which overgrown by weeds and old withering willows, spanned several acres on either side. Bordering an immense ravine to the immediate rear of the property it provided a lovely view of the valley beyond. At the bottom of that ravine, and just beneath the ruins of an old wooden trestle, lay the rusting hulk of an old locomotive. It was never part of the Kettle Valley Line and its presence was never explained, but I once played there as a boy. The last time that I'd seen the old place I was fifteen years old. It was Halloween, and involved several cartons of very rotten eggs... Looking back now, and aside from our personal differences, I felt terrible for having done it.

"I swear to God, Tim's even slower than his clients!" Harry cursed, as ringing the doorbell for the second time, shouted, "If he doesn't open this door soon, we might end up being his next customers!"

"From the looks of things he could use the business." Peering into one of the large windows, I tried to look past the heavy and dark draperies, and said, "He probably doesn't have to be in much of a hurry around here?"

"Oh and Mike—please?" He gestured with both hands in a calming fashion, and said, "I know that there's a lot history between you two. But trust me on this—just give him a chance, okay?"

"Oh? What? So, now I'm the bad guy here?" Insulted, I looked the other way, and grumbling, said, "Gee thanks, that's real nice, Harry."

"Hey, that's not fair, and isn't what I said." He suddenly clammed up as a loud click announced the unlocking of the door behind us.

Having turned with the intention of a polite greeting, my jaw dropped open.

Tim? No, this couldn't have been the same person...

The once broad shoulders drooped, and his previous athletic physique was now drowning in the folds of an ill fitted, and cheap black suit. The familiar coarse black hair was gone, as thinning and grey, was trimmed all too short. Clean shaven with exception to a neatly trimmed mustache, youth had seemingly and utterly abandoned him. Adopting a gaunt and sickly pallor, he stared blankly through wearied brown eyes that appeared far too large from behind black, horn rimmed glasses.

A moment of awkward silence passed, and then abruptly extending a hand, he said, "I don't believe it! Mike—it's wonderful to see you again!"

"Hello, Tim--," I shook his hand, and uncertain of what to say, just blurted out the first thing that came to mind, and said, "I hardly recognized you."

Noticing the cynical manner in which I now examined Tim, Harry had immediately intervened and leaping between us, said, "I hope that you've got the coffee going? I'm freezing my butt off and could sure go for a nice hot cup right about now."

"Of course—what was I thinking? Please—come in." Escorting us into the house and hurriedly closing the door, he apologized, and said, "I didn't hear the bell—I was finishing up with--."

"No need for details." Harry waved a hand in gesture, and forcing me onward with a nudge, pushed me along while saying, "We all know what goes on in these places…."

"I was just scrubbing the upstairs tub and had music playing--," Tim shook his head, and eyeing Harry with a certain amount of sarcasm, said, "You know that I never discuss the business end of what goes on, down there."

"I wasn't thinking--," Harry shrugged in apology, and said, "Things have been crazy, as you already know, and I haven't had a decent night's rest in months."

"You're not the only one…" There was a nervous flash behind those dark eyes, and I knew that was afraid…

As Tim directed us down the corridor I noticed that he suffered a prevalent limp. Watching his movements, I soon discovered that it wasn't an injury at all, but the poor condition of his shoes. The right heel was worn far more than the other and thus, caused him to compensate. I had no idea of how bad things had become for him…

I found no victory within these discoveries, as instead, now felt sincere pity for the man.

"I just brewed some fresh coffee." He proudly announced, as looking back with a child-like grin, said, "And you're in luck Harry! I even have a few of those blueberry muffins that you like so much. I picked them up just the other day."

The lower half of the corridor was covered in ornate, and dark stained oak panels. The upper portion was papered in emerald, with a golden Damask pattern. There was a faded and wine colored carpeting throughout, and color matching, velvet draperies.

Following Tim, I couldn't help but notice several rooms in passing. There was a large beautifully decorated chapel, an office, a public restroom, a family parlor and of course, a casket viewing room.

The shadows lay deep within that place and it smelled of

embalming fluids and disinfectant.

For a moment I tried to imagine what it must have been like for him as a child? A life spent in a place where as darkness fell, and the lights burned low, he slept where the dead reposed in rooms just below. It was no wonder that he had withered so much in such a short time. After all, how much of a life could one expect from dwelling among the dead.

"Here we are," Tim smiled, leading us into the lunch room, and tripping and yelping as he fell heavily to the floor.

"Tim!" Rushing forward, I gently grasped the man by the arm, and assisting him from the floor, dusted him off, asking, "Are you alright?"

"Thank you, but I haven't been alright for a very long time now."

"None of us are getting any younger--," Gently patting him on the back while putting our differences aside, I smiled, and said, "You should see me trying to get out of bed on some days. You would think that I needed a crane."

"He's not kidding." Harry smirked, and said, "I had a hell of a time dragging his butt out of that motel room this morning."

"The Western Star--," The words invoked a painful memory, and smiling sadly, he looked to me and almost whispering, said, "Room 105, right?"

Immediately seeing that I was uncomfortable and unwilling to pursue the subject, Harry interrupted, saying, "I called Mike and asked him to come home. I've told him what's been happening, and we're going to work on this together."

"And you came back--," Tim didn't seem surprised at all, but said, "Under the circumstances, most people might have steered clear."

"Mind if I smoke?" Harry waved a cigar as we were all seated around a table in the center of the room.

"Not at all, I'll just open a window." Tim nodded, and turning to retrieve an ashtray from the kitchen counter, said, "It's nasty business, really." He went to the window and opening it just a crack, glanced back at me, saying, "What happened to Connie, and poor old, Shirley…"

"I'll feel a lot better when we start getting some tangible answers." Thinking briefly, I peered back at Tim, and asked, "Didn't you use to smoke in high school?"

"No, I never really developed a taste for the stuff. But my father smoked like a chimney. I suppose that's what contributed to the heart attack in the end?"

"I'm really sorry to hear that." Shooting a glance toward Harry I suddenly realized what he'd meant, and asked, "How long have you been living alone here now?"

"Oh—it's been over two years now. But it feels like a lot longer. There's just something about an empty house that leaves a person with too much time to sit around, and think about life…" Bringing a tray with coffee and blueberry muffins to the table, he took the chair closest to mine and frowning, said, "And that's another thing, Mike… Listen, I know that we parted on bad terms… but--…"

"I'd rather not get into the past--," Interrupting him, I suddenly felt a sharp jab in my left calf as Harry kicked from under the table, and changing my mind, said, "But, if it's really that important to you? Go ahead…"

"Yes—it's really is important to me--," He began, saying, "I've been trying to find some way, for many years. Some way to tell you what really happened that day?" Removing his glasses and rubbing at his eyes, he said, "That day—July eighteenth, nineteen forty seven. When you drove passed us in the park. I know that you'll find this hard to believe? But that was Karen's idea. It was all just a set-up to make you jealous."

The exact date, I couldn't have remembered that if my life had depended on it! Somehow, I suspected that he'd suffered for this even longer than I had…

"A set up—I don't know what you're talking about?" I swallowed back the anger and frustration with the memory, and speaking calmly, said, "You two—honestly looked like an item too me. I mean, if you hadn't been all over each other? I might've--."

Harry grumbled, his eyes bulging as buttoning my lip I politely motioned for Tim to continue.

"Do you recall a girl named Elaine Warner?" He slowly repeated the name as though it were a poison on his lips, saying, "Elaine—Warner, think about that for a minute."

"Elaine—sure I do. She was that little brunette that worked at Phil's service station—what about her?"

"She told Karen that you and her--," He frowned, appearing

nervous as he said, "Well, that you two had a thing going on—you know?"

Laughing, I could only scoff at the ridiculous accusation, saying, "The only thing that we had going was an order for a carburetor gasket for my 34' Chev coupe. You guys remember that thing. I was always getting things chromed, or buying something for it. As a matter of fact, I must've gone into that station about fifty times in the last two weeks to ask--," The realization suddenly struck me, as looking between my friends, slowly shook my head, and said, "Oh no..."

"Karen didn't know anything about the gasket kit. All that she knew was Elaine had her eye on you, and that you were in there all of the time. All that she wanted to do was make you jealous. She just wanted to make you sorry—and make you talk to her." Tim's eyes reddened as his expression became one of sincere heart-break, and struggling with the words, said, "And instead, we all lost each other..."

"If that's really the truth--," I turned away, and fighting with a frog in my throat, said, "Then how would you explain the fact that you married her just a few months later?"

"Mike, for once in your damn life--," Harry leapt up from his chair and slamming a fist on the table, said, "Could you please just shut the hell up, and listen?"

It was happening again. The hurt and anger was forcing me to run from the answers. In the end, it had always been easier to suffer in doubt than facing the cruel truth.

"Fair enough..." Sipping at his tea, he looked me straight in the eye and without flinching, said, "Did you ever stop to think that all those nights you spent together in that hotel, could go on forever without consequences?"

The thought had honestly never occurred to me. I was young, the world was new, and I had never even considered the possibility....

"When Karen came to me and said that she was pregnant, neither of us knew what to do? You know what small towns are like for a single mother, especially back then. So, we agreed to stay together. I know that it was wrong, but you were long gone, and she was too terrified to tell your mother."

"Did you know about this?" I looked to Harry.

"Not, not until recently…"

"Her mother and father despised me, but tolerated our being together because of the baby." Tim cursed from under his breath and shaking his head, said, "And then, after being married for only two months, we found out that it had been a false pregnancy… Well, at that point, we both just fell apart. She started drinking pretty heavy, and I couldn't really blame her? It's not like we could've just gotten the marriage annulled and walked away from everything. So, we spent the better part of twelve miserable years together. It wasn't love, and we didn't have a relationship to speak of? I suppose that we were both just terribly alone? And then one day—I came home and she was gone."

"Why didn't anyone say anything to me?"

"Because you're as bull-headed as the day is long. Hell, you'd just run off on another one of your little tantrums just before that. So, who in their right mind would've even considered approaching you?" Harry cursed, as shaking his head, said, "Especially Tim or Karen. Knowing that temper of yours, you would've shot first and not even asked any questions later."

There was little point in arguing as it was the absolute truth. I'd always run from my fears and in this case, it had cost us all dearly…

"Harry hadn't spoken to me in years. That stupid stunt at the park that day tore us all apart. Oh God--," Tim sniffled, and wiping the tears from his eyes with a trembling hand, looked to me, and quietly said, "We lost the best years of our lives over a terrible misunderstanding. And, I guess that what I'm really trying to say is how very, very sorry I was, and still am, after all this time…"

There were no words that could have properly expressed how I felt in that moment. The realization tore me apart, as assuming responsibility, and realizing the suffering that it had caused, I was utterly devastated. Slowly moving from the seat as he climbed from his chair, we looked to one another, and embraced. We held each other as old friend would, reunited, and releasing the ghosts of a most turbulent past. A great weight lifting from our hearts and souls, we returned to our seats, and fell utterly silent.

Extending his hand into the middle of the table, Harry looked between us, and said, "Unus pro omnibus, omnes pro uno."

"One for all --," Tim accepted the bond as reaching outward I did the same, as remembering our boyhood pledge, said, "And—all for one. Do you guys realize that we made that oath almost thirty years ago?"

"It does seem like forever now?" Tim sniffled, as rubbing a tear from his eye, said, "I'm so glad that we finally had this opportunity, even if it almost took a lifetime to happen."

"My biggest regret is that Karen wasn't here to share the moment. I wish that we could've at least talked—one last time, and sorted this out between the four of us."

Harry shot a reluctant glance at Tim, as clasping his hands together on the table before him, said, "I figured that you might say something like that. Mike--," He frowned, as slowly shaking his head, exhaled deeply before saying, "Karen died in a drinking and driving accident a little over a year ago. I'm sorry…"

It felt as though a sudden weight had crashed down, crushing my heart and knocking the breath from out of me. Though it had been a life-time ago, each and every special moment that we had shared flashed through my mind within the finality of it all.

"For what it's worth--" He looked away, and clearing his throat, said, "The police report said that death was instantaneous—and that she didn't suffer."

For a few moments my mind ran blank. All I could do was look around the table as we all struggled to hold back the emotions.

"So it's just the three of us now." Tim nervously fidgeted with his tie, and peering up at me, said softly, "If we're going to make the best of the time that we have left together? As much as it hurts—we'll have to let go of the past and allow Karen to rest in peace."

"Amen…" I felt my heart skip a beat in her loss.

"Amen…" Bowing his head, Harry looked away.

They say that you can never go back, but for that moment and gathered in the company of old friends, I'd finally come home...

12:22 p.m.

Putting Karen and the past behind us, duty called our attention to far darker matters.

"I'm afraid that things are a little over-crowded down here at the moment." Descending the stairs into the basement, Tim glanced back, and apologizing, said, "I'm afraid that the weather has complicated things terribly, and I haven't been able to attend grave-side services since the coach broke down."

The penetrating odor of embalming fluids assaulted my senses, and attempting to shake off the affect, I looked back at Harry. He followed from close behind but didn't seem bothered in the least. In fact, it wasn't until we had entered the Morgue that he'd recoiled to the stench of human decay. Shoving a sleeve to his face, he'd coughed while attempting to catch his breath.

"I'm afraid that I can't do much about the smell, at the moment." Frowning, Tim motioned toward the morgue door, and said, "The cooler's been acting up. It doesn't retain a steady temperature anymore, and I have to keep readjusting the thermostat. It's just expensive to replace, and at the moment, I can't afford the repairs."

"I'd say that you should get that Hearse fixed right away." Harry coughed, and with his eyes watering with the stench, said, "Once the cooler gets emptied out, you can deal with the repairs. Still, if I was a repair guy, there's no way that you'd ever get me in there."

Admiring the black 1964 Cadillac Superior Hearse, I walked over to where it was parked in the shadows of the bay. It was a classic with a 3-way table, appeared pristine, and was obviously well maintained. It was the last year of true fins in Cadillac. The body had the same high design and styling as the 1959 but the fins were much lower and sleeker than they had been in 1963. With LaSalle bars, Gothic chrome lanterns, quad lights, elaborate grill and massive bumper, it was unique by all standards. It's wasn't just a car—it was a mechanical masterpiece of the macabre... These vehicles were hardly ever driven, and with such low mileage, rarely broke down. It was a quality vehicle, and I couldn't even begin to guess what might be the problem with it?

"Well, what seems to be the trouble with it?"

"I don't know? I'm beginning to think that it just doesn't like me?" Scratching at his moustache, he thought aloud, saying, "So far, I've replaced the battery and cables, starter, alternator, done the brakes, and had all the wiring tested for shorts. It just doesn't want to work for me."

"With all that service it should be like a new car." Unable to detain my enthusiasm any longer, and running a hand the length of the fin, I looked back, and asked, "Do you think that it'll start?"

Without reply, he wandered over to the counter and retrieving a ring of keys from a drawer, tossed them at me, saying, "Honestly, your guess is as good as mine, Give it a try?"

Climbing into the coach and shoving the key into the ignition, I was shocked as it started upon the first attempt.

"Now isn't that a bitch?" Harry laughed.

Turning off the engine and climbing out of the car, I walked over to where my friends stood together, and said to Tim, "I think that what you really need is a newer model."

"I couldn't afford it at the moment." His eyes reflected utter destitution, as frowning, he said, "I'm so far behind on everything, and with the--."

Drawing the car keys from my pants pocket, I jingled them before his eyes, and said, "There's a 1972 Cadillac, Superior coach parked at the Western Star motel. It had less than three hundred miles on the odometer, and I just brought it home from the dealership a month ago. If you want it, I'll trade you straight across for your old one."

"You're serious?" He stood awestruck, as looking to Harry, said as though questioning my sanity, "Harry, he's serious?"

"Yeah—he's serious alright." Harry nodded at him, and looking between us with a facetious grin, said, "Besides, the old wreck must've felt that he appreciates that rolling, spook-show more than you ever did."

"It's a three-way loader." Tim pointed out, as moving around the side of the car, opened both driver's side doors, saying, "It was the top of the line for this model and year. It has power windows, door locks, and a three hundred and ninety cubic inch engine with factory dual exhaust."

"Well what do you know—a hearse with suicide doors?" Harry scoffed, and looking to Tim, said, "I'll need to use your phone if you plan on getting that thing out of here. I have to call Lenny, and have him come down with his plow to clear the lot."

"Sure thing, it's on the wall beside the counter, help yourself." Tim turned toward me and hesitating, asked, "Are you absolutely sure that you want to do this? Because, I don't know if you'll even make it back into town with the car, much less taking on the highway back to Vancouver."

"Yes, I'm absolutely sure about this. Once I get it into town I'll run it over to the station, fill it with Premium, and have them check everything before I take it home with me. Don't worry so much."

"Lenny's on his way." Harry announced, as hanging up the phone, stumbled, cursing aloud, and saying, "Stupid cat! Where did he come from?"

It happened so fast that I hardly even saw the blur that vanished beneath the Hearse. Leaning down and peering into the long shadows beneath the coach, I laughed as a pair of green eyes blinked back.

"That's just poor old, Merlin." Tim explained as with its tail held high in the air, the large feline crept from out of the darkness and began affectionately rubbing against my leg.

"Aren't you a cute little thing" I scratched under his chin, amused with the loud rumbling purr.

"Cute little thing? Yeah right. I wouldn't get too close to him if I were you?" Harry grumbled, and pointing down at the cat, said, "That cute little thing gets into everything around here. And I mean everything--," Harry nodded in gesture toward the morgue door, and said, "If you catch my drift?"

"Oh, he gets into—everything?" The thought causing me to immediately recoil, I looked to my hands and then Tim, asking, "Is there somewhere where I can wash up?"

"Of course—this way please." He directed me toward a large metal double sink, and handing me a bottle of disinfectant soap and a towel, said, "It's almost impossible to keep him out of things. He has an uncanny way of getting into some of the worst places and things. I feel badly that I never have any time for him. But even so, I just don't have the heart to get rid of him."

"Well the little skunk sure seems to like you?" Harry pointed as the cat continued its affectionate advances, happily rubbing against my left leg. Looking down disapprovingly, Harry peered back at me and wincing, said, "But, after seeing some of the places that he's been into? I'd seriously consider burning those pants."

Retrieving the animal and hurriedly removing him from the room, Tim closed the morgue door. Apparently embarrassed with the creature's presence, he said, "I never allow him down here, but like I said—he just always seems to find a way?"

"Well you have to admit--," Harry coughed, as looking around the room with an obvious sense of disgust, said, "It does kind of smell like rotten old cat food down here?"

There was a moment of discomfort as we all looked at each other.

"That's a nasty looking piece of machinery." I directed their attention to the crematory on the far side of the bay, asking, "Are you running it right now?"

"It's always working. It's the last of the great man-eaters." Tim exclaimed, as tapping a finger against the temperature gauge, said, "After all these years—she still runs like a top."

"I'll never get used to those things." Harry shuddered, and lighting a cigar, coughed while saying, "The thought of burning folks up like that, it's just too damn creepy."

Merlin suddenly reappeared from out of nowhere, as racing past Harry and Tim, affectionately rubbed against my leg.

"Where the heck does he keep coming from?" Harry glared down at the large cat, and cursing, said, "There must be a hole in one of the walls? Maybe where the plumbing comes through from under the sink?"

"You never did mention how long he's been with you?" Accepting a pair of gloves from Tim, I knelt down, and gently stroked the animal.

"He's been around for a little over three years." Tim appeared somewhat apprehensive, as looking down at the mangy old feline, said, "He turned up right here in the bay one morning when I was cleaning. He stayed—so I just started feeding him and he's been here ever since."

"Um Tim—does he ever go outside?" Harry re-lit his cigar, and squinting suspiciously, said, "Do you put him out at night?"

"You know, that's the strangest thing?" Tim paused in thought while walking toward the morgue door, and saying, "He hasn't left the building in almost two months now. I've opened the door for him, but he just sits there... probably doesn't care for the cold too much?"

"Or he's smarter than he looks." Harry's eyes became slits in the dim glow of the fluorescent lights.

"You might want to take a deep breath before I open this?" Tim warned, as slowly reaching for the cooler door, said, "Like I said earlier, I've been having some trouble regulating the temperature in here. So, it's a little—ripe."

Accepting a handkerchief from Harry, I shoved it to my face, watching as Tim opened the cooler door and reeled back with the sudden stench.

"Just a little ripe you say?" Harry gagged, as pointing downward and shouting, said, "Tim—that fat little creep just followed you in there!"

Returning from the cooler with a gurney, Tim shrugged, and said, "I wouldn't worry about it too much. He just pokes around and comes right back out."

"Alright--," Harry watched the cat following along behind Tim, and said, "But don't cry about it to me when the little ghoul runs of with somebody's nose!"

The thought hadn't bothered me half as much as the sight of the bloodied sheet covering the remains that Tim now wheeled out before us.

Switching on a large overhead light, Tim looked between us, and said, "I thought that it might be better if we began with Mrs. Conrad, and looked at Connie last?"

"I'd have to agree…" Judging by Harry's expression I was already expecting the absolute worst.

Adjusting the large lamp over the front of the gurney, he slowly drew back the sheet, staring up at us while revealing the head and shoulders of the corpse. Having expected to witness poor old Shirley within silent and peaceful repose, I wasn't even remotely prepared for the thing that now stared back from that gurney.

"Oh—oh my God--," Covering my mouth with a trembling hand I looked away, gagging while fighting back the bitterness of the hot bile that now surged in my throat.

"That was my first reaction too." Harry puffed at his cigar, and nodding at the remains, said, "As you know, the surgical incisions were all post-mortem, but the majority of the damage is pretty much the same as how we found her."

Her long gray hair hung in bloodied clumps that dripped into a dark and coagulating pool on the gurney. It took everything to force my gaze to where the yellowed and leathery skin, stretching like elastic, hideously contorted the left side of her face.

It looked as though something had reached into her mouth, and literally ripped her face half-way over the back of her head.

Momentarily closing my eyes, I tried to examine things from a scientific perspective, but the personal memories of the kindly old woman were making it impossible.

Easy Mike, it's just dead tissue—a shell. No big deal, just a broken down house that's been abandoned by the previous tenant. We're just here to assess the damage. Now—light a cigarette, don't breathe too deeply and let's get this over-with.

Lighting a cigarette and clearing my throat, I returned to the gurney, and swallowing hard, gazed down upon the corpse.

Although I had never had any previous medical or forensic training, it wouldn't have taken a genius to see that this injury could never have been sustained in a simple fall. A blunt instrument could never have caught and ripped the flesh like that. It looked more like someone had used one of those huge hooks that you see on crabbing boats, and literally ripped off her face.

The gaping wound began just beneath her left upper lip. It had broken out several teeth on entry and shattering the jaw, splintered the skull in a bone crushing arc, taking her face with it.

"I thought that you'd said--," I swallowed hard as forcing back the acid accumulating in my throat, gasped, saying, "That she'd fallen and hit her head?"

My eyes returned to the pulverized and bloody mess that had once been Shirley's face.

"If I'd believed that for even a second—we wouldn't be standing here now, would we?" Harry waved the smoldering cigar at the corpse, and said, "Like I told you earlier, you needed to see this for yourself…"

There was a sudden silence in the room, as looking between the corpse and each other, the examination had ended as the vomiting began.

Turning and rushing toward the sink, I threw my head downward, violently heaving. It was mainly fluid, and I was grateful that we hadn't eaten before we came.

I felt Harry gently supporting my forehead with a hand, and coughing, said, "Sorry, this one was just too personal…"

"I know it—I loved the old girl too."

Rinsing out the sink and splashing cold water on my face, I looked up at him, and said, "If it wasn't someone that we had known for so long, I would have managed."

"Now you know why I didn't take you for breakfast before we came out here." He frowned, and gently slapping me on the shoulder, said, "You'd better take a breather before we finish up here. It's going to get a whole lot uglier before we're done…"

"He's right, Mike--," Tim re-covered Shirley's corpse, and wheeling the gurney back toward the cooler, said, "I've seen a lot in my time, but wasn't prepared for anything like this..."

"Harry, it seems pretty obvious that Shirley's death wasn't caused by a simple fall." Coughing with the stench of the open cooler, I said, "But what I'd really like to know? Is why and how the damn coroner could just pass it off like that? Don't the police question or investigate things anymore?"

"We can discuss the details when we're done here." He frowned.

I was beginning to suspect some kind of strange conspiracy. Feeling sick to my stomach, leaned back against the counter for support.

"I'll be glad when we can finally put these poor ladies to final rest." Tim cleared his throat, and shaking his head remorsefully, said, "It was bad enough that the coroner took so long before we got them back. But, they were both scheduled for cremation over a week ago. Harry had me tell the families that the crematory was undergoing a routine inspection."

"Well, as brutal as it may seem--," Harry puffed at his cigar, and peering over at me, said, "I wanted you to see this, so that you would understand what I meant in saying, no man did this..."

"I'm no genius, but it seems pretty clear that Shirley wasn't just the victim of an accident."

"Come on, Mike. Let's get this over-with so that we can get the hell out of here." He pointed toward Tim and the next body.

Swallowing hard, I looked down at the gurney, noticing the small and twisted form that was hidden just beneath the blackened, and blood soaked sheet.

"Are you ready?" Harry leaned closer, a sincere remorse reflecting in his eyes, as he said, "I'm really sorry to have to put you through this. But I'm sure that you understand why this was so important."

Brushing the hair from out of my eyes and adjusting the collar of my coat, I nodded in reply.

"Okay Mike--," Harry rested a hand on my shoulder, his voice trembling with fearful anticipation as grimacing, he said, "You might want to stand back a little for this one?"

Immediately taking his advice I stepped away, reaching for a cigarette and lighting it before nodding at Tim, said, "Okay, let's have a look."

Inhaling deeply, I held my breath as he struggled with both hands to tear the gore encrusted sheet from the corpse. Tugging, ripping, and pulling, he folded it ever downward, until finally revealing the nightmare that lay beneath.

"Oh, dear God..." Nothing could have ever prepared me for the sight that now met my wide and staring eyes. Gasping, the pen and note pad slipping from my grasp, and clattered to the floor.

"Once again—except for the post mortem incisions--," Harry gestured with a finger toward the deep Y-shaped cut that led from the collar bones to the sternum, saying, "And the back of her skull--," He motioned to the loose skin at the back of her head where the coroner had removed the rear plates of the skull to examine the brain, he said, "The rest of the damage was inflicted at the scene."

The overwhelming stench of decay had caused me to back away, but my eyes remained horribly fixed on the gruesome thing. In the bright glow of the light everything appeared hauntingly radiant. The flesh was far brighter, the blood and wounds much darker. Steam drifted from the gaping wounds as oozing things dripped, pooled around what remained of little Connie Shepherd.

Glazed eyes stared up from beneath heavy lids, the jaw hanging open revealed a blackened, bloated, and hideously distended tongue. The long and curly blonde hair was gathered in clumped masses, and hung about what remained of the torn throat, and shredded flesh of the shoulders.

There had been massive tissue loss around the thighs and lower abdomen. It was apparent that she's been eviscerated, and I could clearly see that the thoracic vertebrae were barely held by what remained of the lower lumbar spine.

"The right arm—," I pointed to the bloody stump from where it had been apparently hacked away from the shoulder, and said, "It doesn't seem to be here?"

"No—and that goes for everything else too. If it isn't here—then we didn't find it."

Briefly averting my gaze I took a deep breath before moving back toward the girl's remains. The lower left breast was gaping wide open and from what I could see, the skin, muscle and fat were literally shredded away from the exposed and shattered ribs. A black garbage bag was partially hidden inside the chest cavity, as wet and dripping, it hung out from the gaping abdominal cavity.

Moving closer, I threw a hand before my mouth. Smelling of soured butter, the stench burned in my nose like acid. The corpse had begun sagging, the limbs and tissue settling as it warmed beneath the hot lamp. That's when I noticed it. Through the bottom corner of the plastic bag, which had been torn on the splintered bone, the swollen and blackening coils of her intestines began spilling out onto the gurney.

Backing off, I looked down and saw that both of her legs had been severed. The bone literally snapped clean through at mid-thigh. With no visible splintering, it appeared to have been done by an industrial press or piece of heavy machinery. What remained of the pelvis had been stripped of flesh, and was filled by the bottom end of that ghastly black bag.

I tried to speak, but only stuttered while choking on the stench, while saying. "There's a trash bag in there... and it's leaking..."

"Oh that—," Harry peered into the open abdominal cavity, and puffing at his cigar, said, "The coroner always takes everything out. They weigh all the organs, run tests, and then it all goes into those bags. Oh, and before you ask? All of her insides were spread all over the place when we found her. So, the fact that we got it all prepackaged just made the job a little easier."

Noticing my horrified expression Tim pulled the sheet back over the remains, and said, "I think that we could all use a little fresh air."

"I'll second that motion..." Harry was pale as a sheet.

Covering the corpse, Tim hurried to the far side of the loading bay. In moments he had raised the electric garage door, stood in the dull afternoon glow. There was a loud rumbling and scraping sound, and as I followed Harry to where Tim stood at the bay door, I saw a plow clearing the lot.

"Tim, in your opinion, what could have caused all the damage to those bodies?"

He seemed immediately disturbed with the suggestion, and looking back at me, said, "My opinion—what on earth for? I'm a mortician damn-it—not a doctor."

"Yes, but you were studying forensic sciences before you got trapped here with your father. If anyone could shed a little light on this nightmare—I'd be putting my money on you."

He had all the appearance of a child awakened from a bad dream but still said nothing...

Making my way back to the gurney, I pointed at the bloodied sheet, and pleading, said, "Tim—I'm not asking you to explain how she died. I was just hoping for a possible answer as to what might have caused those wounds?"

"Just between us—I swear." Harry's stern gaze seemed to offer Tim the reassurance that he had needed.

Moving to the head of the gurney and slipping into another pair of gloves, he nodded, saying, "Okay then—let's take another look..."

To my absolute horror the blood soaked sheet had begun drying upon the corpse. The resulting mess forcing Tim to tug even harder, as struggling, almost pulled the entire gruesome mess from off the gurney. Stepping away from the gurney his expression had become barren of any emotion. It was something that I'd seen in many professionals and was an ability that I truly envied. Then again, death occurring in its many guises was something that I could never grow accustomed to seeing. Retrieving a magnifying glass and forceps, he began gently poking and pulling at the dangling flesh around the wounds. He did the same while examining the areas of the missing limps, and lower Lumbar region. The entire ghastly affair had lasted only a few minutes, and then turning toward us, he finally spoke.

"It's possible for these wounds to have been caused by a hit and run. But if they were, my guess would be that she must've been struck by a snow-plow or some other kind of heavy equipment?"

Directing a finger around the upper thigh area, he motioned toward the severed bone, and pressing into what remained of the surrounding soft tissue, said, "If you look closely? You can see that this area is all hemorrhaged. It's darker than the rest because the blood's pooled here. It almost looks as though the flesh was pinched.

Like the leg was literally—crushed off at this point."

"I've seen something like that before." Harry cleared his throat, and peering down at the corpse, said, "But it was an industrial accident. One of the guy's down at the paper mill got his arm stuck in a press—poor bastard."

"Like I said, it's just an opinion?" Tim motioned toward the girl's right shoulder, saying, "The upper humerus is sheared clean off, see here?"

"It almost looks like someone used a huge pair of steel shears." Harry spoke the words in the same moment that I had thought them.

The cigarette fell from my mouth as Tim, tugging at the broken humerus, caused blood to squirt from a severed artery. The result was a jetting stream that barely missing Harry, splattered against the wall behind us.

"Sorry, I should've expected something like that..." Turning back to the examination, he directed our attention back to the humerus, saying, "This definitely doesn't look like it was done by any conventional tool. The arm appears as though it were pinched—and severed by extreme force. Oh—oh my, that can't be right?"

"What—what's wrong?" Harry rushed around the gurney, and leaning down, curiously peered between the bloodied stump and Tim, asking, "What did you see?"

Quietly moving toward a table containing several surgical implements, Tim grabbed something from off the tray and hurried back. Without a word, he gently raised the arm, running a long Q-Tip inside the shattered bone, and saying, "It's not what I saw—it's what I didn't?"

"No riddles--," Harry growled through a cloud of cigar smoke, and said, "Just tell me what the hell is going on here?"

Withdrawing the Q-Tip from the stump he turned, and holding the cotton tip into the light, said, "Whoever or what-ever did this? Drained all the marrow from out of the bone..."

"It did what?" Harry coughed, the cigar falling out of his mouth. Stooping while intending to pick it up, he stopped dead, noticing that it had fallen into a pool of thick gore that was dripping from off the gurney.

"It's the same thing over here." Tim motioned while shoving a fresh Q-tip into the broken femur on the opposite side. Closely examining the end, he held it up for us to seem and said, "It looks like—the marrow's been completely sucked out?"

I had heard more than enough, as pointing toward the steaming and thawing corpse, I said, "Could it have possibly leaked out? I mean, the body's been hauled all over the place and God only knows--."

"No it couldn't have." He cut me off, his features becoming almost sinister in the pale glow of the fluorescent light, as he said, "After death, and especially in the cooler, it becomes like a thick, cheesy paste. It would never—just spill or drain out…"

It becomes a thick, cheesy paste. The words hung in my thoughts as I felt my empty stomach convulse.

"So what the hell are we dealing with here?" Harry looked utterly lost, as glancing between Tim and the corpse, said, "Is it animal, vegetable or mineral?"

"I don't have the foggiest notion of whom or what could have done this?" Tim wandered away and dropping the Q-Tips into the garbage, ripped off his gloves, and said, "All that I do know is that the wounds are consistent to the damage that might be inflicted by heavy machinery. If you asked me--," He went to the sink and washing his hands, looked back, and said, "I would've guessed that it was something with a heavy curved blade. Like a snow-plow."

"So--," I turned to Harry, saying, "Maybe that coroner wasn't completely off track?"

"Well—yes and no--," Tim interrupted, as returning and peering down at the remains, said, "The injuries do have the appearance of having been inflicted by heavy machinery. But that doesn't account for the massive tissue loss, lack of physical evidence, or missing bone-marrow."

"Or that she was found seven miles away from home." I added in thought, and looking to Tim, said, "We seem to be missing a very big piece of the puzzle?"

"Well—she had been walking home in the dark and along the highway." Tim demonstrated as utilizing his hands in the fashion best illustrating his theory, said, "A plow must have come along. The driver may not even have seen her? She would have gotten caught in the blade, pulled under, and then shoved off to the side. The bottom of the blade would have done most of the damage—and maybe animals got to her afterwards?"

"I hate to spoil the party--," Harry wandered away from the gurney, his attention focused on the blood splattered wall, as he said, "But Lou checked for traces of animal saliva around the wounds and didn't find anything. I know, because I specifically asked him about that."

"And what about the missing body parts? I mean, seriously, those legs and the arm must have gone somewhere?" I felt at a total loss.

"Maybe she was somehow dragged and the missing parts are spread over a seven mile stretch?" Tim looked to Harry.

"Lenny is the only one that we know around here with a plow." Harry took a long pull from the cigar, and said, "But I checked into that to. He was working at the station on the night that she walked home... And, that still doesn't explain the missing pets, the incident with the boar at Barry's farm, or what happened to poor old Shirley at the cemetery. Not to mention—the coroner's report never mentioned the missing marrow, so who knows what else he might've missed?"

"Well, if it wasn't Lenny—who else could it have been?" Tim was grasping at straws.

"It had to have been the department of highways." Harry cursed under his breath and said, "They have trucks running up and down the highways day and night. Half those guys are over-worked and half snow-blind from staring at drifts."

It was all beginning to really bother me. Not because it was my hometown and friends that were involved, but because it all just felt completely wrong. So wrong in fact, that I suspected that we might be up against something completely unexpected. After the incident at the house of McCreary I wasn't taking any chances...

Tim motioned toward the gurney and receiving a nod from Harry, switched out the light, and quickly covered the corpse.

"So what do we do now?" I looked to Harry as Tim wheeled the gurney back into the cooler.

"We go for a ride..."

CHAPTER SIXTEEN

2:45 p.m.

The fresh air had done us both a world of good. With the nausea of the morgue having passed and the lot being plowed, we had decided to find a little lunch before doing anything else.

Sniffing at my coat collar and shirt I suddenly became aware of a distinct odor. Groaning, I looked to Harry and said, "Oh no—that death smell, it's on everything..."

"Yeah, it tends to get into the fiber of everything. It'll even take a few days before the smell fades off your body and out of your nasal passages." Grimacing, he rolled down the window and sticking his head out, gasped at the icy air, while shouting, "Well—if you don't mind holding off on lunch for just a little longer? We can go over to the cemetery and I'll show you where we found Shirley. We should really run home after that, grab showers, and get changed before we get food. I really hate the idea of stinking like this, especially in the diner and while we're trying to eat."

"That makes sense. But, although I brought a change of clothes, I didn't think to bring a spare coat. And from the way this one smells, I might have to burn it before I leave town..."

"We can drop your coat at the dry-cleaner. I'm sure that I've got something that I can lend you for the time being."

"Thanks, I'd really appreciate that." Choking, I shoved my nose out the partially open window, shouting, "Listen Harry, I was thinking about taking my coach over to Tim after dinner. If you wouldn't mind, could I get you to follow me when I drive his hearse back to the motel?"

"I was thinking the same thing. And besides, that'll give Lenny a little more time to clear the road for us. Let's just pray that the weather holds out. The weatherman's predicting flurries some time tonight."

"Great and you know how much I just love the winter, and snow..." Searching around the dash, I turned and asked, "You wouldn't happen to have any cologne or air fresheners, would you?"

Reaching over and pulling an air freshener from the glove compartment, he grinned facetiously, and said, "Its pine scented. Fill your boots."

"Good enough." Grabbing it from his hand, I proceeded to smear my sleeves and especially the area around my collar. It was strange. The further that we drove away from that morgue the more apparent the stench seemed to become. I knew that it was just my senses recovering, but found something haunting in the thought… It was like death now followed us home…

"Toss a few of those around the car, would you?" He cursed under his breath, saying, "I sure hope this damn stink doesn't get into the upholstery?"

"If I were you, I roll all the windows down and leave it sitting through the night." Noticing the curve in the road ahead, I pointed, saying, "That looks a little sharp for this speed, don't you think?"

"For Pete's sake, will you just relax and let me do the driving? I already told you--." He started to say, "I've driven these roads my whole life and through all kinds of weather, and I know them like the back of my--…"

It was at that moment, and while looking at me instead of the road, that Harry hit something concealed beneath the snow!

Lifting upward as we drove over the obstruction, we sailed through the snow. Closing my eyes and tightly gripping the seat-belt, I braced for the impact! The vehicle came to rest nose down in a shallow ditch, the rear wheels still spinning as we were helplessly suspended in the air.

"Holy freaking Hannah, what the hell did we hit back there?" Startled and staring wildly, he looked to me, and asked, "Are you okay?"

"I'm not sure but it was big. It must have been a dear that was hit on the road, and buried in the snowfall."

Retrieving the police radio from the dash he proceeded to call into town for a tow truck. It was obvious that he was still just as shocked as I was, and as he spoke into the radio, he leaned from the window to examine the car, saying, "Well, it doesn't look like we did any serious damage to the old girl. How does it look out your side?"

Frustrated with his carelessness and feigning a smile, I leaned out and looking around, said, "You can be grateful for all of this snow. It seems to have cushioned the impact?"

"Thank Christ--," Hanging up the microphone, he switched off the ignition and sighing deeply, looked to me, and said, "The boys are on their way as we speak, and they'll have us out of here in no time."

Noticing the old sign that stood almost directly in front of where we were stuck, I pointed, saying, "Well, we made it to the cemetery. Why don't we take advantage of the daylight, and just run over there while we're waiting?"

"Good idea." He pulled out a notepad, and scribbling something on the page, tore it out, and presumed to pin it to the windshield with one of the wipers.

"I'm just letting them know that they can find us over at the cemetery. They're nice guys but not two of the brightest."

"Did you leave the keys in the ignition for them?"

Snapping his fingers, he pulled them from his coat pocket, and hurried back.

Climbing from the car, I paused to look down. The angle wasn't severe, but I had no intention of falling into the ditch, and down into where the car had broken through the ice. It was only a small stream, but I knew better than to get wet in this weather. Climbing the small embankment, I stopped on the road to look around. There was a grisly crimson trail from where we had impacted the thing on the road, but the body was missing. Noticing what had caught my attention, Harry followed the trail to where it disappeared near the edge of the ditch.

"Well whatever it was—it's gone now?"

"How could it just be gone?"

There was no reply from my friend and only an empty stare.

"Let's just get to the cemetery." I had no intention of waiting around to see what might happen next. I remembered that old cemetery road better than most because it had always haunted me. It was amazing how good memories always faded with time, but the painful and worst seemed to last forever. It's been years since the mine accident, but I sure miss you dad. I wish—no, leave it alone, Mike. That's the main reason mom moved to Vancouver. You can't really keep living when you're standing too close to the end of the road... In the many years that passed since his death, this dismal and silent place had not changed. Still, the dense pines crept ever forward, the brush embraced the road on either side, and winter brought death to that place. With the grey heavens, and heavy snow blanketing everything in a pale shroud, the forest was blurred into a pasty and charcoal haze. I felt suddenly claustrophobic, and suffocating in that most dismal atmosphere, felt the world begin to spin.

"Mike—you okay, buddy?" Harry stood beside me and looking n with obvious concern, gripped my shoulder with a hand, saying, "You didn't get too shaken up back there, did you?"

"No, I was just looking around, and remembering…"

"Yeah, I remember your dad's funeral too… I leave flowers on his grave for both of you, every year."

Something had died in me when we lost him to that mine accident. Even worse, was the memory of having almost perished in that same cavern not even a few years later… There were no words exchanged in that moment, I had only nodded in thanks.

"We should get moving--," He pointed ahead, and to where the cemetery gates appeared on the left side of the road, saying, "Just so you know? We won't be going anywhere near your father's grave. I know how you feel about it. Clark is buried on the opposite side, and near the fencing."

I had always avoided that place. Not because I'd held any angst against my father, but because it was like staring mortality in the face. Our mother and father bring us into this world, and when they depart, they take some intimate piece of us with them. Flesh, blood and soul, we are forever bound unto the grave. For this reason alone, I could not bear to bring myself to gaze down upon his ending…

After making our way through the rear entrance gates, we began the journey up the stone walkway. Nothing had really changed with exception to a few new grave-stones

Completely surrounded by a six foot spiked iron gate, the memorial grounds extended east and west some sixty yards in width. The incline being unusually steep and filled with assorted trees, gently ascended another two hundred yards before finally meeting the road at the very top. There were small stone pathways leading from either side, and traveling in between the graves every ten rows. This offered easy access to a loved one without walking over too many others.

From where we stood at the rear gates, I could barely make out the new entrance-way somewhere high above.

"It's a bit of a walk--," Harry gasped, as struggling through the knee-deep snow, said, "As you know, when they first built this place, the main gate was down here. They changed the entrance because as they moved up over the years, all the newer graves are at the top."

I could see the old willow that stood near my father's headstone. A huge part of me desired nothing more than to have the opportunity to say goodbye, but the thought broke my heart.

"We're almost there—." Harry had noticed, and drawing my attention, pointed toward the far eastern corner, saying, "Clark's buried up there."

It was less than fifty yards distance from where we stood, but in the deep snow might just as well have been miles.

The iron fencing that traveled the eastern edge of the grounds had been overcome by huge trees in places. I could see that wherever the pines pushed and branches swung low, that certain portions were bending inward and being crushed beneath the immense weight.

Removing the camera from the case that hung around my neck, I poised, snapping several shots. It was a strange sight, as beyond the old and leaning headstones, and to where the path traveled closest to the fence, a deep shadow blocked all view.

An immense pine stood in that place. Far older and taller than all the others, its broad and lower branches had been trimmed some eight feet from off the ground. It was these lower and over-hanging limbs that formed a kind of natural canopy, and caused that impenetrable shadow.

I could see that the snow was much lighter in that place, as for obvious reasons, the path had been recently cleared. Crime and accident scenes usually were…

"It doesn't look very well maintained, does it?"

"Oh, don't kid yourself." He adamantly disagreed, saying, "It's just the recent snow-fall. The church takes really good care of the place. Especially, since they put the new road through, about four years ago. Truth be told, and as much snow as we see here, the walk-ways are safe as can be." He tried unsuccessfully to skid on the obviously well salted and sanded walk-way, and looking at me suspiciously, said, "It kind of makes you wonder, doesn't it? If I can't do it intentionally, then how in the hell did old Shirley manage to slip on this stuff?"

"The more that we find out the less that any of this is making sense…" Halting to catch my breath, I muttered in thought, saying, "Maybe, it's not that we're asking the wrong questions, but looking for the wrong thing…"

The comment bothered him. It was apparent just in the way that he placed his hands on his hips, and nervously looking around, quietly asked, "So, what do you think we should be looking for?"

Looking into the distance and over the dark tree-tops I shook my head, as looking back to him, said, "Maybe, instead of considering the obvious, we should be looking into the unknown?"

"What—like aliens and Bigfoot?" He shrugged it off, as continuing along the way, I followed in swift pursuit.

"Harry, you've already said that whatever did this to Connie and Shirley, wasn't a man. Just listen to me here. We might be dealing with something that no one else has ever seen, or lived to talk about… That would explain why all the clues lead up to one big fat zero, zilch, and nothing."

"I'm not saying that I'm completely disagreeing with you here--," His entire demeanor changed, as speaking calmly and quietly, he motioned for me to settle down, and said, "But, I have to write reports too, and I can't justify running off on some kind of a monster hunt, or chasing the boogeyman."

Pointing an accusing finger, I argued, saying, "Isn't that why you called me, and dragged me all the way out here in the first place? Because deep down, Harry--," I poked him in the chest, saying, "In that great big heart of yours, you know that something is very wrong about all of this. And, that it's going to take someone with a pretty damn open mind to come up with answers, even if they aren't what anyone wants to hear."

"Okay, so you're right… but for the moment, just bear with me, okay? Let's look over all the evidence first, and then see if we can figure this thing out somehow."

"Fair enough--," I followed after him to a grave-side, saying, "But Harry. I don't think that anyone will like the answer if it finds us first…"

The wind whipped the hair about my face, and adjusting my

sunglasses, simply stared back at my friend.

"The caretaker managed to scrub off most of the blood, but you can still see the stains." He directed my attention the gravestone before us, and saying, "She was found lying across the grave with her face pressed against the stone. Oh and Mike--," His eyes narrowed suspiciously as he fumbled for a cigar, and lighting it, said, "We didn't find any prints in the snow—except for hers."

My immediate and instinctive reaction was to turn and follow her path back toward the road above. Unfortunately, it had snowed long since the old woman was discovered there.

"There wasn't any snow from between the time of the accident and our finding her body—so it was pretty clear." Harry pointed while explaining, and said, "So, retracing her steps from the top, and where she'd parked the car, I followed them right to here. From what I gathered from the scene--," He puffed at the cigar, and squinting while peering up the path, said, "She must've came down the path, and then stopped over there by the fence, for some reason?"

"Where exactly—did she stop?"

Pointing behind where we stood and motioning several yards up the path, he sighed deeply, and said, "Oh, and that was another thing... For some reason, and judging by the distance between the steps, at some point, she took off running... and inevitably, ended up falling here..."

"See—that's exactly what I was talking about! We both know that she was obviously running away from someone, or something." Turning to where the dense thicket pressed tightly against the iron fence, I placed a finger before my lips, and said, "And from the looks of that bush, nothing bigger than a rabbit would have a chance of ever getting through there."

"Well whatever it was—it didn't leave tracks on either side of that fence, because I checked..."

Taking several pictures of the fence, grave, and marker, I focused the lens on the pathway, and asked, "Harry, did you notice that before?" I pointed to where the fence seemed to bend inward further than the rest, saying, "I realize that the forest is slowly forcing the fence inward—but there's nothing resting against that section."

Hurrying toward the fence he leaned down while closely examining the twisted rails, and cursing, said, "Son of a bitch—

you're right! It looks like something heavy slammed against it from the other side. It's all bent to hell! I don't know why I never noticed this before?"

"What do you suppose could do that to an iron fence—without leaving prints or tracks of any kind?"

Leaping back suddenly, and to the sound of a blaring horn, we noticed the car and tow-truck at the bottom of the hill behind us. Waving at them, Harry's expression filled with a sudden urgency, and growling, he said, "Let's get the hell out of here…"

7:13 p.m.

With the exception of a small dent in the driver's side fender the only real damage had been to Harry's ego. With bigger concerns and that horrid stench still on our clothes, we had returned home for showers.

When he had dropped me off at the motel he mentioned having to take care of some things first. Usually, I wouldn't have minded just waiting around, but I was cold, tired, and hungry. So, sooner than sitting around and waiting, I agreed to meet him at the diner.

Swiftly disrobing, and utterly disgusted with the smell, I hurriedly placed my clothing into a plastic bag. Although it seemed impossible, that smell was permeating the room even through the plastic. It was a sad day when I put that bag outside my room, because somehow I knew that it was the ending of that suit and coat.

After a long hot shower, fresh clothes and far too much cologne, I suspiciously sniffed at myself.

Through everything, although it was feint, my nose still burned with the cheesy, ammonia stench of death.

Was it still in my hair, or had it somehow been absorbed into my skin. Wearing only a black turtleneck sweater, brown corduroy pants, and winter boots, I quickly made my way outside. It was bitterly cold, the wind was unbearable, and I had to second guess my decision about going out. It hadn't taken long. I was starving… In the end, and grabbing the bag outside my door, I bid farewell to the old suit and coat. The whole kit-and caboodle went into a dumpster on my way to the restaurant.

CHAPTER SEVENTEEN

Crossing the road from off the highway, I hurried along and toward the welcoming lights of the diner. It was a short walk, as walking up the main street and passing a strip of small businesses, soon arrived at my destination. I was actually climbing the front steps to the diner when a honking caused me to turn, and look as Harry pulled in and parked behind me.

"What the hell are you doing?" He slapped his brow while climbing from the car, and saying, "When I dropped you off I forgot that you didn't have a coat." Moving to the rear door, he went into the back seat, and producing a dark green Parka, waved it, saying, "But, I remembered to bring this for you."

"You're a real gem, Harry, thanks" Accepting the coat from him, I held the door for him before entering the diner

The place hadn't changed much at all since I was a kid. It had the same old red leather booths, black and white checkered tiles, but those curtains? I didn't remember them being that shade of pink? Oh wait—they were just faded over the years. Yes, the same old red curtains too.

Waving as we passed the front counter, Harry smiled at the waitress, and said, "Coffee for me and tea for him, and menus please, Linda."

At first glance she reminded me of a slightly heavier, Mae West. She was tall, curvy, and had bleached blonde hair that was tied back in a tight ponytail. Her eyes were bright blue and stared back from a rounded face, buried beneath far too much makeup. She appeared to be mid to late forties, had bad skin, and in all truth, I'd seen department store mannequin's with more natural appeal.

"Be right with you, honey-pie!" She adjusted an apron that partially covering a pink angora sweater, revealed bulging rolls that spilled over her tightly fitting, black slacks.

Seating ourselves at a booth to the rear of the diner, I parted the curtain slightly to peer out into the empty parking lot.

"Sure is a beauty, isn't she?" Harry beamed, as reaching for a cigar, looked out at his Chrysler, and said, "They sure don't build them like that anymore."

Misunderstanding while caught in another thought, I had just looked to him in question.

"The car, dummy—I meant the car." He muttered under his breath, as smiling and accepting coffee and a menu from Linda, said, "Ad how are you doing on this fine, frosty night?"

"Just fine, darling--," She gleefully chewed at a mouthful of gum, and asked, "Now what can I get for you boys. Say Harry—aren't you going to introduce your friend?"

Before he could even respond, recognition glittered in her eyes and she snapped her fingers. "Mike Schreiber, oh my goodness, it is you! After all these years… what brings you back into town, sweetie?"

It all came back in one vast and nauseating flood. Linda Evans had once been a cheerleader for our school football team, but I barely recognized her now.

"I'm just visiting with some old friends." I smiled up at her, and shrugging, said, "It's been some time, and I thought that it would be nice to just kick-around, and see the old stomping grounds again."

"At our age they call that a mid-life crisis, honey. Take it from me. There are far better things to fill that cute little head with." She poked a finger into my chest and laughing, said, "I don't see a wedding band—does that mean that you're still open for takers?"

"Linda, please--," Harry smirked, as raising an eyebrow at her indiscriminating behavior, said, "He just got into town, don't scare him away already."

"Oh, you are still the worst, party-pooper--," Slapping playfully at his shoulder, she pulled out a pad and pen, and winking, asked, "So what can I get for you boys?"

"Is there a special tonight?" Jabbing a thumb back toward the front counter, I explained, saying, "I was in a hurry to get out of the cold and forgot to look at the menu board."

"There sure is sweet-stuff." She pointed toward the front counter as though any of us could even see what was written on the board, and said, "The roast turkey dinner's on special. It comes with stuffing, mashed potatoes or fries, mixed veggies, and dessert. The dessert tonight is apple pie a la mode. And that's five dollars and forty nine cents. Or--" She beamed joyously, jabbing a thumb over her shoulder and into the kitchen, said, "Gene just dropped off some lovely fresh venison. Old Bert's back there right now, cutting up some real fine steaks."

The sound of a meat cleaver in the back caused me to wince at the thought of fresh meat. In that same moment, visions of Shirley and Connie's remains steaming beneath the hot lamp flashed through my mind. I'd never cared for wild meat anyway, but couldn't bear the thought of anything even resembling it.

Stuttering, I said. "I'll be fine-fine—I mean, fine with the turkey, thanks."

"Fresh venison--" Harry placed a finger to his lips in thought and noticing my expression, courteously declined, saying, "Well— maybe next time. I'll just have the same as him—but with extra mashed potatoes and cranberry sauce."

"You got it, sugar." She winked, and retrieving the menus and flashing those mascara covered baby blues, said, "Are you going to be in town for a while? I have a trailer down the road from here. It's the Golden Acres trailer and RV Park? You can't miss it. It's the only one in town." Scribbling her phone number onto the note pad, she tore out the page, and shoving it into my open hand, said, "You can call any time. I'm usually around in the evening, and I stay up late on most nights."

Thankfully, there hadn't been time to respond. The door slammed suddenly from behind us, and turning, we were surprised to see Tim hurrying toward our table!

"I had a feeling that I'd find you boy's here!" He dropped into the booth beside Harry, and grinning from ear to ear, said, "I managed to drive the old coach down here! I couldn't believe it? The darn thing started without any trouble and made it all the way here."

Glancing out the window and into the empty parking lot, Harry squinted suspiciously, and looking back to Tim, asked, "So where is it?"

"Oh well—that?" Tim groaned, as clasping his hands together and cursing under his breath, said, "Well—everything was fine until I parked the damn thing at the motel. I thought that I'd pick you up?" His looked to me, his eyes rolling in his head, as he said, "But I guess I'd just missed you? And when I went back to the car it wouldn't start."

"No problem." Harry winked, and looking to me, said, "I'll follow

Tim back to the funeral parlor after I'm done eating."

"Oh, you needn't bother. Lenny managed to clear the roads--," Tim interrupted, saying, "I had no trouble getting into town and should be just fine going back."

"I'm sure that I still have some extra transfer papers in my bag at the hotel. We can stop there after we eat, and get the titles of ownership sorted out."

"I'll get the boys to tow the 64 over to the service station in the morning--," Harry nodded at me, and said, "I'm sure that Lenny can get that old pig running again."

"Can I help you—Stinky." Linda chuckled at Tim, her expression revealing an obvious loathing.

"Please don't call me that." He became rigid, slowly looking between us while averting his gaze from the large woman.

For obvious reasons, it was the nick-name that had followed him all through high school. Usually I felt bad for him, but at the moment and feeling self-conscious, both Harry and I nonchalantly, sniffed at our-selves.

"Oh, can't old friends make a joke now and then? Lighten up, why don't you?" She winked as though having scored points for bashing him, and said, "What can I get you, Tim?"

"Coffee—," He refused to even look at her, staring down at his clasped hands upon the table and fidgeting, he said, "And maybe a slice of apple pie, please and thank you."

"So how would you like that pie? Heated with ice cream… or just plain cold?"

"Heated and with ice cream—please."

Linda had been one of the many girls that had been unrelentingly cruel to Tim all through school. It was sad how certain people never changed. I understood why some guys had simply lost their minds, and why women like Linda regularly turned up on the Missing Persons list.

The door to the diner suddenly flew open in a brutal and chilling gust, and once again, we all turned to look.

"Well I'll be damned! Steve—you made it!" Harry leapt up from the bench, and hurrying toward his friend with an extended hand, said, "I was beginning to wonder if you were going to show up!"

Sergeant Steve Harris was an imposing figure of a man. The only son of a Black father and Japanese mother, he bore the finer characteristics of both. Broad shouldered, muscular, and well over six feet tall, the floor shook beneath his mass as he approached the table. In his left hand was a large black duffel bag, and as he turned toward us, I felt slightly intimidated in his presence.

Tanned, his black and greying hair was cut short, and he sported a Texas style, handle-bar mustache. His features were stern, but there was a kindness residing behind his deep brown, and almost black eyes. As he walked, the long black leather cloak whipped behind him, and slipping aside, I caught a glimpse of the shotgun gripped within his right hand. It was a Winchester model 1200 Defender with extended tube magazine. I knew the weapon because it was a slide action riot gun which introduced in 1964 was used by police.

"It would take a lot more than a little snow to stop me." Steve's deep voice boomed in the little diner, as dropping his bag and stomping the snow from his boots, he heartily slapped Harry's back, saying, "But, I could sure use some coffee and hot food."

"Michael Schreiber, meet Sergeant Steve Harris from the Penticton detachment--," Harry proudly introduced us, and as we shook hands in greeting, said, "We've been friends for close to eleven years."

"Sure—the writer that you've been telling me about--," Steve grinned and his smile became huge beneath that black mustache, "It's a pleasure to finally meet you, Mike."

"Thank you, the pleasure is mine, sir. I've written a few short stories for magazines but nothing really prolific." Sipping at my tea and reaching for a cigarette, I paused and said, "I'm actually working on my first full length novel right now."

Steve looked around the table, a deep and throaty chuckle breaking the tension, as he said, "Well, that's definitely better than having a real job." Looking at Tim he extended a hand and grinning, said, "And you must be, Tim—the mortician..."

"Yes, the mortician." He sighed.

"Good to meet you." Steve coughed, and slipping the hand beneath the table, casually wiped it against his pant leg.

"Mike writes ghost stories--," Harry changed the subject, and waving for Linda to bring more coffee, said, "You know, stuff about spooks and other imaginary things that go bump in the night."

"Not everything that goes bump in the night is imaginary." Tim stirred cream and sugar into his coffee, and turning in my defense, said, "There's an entire field of research dedicated to the study of mysterious monsters, mythical beasts and animals reported, but never seen again."

"They call them Cryptids, and that field is known as Cryptozoology--," Steve informed us all, and leaning back in the seat beside me, said, "You know, there was a time in my life when I didn't believe in anything that couldn't be proven. Hard facts, straight goods, and that's all there was too it. But now--," Something dark flashed within his eyes as he said, "I'm not quite as quick to dismiss things…"

"With all due respect--," Fascinated, Tim curiously observed Steve, saying, "But, you just don't strike me as the type of person who would be interested in such things?"

"You might be surprised as to what I might be willing to believe…"

"I called Steve a few days ago--," Harry explained, as speaking in low tones to remain discrete, said, "He's got something of a personal interest in this matter." Nodding at his friend, he said, "You can speak freely, you're among friends…"

There was reluctance at first, and it was evident that whatever it was, that it truly frightened him. Then tightly clasping his hands together upon the table, he solemnly said, "What I'm about to tell you will likely sound completely insane. But I swear that to the best of my knowledge, it's the absolute truth…"

"Do you might if I make some notes for my own, personal use?" I looked between Harry and the big man sitting next to me. Patting at my sweater, and realizing to have forgotten the pad and pen in the motel, I drew a blank.

Without hesitation Steve reached inside his coat, and producing a police issue notepad, dropped it on the table before me, saying, "If anything about this ever leaks out, I'll lose my badge, and be looking for you…"

I could see by the stern reflection in those black eyes that he was dead serious. Swallowing hard, I nodded with the understanding, and said quite nervously, "Of course—I understand…"

There were several moments, where returning to refill our drinks, Linda made something of a nuisance of her-self. Then sensing she'd warn out her welcome, hurried off again.

"Sunday November the fifth. It was just shortly after two thirty in the morning when I was called out on an MVA." Steve spoke so quietly that I had to lean closer to clearly hear him. Looking at Harry, he added, "You know what those are always like around the holidays. It's usually just some drunk stuck in the snow or kids fooling around."

As he spoke, he nervously peered out, and into the heavy snowfall beyond the window, and said, "It was a night a lot like tonight. There were heavy flurries, poor visibility, and strong winds."

Staring out the window Tim's expression paled. It was apparent that he was now dreading the drive home.

"The accident was reported less than five miles out of town, which is about halfway between Penticton and Summerland. Like I said, the snow was so bad that I couldn't see five feet in front of the cruiser. So, I didn't arrive at the scene until twenty minutes later. I was supposed to meet Willy Downs—my duty partner that night. We'd known each other for almost ten years. He'd radioed on route that night, and said that he didn't like the idea of being alone out there, and in that storm. He never said things like that—so I had a gut feeling that something wasn't right."

"Were you the only two members patrolling that night?" Scribbling in barely comprehensible abbreviations, I glanced over at him.

"There were two others stationed in town, but Willy and I were usually assigned to respond to highway calls."

"Sorry for the interruption--," Waving the pen, I politely encouraged him, saying, "Please continue."

"When I finally arrived on the scene I noticed that there were two vehicles. Will's patrol car was parked on the South side of the highway, and there was a black 1953 Buick sedan, which had gone off the road and into a snow-bank. The beacons were flashing, and the spotlight on Will's cruiser was directed on the Buick. At that time, I didn't see anyone out there? So, I let off a few blasts on the siren... but no one came. I've never been scared on the job but something felt different that night. I wasn't sure what was going on, so I called in for road-side assistance, grabbed my flashlight, and went for the shotgun in my trunk."

Moving ever so slightly in the seat, I saw that his foot contacted the duffel bag and shotgun. It was obvious that he found comfort in the weapons presence.

"When I got closer to Will's patrol car, I noticed that the driver's side door was hanging open... and that the car was empty. The snow was getting worse. I followed Will's tracks from the cruiser. They were almost filled, but I could still make out the shapes. They led directly to the driver's side door of the Buick, but it was empty too. The keys were still hanging from the ignition in both vehicles, but there wasn't a single living soul in sight. My first instinct was panic, and I felt like I had to get the hell out of there real fast. But I couldn't do it, and especially not without trying to find Willy first."

"Okay boy's—dinner's here!" We were interrupted as Linda reappeared, and placing down our supper plates, asked, "Can I get you fella's anything else?"

"No this is perfect." Harry sniffed at the steaming plate of food.

"Would you like to try the Venison steak?" She looked to Steve.

"Not tonight ma'am, thank you—maybe another time." He was polite, but his thoughts and attention remained beyond the window, and deep in the storm...

"Alright then, you boy's just shout if you need anything."

I watched as she hurried off, and clearing and wiping off the tables, made her way behind the counter.

"You were following Will's tracks." I reminded him, as glancing to where Linda now disappeared into the kitchen, said, "What happened then?"

"The tracks—," Steve thoughtfully tapped a spoon against his coffee mug, and said, "They led into the forest for about ten meters. That's where I found the third vehicle. It was a family car, a two-tone green and white 58 Plymouth wagon. I reached for the driver's door in the dark—and my hand slipped off the handle. I looked down." Raising a trembling hand before widening eyes, he stared into the palm. There was a moment where vividly remembering the experience, he shook his head in disbelief, and then turning wide-eyed, said, "There was so much blood." He kept shaking his head, and, "I've never seen so much in my life.... There were frozen rivers running all down the door, and these huge smears across the front fender and hood. I was stunned—so damn scared that all that I could do was point the flashlight into the window, and stare. It took a moment, but then—reaching out--," He motioned with his hand, and making a clutching motion, said, "I opened the driver's side door."

His face grew pale, his eyes darting rapidly between us, as he said, "When the interior light came on—I swear to God. It looked like someone had just exploded in there. Everything was soaked and dripping, every inch of those seats—the dash, headliner. I knew that someone had been literally shredded in that car, and could even make out, pieces of people…"

"Pieces of people--," Tim repeated the words, and removing his glasses, wiped at the lenses with a napkin, asking, "Can you expand on that a little?"

"It looked like a tub full of blood, shredded guts--," Steve almost choked on the description within memory, as whispering, said, "And tiny, bite-sized pieces of several people…"

Glancing down into the coagulating gravy on my plate I suddenly lost my appetite. Usually I wasn't that sensitive, but after the events of the day and still smelling of death, it was just too much. Sliding the plate away I returned to my tea.

Oblivious, Harry had gestured at my plate with a fork, and asked, "Aren't you going to finish that?"

"Too much garlic and sage--," I lied, as sliding the plate across the table for him, said, "Please—feel free. I'd hate to see it go to waste…

Abandoning the meal for the safety of a cigarette, I turned to Steve, and said, "You were saying something about the interior of the car?"

"It was an absolute nightmare." The horror reflected in his eyes as while directing his attention back to the window, he continued, saying, "It was so dark that I didn't have any other choice. I reached inside that car and turned on the head-lights. It didn't help much while reflecting in all that snow. I felt like I was looking into a wall of nothingness."

Sipping at his coffee, he said, "I drew my service revolver at that point, and began making my way around the car. That's when I stumbled and found Will's revolver… It was lying in the snow near the passenger side, rear door…"

He shook his head in disbelief, and said, "I looked in the chamber. It hadn't even been fired. That's when I knew it. I knew that Will was dead, and that I'd walked right into the middle of something... Nothing made sense, and all that I could do was just stand there, staring down at his blood covered, thirty eight special. There was a movement. I caught it in my peripheral vision. But it happened so fast, that I knew it couldn't have been a person or animal. It happened again, only closer. A second later, and I was panicking— aiming blindly into the blizzard from all around me. I didn't see a damn thing out there, just endless, and blinding snow… But I knew something was out there…"

Gazing into the pale and blinding storm beyond the window, he slowly shook his head in disbelief, and said, "It's a strange thing— the way that snow muffles everything except for the sound of your own pounding heart. I was scared to death, but I've been a hunter all my life. I learned a long time ago that you never run in a situation like that. So, scared or not, I just started to slowly back away. Somehow, and in all the confusion, I was blinded by the Plymouth's head-lights, and went off the beaten track. Somewhere between the path that I'd made earlier and the direct line of the light, I stumbled over something buried under the snow. That's where I'd found what was left of Will. He was torn to--…" Words failed him and his eyes became wide and glassy.

"There was nothing that anyone could have done." Harry tried to comfort his old friend, saying, "It was over long before you'd even gotten there... Just finish the story…"

Slowly wringing out his fingers and cracking his knuckles, Steve cleared his throat, and quietly said, "I was moving backwards, slow and steady, when I caught a movement in the beam of my flashlight. It was something big, but it was just a blur in the corner of my eye. I couldn't tell what direction it'd come or where it'd gone? I knew that if I didn't get out of there soon, that whatever had gotten to Will and the others would be coming for me. I'd just turned to move… and it all happened so fast that I didn't even see it coming."

"One second I was turning to walk—and the next thing that I remember is a shadow in front of me. Then something just grabbed me." He gestured with his arms, as making the motions of being tightly embraced, said, "It was huge, powerful, and cold as ice. It felt like being caught in a steel trap. I was completely helpless and couldn't even fight back. There was an incredible pressure, pain, and

I couldn't breathe. It felt like every bone in my body was about to break. Then I heard gunshots, I blacked out, and all that I remember is waking up in an ambulance."

"Sergeant—if you don't mind me asking--," Nervously chewing at a fingernail, Tim peered over at him, and said, "What exactly do you mean by huge? I mean—you're a very big man compared to the rest of us."

"Whatever it was--," Steve leaned closer and speaking in a barely audible tone, said, "It was big enough to lift me clear off the ground--, He made a grasping motion with both hands in the air before us, and clasping them tightly together, said, "And crush me like I was nothing more than a toddler..."

"So we're obviously dealing with some kind of an animal--," I turned to look at Harry, and said, "It may even be a Grizzly. They've been known to crush people in a similar fashion as to what Steve just--."

"It wasn't any bear or animal that I've ever seen." Angered, Steve promptly removed his coat, unbuttoned his uniform shirt, and parting it to reveal his chest, growled, saying, "You tell me— what kind of an animal leaves marks like this?"

All that I could do was sit and stare in absolute shock and amazement. On either side of his broad and muscular chest, and running the length of his ribs to waist, were a dozen deep red scars. It was apparent that they had required numerous stitches, as easily an inch in diameter, appeared as large, round, and progressive punctures. In all respects, he truly appeared to have been caught in an animal trap of immense proportions...

"Dear God--," Tim covered his mouth with a hand, and shaking his head, said, "I've never seen anything like that before."

Cautious not to alert Linda who stood bored behind the counter, Steve slowly turned to the right side, and directing our attention to his lower abdomen, said, "It took sixty eight stitches to close that one." Peering down to where multiple wounds formed a circular scar on his stomach, he looked up and said, "It almost gutted me like a fish."

"How could something that big, move so fast, and catch a person unaware like that?" Tim's eyes bulged.

"It must have been in the trees? That might explain why I never saw it coming."

"The trees--," Sliding my empty yea cup aside, I turned toward Harry, and said, "We never even thought of that? At the cemetery—that would explain why there weren't any prints. That might also explain the reason why that fence was warped. What if something came out of the trees, and the reason that you never found any tracks, was because it used the fence as a method of travel?"

"That young girl and the elderly woman wouldn't have stood a chance--," Steve grumbled while tucking his shirt into his pants, and saying, "And I Likely wouldn't be sitting here tonight either, if it wasn't for old Harry--," Slipping back into his coat, he scowled, looking around the group, said, "I'd just be another unexplained statistic."

"Harry?" The statement took me by surprise, as looking to my old friend, I asked, "Harry—what does he mean?"

"Well, I told you that I was in Summerland over Christmas. I was with Irene for dinner, remember?" Shrugging, he said quite modestly, "I was one of the attending officer's that responded that night. I never said anything because I just thought that it would be better if you heard this right from Steve."

"Did you see anything out there?" Tim's features twisted with a strange and rather morbid fascination.

"It might be better if you just start from the beginning." Puffing at my cigarette I sighed deeply, and looking to Harry, asked, "How exactly did you become involved?"

"Like I had said before--," Harry finished eating and sliding his plate away, looked to me, and said, "I was in Summerland visiting Maureen over the holidays. I was just getting ready to leave when I heard the call on my police radio. It was Steve, so I figured what the hell—I'm out here anyway? Penticton is only seven miles west, so I figured I'd meet him half-way? Maybe stick around for a quick donut and coffee before heading home?"

Re-lighting the stub of his cigar, he shrugged, saying, "When I got to the MVA scene and found both cars abandoned--," He hesitated as Linda hurried past with an armload of napkins and clean cutlery, and leaning closer, said, "I saw the headlights of the car in the woods, so figured that Steve and Will might've been there. Like he said, the snow was pretty bad, and it was almost impossible to see anything. It was freezing. My hands were shaking so bad that I could hardly hold the shotgun. I followed the light and must've been less than ten feet away when—it happened."

Tapping the glowing ash from off his cigar he swallowed hard, and staring as though invoking a nightmare, said, "I saw Steve—and something huge swung down. Like he said—it was a shadow and just came out of nowhere. They were both in the headlights, but the cold had fogged up my glasses, made everything look like shadows. I just aimed at the thing and started blasting away. It let go of him— and disappeared just as fast as it had shown up. I didn't hang around to see any more. Just grabbed Steve, and high-tailed it out of there. As you've both seen, he was hurt pretty bad…"

"The ambulance guys told me that Harry carried me out of there that night." Visibly emotional over the incident, he nodded at Harry, and swallowing hard, said, "I still owe you one, old buddy."

"Bullshit." Harry rubbed at his eyes and looking to Steve, said, "You would've done the same for me."

"Can you describe what you saw?" Tim was obviously horrified beyond his wits, his eyes glistening with fear, as he asked, "What did it look like?"

"All that I saw were two sparks of light and some kind of huge, blurry shadow." Harry sipped at his coffee, and said, "I aimed for those lights—and just kept firing."

"And with all that gun-fire--," I looked to my friend and asked, "You didn't manage to injure—or find any evidence of this thing?"

Slowly shaking his head, he puffed at his cigar, and said, "Not a single, damn thing. I didn't even get a clean shot. Too many trees and all that damn snow."

"What about the occupants of those two cars?" Tim adjusted his glasses, and looking between the two men, asked, "They must have found—people?" He looked to Steve.

"No--," Steve tapped a finger against his mug and looking down briefly, glanced back at Tim and said, "Not exactly…"

"Not exactly--," It wasn't what he had so much as how he'd said it that stopped me cold, "Well, what about the victims? The authorities obviously know their identities, right?"

"The motor vehicle board ran the plates." Steve nodded, saying,

"The driver of the Buick was Paul Brunner. A sixty two year old Kelowna, bank manager on his way home from visiting family. According to his wife, he never returned home. I talked to her last week—still no sign of him. The occupants of the Plymouth station wagon were a father and mother, Philip and Dorothy Turner." A shadow crossed his face in reflection as solemnly, he said, "And Melissa, their six year old daughter."

"Oh my God--," Tim threw a hand before his mouth, and whispering said, "She was just a baby."

Taking a long pull from my cigarette and flicking an ash, I looked to Steve, and asked, "And the official police report? How did you sum that one up?"

"Under severe weather conditions, the accident occurred when a southbound vehicle collided into a vehicle in the oncoming lane. Occupants of both vehicles were missing at the scene... the body of an attending officer was discovered near one of the cars... and the investigation is still pending."

"And what about all the blood and what happened to you?" Pausing in my notes I looked to him for answers, asking, "What did the coroner have to say? I mean—they obviously examined the vehicles, didn't they?"

"Well, from what I read in the report, the Buick was clean." Steve shrugged, saying, "Just looked like any other abandoned vehicle. But that old Plymouth station wagon? It didn't have much damage at all. There was a slight dent in the driver's side fender, a little bent chrome, and a broken headlight. But inside—well, that was another story...."

"Pieces of people..." Tim's eyes widened.

"Um--," Steve's entire demeanor seemed to change. His features twisted with grief as struggling for the words in description, swallowed hard, before saying, "In the front seat—they identified two blood types. A man and a woman, I'm not sure if it was verified, but I think we can all safely assume that it was obviously the girl's parents."

"In the blood and entrails on the floor of the back seat... they found a child's pink bow, clumps of blonde hair—," He stuttered and faltering briefly, said, "And several small, human teeth."

"Dear God in heaven..." Tim became sickly pale, as covering his mouth with both hands and sniffling, turned away and looked toward the window.

"No other evidence of their bodies was ever found. And believe me—it wasn't for lack of searching. I must have run that dog-crew all over that area for days. Nothing but blood... it was like everyone involved that night—had just vanished into thin air?"

"Is there any possibility that this Paul Brunner character might have murdered the family—and hidden the bodies?"

Shaking his head, Harry tapped his cigar into the ashtray, and without making eye contact, said, "No, I did some private background research on Paul character. He's so clean that he squeaks. Without doubt, he was definitely just a victim in this mess too."

Dropping the pen onto the pad and crossing my arms, I looked between my friends, and said, "Well, I don't know about the rest of you? But this little police investigation of yours is starting to look and sound a lot more like a monster hunt to me..."

"The weather is beginning to look pretty nasty out there, fella's." Linda approached our table, her fleeting glances all too obvious, as smiling, she said, "It's a good thing that I don't live too far away? All the same—I'd like to be getting home soon—if you boys are ready to settle up the bill?"

"I'll cover for everyone--," Harry gestured with a hand around the table, and said, "But I'd like one more coffee before you toss us out into that blizzard, if you wouldn't mind?"

"You got it sugar—I'll be back in a flash--," Gathering our empty plates, she looked about curiously, and asked, "Did anyone need anything else?"

"Just that coffee would be great." Harry spoke for all of us.

Waiting until after she had refilled our cups and left before saying anything, I finally looked back to Steve, and rather coyly, said, "You know, you really don't strike me as the type of person to allow anything to slip past, unnoticed..."

"No sir, I am most definitely not. That's why—when they finally released me from the hospital, and still in bandages, I went back out there with the dogs to have a look around."

"Released you, my ass," Harry scoffed, saying, "I heard that you left against doctors' orders."

"It doesn't matter, Harry." Steve's eyes narrowed as clenching his fists angrily, turned back to me, and said, "The fact remains the same—we searched that whole place from top to bottom for days…"

"Nothing, not even a print or sign of a single living thing--," Harry frowned, as finishing his coffee, said, "Come to think of it—it was so still that you could've heard a pin drop."

"No offence--," Nodding respectfully at Steve, I asked, "But what about your partner. Did the coroner find anything that might help identify his attacker?"

"No—they didn't." Steve interrupted, a sinister shadow darkening his features as he said, "His body was missing by the time other members arrived on the scene."

"Before we go, can I ask you both to do something for me?" Retrieving the notepad and tearing out several sheets, I slid them each a page, and said, "Without comparing, would both of you draw a sketch of what you think you might have seen? But please? Don't draw anything that you're not absolutely sure of—everything else can be scribbled or just left blank."

Reluctantly at first, they each took the page and leaning in such a way that neither could see the others rendering, immediately etched images.

"And if you wouldn't mind?" I added in thought, saying, "I would prefer that neither of you saw the others work until tomorrow. I'd like a chance to try to make some sense out of this—if it's possible."

Harry nodded, as flipping his page upside down and sliding it across the table, said, "That's the best that I could come up with. Like I told you before—I couldn't see a damn thing out there. So it might not help much."

"Same here–," Steve folded and offered me his drawing, saying, "It just all happened so fast. Christ—all I can remember is being crushed against that cold, hard surface."

"What?" The description sent a shudder the length of my spine, as turning back to the Sergeant, I said, "You never mentioned that before?"

"It just came to me now--," Gently rubbing at the scarred area of his stomach wounds, he said, "It was like being crushed against a frozen shell…"

A moment of stillness and Linda politely called from the counter. "I'm ready whenever you are?"

Intending to return Steve\s pad and pen, he insisted that I keep it. This saved me from tearing out all my notes, and presented a memento in meeting. Retrieving the pages from the table and neatly folding them, I slipped them into my pocket.

Gathering our belongings, in moments I wore the Parka that Harry had brought, and we all stood before the front counter.

"What good are those going to be?" Tim leaned close and inquired in less than a whisper.

"I'm not sure?" Butting my cigarette in an ashtray on the counter, I looked back to my friend, and said, "But you can't build a puzzle without pieces…"

CHAPTER EIGHTEEN

10:30 p.m.

There was a strange and lonely aura hanging over the little diner that night. Walking away and squinting through the blinding flurries, I watched as the lights blinked out. With exception to the tiny light above the door, and the flickering glow of the neon signs, the place looked utterly destitute. It reminded me of a tiny light-house, which swiftly fading into the fog, vanished upon some dark and distant shore. Parked directly beside Harry's Chrysler was Steve's brown and cream, 1971 Ford LTD sedan. Rather than using both vehicles, Harry had insisted that Steve travel with us while following Tim home in the coach.

"We picked a pretty lousy night to do this car trade—didn't we?" Harry cursed, as we slowly pulled away from the diner.

"It'll probably be just as bad—if not worse tomorrow?" My eyes burned in the sudden warmth of the car, and I worried that I'd caught a chill earlier.

"I guess you're right? But all the same--," He chuckled, and looking over his shoulder at Tim and Steve in the back seat, said, "You guys are both welcome to the couch's at my place."

"If it's all the same to you--," Tim appeared strangely nervous, and with his glasses still fogged from the cold, said, "I'd sooner get home. I don't like leaving the parlor empty for too long."

"Damn wipers--," Harry rolled down the power window, and brushing a hand across the freezing slush on the windshield, said, "I hate it when that happens!"

"At least I'm home for the night." I nodded toward the dim lights of the little hotel as the dark shape of the 1964 Hearse caught my immediate attention. Parked in the darkness beside my newer coach, it was barely visible through the falling snow. The long fins, high top and curved lines gave it an almost sinister appeal within comparison.

Suddenly remembering that we still needed to sign transfer of ownership documents, I looked into the back seat at Tim, saying, "I've got transfer papers in my bag—we should have done this at the diner, but it slipped my mind."

"We weren't expecting Tim so soon." Harry spoke in my defense, saying, "And besides, we can leave the paperwork until morning. Both cars are insured—and we're the only cops in town, anyway."

"Good enough." Tim thanked Harry, and pausing, said, "If you boy's want to go home I should be okay from here."

"Not a chance, amigo." Harry laughed, as looking out and into the flurries, turned in the front seat to look back at Tim, and said, "I know that you can manage, but with everything happening the way that it is around here, I'll feel better if we follow you home."

With a nod of thanks, Tim hurried out of the car and rushed over to my old hearse. In a sense I was sad to see Lilly leaving, but it was justified within a good cause.

"Thanks for coming out to be with us--," Harry leaned over the back seat to look at Steve, saying, "All things considered, I know that life has dealt you some pretty bad cards lately."

"I appreciate that—and the feeling's mutual." Steve frowned as looking out into the steadily growing flurries, he said, "With Lorna leaving me the way that she did, and me losing the house? Well, let's just say that between the hotels and endless motels, it's good to feel at home somewhere."

I looked into the back seat and sighing deeply, said, "It seems that we've all got a few things in common."

"We're just a bunch of lost souls traveling a lonely highway." Harry sighed, and looking back at Steve, said, "But hell—it'll be nice to have someone to play chess with. Maureen say's I cheat—so she won't play me anymore."

"In all the years that I've known you—I didn't know that you played chess?"

"Well, to tell the truth, I just started learning a few months ago--," Yawning and stretching his arms back, he said, "Lenny's been teaching me down at the service station on slow night. He's been showing me some new and fancy tricks." He gestured with his hands, motioning the moves as he said, "Some fancy switch-around thing that they do with the rooks—crossing them over and other such baloney."

The night suddenly became bright beside us as Tim, putting the coach into reverse, began slowly backing out.

"Anxious little bugger, isn't he?" Steve smirked.

Tim slowly eased the coach out, and cautiously moving out of our way, passed from behind, and through the deepening snow.

"It looks like he's playing with your radio." Harry snickered, pointing to where a light brightened through the rear window of the coach.

Tim had switched on an accessory light, and though we couldn't clearly see him, it was obvious that he was busy with something in the front seat.

"That won't get him too far. I doubt that he'll get much reception in all of this?" I suddenly remembered the *Ventures* eight track tape, flashlight, and bottle of Brandy that I kept in the back for emergency purposes.

"That reminds me? I still have a few things to clear out of there."

Following Tim from out of the motel lot, Harry peered over at me, and said, "I guess that's better that being put in there?"

"Good old, Harry, always quick with a joke!" Steve patted him on the shoulder, and looking into the storm, said, "This weather is looking worse by the minute."

We were two car lengths distance from Tim and already moving slower. It seemed that Harry had learned from our little incident earlier that day. All the same, I wasn't complaining.

In good conditions the drive would only take ten or fifteen minutes, but tonight, it was almost double that before we'd almost reached the parlor.

There was a sharp bend in the road, and as the tail0lights of the hearse disappeared into the turn, I saw something in the last second.

"Watch out!" Bracing for impact, I grasped the dash with both hands as something raced from out of the forest! Leaping over the tall drift, it sped across the road directly in front of us! In the headlights and with the heavy snowfall it was nothing but a blur. It traveled blindingly fast, passing between both cars before vanishing into the frozen night!

We drifted sideways as Harry, avoiding the use of the brakes, mastered the slide and corrected the vehicle's course with astounding expertise.

"That wasn't any deer! Steve was half-way into the front seat and staring wildly.

"I didn't even see the damn thing coming! What the hell was it?" He turned to me for an answer, and still gawking, asked, "Did you get a look at it?"

"No—I just saw something moving really fast through the snow."

My attention was immediately drawn to the steep embankment, and dark woodland surrounding the empty old road on either side.

"Well its long gone now--," Steve eased the shotgun back down onto his duffel bag, and said, "Whatever it was…"

The dim glow of the parlor lights brought our little convoy to an abrupt stop near the top of the driveway. Unwilling to chance getting stuck in the parking lot, Harry waited on the road as I climbed from the car and hurried after Tim.

Within the few minutes that it had taken to collect my belongings from the coach, and bid farewell, the heavy flurries had almost entirely covered our previous tracks. There had been very little discussion during the return voyage as Harry concentrated while cautiously navigating back through the deepening snow. Steve had drifted into a disturbed slumber, and the sounds of the pulsing wipers thundered in my thoughts. Glancing at my silent friend, I pondered the passing years in the lines of his wearied features. Time had not so much wrinkled his flesh, but etched and defined his character. It was mortality's way of baring the truth of the soul for all to see.

From the stern bridge of a hawk nose ran lines that revealed much laughter and many smiles. His brow had a depth of thought, the lines residing there expressing deep contemplation, and sincere concern. There was a type of kindness, that revealing courage of conviction read clearly within his face. My mind swam as the snowflakes reflected like billions of tiny stars in the headlights. The heat sending me into a fatigued delusion, imagining that we traveled the endless depths of space. It was so quiet—so cold, dark and seemingly empty. How could anything exist in that barren and bitter cold wilderness. Certainly nothing human…. I suddenly became aware of a burning pressure in my bladder, and squirming with the realization, watched for any sign of town.

"It'll just be a few minutes now, we're almost there." Noticing my discomfort, Harry gestured with a nod of reassurance, and said, "My bladder isn't what it used to be either."

In minutes we pulled in before the motel, and parking beside the hearse and before my room, Harry said, "I'll be around for you in the morning. Try to get some sleep—if you can?"

Glancing to where Steve slept soundly in the back seat and reaching for the door handle, I glanced back at Harry, "Do you really believe that there's some kind of monster out there somewhere?"

"Just don't go wandering around out there by yourself, okay?"

"Drive carefully." Gently patting at his shoulder, I climbed from the car and glancing back, said, "I'll see you for breakfast."

"Night friend…"

The icy wind whipped the fur collared hood against my face as I silently watched them depart. The old Chrysler slowly creeping through the deep and drifting snow, I waited until the tail-lights vanished into the blizzard.

"Oh geez–," I spun toward the door, and with my bladder threatening to explode from the pressure, fumbled with the keys. From behind I could hear the immense pines creaking and groaning as they swayed in the bitter gusts. Unlocking the door, something caused me to turn and look back into the darkness. The gusts whipped at the piling snow, drawing long and deep drifts from across the empty lot. Cringing before the door, I gazed wide-eyed into the icy wasteland beyond. The lamp-post swayed ever so slightly as long shadows crept from all sides. I couldn't see anything, but sensed that something now watched from the blackness of the forests edge…

With a racing heart, icy fingers and frost-coated face, I quickly hurried inside. Locking the door, I kicked off my boots and coat, and switching on the little lamp that stood beside the bed, rushed into the bathroom. During the few moments that I spent in the little room I detected a foul odor. It was the sour and lingering stench of death… Realizing that the stink from the funeral parlor had remained in my hair and skin, I quickly climbed into the shower. It took several thorough scrubbings with soap and hot water, but after a short time I was satisfied that the odor was gone. Stepping out, I caught the slightest scent from under the soap smell and thought about staying in that shower for a week…

In moments I had slipped into my favorite blue flannel pajamas, slippers, and black robe. Unsettled with the haunting sounds of the wind I had gone to the window, and parting the curtains ever so slightly, peeked out. Adjoining a main avenue of the little town the motel was on the far eastern edge, and was bordered on three sides by a vast forest. The location had provided privacy by being several hundred yards from the main business route, but now left me feeling vulnerable. The motel was virtually empty with exception to my hearse, the owners fifty-nine Buick Electra, and the forty-seven Dodge Desoto sedan belonging to the only other patron. The town was literally barren after dark due to the weather, and with exception to Gordon Farrell, the elderly owner, I was utterly alone.

Moving toward the door, I hesitated before unlocking and opening it just enough to see outside. Peeking from between the slight crack that I had permitted between the frame and door, I winced in the bitterly cold gusts. Watching the enormous flakes slowly spiraling downward, I perceived them as the ashen leaves of a pale oak that stood in death's, winter garden. The wind had faded but the snow continued… that huge, swelling white mass, engulfing and smothering all within its path. There were few words that could properly describe those forlorn, frozen, and desperate moments of silent despair.

Closing and locking the door I returned to the bed. In moments I was comfortably covered in blankets, and was quietly comparing the sketches that my companions had drawn. Harry's illustration resembled an oddly formed, fur covered, balloon, where twin stars, assumedly the eyes, appeared at the base.

"Now, what do you have going on here?" Carefully scrutinizing Steve's rendition of the creature, I turned the image around while examining it from different perspectives.

"It looks like an old tree stump? Were you somehow, caught up in the branches? A branch—that's possible. A branch might have broken—you did say that there was a lot of snow. If you were panicking, you could have imagined anything. Like they say—the eyes are only a mirror to the mind. It can only translate information according to previous experience, and known imagery. Which might explain these drawings—but then again? Maybe neither of you could draw a straight line without a ruler?"

How was it possible for both of them to have witnessed a single creature, and drawn two completely different images? In fact, the only real similarity was those eyes, those large and round, brightly glowing eyes.

"It might have been ice—yeah that might've done it? It could've been a reflection—maybe the headlights of one of the vehicles. That would make sense—two bright and glowing eyes. Maybe when Steve turned to run he was caught in some old branches. But those marks on his back and stomach were symmetrical. And even a dummy like me knows that there aren't two branches that are exactly alike. Okay Mike, just think for a moment—there must be a perfectly logical answer to all of this… something that nobody's thought of yet? Something simple… Aw hell—who am I kidding? If the damn police and trained professionals can't figure it out, then what chance do I have?"

My head ached, and the familiar sting of dust in my nasal passages brought on an immense sneeze. Hurrying into the bathroom and grabbing some toilet paper, I blew my nose, glancing down at my watch.

"Oh shoot—it's after midnight already? Knowing Harry, he'll be here bright and early. I'd better grab a little sleep while I can."

The door suddenly rattled in the frame, and I turned while feeling an icy gust. The door visibly shook, as the wind, forcing its way beneath, came through all the unsealed cracks and crevices.

"That's a flimsy and improperly sealed door." My attention was like-wise drawn to an old and very heavy looking bureau.

It had taken a considerable effort, but after sliding the sturdy old bureau across the room and pressing it tightly against the door, I stood back and smiled. The victorious grin swiftly fading while noticing the large window, and saying, "Well, that's just terrific. I've managed to block myself from escaping out the door, while leaving space for something to come in through the window…."

Snapping my fingers, I hurried across the room and toward the wardrobe. Like the bureau it was old and made of solid oak. It was quite tall, and though easily blocking the window, far heavier than anticipated… Setting about the task of slowly dragging the old wardrobe across the room, I groaned with the weight. It teetered dangerously, and after having almost dropped the monstrosity on myself several times, finally used a shoulder to force the antique against the window.

"Good enough. That should hold just fine!" I stopped as looking between the door and window, sighed and thinking aloud, said, "Besides, anything strong enough to get past that—could break through the door just as easily."

Shaking off the thought, I hurried toward the bed, and removing my robe, kicked off my slippers before slipping beneath the heavy comforter.

"Oh geez—I forgot the lamp." It was on the night-stand next to the bed and easy enough to reach. Yet, something halted me. I was feeling uncomfortable with the thought of being in the pitch-dark...

"It's not that bright ," Briefly admiring the dim yellow glow I shrugged, as squirming back under the covers, said, "I'll leave it burning—just for tonight."

The wind whistled, as rattling the pane of the small window above the kitchen table, caused me to sit up and look. It was a lot smaller than the main window, but still large enough for an average sized man to climb through...

"Oh for crying out loud—how could I have forgotten that too?" My eyes were glued to where the night crept in from between the inch-wide spaces on either side of the curtain. Although quite small, it was just enough space for someone or something to see clearly into the dimly lit room.

"I should at least close the curtains." Climbing from the bed and shivering in the chill, I looked over at the lamp, and reconsidering, said, "And on second thought—it might be better to turn out the lights? I can't see out there—but something might certainly see me... No need to get out of bed again..."

I had just reached over and switched out the light when something suddenly pounded against the window! Startled, I spun toward the source of the sound in the darkness! It was a dull thud, the type that you might expect to hear if a small bird flew into the pane...

A moment of silence and then it came again, only louder this time. The effort became more aggressive, brazen, as it now shook the little kitchen window.

All alone and someone or something is out there... It's testing the glass—and trying to find its way inside...

Ever so slowly I crawled out from beneath the covers, as cautious not to make a sound, reached for the bag beside the bed. Without taking my eyes from off that window, I reached into the doctor's bag. My fingers finding the weapon, I drew it out as gripping it tightly within trembling hands, silently slipped from off the bed.

Oh God—my hands are shaking so bad that I can hardly hold the damn gun! Steady man—calm down—you have to try to remain focused. It's your only chance…

Trembling uncontrollably, I slowly made my way across the room. Cautious of each step, and lingering in the deepest shadows, I slowly approached the window. Swallowing hard and gripping the revolver with a finger on the trigger, I slowly reached a trembling hand toward the curtain. The cold glow of the lamp-post shone through the gently falling snow, casting long shadows through the thin material. At first, I had aimed the weapon into the darkness and just below the pane. Then, reluctant to fire blindly, decided to take a stand and make every shot count. I steadied myself, and gathering what little courage that remained, slowly reached out. In a moment of sheer fright and adrenaline, I tore the curtains away from the window, and shoved the pistol into the face of the thing.

There was a deafening shriek as the weapon suddenly went off in my hand! The terrified wail of poor old Gordon Ferrell, as dropping to his knees, the glass exploded above his head.

"Oh my God—Oh no, I'm so sorry!" Rushing across the room and struggling with the heavy bureau, I threw the door wide open!

The old man still cringed in the deep snow beneath the window as while gripping his head with both hands. In bare feet, I went to his side and carefully drawing him upward, apologized in a stream of stutters and curses.

"I'm so sorry Mr. Ferrell—but I heard a sound and thought it might be a burglar--," Gently assisting the terror-stricken man, I hopped about in the deep snow while inspecting him for injuries.

It was as though he had been awakened from a bad dream and had suddenly come to life! Balling a fist and punching me straight in the nose, everything suddenly went black as dropping the revolver, fell backward and into the deep snow.

He was lean and a lot faster than I might ever have expected. An old prospector with white and wildly flowing hair, he gazed ominously down with steel grey eyes, and waving a fist, said, "You stupid bastard! You almost blew off my damned head!"

Cupping a hand over a painful and bloodied nose, I crawled back to my feet as dizzy, shouted back in anger, "Well—what the hell were you doing sneaking around under my window in the middle of the night?"

"Coons--," The old man tugged at his suspenders, and pulling up the collar of his winter-coat, pointed toward the edge of my doorway.

"I was throwing snow-balls at the raccoons. You must've left garbage or something out here—because the dang varmints were just going nuts at your door. I don't want them around here. Little shit-heads get into everything. Wreck stuff and piss all over the place. You ever smelled coon piss, son? It's nasty business, especially when they get into the rafters!"

It wasn't garbage that had drawn them, and I wasn't about to explain it to the old man either. He was already angry enough.

"Mr. Ferrell—I am so, so very, terribly sorry." Realizing that the fault had been entirely my own, I accepted his hand, and climbing back to my feet, said, "I really had no idea of what was happening."

Dusting the snow from off my shoulders, he grumbled, and eyeing me up suspiciously, asked, "You aren't going sue me--," He gestured toward my nose and squinting in the bitter wind, said, "For poking you one in the snoot, are you?"

Shaking uncontrollably in the bitter cold, we had looked each other over, and I said, "No sir—I had that one coming."
Picking up the revolver from where it had fallen in the snow, and offering it back to me, he said, "How about this? You forget the poke in the nose and I'll forget that you took a shot at me," Guiding me back into the room and closing the door behind us, he looked to me, and pointing an accusing finger in my face, growled, saying, "But you're sure as heck paying for the busted window."

"Of course—fair enough. Um, would it be possible to get a room a little closer to the office?"

"Well, seeing as this one's got a hole in it now, it not like you can stay here. Tell you what? I'll give you the room next to mine, but that old meat-wagon stays back here. Things are tough enough right now and I don't need you spooking my customers off."

"It's a deal."

"Alright then--," He turned back toward the door, and said, "Gather your goods and let's get you settled in again…"

Thursday January 4, 1973.
9:35 a.m.
Awakened by the sound of heavy pounding on the door, I rolled over and shoved the pillow before my face. My head felt like it was filled with rocks, and my mouth was so dry that I croaked while trying to speak, "Hang on a second—I'll be right there!"

Sluggishly moving from off the bed I pulled my robe closed, while blindly stumbling toward the door.

"Ouch—damn it!" I stubbed a toe against the bureau, as pulling it aside, groaned while opening the door. Although being directly beside the office, I'd still done a little re-arranging of the furniture before for bed.

"You know—when I gave you that gun it was supposed to be for self-defense--," Harry grumbled, as carrying a tray of Styrofoam cups filled with hot drinks, said, "Not shooting at the locals."

"It wasn't my fault. The old boy scared the daylights out of me last night, peeking in windows…"

"We heard." Steve gestured at the wardrobe, and taking a seat at the little table beneath the kitchen window, asked, "Did we miss something?

"You look like hell. This one's yours--," Harry pulled the cups out of the little card-board tray, saying, "Three hits of sugar and far too much cream."

"Perfect." I thanked him as sitting on the edge of my bed and looking back, said, "I hardly slept. I suppose that everything has got me jumping at shadows now?"

Grabbing my cigarettes from the night-stand I fumbled with the Zippo, almost dropping both in the process. It was apparent that my nerves had taken a real beating.

"You weren't the only one." Steve admitted, sipping at his coffee as he said, "I couldn't have slept more than three hours, altogether."

The telephone rang and startling all of us, I reached toward the night table and grabbed for the receiver.

"It's probably Tim." I answered, pausing to look at Harry before extending the receiver toward him, and saying, "It's for you?"

"Oh yeah—I told Barbara down at the office that I'd be over here."

He answered the call, the conversation brief, he handed the receiver back and frowning, said, "God have mercy—here we go again…"

"What's happening?" Steve began to move from his chair but Harry had halted him with a hand, saying, "It's not definite yet? But Marlene Keller didn't make it home from work last night. Her mom's calling around town right now." He paused, and rubbing at his eyes, said, "She's sixteen years old—and works for Lenny down at the gas station. She was on a late-shift, they close at nine. Being on the highway they're always hoping for a little extra traffic."

"Why wasn't it reported sooner?" Steve appeared angered.

"Being that late—and in such crappy weather--," Harry grumbled, and cursing under his breath, said, "They likely figured that she stayed with a friend. Either way, if her parents don't find her soon, Barb will call us back. The whole family and some of the neighbors are out searching for her right now. It's a small town, if we don't hear back from Barb in a few minutes we'll head out there."

"You would think that with the recent events--," Steve drew the curtain and suspiciously peering out the window, said, "That people would be more concerned about where there kids are at night?"

Harry looked over at me, and sighing deeply, said "You'd best be getting ready. Dress warm—it might be a long day?"

"Marlene Keller--," Butting the cigarette and pausing before the bathroom door, I turned to look back, and asked, "Her mother isn't Kathy Keller is she?"

"Yeah—she got knocked up by a mysterious stranger." Harry shrugged, and said, "So after she had the baby she stayed with her folks. They're all still living in the old homestead."

The thought of a missing girl had been bad enough, but Kathy had always been one of the nicest girls in school. It just didn't seem fair.

10: 25 a.m.

Parking at the service station and behind an old Dodge camper truck, we climbed out to greet the others that already stood waiting. It was a small gathering, but all carried rifles and looked anxious.

From behind the crowd, a man restraining three of the largest hounds that I'd ever seen struggled toward us.

"Its old reliable and his dogs--," Harry nodded at the man, saying "That's Gene Doherty—don't let the hounds spook you, they're regular sweeties when you get to know them."

Gene Doherty was a middle-aged man of medium stature. Dressed in Canadian military fatigues, a heavy green Parka, and sporting an excessively long mustache, he wore aviator style sun-glasses. His features were strong, his eyes blue, and a light brown pony tail hung from beneath his green beret. Upon his right hip rested a Smith and Wesson, 45 caliber, M1917 revolver. It was known for its use from World War 1 and even carried by the infamous 'tunnel rats' in Vietnam. On his left hip hung a short but sturdy machete', the bottom end of which was securely fastened with straps to his lower calf. There was absolutely no doubt in my mind that this man meant business, and was more than capable.

"Gene Doherty--," Harry motioned while introducing us, and said, "These are my friends, Michael Schreiber—and you remember Sergeant Steve Harris, of course."

"Yes sir--," Gene respectfully saluted, saying, "The incident from last November."

"Gene brought his dogs to the scene and assisted with the search." Harry informed me, as turning back to Gene, asked, "Did you manage to get something personal from the family, something that we can use to pick up her scent?"

Pulling a plastic bag from one of the large pockets of his parka, Gene reached inside, and producing a long pink gown, said, "Her Mom gave me this—it's her night-gown."

The chime of the service station bell had caused us all to turn. We were approached by an elderly man, who shaking off the cold, looked toward us expectantly. He was a large fellow and judging from the oil-stained blue cover-all's that he wore, was still doing his own mechanical work.

"Harry--," Extending a hand in greeting, he anxiously looked around the group, and asked, "What's happening—has anyone heard anything from Marlene yet?"

"No—not yet, Lenny--," Harry answered, biting down upon his lower lips as scanning the nearby highway, said, "But we're doing everything that we can."

Leonard Rosenberg was a kindly old soul. I still remembered him from his younger years. He'd provided job opportunities for many of the local teens and always supported the church and other community functions. Sadly, and even under the circumstances, I was a little disappointed that he hadn't recognized me.

Catching a flurry of movement in the corner of my eye, I looked over my shoulder, noticing the arrival of several vehicles and a sudden accumulation of people. The news was out and as was often the case, the entire community was now responding.

"A few quick questions--," Harry fumbled with his notepad in an icy gust, looking to Lenny, and asking, "Do you remember anything at all that might help us here? Maybe she mentioned meeting someone, possibly even a friend from out of town?"

"The weather was very bad--," Lenny thought briefly, his deep brown eyes filling with tears as trembling, and he said, "Oh Harry— I told her that she could go home around seven last night. But she wanted to stay."

I watched as the old man leaned past Harry to look down the road, and sniffled as he said, "It's so close—you can see her house from here. I thought that she'd be okay? I watched her walk out from here... Oh, merciful God in heaven—help us..."

"It's not your fault--," Harry reassured him, and asked, "Was there anything that she did different from other nights? Maybe she used the phone to call someone before she left?"

"No—she talked to her mother as usual." Lenny scratched at his bald head, and shrugging, said, "She called home to let her mother know that she was on her way. I do that with all the kids—just to be sure. You know that."

Harry nodded, squinting in the bitter wind as he said, "Of course you do, and I remember. I worked here for over the summer when I was seventeen, remember?"

"Well, how about that." Lenny's eyes brightened although it was quite apparent that he couldn't recall that far back.

"So she left at seven." Harry paused while obviously double-checking the accuracy of the old man's information and memory.

"No—she stayed until--," He looked in the window at the old clock as though uncertain, and then nodding, looked back at Harry, and said, "It was nine." Lenny put a finger to his lip in thought, and then nodding, said, "Yes nine, I remember, because I was standing right here. I watched her walk up the road. I watched until she disappeared into the snow—into the dark..."

"Don't worry, Lenny—we'll do everything that we can to find her." Harry gently patted the old man's shoulder and turning, pointed a finger at Gene, and asked, "Is Wayne on the other end?"

"Yeah—he's on his way to the Keller place with his hounds. I just talked to him on the station telephone about fifteen minutes ago."

"Well—if everyone's ready?" Harry's drawn features faded into shadow as the sun disappeared behind dark clouds, and he said, "Let's get out there and find her..."

No sooner had Gene waved the night-gown before the snouts of those immense hounds, than did they start baying, and surge forward with certain purpose! My heart leapt into my throat as the desperate chase began.

The little service station lay on the far western edge of town from where the main road became the highway. Being on the opposite side of town and from where I was staying, it was also bordered on either side by the forest. Crossing to the south-western side of the highway and following the hounds ever westward, I had glanced at both Steve and Harry, but they had taken little notice. Staring straight ahead their expressions were cold reflections of uncertainty and morbid desperation. I already knew that they were expecting the worst... Without even thinking I suddenly looked up the road, accounting for the distance and every little detail in between. I had been making notes through-out the experience, as compiling material for a new story, now absorbed all and any pertinent information.

There was a tall fence-post with a flood-light that marking the end of their driveway, was less than sixty yards away from the station. Is this what she'd seen in those final and desperate moments? In the pitch-dark and in the middle of that blizzard, the light might have seemed much closer than it actually was. The thought had barely concluded when Gene cried out! Then losing his balance as the hounds veered sharply from off the highway, he was dragged into a deep embankment.

"Hold on! Keep going!" Harry shouted while following the struggling Gene who still desperately clung to the leashes. With the dogs pulling him head-long through the knee-deep snow, he was literally dragged toward the forest.

My heart thundered as my mind was swimming through an icy and fear-filled delirium. I fought back the sting of tears while envisioning the terrified girl, as helpless and alone, she had stumbled blindly through the storm with the devil close at her heels!

The blizzard winds and snow-drifts may have covered what-ever tracks she had left during the night, but the burning scent of fear still lay heavy in the air. It was like a strange static electricity, a terrifying excitement that drove us all onward.

Choking and coughing on the freezing air I fought to keep up. Years of smoking and a poor diet now strained heavily on my lungs, ligaments, and every aching and burning muscle. We had barely entered the forest, passing several small pines and coming into a wide clearing, when everything came to a sudden stop.

"There!" Harry pointed ahead as gasping for breath, shouted, "There's something over there!"

Gene stumbled as fighting to catch his breath, stopped in a small clearing and motioning with a hand, called back to us, saying, "In there! I can see something—in there, by the big tree!"

There was an utter stillness as the baying and whimpering of the hounds suddenly ceased. All that remained was the steady pounding of my heart, and the lonely whisper of the cold wind in the ancient pines.

"I can see something! Yeah—it looks like a piece of clothing!" Gene pointed into the sparse brush, grabbing the whistle that hung from around his neck, and shoving it into his mouth.

"No--," Harry grabbed at his wrist, slowly shaking his head, and saying, "Not yet, let's make sure about this first."

I followed after Harry and Steve, struggling through the knee-deep snow as Gene waited with the dogs. My lungs burned and the bitter cold gnawed at my fingers and face, but desperation drove me onward.

"It's a scarf alright." Steve cursed, directing our attention to where it lay partially buried beneath the snow, and near the foot of an immense pine

I could hear the crazed baying of Wayne's hounds as the hunters were getting closer. The idea of seeing Kathy Keller again had caused icy butterflies in my stomach. But the thought of finding her daughter buried under that drift? Well, there just aren't words to explain the horror that I was feeling. Inhaling deeply, I struggled with the fear and nausea.

I could see the pink scarf in the snow-drift and watched as the wind tossed it from side to side... It was almost as though it wanted to be found. It's just a scarf—someone could have lost it? It could have been blown here in those frozen gusts... Please God—don't let it be whatever's left of that little girl... Please... Scowling while taking a long pull from his cigar, Harry looked to Steve, and quietly said, "The rest must be—underneath the snow." He moved toward where the material breached the snow's surface and pausing briefly, reached down while gently tugging at the pink scarf. My eyes bulged as it pulled free and Harry stepped back, staring down at the thing in his hand. I couldn't see what had happened and then turning, he waved the scarf, calling back and saying, "Nothing—there's nothing here?"

Dropping to his knees in the deep snow, Steve began digging with his hands, pleading as he said, "She has to be here, somewhere. Where else could she have gone?"

One of Gene's hounds suddenly tore loose as baying wildly, it charged through the deep snow and directly toward where we stood. Thinking the beast to have suddenly gone mad, Steve leapt back and drawing his revolver, stepped defensively before me.

Racing passed where we stood, the animal began leaping and howling at the base of the gigantic pine.

"I've got him!" Steve waved at Gene, as hurrying forward and taking the hound's leash, he suddenly looked back at us, and startled, said, "You guys might want to come over here and have a look at this?"

A moment later and we all stood and stared. Our eyes fixed on the lower portion of the tree trunk.

"There's no way that a man could have done that...." I spoke out of thought rather than intending to voice my opinion, and looking to Harry, said, "Or any animal that I've ever seen..."

Peering upward at the torn and mangled trunk of the pine, Harry closely examined the splintered bark, running a hand across the long and deep gouges.

"Well—whatever the hell it was?" He looked high into the branches, and almost whispered as he said, "It was sure trying to climb this tree for some reason?"

The lower trunk of the tree had been almost entirely stripped of its bark. The branches were broken, splintered away, and it bore huge gouges as though some immense claw had gripped, and then torn at it. Pulling a napkin out of his coat pocket and wiping the sap from his fingers, Harry shook his head, saying, "Whatever it was? It was real heavy and one powerful son-of-a-bitch. Those gouges in the trunk—they must be ten inches long and five inches deep?" He thought for a moment, as pulling off his hat and wiping the sweat from his brow, said, "Not even the biggest Grizzly could do that…"

"Hey watch out guys!"

I had heard Gene's warning but it had come far too late. The world suddenly becoming dark as I was crushed downward by an icy wave from above! The combined weight of the mixed ice and snow had buried, and left us all cursing and struggling to escape Burrowing our way free of the frozen down-fall, we scrambled away from the huge tree. Gathering as we turned to look back, Harry dusted the snow from out of my hood.

"Now where do you think that came from?" Stepping back, Steve raised a hand, as shielding his eyes from the mid-day sun, stared high into the branches.

"What the hell is that?"

Before I could even react, he shoved the dog's leash into my hand, and scrambling through the broken branches, began climbing the old tree. The sun momentarily escaping the clouds, blinded and obstructed all view while reflecting from off the snow.

"Watch it!" Harry pulled me aside as huge drifts of ice and snow fell, and our friend vanished into the dense branches somewhere high above.

The sounds of Wayne's dogs and excited voices caused me to look back. An immense crowd was now gathering as Wayne's search party now collided with the clamor of the swiftly arriving town's people. It looked more like a lynch mob than a concerned community, but at this point I really couldn't blame them. Someone would have to account for these events.

"Aw—dammit! That's all that we needed now!" Harry moved back toward the crowd, and waving with open hands, shouted.

"Please stay where you are! We need this area quarantined for police investigation!"

Heedless they flowed forward, halting abruptly as a gun-shot ripped through the chill.

"You all heard him people!" Gene held the smoking revolver high above his head, and looking toward the others, calmly said, "We know how important this is to everyone—and we all love her. But if you all disturb this area, it'll ruin our only chance of finding out what happened here. Now—do you all want that?"

There was a moment of confusion before retreating between curses, grumbles, and tears of frustration, the crowd started to back off and disperse.

"Thank you—please return to your homes. The Sherriff will let you know what's happening just as soon as this is figured out!"

Harry winked at Gene who lowering the revolver, tipped his beret before slipping the weapon back into its holster.

"Harry—call for an ambulance!" Steve bellowed from somewhere high above. His voice piercing and shrill, as gasping and out of breath, he cried out, "Get a God-damn ambulance here, now!"

Ripping the hand-radio free from where it hung on his belt, Harry began desperately switching through fields of static. With the sun disappearing behind the clouds I looked up and into the branches.

"I'm almost down!" Steve called, as sliding between the branches and almost falling, dropped safely into the deep snow. Held securely within his arms was the girl. With her arms wrapped tightly about his neck, and her face buried into the warmth of his coat, he now ran toward us.

"Oh, thank God." I looked away, sniffling as leaning into Harry I fought back the emotions.

"My baby—oh my God—Marlene!" A middle-aged woman burst from out of the crowd, and weeping hysterically, ran and fell into Harry's open arms.

"It's going to be okay, Kathy." He reassured the terrified woman, holding her close and patting her on the back. In that moment he had turned and glanced over at me. I saw the lost look in his eyes and knew that we were now hunting a monster...

It seemed like an eternity since I'd last seen her. I recognized Kathy immediately, but in the panic and ensuing confusion she'd passed me without a second look.

She was still the same tall and somewhat lanky, short-haired, brunette. Under different circumstances I might have felt some kind of nostalgia. Yet, all things considered, I could only swallow the guilt of being grateful that she hadn't noticed me.

Harry hugged the tearful woman, as assisting her into the ambulance with her daughter, stepped back as with lights and sirens blaring, they raced off.

There was no victory for us that day, as suffering from severe frostbite, no one knew if the girl would even survive the night…

2:45 p.m.

Ordinarily I always loved desserts. But, as I sat there picking at the warm apple pie and watching the melting ice cream, all that I saw was endless snow…

Leaning back in the booth, I looked across the table at Steve and Harry, and asked, "So, is there any word yet, on how she's doing?"

Steve looked up from where he had been indulging a big pancake breakfast, and wiping syrup from his lips, said, "The doc said that she's lost most of her fingers and toes, and will need some facial reconstruction due to soft tissue damage. She's still in shock from being up in that tree all night. So she'll have to stay in the hospital for some time still…"

Sliding the pie away and lighting a cigarette, I looked between my friends, and said, "When you brought her down from that tree. You mentioned her saying something about—coyotes, or wild dogs?"

"Not exactly--," Harry broke from his trance, as clearing his throat and reaching for his coffee, said, "All that she said, was that on her way home, she'd seen shining eyes. Eyes that she figured might've been coyotes. It scared her bad enough that she'd ran—that's how she ended up in the top of that old tree."

"Correct me if I'm wrong?" I tapped an ash, and leaning back in the booth, scrutinized my friends before saying, "But aren't animal eyes just reflective? I mean—they don't actually glow without a direct light source, right?"

"Mike—before you even start?" Harry growled, and turning to look at Steve, said, "I'm pretty sure that we all have our own opinion on what might have happened out there? And it certainly wasn't coyotes, wild dogs, bears, or any damn snow-plow."

Dropping his fork on the plate Steve wiped at his mouth with a napkin, and said, "Those marks on the tree weren't made by man, animal, or machine. She said that she's heard barking? Well—we all know that dogs bark—not coyotes. She was in shock, and I could barely understand anything that she was saying."

"What if the barking dog had nothing to do with what went after her?" I stared from out of a stream of cigarette smoke, and looking between my friends, said, "What if—whatever that thing is? It was climbing that tree to go after the girl—then settled for a dog instead?"

"Well—we never found any damned dog." Harry grumbled as re-lighting his cigar, pointed an accusing finger at the window, and said, "The only thing that I know for sure? Is that whatever the hell this thing is? I'm going to kill the bastard and hang its sorry ass on my trophy wall."

Noticing the snow growing steadier by the minute I felt the bottom drop out of my stomach, and looking to Harry, said, "And we also know that it's a climber…"

"Or not--," Harry stirred cream and sugar into his coffee, and said, "It sure didn't have much luck getting up that tree."

"Don't be too sure of that." Steve muttered as licking maple syrup from his thumb, raised a finger in thought, and said, "Maybe Mike has a point? Keep in mind that we weren't there—and there could've been extenuating circumstances?"

"What kind of extenuating circumstances?" Nervously tapping my fingers against the coffee mug, I squirmed in the seat. It seemed that the chicken salad sandwich and fries that I'd had for lunch weren't sitting too well.

"Well—like you'd said" He pondered before saying, "What if— the animal, or whatever it is, was interrupted, or somehow disturbed in the process of going after the girl?"

"We can rule out people or cars--," Harry looked around the empty diner, saying, "No one's ever out that late around here and besides, with all the snow, the highway's been pretty much empty."

"What about the dog?" Taking a long pull from the cigarette I burped up something acidic, and excusing myself, said, "You said that she'd heard a barking dog. Maybe we should look into that, somehow? If that thing got a hold of someone's dog, there's no way that animal made it home that night either."

"Which means--," Steve raised an eyebrow, and said, "There's a missing dog out there that's been gone since last night."

"We need to ask around and see if anyone is missing a dog." Harry agreed, saying, "It shouldn't be that tough. Most of the cats and dogs went missing around here a few months ago…"

The little bell above the diner door rang. The place having been basically abandoned due to the weather, curiosity had caused us all to turn and look.

"Tim." I was both surprised and pleased to see him.

"Hello again--," He nodded, as stamping the snow from his boots, hurried over and sliding into the booth beside, asked with a certain sense of urgency, "I heard about the Keller girl—how is she doing?"

"She's alive but suffering from extreme frostbite—," Steve quietly informed Tim, and said, "Even if she makes it she's never going to be the same…"

"Oh my God…"

"How did you manage to find your way back here in all that snow?" Harry asked while curiously peering out into the parking lot as the door-bell rang;

"Smitty and Blake gave me a lift. Their tow-truck's the next best thing to a plow."

Simon aka "Smitty" and 'Blake Blanchard' were brothers and new-comers to Hedley. Although they had rescued us from the snow-bank outside the cemetery, I didn't trust them as far as I could see them.

Smitty was the elder by several years. Short, over-weight and unshaven, his laughter echoed madness and his behavior was even worse. His brother Blake was taller, gaunt, not the brightest bulb in the batch, and strangely quiet.

Dark haired and brown eyed they were easily identified as having been related. In fact, I suspected that their parents may have been as well. The pair were dressed poorly, covered in grease stains, motor oil, and other, thankfully, unidentifiable filth.

"Good morning to you all." Smitty snickered, as tugging at the visor of his black baseball cap, curiously looked back at our table, and asked, "Say Harry, are you fella's having any luck with those disappearances?"

"Not as much as we'd like to be--," Harry butted his cigar, and peering over at the two brothers, said, "But things are slowly coming together. Why, do you boys have something on your mind?"

Turning on the stool where he sat beside Blake at the counter, Smitty promptly said, "As a matter of fact—yes I have." His upper lip became tense, but that ugly grin never left, as he said, "Something broke into our freezer last night—and made off with almost half a buck."

"Where do they live?" Steve looked to Harry in question.

"An old ranch along the highway—about a mile and a quarter West of the service station," Harry muttered, as turning to look back at Smitty, asked, "Do you have any idea of when it might've happened? Was it early evening, late night?"

"Seems to me--?" Smitty scratched at the stubble upon his cheek, his shifty and dark eyes rolling as he thought, and said, "Things were just fine when we went to bed. Guess it must've been after eleven some time? Yeah–," He snapped his fingers, saying, "Because I stayed up to watch the news, so it had to be after eleven. But it was before twelve. That's when we got woken up by the noise and went outside."

Sipping at his coffee, Steve leaned back in the booth, crossing his arms over his chest and staring suspiciously, asked, "Why didn't you report the theft last night?"

"Well, that's what I'm doing, right now." Smitty appeared increasingly aggravated, as cursing under his breath, said, "The buck was payment for some work that we did—and was our winter meat. I don't have any bills or receipts for that—so it isn't like I can prove anything."

"It's alright, Smitty, I'll take your word for it." Harry slowly nodded, his eyes narrowing as he asked, "Did you find any foot-prints?"

"Hell no—snowed all night. Everything got covered up--," Blake finally spoke up, his voice sounding more like a whine than a rant, and he said, "And the jack-ass tore the living hell out of our freezer. It isn't worth a shit now, just more scrap."

"Have a little respect Blake—we're in the company of a lady." Smitty noticed Linda at the counter, and gesturing with a hand, looked at his brother and said, "Keep a civil tongue in that head—or I'll knock it off for you," He cuffed at his brother's ear, turning and shrugging apologetically as he said. "Sorry about that people--," He jeered at his brother before peering back at me, and saying, "Sometimes he's a little dense—dumb fucker."

"Alright—I'll make a note of this." Harry promised, as documenting the incident and time into his notepad, looked back at them, and said, "If you boy's should happen to notice anything else? Anything strange, please let us know, right away."

With a nod, and grinning mischievously, he leered up at Linda who served them coffee. She was polite, but it was obvious by her expression that she would have much rather been somewhere else. Anywhere else…

"Do you think that the incidents might be related?" Uncomfortable, Steve moved around on the set beside Harry while adjusting the holster on his hip. I noticed that it was unusually longer and unlike the standard .38 caliber police issue. It was a Remington .44 Magnum, a virtual hand-cannon.

"I'm not sure—but I'd like to have a look at the freezer before we start assuming things." Harry nodded as Linda poured fresh coffee, his eyes following her away from the table before he said, "On the bright side, if it was related, at least its sticking to the main highway and not coming into town, yet."

He said it as though he was expecting it to happen, and my gut-instinct was telling me the same thing…

"This whole town is built along the highway--," Tim muttered from under his breath, reminding him, and saying, "And in case it failed to catch your attention, Harry?" He leaned very close, and speaking in a whisper, said, "If the Keller girl was chased by our suspect shortly after midnight?"

"It would've been impossible for it to have been at the Blanchard place at the same time." Harry grumbled, and nervously tapping a finger against his mug, said, "I know… that's what's bothering me…"

Looking at his watch, Steve shook his head, and said, "If it had been our suspect? It would have had to travel almost seven miles through deep snow, during a blizzard, in less than ten minutes."

"That's sounding very familiar--," I peered fearfully between my friends, and said, "Isn't it?"

"What if we're dealing with more than one here?" Tim said what we had already been thinking. The expressions said enough without anyone having to speak. It was apparent that we all suspected and feared the same thing.

Startled as Blake squawked as Smitty elbowed him at the counter, I cast a nonchalant glance in their direction.

Slapping Smitty back, Blake complained in a high-pitched whine, saying, "Hey—keep your dirty fingers out of my coffee, Smitty!"

They slapped and poked at each other like children. It was ridiculous and yet pathetically amusing at the same time.

Sliding his empty plate across the table Steve turned back to Harry, asking, "So where do we go from here, Harry?"

Harry spoke quietly, as appearing at a complete loss, said. "I'm not exactly sure at the moment? No one's seen anything—and even if they had, the snow keeps covering up the evidence... I'm beginning to think that unless Marlene recovers, and can tell us something, that we're out of luck..."

Leaning closer to the window to look out into the parking lot, my attention was drawn to the Blanchard's late model, Ford tow-truck. It wasn't so much the state of the vehicle itself, but that huge, low and rusty old bumper... If the incident with Connie had truly been a 'hit and run' I would've suspected them a lot faster than poor old Lenny...

"You boys have a good day—and happy hunting!" Smitty shouted from across the room, as laughing, he shoved the stumbling Blake out the door ahead of him.

"Smitty--, Harry waved and catching him at the door, said, "I'd like to have a look at that freezer of yours."

"Sorry, we scrapped it this morning." Smitty snapped his fingers and made a tossing gesture from over his shoulder, saying, "It's like Blake told you, after last night it wasn't worth shit."

"Alright then, you boys just be careful out there. And remember what I told you. If you see or hear anything strange, call us right away."

"You got it, boss." Smitty winked, and aiming an imagined finger revolver at us, pulled the trigger with a laugh, saying, "You have yourselves a good afternoon, gentlemen."

Watching as he went out, and began running around their truck while throwing snow-balls at each other, I realized they were little more than children. Yet, for some reason, I just couldn't stop looking at that huge and rusted old bumper and wonder if those reddish stains were only rust.

"It couldn't have been them." Harry jabbed at me with an elbow as if having read my thoughts, and said, "They were hanging around at the gas station the day Connie went missing."

"They lost their parents to a house-fire three years ago." Steve explained, saying, "And used what little money they had left to buy that tow truck and get settled here. Their house is old and barely livable and old Lenny feels sorry for them. He buys them dinner and feeds them free coffee and donuts. They do pick-ups on the highway and other work for him. So, as bad as they may seem, they're darn good mechanics and they're always willing to help out."

Noticing my expression of surprise and appearing a little guilty, Harry shrugged, and smirking, said, "I took the liberty of asking Steve to check them out for me. That way they wouldn't have any hard feeling if they found out I was asking questions."

"Alright then, I won't feel bad for being suspicious of them."

"Mike, if they accidentally hit some girl on the highway, I wouldn't put it past them to get scared, and try to cover it up." Harry stirred additional sugar and cream into his coffee and looking up at me, said, "But, they've got a perfectly solid alibi. Not to mention the fact that they don't have the brains of a squirrel between them." He looked out the window as slipping in the snow, Smitty fell and his brother jumped on top of him.

"Sure, they may be a little dirty and rough around the edges." Steve agreed, as looking out and laughing as Smitty shoved a glove-full of snow into his brother's face, he said, "But they don't have criminal records and never cause any trouble around here."

First impressions having been bad I could clearly see and understand what they meant.

"Gene just showed up--," Harry motioned with a finger at the window, saying, "And it looks like something's got his feathers ruffled?"

When the door opened and Gene stepped inside, the intense look in his eyes spoke volumes. He looked like he'd just witnessed the end of the world.

"Harry--" Rushing toward our table and wild-eyed, he was trembling but managed to remain calm, and speaking quietly, said, "Can I talk to you alone for a second?"

"Speak your mind--," Harry reassured him, waving a hand around the table and saying, "Don't worry, we're all in this together."

"Okay, any of you boys—," Gene squatted at the tables edge, and looking between us, visibly shook as he said, "Ever seen that big old Irish wolfhound that Marlene's mother owns?"

"What, Viking?" Looking around the table Harry scoffed, and nodding, said, "I sure have. Who could miss him—he's big as a horse."

"Well, I just found what's left of him."

"What's left of him?" Harry's jaw dropped.

"I took my hounds back out there today—after everyone left." Gene accepted coffee and a chair from Linda, and waiting until she had left before speaking again, said, "I found old Viking about a hundred yards, north-east of where we found Marlene. He was torn up real bad. My hounds wouldn't go anywhere near him."

"The snows getting worse--," Steve grabbed for his coat, and intending to slip out the booth, said, "We need to go back out there—and take a good look at the dog."

"There's no need--," Gene coughed, as holding his mug with trembling hands and sipping at the steaming coffee, said, "I figured that you boys might want to have a look at him, so I brought him back with me. He's outside—I've got him wrapped in a tarp in the back of my truck."

Grabbing at Harry's shoulder while he tried to move out from the booth, Steve insisted, saying, "Harry wait, think about it for a moment. You do not want to open that package outside of this damn diner."

"He's right, Harry--," Gene's eyes were huge as shaking his head, said in warning, "You really don't…"

"Listen, I need a ride back anyway--," Looking across the table at Harry, Tim said within suggestion, "We could take it back to the parlor where we can examine it properly and in private. I've got the facilities and the right equipment there."

A young family with two little children entered the diner, and as the bell rang from above the door, Steve stared back at Harry in horror.

"Let's finish up here and get over to the parlor before dark…" It hadn't taken long for Harry to make the decision.

CHAPTER NINETEEN

Versailles Funeral Parlor
4:15 p.m.
The loading bay was cold and the stench of death still lay heavy. With little time and another blizzard building at the back door, we quickly set about the grim and ghastly task.

"It must've been one hell of a battle." Gene stepped away from the gurney as Tim tore the canvas away from the huge animal's frozen corpse.

"Well, I think that we know where that barking that Marlene heard was coming from?" Steve surmised, as looking to Harry, cursed and said, "It probably saved her life…"

"Whatever he was fighting must've been one huge mother?" Nervously shoving a stick of gum into his mouth, Gene just stared down at the corpse, and quietly said, "I've never heard of a big dog like this losing to anything short of a grizzly."

Rolling the overhead lamp close to the gurney and switching it on, Tim stepped away as we were all momentarily blinded.

"Oh—oh God, no…"

His reaction hadn't quite registered until I saw the thing on the gurney. I say thing because it wasn't immediately recognizable? What remained of that poor animal was nothing more than a mass of fur covered, mangled flesh, broken and protruding bones.

"Jesus H. Christ--," Harry shoved a hand before his mouth and gasping to catch his breath, said, "It looks like the poor bastard got caught in a hay baler—got chewed up and spit out…"

"If you'd seen the spot where I dug him out--," Gene chewed feverishly at his gum, his eyes flashing between Harry and the corpse as he said, "It was so dense you couldn't have gotten a skidoo in there… I had to drag him…"

An eerie mist began rising from off the frozen body as it thawed from beneath the heat of the bright lights. There was a musky scent of wet fur, the sour stench of exposed fat, and the disgusting odor of feces spilling from out of torn intestines.

"Are you okay?" Gently grasping at my shoulder, Harry reached into his breast pocket for a fresh cigar, and said, "If you need to— just step out for some air."

"No—but thanks… I'll be fine in just a moment…"

"Just as I thought--," Tim tapped a scalpel at the base of a femur bone, his features paling within observation, as he said, "It's the same as what we saw with Connie and Shirley." Forcing the broken femur downward with a hand, he pointed a scalpel within the broken fragments of the bone, saying, "As you can plainly see, the bone has been literally, crushed apart…"

Grabbing a long Q-tip from his assortment of embalming tools he shoved it inside the broken bone. A moment of swabbing and retracting the Q-tip, he raised it before us, and said, "It's completely dry. Something has sucked all the marrow out of these bones."

Gene moved closer, his eyes widening as he looked up at Harry, and asked, "What is he saying about Shirley and Connie? And what the hell kind of an animal does a thing like that?"

I suddenly realized that Gene hadn't been informed of the recent developments.

"I didn't trust the coroner's results. So I asked Tim to do a little checking for me." Lighting a cigar and stepping away from the gurney, Harry said, "We still don't know what did it—but the test results are the same on all the bodies. Whatever killed old Viking was also responsible for Connie and Shirley's deaths…"

The look of absolute horror in Gene's eyes was almost indescribable, and at one point, almost choked on his gum.

"If it hadn't been for this animal--," Removing his plastic gloves and tossing them into a waste basket, Tim sadly looked down upon the corpse, and said, "We'd likely be looking at Marlene right."

A sudden anger flushed Gene's face, as looking wildly about the group, he said, "When it comes time—I want a piece of the dirty bastard that's done this…"

"You'll get your chance." Harry took a long pull from the cigar and wincing at the sight of the thawing dog, said, "We all will…"

"We already know that these weren't isolated incidents--," Staring down at the mangled remains of the dog and visibly horrified, Steve, said, "And likely won't be the last before we get this thing."

"We'd better get going before we all get snowed in here." Harry motioned toward the partially open bay doors, saying, "We can't seem to get a damn break from anything."

"Before you leave--," Looking between us in a rather desperate plea, Tim pointed and asked, "Would you please remove and dispose of the carcass…"

"Sure thing—I'll bury him out on my farm," Gene quietly agreed, and looking to the steaming remains under the bright lights, said, "Its best that Kathy and Maureen never find out—or ever have to see this, anyway…"

Hedley Diner
7:35 p.m.

The greasy fried chicken dinner that I managed to choke down was now sitting in my guts like a lead weight. It wasn't that I'd actually even had an appetite. I was just feeling unusually weak, and was obligated to add a little fuel to the proverbial furnace. The four of us sat around like lost souls, picking at apple pie a la mode, and watching the blizzard from beyond the window. There was a distinct sense of helplessness, and we were all just waiting for something to happen. I had a feeling that we wouldn't be waiting long…

Terrified of being alone that night, Tim had returned to the diner with us. Although he hated leaving the parlor unattended, there were worse things to be concerned about. Under the circumstances I really couldn't blame him.

Tossing his fork down on the plate and sliding the half eaten pie away, Steve cursed, and said, "It's so hard to just hang around here waiting for the next thing to happen. I feel like we're all just sitting ducks…"

"At the moment there's not a damn thing else that we can do."

Harry was right, but I felt the same way about things as Steve.

"Are you spending the night on my couch?" Harry asked Tim but was kindly offering.

"He can take the room next to mine at the motel--," I suggested and thinking for a moment, said, "I doubt that we'll get much sleep. We can sit up late and watch television."

"That sounds great—we can catch something on the Late Show." Appearing pleased with the idea, he soon nodded in agreement, saying, "That's exactly what I'll do."

"I was looking through the TV Guide last night. There's a good old horror film playing after midnight." He suddenly stared into oblivion, saying, "It's another one of those cheesy 50s horror flicks… about space-aliens terrifying a small town…"

"Maybe we'll just play cards…" I suddenly lost all interest in watching television.

"Well, with this weather being the way that it is—I doubt that anyone or anything will be doing much tonight." Steve just stared as while appearing to have some dark fascination with the storm. I suspected that it reminded him of that fateful night on the highway.

"Lenny's going to have a busy night--." Harry grumbled as shoving a fork-full of ice cream and pie into his mouth, spoke between gulps, saying, "Let's just hope and pray that he doesn't turn up missing next."

"Oh no—that just reminded me!" Tim cursed, as slapping a hand to his forehead and appearing desperate, looked to me and said, "I forgot poor old Merlin in the cleaning closet the other night. It's freezing down there and he hasn't eaten in days…"

Steve appeared horrified with the cruelty. "What on earth would possess you to lock a defenseless animal in a damn closet?"

"Believe me—you don't want to know." Harry looked a little green around the gills.

"I'll go back with you." The thought of traveling in that snow bothered me, but not half as much as leaving the animal to freeze to death.

"To be honest—I just can't keep him any longer… I'm just too forgetful and don't have the time." I knew what Tim was going to suggest even before he said it.

"Is there any chance—that you might consider taking him?"

"Well, you do live alone—and the little stinker seems to like you" Harry shrugged and appearing rather amused, smiled as he looked over curiously, and said, "I'm sure that if you bleach the little bastard a few times and keep him inside, that it wouldn't be so bad?"

"You know what Harry?" I pointed a finger at him from across the table, and frustrated for being put on the spot, said, "I just might do that!"

"Oh, thank you! You don't know how much I appreciate this--," Tim gasped in relief and hurriedly finishing his coffee, said, "You know what? I've even got one of those fancy kitty-cat carrying cases. So it won't be any trouble at all."

"I'll call and have Lenny lead you down in his plow." Harry offered, saying, "It might take you a little while, but you'll be safe there and back again."

"Oh, and make sure to call us the moment you arrive back at the motel--," Steve insisted, saying, "I know that I don't need to remind you, but the snow isn't the worst thing going on out there…"

"And you know me--," Harry agreed, saying, "You don't want to get me worried and worked up, or I'll come looking for you…"

"We'll go straight there and back again--," I promised, saying, "Don't worry—what could possibly go wrong?"

Nothing was said, but the expressions that were exchanged would have been a mouthful, to say the least.

8:40 p.m.

The old hearse started on the first attempt and Harry just shook his head as we backed out, and began pulling away.

Lenny had already begun plowing the route to the funeral parlor, and to Tim's shock and amazement, we had no trouble with his old coach, whatsoever. The lights worked, wipers fought off the blizzard, and we were soon comforted in the streaming heat.

"I'm not complaining—but if I love to be a hundred I'll never understand this car." He was visibly disappointed.

"Don't bother yourself with the little things—we've got enough real trouble to be concerned about right now. Besides, you've got a new model now—so won't ever have to worry about this one again."

Satisfied with the thought, he slipped back into the seat and fell silent. In that moment I couldn't help but smile. Even through the horror of it all, something good had come of our reunion, and I was glad that we were friends again.

Lenny had traveled slow and steady and it had taken almost thirty minutes to reach the parlor. The storm showed no signs of letting up, and as Lenny pulled away, I was concerned that we might become trapped there.

When we entered the building and Tim had slammed the door leaving the blizzard behind us, he looked about strangely.

"Is it just me? Or is this place absolutely freezing?"

With the breath visible before us the answer was quite clear. Dusting the ice and snow from out of my hair, I rubbed my hands together for warmth wile following him down the corridor.

"Maybe the power went out during the night?"

Hurrying down the hall, he paused to examine the thermostat, and appearing confused, turned and said, "Now that's really odd? The temperature hasn't been changed—it still registers at twenty five."

"That can't be right—this place is as cold as the North Pole." Rubbing my hands together I hurried into the kitchen and to where an old barometer was hung, reading the temperature and shivering, I called back to Tim, and said, "Well according to this thing it's only three degrees in here."

"That's not possible--," Tapping a finger on the thermostat housing as though expecting it to magically come to life, he frowned and said, "The furnace is brand new—it's only a year old. It cost me a small fortune and left me in debt…"

Leaning down and shoving a hand before the heater grate, I felt warm air, and looking back at my friend, said "The furnace seems to be working fine."

"Maybe—there's a broken window somewhere--," His face paled as he quietly said, "Or possibly an open door?"

Moving down the corridor we began turning on lights, looking into the adjoining rooms, and checked all the windows. Everything was tightly sealed, there were no drafts, and we could not define the source of that strange and bitter cold.

"It seems to be coming from down here--." Shivering as he stood in an obvious and frozen gust in the doorway that led down to the basement, he turned to look back at me, "It must be the bay doors…"

Drawing the revolver from out of a coat pocket, I held it down while moving toward the basement stairs.

"You'd better let me go first."

Stepping aside to allow me past, he followed closely from behind.

Tightly gripping the revolver and shoving the door open, I reached into the blackness and switched on the lights. Too terrified to say anything, and ever so cautiously, I began descending the old wooden steps. My heart jumped into my throat as beneath the dull glow of that single and swinging bulb, the old wood squeaked loudly beneath our weight. I grit my teeth as each and every step seemed louder than the last. The stench of death was now unbearable and seeming far worse than even before. Tim followed closely as we came to the bottom stair, and slowly turning, we looked down the hallway. In the deep shadows and at the end of the hall, we saw the partially open morgue door, swinging slowly open and closed…

"Whoever or whatever has gotten into the bay—," Tim leaned close and whispering into my ear, said, "It's too dark to see anything in there. The light switch—it's by the sink and against the far wall."

Ever so slowly, he moved down the last step, and slipping into the dark hallway, retrieved the fire-axe from an emergency box on the wall. Nodding toward the open door and speaking in less than a whisper, he said, "I'll go for the light—you cover me…"

The dull glow of the little bulb cast a sickly yellow haze. The shadows were deep, our movements slow, and each step calculated.

We had no plan beyond the obvious. When he reached the open doorway, he looked to me and raising the axe high above his head, suddenly rushed into the room.

Running blindly in behind him, I heard him cry out, the sound of utter chaos, and things falling in the blackness.

"Tim! I'm coming—hang on!" I could barely see a thing! The dim glow from the hallway cast a singular beam into the bay as hysterically rushing inward, I suddenly slipped, and falling, crashed heavily to the floor! The gun fell from my hand, and desperately scrambling on the wet surface, I searched for the weapon!

"Mike—don't move, stay exactly where you are!" He shouted from somewhere close-by. His voice shrill and desperate as calling out, he said, "For God's sake, hold still—I'm going for the lights!"

Struggling and soaked in something sticky that I had apparently spilled during the fall, I shouted back, "I'm not going anywhere—but I've dropped the damn gun!"

There was a sudden and blinding flash, the lights came on, and I stared in wide-eyed horror at the nightmare surrounding us.

Without warning and doubling-over, I wretched violently while heaving the steaming contents of my stomach onto the gore covered floor! Reeling and almost falling amid the gruesome mess, I fell back against the sink and counter.

In a history of nightmares it was the worst that I had ever seen! The heavy bay door was literally ripped, and bent inward from outside. The cooler was torn clear from off the hinges, and the contents emptied out. In a ghastly and gore imbued ocean of organs, and spread across the bay, were sprawled the putrid, mangled and disemboweled corpses. Many of them had been hideously dismembered, torn beyond recognition, beheaded and crushed! The parts and pieces of which were floating among bloated entrails, a cold, vile and rotting, human soup…

"Mike—I'm over here--," Slipping and skidding through the rotting filth, he came to where I rested again the counter, and looking into my face, said, "it's okay, whatever did this seems to be gone?"

Still utterly shocked by the absolutely gruesome sight, I struggled while unable to find the words to express my horror. Running water in the sink behind me Tim soaked a towel and began washing my gore soaked hands and face.

"Let's get you cleaned up a little--," His eyes darted wildly about the room while focusing upon the bay door, as he said, "Then we better take Merlin and get the hell out of here before that thing comes back."

It was everywhere, soaked and sticking through my pants, dripping and oozing, it coagulated on my clothes and was crusting and clotting in my hair! Gagging, I spat while on the verge of vomiting again. Choking with the bitter taste of human decay, I desperately wiped at the filth covering my face.

"Mike—you need to calm down--," Shoving my head into the sink and running warm water through my hair, he used soap to scrub and rinse the gore out.

"I'm sorry—I'm just having a little trouble with all of this."

"I know what you must be experiencing—but we can't afford to blow our cool now. Just try to imagine them as mannequins or dolls—just until we can get out of here… okay?"

Wiping at my face with a fresh towel and standing me upright, he stared, and said with a frown, "That's done the trick—there's a shower down here and I've got spare smocks. Let's get out of these clothes, get cleaned up, and we can find something to wear upstairs."

"What in God's name are we up against…?" They were the only words that I could choke out while gazing upon the torn and twisted bay door.

"Please--," He took me by the arm and attempting to lead me away, said, "Let's just get cleaned up, take Merlin and get out of here."

Looking down and noticing the thick veins in a fatty yellow clump that was stuck to my shoe, I heaved. Gagging and throwing off my blood soaked shirt, I fell back against the counter.

"Mike!" He grabbed me from under the arms, and supporting me, literally dragged me from out of that nightmare, and to where we fell against the wall in the outer corridor.

In that same moment something caught my eye, and raising a hand, I pointed, saying, "There—and where the blood pooled around that arm."

He looked to the corpse and making certain that I gained my footing, went to closer observe the floor. It only took a moment before he turned back in astonishment, and said, "It's some type of a print?"

Directing his attention as while pointing from between the corpse and bay door, I said, "They're scattered and hard to see in all of this—but they travel from the cooler back to the bay."

"It almost looks as though something was being dragged off--," Tim followed the strange patterns through the blood, and calling back to me, said, "I've never seen prints like this before…"

Compelled to examine them closer, I struggled to force myself back into the room. Using a hand and the wall for support, I gazed down into the pooling organs and gore…

At first glance it appeared as little more than a wide and bloody smear, but moving closer I could make out a distinct pattern in the thick and clotting trail. The prints were a strange semi-circle shape with what appeared to be three-pronged endings? Completely unfamiliar I was convinced that they were indeed, nothing of this earth…

Without comment, I moved closer to the gate and assessing the torn hole to have been roughly four feet in diameter, said, "Whatever it is—it must be huge?"

"What this?" He directed my attention to the torn and glistening steel edges of the gate, and leaning closer, suddenly stared up at me.

Leaning down, I suddenly saw what had so terribly upset him. Caught and still hanging from the jagged edges, was a clump of brown hair, and torn flesh from of a body that had been dragged away…"

"If I had to make an educated guess, I'd have to say that this came from Connie's corpse."

"What would make you assume that?"

"Because its missing--," Gazing among the strewn and torn parts, he shook his head in the bitter gust blowing in from that hole, and said, "She's just gone…"

"Well I've seen enough--," Directing him away from the gate and back across the room, I suddenly stopped to look back in question.

"Did you hear that?"

The wind whistled hauntingly through the gaping tear in the gate from behind us, and we stood quiet and listened. It came again. It was the sound of something sharp, something that was scraping against the wooden surface of a door. Far worse though, was the fact that it came from directly before us… It was blocking our only route of escape from the morgue...

Thump—thump—thump it suddenly pounded, the efforts increasing with each attempt. Grabbing the axe from where it had fallen on the bay floor, Tim raised the weapon and stood ready. Having lost the revolver in the ensuing chaos I stood virtually helpless. A thousand terrors flowed through my mind in that moment and I was at a complete loss as to what to do.

"Mike—," He whispered, the axe shaking dangerously in his trembling hands, he said, "We don't have any choice now."

Nodding at my terrified friend I knew that he was right. One way or another we had to pass through that corridor… Taking a deep breath and holding it, we both plunged head-long into the hallway! Soaked with rotting death and out of our minds with fear, we leapt shrieking into the hallway. Nothing but darkness as the sound had suddenly stopped… Noticing a shadow move from beneath a hall door, I looked to Tim while pointing and drawing his attention. There was a moment of absolute still, and then it happened. A black paw reached out from beneath that door, and clawing at the bottom of the wood, Merlin pleaded in a loud and desperate meow.

"Oh—," Tim hurried to release the cat but I stopped him while gesturing toward the open morgue, and saying, "We don't want him running around loose in here."

Opening an opposing door and retrieving a large cat cage, he looked to me, and said, "This won't take long."

Within a moment he had Merlin in the carrier, and hurrying upstairs, we closed and bolted the basement door behind us. It became a mad race for time after that point. The coagulating gore was causing the clothes to stick to my skin. The putrid stench accompanied by a terrible itching now had me afraid to scratch for fear of infection. Although completely terrified, I just couldn't put off the shower. Every moment felt like an hour as watching the clotted blood, hair and other unmentionable particles flowing down the drain, I fought against an overwhelming nausea

After the fastest and hottest shower of my life I waited with Merlin while Tim got cleaned up. He was even faster than I was and I suspected that fear had a lot to do with it…

Rummaging through the closet, and to my utter dismay, I found nothing even close to my size. Desperate and destitute, I turned as Tim rushed in from the other room.

"I couldn't find anything suitable." He approached quickly and while saying, "But this work until we get back to the hotel."

Without hesitation I accepted the pajamas and blue bath robe, and slipping into them, hurried toward the door.

"Alright—grab the cat and let's get out of here—we've already been here too long for my liking."

Taking a firm hold of the carrier and terrified feline, he raced out after me, as rushing down the stairs, made our way to the front door.

"Oh no--," He halted me as I was reaching for the door handle, and said, "You'd better call Harry real quick—and let him know what's happened. We've been here for a while--," He looked at his watch, saying, "It's already after nine."

The thought having completely eluded me I immediately moved toward a phone on a nearby bureau. Grabbing at the receiver, I quickly dialed out.

"There's no answer… They must still be over at the diner?"

"Then we'll just meet them over there after we go back to the hotel—and you get some clothes."

The large cat suddenly growled. It was an unnerving and guttural sound at which point, hissing, I noticed his weight shift as he firmly pressed himself away from the cage opening. Just in the way he was behaving I already knew that we were no longer alone…

"Somethings coming…" Tim stepped away from the door as we

both stared in horror, and shadows moved in the glare of the external light.

In the stillness we suddenly heard something moving in the deep snow beyond, as swiftly approaching, moved onto the doorstep!

A loud banging sent backward and into the hall, as raising the axe above my head, I prepared for whatever broke through that door!

"Wait!" Tim grabbed my wrist.

The door thundered to a violent pounding and he looked to me, saying, "That doesn't sound like something trying to get in—it's a knock…"

Rushing forward, he unlocked, and threw the door wide open! Wind and snow blew into the corridor as through the blizzard, Harry and Steve almost fell into the hall before us.

"What the hell are you doing?" Harry bellowed as barely catching his breath, came forward and embracing me fearfully, said, "You son of a bitch—you were supposed to call! We thought that something had happened to you guys."

"We thought you were both dead." Steve drew his 44 Magnum, and looking nervously toward the door, said, "Your motel room was completely trashed and everything was torn to pieces."

"Your luggage is history but I saved your bag and typewriter--," Harry noticed the pajamas and robe, and looking between us said, "What's going on here?"

"Something tore a hole through the bay door and made a nightmare out of the morgue…" Tim moved the cat carrier out of the draft, and closing the door, said, "It looks like a bloody Hell broke loose down there."

"There are prints of some kind--," Directing them down the corridor, I pointed, saying, "They aren't like anything that I've ever seen before, but they're definitely prints."

"Let's be quick about this--," Harry quickly followed, saying, "Your hearse is already stuck out there, and our car is up on the road. If we don't move fast, none of us are getting out of here."

We never hesitated for a moment as we all knew that he was right…

The experience had almost been too much for all of us. The only advantage they had was the fact that we had warned them of what to expect. Even then it hadn't been enough… When they witnessed the horrendous chaos in that room the prints hadn't come as such a shock. We all knew that something huge had torn its way into the place, and was powerful enough to shred human bodies like paper.

By the time that we left that place the snow had almost stranded the Chrysler in the parking lot. Harry had only barely escaped the steep driveway, and it was a struggle to make it back into town. Unable to return to the motel, Harry had insisted that we all remain together. Needless to say, I felt a lot safer somewhere else and surrounded by heavily armed friends.

Smoking my last cigarette of the night my thoughts drifted through the long shadows of Harry's living room. It was much smaller than what I was used to but comfortable all the same. There was a certain sense of security knowing that we were now in the center of town. With additional lighting and neighbors just a shout away, it was a little easier to settle down for the evening.

"I feel a lot safer here--" Tim whispered as rolling over in the bundle of blankets that he occupied on the floor, said, "It was nice of Harry to let us stay with him."

"Well, after what happened at the hotel—and the look on his face when he saw your morgue?" I adjusted the pillow as leaning closer to the dimly glowing hearth, said, "I don't think that we had much choice?"

Butting the cigarette into an ashtray on the table next to the couch where Steve slept soundly, I peered out from beyond the partially open curtains.

"Hey—are you alright?" Tim rolled onto his stomach.

"I'm not really sure? I'm still a little freaked out about the hotel room being torn apart like that." I sat up and leaning with my back against the stonework of the hearth, quietly said, "It just doesn't make sense? How could that thing have known where I was—and why did it come after me?"

"It could have just been random--," Turning and raising himself on an elbow he peeked over the far side of the table edge, saying, "Or maybe it's staked out the motel for some reason?"

"There was another persona staying there--," The thought terrified me beyond words, and I said, "He was in the room three doors down from me. I saw his car last night."

"He left this morning--," Steve muttered, his eyes glistening in the darkness from where he had been listening, and he said, "And as for our animal? Most predators stalk and choose their prey. So, you might've been marked for some reason?"

"It couldn't have been stalking me—I would have seen it Old Gordon Farrell is always wandering around the property at night. Someone would have seen something?"

"Maybe this one is different?" Tim tapped a finger to his forehead, saying, "What if this thing doesn't hunt by sight—but by scent?"

"Why would you assume that?" Steve sat up and reaching for a cup of cold coffee that sat on the table before him, gulped it down.

"Well—think about this for a minute." Tim climbed out from under his blankets, his eyes bright with morbid fascination, and he said, "There might be a way to connect the events involving Shirley, Connie, and even Marlene. We just didn't think about it before." He stared as though having fallen upon some great revelation, and said, "Instead of looking for the clues that weren't there, maybe we should have considered the obvious… what did all three women have in common?"

"Aside from the fact that they were all women and living in the same town--," Steve scratched at stubble on his chin, and shrugging, said, "I don't see any obvious connection?"

"They were all wearing a strong and sweet smelling perfume–," Harry pulled his bath robe closed, as tying the belt and wandering out of the adjoining bedroom, said, "You could smell them a mile away…"

"No shit--," Steve leapt up as Harry dropped on the couch beside him, and he asked, "So if that had anything to do with their murders—why did the thing go after Mike?"

It was easy enough to answer that question myself,

"You know—I would never even have thought of that until you mentioned the perfume!" Snapping my fingers, I pointed at Harry, and said, "After we left the funeral parlor—the pine scented air freshener."

"The morning that we came back from viewing the bodies--," He explained to Steve, saying, "Mike rubbed him-self down with an air freshener. It's not exactly perfume—but I'm sure that's what must've done it."

"So if this thing is really following smells?" Steve stared at Harry in the deep shadows, and said, "Why did it break into the funeral parlor?"

"Somehow, it must've picked up the smell on Connie and Shirley's bodies." Harry puffed at his cigar, the brightly glowing ember reflecting eerily in his eyes.

Nodding, Tim peered suspiciously at the window, his wearied expression hinting of obvious though unspoken fear, as he said, "It's not that far-fetched—when you consider that sarcophagus flies can sense and find their way to a rotting body... from over five miles away."

"Five miles--" I had never heard that before, and looking to Tim, asked, "What kind of fly?"

"The Sarcophagus flies--," Tim rubbed at his sleep filled eyes, and said, "Any of the flesh flies really—even the green or blue bottle-fly. Did you know that the green bottle-fly will only lay its eggs in the light while the blue bottle-fly prefers the shade?"

"Bugs give me the creeps...." Shuddering at the thought, Harry looked over at Tim, and said, "We had to take a course in entomology to pass the final exam. It left me with my guts turning... I still can't look at rice or vermicelli the same way..."

"I still don't know how anything could survive out there, and in that cold?" Steve grumbled, pointing at the window and nervously shaking his leg, said, "And if it's as big as we're guessing? How the hell is it getting around without someone seeing it?"

"Maybe it isn't always out there?" Harry drifted in thought, his attention drawn into the ensuing blizzard, as he said, "Some things live in burrows, caves, and possibly even abandoned farms and houses?"

"Or maybe even—at the bottom of an abandoned mine?" His words seemed to resonate in mind. The fear of what had happened during my childhood, the horror of being lost in that mine all flooding back, coming back to haunt me! It was possible...

"No one ever knew what caused that mine accident..." Tim looked to me in apology for bringing up the subject, and said very sadly, "Maybe they went to deep and ran into something down there?"

Merlin crept out from beneath the couch, as slinking toward where I was leaned against the hearth, dropped onto the blanket beside me.

"Oh Geez, you let that thing loose in my house?" Harry cringed in disgust.

"I washed him in your basement sink, twice, and with a lot of soap." Tim reassured him, saying, "He hated every second of it, and I was soaked, but he's seriously clean as a whistle now."

There was an immediate and obvious dislike between Harry and the cat, and it showed in the way they suspiciously eyed one another.

Gently stroking Merlin's thick dark fur, I felt him lean closer. The purring becoming a deep rumble as closing his eyes, he settled against my leg.

"Speaking of smells?" Steve directed our attention back to the conversation, and said, "If this thing is attracted to specific scents? Can't we just bait a trap using Connie, Marlene, or Shirley's perfume and wait for it to show up?"

"If this thing is that sensitive to odors--," Tim thought for a moment and looking to Steve, said, "It might be more aware of us than we think, and realize what we are doing."

"Don't start attributing too much intelligence to this thing—after all; it's still just an animal…"

Searching through the accumulated contents on the coffee table Harry located a packet of matches and lighting a large candle, placed it down in the center of the table.

"A bear trap with a gallon of perfume poured over a deer carcass would do the trick--," Tim thought aloud, saying, "It would be irresistible to that thing."

"Traps are far too dangerous." Harry disagreed, shaking his head and saying, "We have a lot of kids, hiker's, guys on skidoos, and hunters around here. I'd rather not risk injuring anyone in the process… But, it might be an idea to take Gene's dogs down to the funeral parlor tomorrow. We may not have a definite scent of the animal, but they'll sure as hell be able to track the body it took…"

"You know?" Tim crawled deep into his bedding as removing his glasses and placing them on the table, said, "There's always a chance that this animal—or whatever it is? Could be intelligent—and leading all of us into a trap?"

"As long as I get a clear shot at the bastard--," Steve growled from out of the shadows, saying, "I'll put an end to this nightmare once and for all."

Cautious of Merlin who slept at my thigh, I drew the blankets up, and said, "For all that we know it might already be out there—and just waiting for us to fall asleep."

There was a static tension in the air, a nervous energy that made my nerves tingle. It quickly filled the room and I knew that it was the fear that we were all feeling...

"Then it'll be getting a big surprise--," Steve grabbed the twelve gauge shotgun from the floor, and leaning over the coffee table and looking down at me, said, "It may be a lot of things? But I doubt that it's bullet proof."

"But then again--," Tim's voice sounded weak as he became invisible, fading somewhere among the heavy down covers, as he said, "It was after Mike—so if Harry's scent theory is right? Even if it does manage to get in here—it'll go straight for him."

"Thanks Tim—I'll sleep a lot better thinking about that..."

"It's not getting in here and if it does—it'll be going out in a million, smoking little pieces." Harry grumbled, nodding at me and saying, "But we can all use some sleep. I'll see you boys in the morning." He yawned as butting his cigar and blowing out the candle, said, "Try to get some rest guys—you're going to need it."

"Don't worry about a thing." Steve rearranged his blankets and winking at me, said, "By tomorrow night this'll all just seem like a bad dream."

"I certainly hope that you're right." Tim's disembodied voice was muffled from somewhere in the heaped blankets.

"Just wait--," Steve climbed into the sleeping bag and working with his back into the couch, said, "If it's the last thing I do? I'll kill that bastard..."

His words echoed in my mind as the darkness slowly closed in from all around me. The shadows drifting, swirling as moving about the entrance to a cavern, I saw something stir within the blackness... It was the mine, as even within dreams I was pursued by the soul rendering terror of the unknown...

CHAPTER TWENTY

Friday January 5, 1973.
10:30 a.m.
The snow had stopped during the night but Lenny still had to clear a path for us. It was a last minute decision that brought us all back to the funeral parlor in an attempt to conceal what had happened there. Desperate and fearing an endless stream of lawsuits, we were only left with the option of immediate disposal. This meant gathering all of the remains and processing them through cremation.

To accomplish this legally, we would also have to provide medical documents verifying the threat of a possible, viral contamination. Fortunately, Steve had an associate working at the Center for disease control. They were dear friends, and after a few telephone calls and additional connections, he managed to attain the required documentation. Guaranteed delivery within days, we were provided with a letter specifying a possible, Cholera threat. It was a common disease, and was caused by bacteria known as 'Vibrio cholerae' which could be found in drinking water. Needless to say, it was dangerous enough to provide the necessary concern without drawing too much attention.

With a nightmare on the doorstep and another storm close behind, we began the grisly task of clearing the parlor bay.

Dressed in hip waders, goggles, and heavy rubber gloves, we dragged large trash pails while gathering remains. Making an attempt to separate and keep appropriate pieces with their associated torsos made the task even harder. It wasn't absolutely necessary, but for moral reasons, we felt that we owed it to the families.

Though we had worn gloves, masks, and other protective gear the stench was horrendous. With tears in our eyes and gagging, we struggled to get through the morning.

"I don't know why we can't just pile this mess into that machine and burn it by the load." Steve had already been sick twice, and fought while gathering parts too heavy for the rest of us to move.

"Because that's just plain wrong--," Tim slipped in the coagulating sludge, and waving an arm that he'd picked up from off the floor, said, "These are all someone's family. Loved ones and friends… we all deserve a little respect, even in death."

Harry cursed, as sliding on the gore smeared floor, stumbled, and dropping a head and torn rib-cage, fell backward into the grisly mess.

"Oh—God, Harry, are you alright?" I ran over and began helping my friend back to his feet.

"No—I am most certainly—not alright" Wiping the clinging gore and blood soaked entrails from himself, he looked over his shoulder at Tim, and said, "I can't even tell what belongs where or to who?"

"Just use the shovel for the squishy and sloppy stuff--," Tim directed while pointing and saying, "And pile whatever looks like it belongs together in separate bins."

"You make it sound easy." Steve frowned as looking into one of the numerous bins, reached inside and said, "This doesn't even belong in here." He pulled out an elderly man's hand and waving it across the room at Harry, said, "There's a woman in this one."

Briefly examining a foot taken out of his bin, harry held it up, saying, "I have a man's foot, approximately in his mid to late fifties. Anyone missing or need a foot?"

"I'm still missing a right arm and head--," Peering down into my bin, I thought for a moment, and said, "Also possibly lungs, heart, and kidneys?"

"All the squishy stuff went into the bins against the wall--," Steve informed me, saying, "Tim said we can skip sorting them…"

"It would take forever—and we still wouldn't get it right," Appearing somewhat disappointed, he shrugged, saying, "We'll just cremate and dispose of the ashes."

"We could always just mix and match--," Steve suggested, as looking between us said, "Just to balance out the weight of the cremains. People will notice if we short them—right?"

"That would defeat the purpose of everything we've done so far." Harry waved around the room, and said, "Let's just get this done before dark… we have worse things to be worried about…"

It took all morning and the better part of the afternoon before we began mopping. With the gore soaked floor entirely cleared of bodies and dismembered limbs, we began the final process to finish the job.

With the cremation machine running, Tim began disposing of all the internal organs first. This cleared a large area, and gave us more space to work. While Harry, Steve, and I worked with buckets, bleach and mops, Tim did a final inspection of the bins.

"Wait a minute—what's this?" Tugging at his heavy rubber gloves and making certain that they were snug, reached into one of the bins. Drawing a small and bloodied fragment from within, he looked at it in utter confusion.

"This isn't part of a human being?"

Dropping what we were doing, we all hurried to where he stood before the bin.

"What is that?" Harry leaned closer.

"It looks like a piece of turtle shell—only harder?" Tim examined the small shard, which no bigger than a silver dollar, appeared sharp as a razor.

"That's another thing?" Placing his hands on his hips, Steve looked to the fragment, and said, "Why didn't it take Shirley as well as Connie? They were both victims, both wearing perfume, and both in the same place."

"Maybe it only took one because it's coming back for the other one later…" Although I had said it they were all already thinking it.

"So why did it do so much damage to all these other corpses?" Steve leaned closer while inspecting the strange and jagged shard.

"Maybe it was looking for something?" Returning to my mop and the pail of hot water and bleach, I said, "It might have some strange type of dietary requirement or just be selective."

"All that I know right now--," Harry pointed to the bloody fragment in Tim's glove, and said, "Is that we need to get that analyzed."

"The roads are bad and the nearest lab is in Penticton." Steve soaked the bay floor with hot water and bleach, and taking hold of his mop, said, "I'd put that thing on ice until we can do something with it."

"He's right--," Tim hurried toward the counter and opening a cabinet, withdrew a plastic container with a lid, and saying, "I'll toss it in the fridge down here until we can figure something out."

"Speaking of bad roads--," Harry went to the gaping hole in the bay door and peeking out, said, "Lenny's got the lot cleared again. You better that Hearse of yours back to the motel for the night. I'm sure that old Gordon won't mind if you park it out back, for a few extra bucks."

"I still owe him for a window—and what happened in my other room."

"It's all taken care of—Harry waved me off, saying, "I've been friends with the old goat since he first came here, nine years ago."

"I still can't figure out why that thing tore this place apart the way that it did?" Tim slipped the plastic container with the shard into a fridge, and moving to look into the entrance to the cooler, said, "It wasn't afraid. Was it mad, frustrated, or desperate?"

"I would assume all of the above--" I gestured toward the battered and bloodied framework of the door, and said, "But wasn't Connie on a gurney?"

"No—I removed her and placed her on a shelf to the back. She was light and compact, and fit on a top rear shelf," He motioned with a hand toward the right and upper rear of the cooler.

"So it had to move everything out of the front first—which would explain the mess." Harry nodded in observation, and said, "And it must've been pissed by then, because it wasn't just pulling them out, it was shredding everything along the way."

"That seems fairly obvious just by looking at the edge of that door frame--," I pointed to where shreds of skin, torn flesh, fat and other greasy reside was caught upon the jagged metal edges, and said, "It looks like a cheese-grater. There must be at least, four or five pounds of flesh, fat, organs and other--." I didn't even have a chance to finish the sentence.

"Whatever it was, the door sure didn't slow it down--," Wandering back to his mop and pail, he looked down into the gore filled bucket, and said, "We need to finish up here and get back into town. I think that it's time that we round of some of the boys, get Gene and his dogs, and go hunting…"

"Hunting for what?" Tim stood and stared.

Emptying the bloody and foaming contents of his bucket into the sink, Steve glanced over, and said, "An animal with some kind of shell, feeds on bone marrow, and is big enough to kill a three hundred pound boar."

"Now, who's sounding like the late show?" Tim attempted to break the tension of what was swiftly becoming the darkest day of our lives.

"Not, sounding like it." Harry finished mopping. Pulling off his gloves, he slammed them into a trash bin and glaring back, spat as he said, "Now, we really are the late show..."

Leaving the crematory machine running while it finished its final cycle of the day, we barricaded the hole in the bay doors. We used an old door that we found in the storage room, and nailed boards up to support it. We knew that it wouldn't keep out the monster, but it served to hold back the brutal elements.

When we left, I had taken Tim in the Hearse while Harry and Steve followed in the Chrysler. Lenny had been busy clearing the snow, ominous clouds darkened the heavens, and town was a welcome sight. Surprisingly enough, and especially after our previous experience, old Gordon Farrell had been more than willing to accommodate me. Agreeing to the sum of twenty dollars for a week of parking, I promptly took the Hearse to the far end of the building. Parked laterally and before a large, side entrance suite, it was invisible from the road and other customers. If things were different I might even have enjoyed being there. Completely private as while bordered by forest on three sides, it caught the morning sun, and was shaded in the pines before noon.

Dispersing with my clothes, all that was readily available was an extra pair of boots, and military fatigues belonging to Steve. Although the clothing was a slightly loose fit, the boots were perfect, and it all seemed appropriate.

After ruining Harry's parka in the parlor incident, he had kindly provided another. The man had a seemingly endless assortment of coats, hunting jackets and fishing vests. It was good to be prepared and he always was. I was surprised when Tim appeared dressed in a similar fashion, and wore the same style and color parka. When Steve and Harry appeared in the same attire it looked as though we were going to war, and in some sense we truly were. Instead of starting the search from a location nearer to town, Harry had decided upon a fresher trail. Using snowmobiles, everyone had been gathered at the funeral parlor, and organized while awaiting dispersal.

Ignoring the threat of extreme weather conditions, Harry had insisted upon still using his Chrysler. For this exact reason, old

Lenny stood ready at a radio in the event that we required assistance. The event was well organized, all possible safety precautions observed, and we were soon underway.

Harry deputized a group of over sixty men that day. All of them were responsible, well-weathered, and capable hunters. Still, and with all due care, I knew that the road to hell was paved in good intentions…

Versailles Funeral Home
2:20 p.m.
"How about getting a picture of us altogether--," Gene waved at the group with a gloved hand, and said, "We use to do this over-seas, and for good luck."

"Sure thing Gene, Just give me one second here." Retrieving the camera from the front seat of Harry's Chrysler, I hurried back as everyone moved into position.

Kneeling in the deep snow I snapped several shots. With the restless hounds leashed and in the foreground, the expressions of my companions varied drastically in contrast. Gene, tightly gripping the leash, glowed with unsung victory, while the terrified Tim appeared to shrivel ever deeper into the hood of his parka.

Smitty just smiled, looking as though he were on the verge of some big pay-off. His brother Blake appeared confused and as though he was trying to remember something that was lost or simply left behind.

Yet, it was with Harry and Steve that my attention was mainly focused. Their features were grim, their eyes dark, and strangely haunting. They looked like two old soldiers facing some final battle from which neither might return. In my heart I now feared and felt the same…

The gathering numbered somewhere around sixty but many of the faces were new or simply unfamiliar. The only thing that they all had in common was weapons, winter, and that look of anxious anticipation. It was a look that most hunters get. I wondered if they even realized that they were little more than bait to lure a monster…

"Hey Mike—you need to get in here too." Gene insisted as motioning for the camera and handing me a rifle, shoved the leashes into my hands, saying, "Okay everyone—get ready!"

The flash went off several times as he snapped numerous images. It was a practice that I could appreciate having done it myself. There was always the concern of losing a moment because of poor lighting, or ruining a shot due to a blur caused by an unexpected movement. It was apparent that military service had taught him that some pictures were final moments for many. It was an understanding that we shared, especially on that winter afternoon.

"One minute guys--," Gene leaned down as constructing a base out of snow and balancing the camera, checked the angle several times, as he shouted, "One second." Setting the timer on the camera he rushed over and taking the leashes from out of my hand, proudly knelt with his hounds.

Feeling rather stupid for staring into the bulb I blinked several times after being blinded by the flash. It wouldn't have been quite so bad but it was a particularly dark afternoon.

"I brought a few things for us to use today." Harry said as moving toward the rear of the Chrysler, opened the trunk to reveal two large military duffel bags. Unzipping them he turned to look over his shoulder while searching through the contents, and said, "It's very important that we don't get separated." He proceeded to hand out police issue hand-radios, saying, "The channels are all pre-set. I'd like everyone to take one. But leave them turned off for now—we need to spare the batteries."

A loud screech caused everyone to turn. "Oops--,"Smitty grinned and shrugging as he switched off the radio, slapped at his brother for laughing at him.

"Everyone take one of these." Harry passed out compasses, magnum flashlights and road-flares, saying, "We may not need them—but it's better to be safe than sorry."

"Um—speaking of being safe?" Tim slipped into a pair of over-sized woolen mittens, waving a hand as he said, "I didn't bring—well? I don't own any firearms?"

Looking at Smitty and Blake who simultaneously shrugged, Harry turned and rummaging through the duffel bags, produced three police issue twelve gauge shotguns. Shoving one into Tim's hands, he said, "Keep the safety on—and do not for any reason, other than my telling you to do so, remove the safety."

There was a solemn moment as Harry quietly looked into the faces of everyone involved, and said, "Okay gentlemen—as you already know, we're looking for a killer. All that we really know is that it's a big bastard and dangerous—so shoot to kill. That doesn't mean that we'll be running through the forest and blasting anything that we see. There are other people out here—so please, let's make sure that we can see our target, and know exactly what we're aiming at before we pull the trigger." Looking at Steve he shrugged in question, asking, "Is there anything that you'd like to add, Sergeant Harris?"

"No sir." Steve solemnly looked away and pulling the hood of the parka over his head, checked his weapons.

"Alright gentlemen--," Harry looked around the group as appearing stern though frightened, nodded as he said, "Let's find us a killer."

A hand in the crowd suddenly halted everything as an older man had called out, asking, "What exactly are we looking for? Is it a person or an animal?"

Harry nervously looked back at us before addressing the man by name, he said, "Well Grant, we aren't exactly sure at this point. But if you run into him—or it, trust me, you'll know it. Don't take any chances. Either subdue the man or kill the beast. There are no two ways about this thing, my friends!"

With that the crowd separated into groups of six, and with weapons and dogs, began the grim journey into that frozen wilderness.

"Are you bringing the camera along?" Gene enthusiastically tugged at my sleeve, grinning as he said, "They come in mighty handy at times."

"Sure—why not?" Slipping the camera strap around my neck and squinting in the icy wind, I couldn't help but cringe, asking, "Does it just keep getting colder—or is there an end to the freeze around here?" Shoving my hands into a pair of black leather gloves I shielded my eyes, watching as a brooding wall of darkening clouds gathered on the gray horizon.

"Yeah–I noticed that too--," Harry zipped up his parka and retrieving a Winchester rifle from the trunk of the car, adjusted his glasses, and said, "We're in for another storm tonight."

"Are you going to be okay?" Noticing Tim stumble in the deep snow, Steve offered a hand in support, saying, "You really don't have to do this."

"We're in this together." Tim shot a nervous glance over his shoulder and looking back at the funeral home, said, "And besides— I'm willing to bet that it's safer than staying here alone."

"Gene—if you're ready?" Harry took a long pull from his cigar before tossing it into the snow, and waving a hand above his head, shouted, saying, "There's bad weather on the way and we're short on day-light! Let's get moving people!"

Needless to say, I was relieved that the trail hadn't forced us to descend into that dismal ravine behind the property. Instead, we travelled directly into the western edge of the forest. After all these years I still couldn't believe just how many places in this town had actually bothered me. That ravine where I had played as a child was nothing more than a deep and dried up river-bed. In the spring it was a mud-hole and through the summer it was nothing more than a dusty pit, filled with cracks and clay-walled crevices. There was an old wooden train trestle that crossed further down, but it had been abandoned long ago. All things considered, the cemetery had bothered me for obvious reasons, and my father's death in those dark, cold and seemingly bottomless mines. It was no wonder that I had been drawn to writing thrillers and horror stories. My life was an endless stream of fear, tragedy, and uncertainty. It was a dark path into the unknown and that I even followed now.

It had been several hours since we had begun laboring through the deep snow. With Tim slowing us even more due to his poor health, we navigated the hills and dense pines until finally arriving at a gasping and heaving halt. Pulling off the leather gloves and rubbing my hands together I cupped them, while blowing warm air into the chilled dampness of my fingers.

"It looks like we're heading upward now." Steve looked down at the sickly dark and yellowing smear that we had been following through the snow. It was the trail that our monster had made while dragging off what remained of little Connie...

"Yeah--," Attempting to light a cigar in the strong wind Harry looked over at me, cursing and muttering under his breath, he said, "Straight toward those damn mines." His attention moved to where Tim, leaning against a tree, coughed while fighting to catch his breath. Sadly shaking his head, Harry turned to me and quietly said, "He doesn't seem to be holding out too well, does he?"

It was true enough. Tim looked awful as sitting on a nearby stump and coughing loudly, leaned forward while resting his face between his hands. He appeared as though he couldn't go another step.

Gene having overheard the comment, quickly turned to look at Harry and asked, "Who's going to meet us up there? I mean—think about it, man? It's going to get dark soon and--."

There was a moment of utter confusion before Harry, realizing Gene's intention had slapped a hand to his brow, and said, "Oh for crying out loud—I never even thought about that! We're going to need a ride. There's no way that we'll have time to walk all the way back from up there, before dark."

"Maybe someone should go back and get the car." Gene pointed in a North-West direction, saying, "There's an old mine service road about three miles from here. It crosses the highway—it should be clear? Lenny's been all over the area, we could meet there?"

"But what about—the animal--," Blake stuttered, his eyes wide with fear as he said, "I mean—for all we know? It could be following us right now?"

"Well we either go back for the car—or all get stuck out here in the dark. I'll go back for the car." Steve volunteered as fumbling to remove his back pack, halted and turned within Tim's approach.

"No—Steve, wait." Tim raised a hand as moving into the middle of where we all stood, he looked up and said, "I'll go back--," A nervous laugh escaped as he looked around the group as he said, "I'm afraid that I'm not of much use here anyway? I'm already falling all over the place" He patted Steve's shoulder, saying, "And besides—they're going to need you here."

"Maybe someone ought to go back with him?" Blake was visibly frightened, and stepped back as his brother interrupted.

Jabbing a finger into his brother's chest, Smitty growled, and said, "Never mind that bullshit—you just stay put, chicken-little. We're in this one together—it's what family does."

"I can do this, really!" Tim insisted, locking eyes with Harry and saying, "Going back will be a lot easier. It's all downhill--," He motioned back with a nod, saying. "And we left a clear trail."

There was a desperate gleam in Tim's eyes. It was something that finally caused Harry, though quite reluctantly, to retrieve the car keys from his pocket and handing them to Tim, say, "Okay then—but the radio's aren't much good after a mile out here? So you'll be on your own..."

"That's fine--," Tim took the keys out of his hand, saying, "I'll meet you on the service road. If it's blocked—look for me at the bottom, because I know that Lenny plowed the new cemetery road."

He was right and I had never even considered that before? The route from the mine led down to the highway. The highway would become the road through town where passing the cemetery, it would continue Eastward and into Penticton. It was a direct line from where it had all started with a mysterious accident?

First there was the attack on Steve in Penticton, then the incident at old Barry's hog-farm on the highway just east of town. Shirley died at the cemetery. Connie was killed just down from Barry's place, and Marlene was attacked on the edge of town.

There was the recent freezer incident at the Blanchard's place, which was in between my motel room and finally, the funeral parlor. There was a distinct pattern to the series of events... and it was the unmissable mark of a predator...

Jingling the car keys and attempting a half-assed smile Tim extended a hand in parting, and said, "Good luck—I'll see you on the other side."

"Don't say it like that." The words were caught in my throat as looking away I slapped his shoulder, and said, "I'll meet you at the service road. Oh and Tim--," He glanced back at me as pointing at him, I said, "Keep that shotgun handy—and watch your back..."

There was an unnerving stillness, a tension which passed over the group while watching as Tim stumbled back down the path. Heavy clouds dimmed the heavens as Tim wandered alone into the dense and frozen wilderness...

"Christ--." Harry cursed as we began moving again and glancing back at me, he said, "I shouldn't have just let him go off alone like that."

"It would've been a lot worse dragging him all the way out there." Fighting to light a cigarette in the frozen gust I gave up, tossing it down and hurrying after them.

"The trail ends just up ahead--," Gene pointed to where the dark bloodied stain faded in the snow, and peering suspiciously into the tall pines, said, "Whatever it was? I must've dragged the carcass up and into the trees?"

Looking into the dark horizon, I blinked as the first snow-flake struck and melted against my face. It was coming…

The dogs suddenly howled, startling us all as baying and veering sharply to the left, dragged Gene down a steep embankment. Bounding through the knee-deep snow in a South-Western direction, the hounds seemed frantic! Gene shouted as stumbling along behind the enormous trio, called out their names while desperately attempting to slow them.

"Digger—Rosie—Diablo, come on, whoa!" He cried out, fighting to keep balance and struggling to avoid losing his grip of the reigns!

Fighting through low hanging and snow-covered pine branches, it was a desperate pursuit. Slowed by the deep snow and stumbling, I fought for breath in the icy winds.

Ever further we traveled into the deepening brush, the hounds baying wildly. We all knew that they had caught the scent of something, but could only wonder and fear as to what...

We had gone some distance from the original trail, when finally entering into a small clearing everything came to a sudden stop.

"Whoa—back off boys and girls!" Gene pointed to where barely visible between the tall pines we saw the shadowy remains of an old cabin.

"What's this?" Harry appeared confused.

"We're here –," Gene spoke while gasping to catch his breath, and said, "And whatever we've been looking for--," He nodded in the direction of the cabin and glaring, quietly said, "Is most likely in there…"

"Gene, stay here with the dogs." Harry motioned at the Blanchard brothers and waving them forward, said, "You two go around the back. If anything other than a man comes out of that place? Don't hesitate—shoot to kill. Mike, Steve, you boys go around the sides… I'll take the front door."

"No—wait a second, Harry." Gene tied the dog harness around the trunk of an immense pine, and drawing his revolver, said, "It would be better if we work in pairs. I'm going with you, amigo."

Pulling the Winchester rifle from his back-pack Harry nodded in agreement, and said, "Okay people, we're aiming to kill, but no one fire until you have a clear target and know what you're shooting at. We don't need to kill each other out here…"

There was a meeting of eyes, the scent of fear, and an apprehension that sent a chill up my spine. The tension was so thick that it could have been cut with a butter knife.

"Okay gentlemen." He solemnly gazed around the little group and motioning with the rifle, said, "Let's do this."

The frozen surface of the snow cracked and crunched beneath our boots. Our every movement, no matter how cautious, echoed like thunder in the presiding stillness. If there was anyone or anything in that cabin it would have to have been deaf not to notice us coming…

"Watch yourselves." Harry warned while pointing toward the remains of an ancient fence that surrounded the old homestead. Digging with a gloved hand into the knee-deep snow, he pulled up a length of rusty and tangled barbed-wire.

"This whole area's covered in wire and old timber." Pointing to where the tops of old posts peeked out from above the snow, Steve cursed, saying, "The only sure way out is back the way that we came."

"Let's keep moving." Harry led us onward.

Trembling in the icy gusts, I looked to where Smitty and Blake now worked their way around from either sides of the cabin.

"Aim high and stay low--," Gene advised while noticing where I was looking, and said, "That way, you won't get caught in a cross-fire and you'll be less of a target…"

"Thanks, I'll try to remember that." The full horror of what was about to happen was finally settling into my mind, and I wondered if anyone had mentioned that little detail to Smitty and Blake? Looking to where they slowly disappeared from around the cabin, I could only pray that they would figure it out on their own.

CHAPTER TWENTY ONE

Moving around the dense pines my eyes remained fixed upon the gray and weathered remains of the old cabin. There was nothing extraordinary about the place. It still looked the same as it had when I was a boy and explored the area.

It was overgrown with dead ivy, and weighted down with heavy moss that caused the roof of the front porch to sink dangerously. The boards were weak and long weathered, and it appeared as though it might collapse at any given moment.

A farmer, his wife and two children had once lived there. It was long ago, and they had all been taken by consumption one winter. Their frozen bodies had been found by Natives, and they were buried not far from the place. I knew because one of them, an elderly man during my childhood, had told me the entire sad affair.

I remembered the place well. So well in fact, that I now squinted while trying to figure out why glass now filled those one broken and barren windows?

Or was it glass? It was reflective and yet flowed uneven while appearing to almost spill out, and creep down the sides of the cabin… The sounds of my friend's movements began to fade and the dogs had become strangely silent. Glancing back, I saw that their whimpering had been replaced by a nervous reflection that lingered in their fearful, though ever watchful eyes. The sudden shrieking call of a raven caused me to look high into the braches of the tall pines. From the heights the massive black bird leaned downward, examining me as though it were warding me off from that place. I knew that this was only a contrivance of fear while desperate to escape, and looking back, saw that it was suddenly gone.

Get a grip of yourself! You're so scared that you're seeing and imagining things now! I had to keep it together.

Nearing the front door and pulling the flashlight from his belt, Harry motioned with the rifle, gesturing for us to hurry around.

"Careful Harry--," I could barely hear my own warning, as looking to the front steps and old porch, whispered, and said, "Those boards are rotted right through…"

With the rifle poised defensively before him, he ever so cautiously began to ascend the old wooden stairs. His movements were stiff and almost mechanical. There was a moment of reluctance as glancing back and taking a deep breath, he turned and suddenly leapt forward!

"Hedley Police—nobody move!" He kicked the door which breaking inward, splintered from its hinges, and was sent crashing to the floor inside!

There was an immediate, suffocating and overwhelming stench of ammonia that sent us reeling backward! With tears in our eyes and gasping for breath, Harry stared back into the dark opening, and said, "What the hell is that?"

Running from above and around the edges of the door was a type of foul, green, and glistening slime. In that same moment we noticed what appeared to have been steam pouring from out of the opening, and just looked to one another.

"Stay close..." Reluctant but determined, he cautiously moved back toward the open doorway.

With Gene close on my heels, we followed after him. Slowly entering into the doorway, Harry leaned away as a globule of that slime dropped, narrowly missing him as it struck the old wooden floor.

There was an immediate temperature change while entering into the cabin, and I suddenly realized why the windows had appeared as they had. The entire interior of the cabin was absolutely coated and covered in that ghastly, running and pooling mucus.

"Sweet Jesus, have mercy." Gene spat, his eyes darting madly about the room a looking back at Harry, asked, "What is all this shit?"

The stench of Ammonia was almost blinding, but I detected something else as well... It was the damp and putrid stench of rotting human flesh... In the beams of our lights I could see the thick mucus that covering the floors, hung from the ceiling. Running from the walls all about us, it formed a thick, crusty, and sticky mess upon the floor.

"That's why it's warm in here..." Steve appeared from behind us, and absolutely horrified, shone his light to the ceiling and windows, saying, "That slime is acting like some type of organic insulation."

"What in the name of Christ have we walked into...?" Harry's eyes were huge as he slowly shone his light around the room, and said, "No one touch anything…"

"Hey—are you guy's okay in there?" Smitty and Blake appeared in the open doorway and making their way inside, stopped as Smitty said, "There's no back door or any side windows—and we couldn't see shit through the front windows. They're all covered in—sweet Jesus--…"

"Yeah—we know…" Gene raised a foot, cursing as the vile stuff clung like glue while dangling from his boot. Scraping it off against an over-turned table, he said, "What the hell is this shit? It hardens like cement when you touch it."

"Don't touch it--," Blake pulled his hand away from the open doorway, and looking into his palm, said, "It might have a re-active agent. Like two-part glue. It stays wet until it mixes with other chemicals or oils…"

We all looked at the man with certain shock and amazement. None of us would have ever assumed that he could spell his own name, much less understand basic chemistry.

"Shut up Blake--," Smitty back-handed his brother in the chest and said, "We have enough problems already without your stupid idea's."

Leaning back as a long and thick clump of mucus slowly dangled while dripping from the ceiling, I watched as it dropped, pooling on the floor.

Watching as the thick mass oozed and congealed as it came into contact with foreign surfaces and objects, I looked to Harry, and said, "This isn't any naturally occurring process of decay—something did this intentionally… I think that it's some kind of nest…"

"A nest made by what?" Smitty slowly turned, and as the beam of his light fell into a far corner across the room, he suddenly froze, and stuttering, said, "There's something moving over there…"

Turning ever so slowly, my eyes followed to where the beam of his light focused. Hidden beneath a wooden stairway leading into an attic, lay the torn and mangled remains of Connie Shepherd…

"Oh shit--," Blake was terrified out of his wits, and stumbling back into his brother, almost pleaded, saying, "No—no—I'm not going anywhere near that thing!"

"That's just fine—," Harry raised a hand while attempting to calm the young man, and quietly said, "You boy's just stay right here."

"If there is anything up there and it didn't see us coming earlier?" Steve pointed out while looking between the brothers and saying, "You can bet you're asses that it's heard us by now." He whispered as pointing toward the open doorway behind them, said, "Just watch your backs, because when we go up those stairs. Whatever made this mess, will probably be coming down from out of one of those upper windows—and be pissed right off..."

It wasn't his words that had terrified me, but the eerie way that his eyes had rolled up into the darkness. His attention entirely focused somewhere near the top of those attic stairs. We had all looked when he had done that, and all watched the oozing trail that streamed down from those steps. Thick, putrid, and glistening in the fading afternoon light of the open doorway...

"Maybe you're right?" Blake was almost hysterical and tugging at his brother's sleeve, said, "It'd be best if we all just stayed together."

Every step was treacherous, as slipping and struggling for balance in that through that ghastly mess, we cautiously began making our way across the room. The further that we traveled into the place, the more pasty and worse it became.

Walking through the ankle deep mucus was becoming almost impossible. Once it came into contact with anything else it quickly began hardening, and more so with applied pressure. In the few steps that we had taken it was a struggle to avoid losing our footwear in the process. Our boots were absolutely covered and each movement was painfully slow for fear of falling. Horrified, I focused straight ahead, and toward the remains of Connie's corpse. Partially crushed and jammed tightly beneath the wooden steps, they glistened and oozed with that hideous slime. I could see that there was a steady stream dripping down from somewhere at the top of those stairs. The residue accumulated near the bottom while forming strange shapes and barriers where the light couldn't reach. It was apparent that the attic was the main source of that foul and gathering pool, and felt like we had entered into a different world...

"I heard something..." Slowly pointing his twelve gauge pump into the dark opening above the stairs, he whispered, saying, "There's something up there..."

Absolute stillness, but then I could hear it? Barely at first, but it was definitely movement from somewhere in the room? Straining to make out the sound, I cringed while realizing what it was. It was the sound of something wet, that sliding, pressed against a sticky surface while making a sickly, sucking sound.

"Oh Jesus—what is that?" The flashlight fell from Harry's trembling hand and sank into the sludge.

Lowering the beam of my light and leaning down ever so cautiously, I peered beneath the steps.

Torn, twisted, and crushed, the rotting thing wasn't even vaguely human anymore. If I hadn't previously seen it in the morgue I would never have known that it was Connie…

The stench was unbearable, and pulling a handkerchief from a coat pocket, shoved it before my nose and mouth. Then I saw what had shocked Harry so badly… Amongst the blood and foaming decay they wriggled, clawing and burrowing ever deeper into the rotting flesh of Connie's back. Roughly the size of a football and baring numerous clawed appendages, the pale and bloated larva were ravenous. Without eyes and having no mandibles of which to cling onto prey, they fed like leeches from an oval, and tooth filled mouth. Covered in patches of coarse black hair, they weren't entirely insect or animal, but some kind of horrific mutation. Shining the beam of my light from around them they cringed ever so slightly. In the pale glow I saw smaller ones which forcing their way into the seething mass, suckled at the corpse.

Sickened with the sight, I turned while fighting back the hot and surging bile in my throat.

"They're some kind of beetle larva--," Gene stared in disbelief, saying, "But they're not like anything that I've ever seen."

"I don't really give a shit what they are!" Smitty cursed, his eyes huge as the rifle shook in his trembling hands, and panicking, he said, "I say that we just clear out of here and torch the god-damned place!"

The repulsive sucking sounds of their frenzied feeding echoed like madness, and I suddenly felt dizzy. Throwing a hand before my face I fought for consciousness, the horror becoming a fevered panic.

"There might be more of those things upstairs." Choking out the words I fought to look away from the horrendous sight.

"Never mind that bullshit!" Harry grabbed me by the sleeve and slowly backing away from the stairs, he said, "I think that we've all seen enough. Smitty is right, let's just torch the damn place!"

"We should at least take a look up there--," Steve motioned with his flashlight to the top of the stairs, and said, "There might be others—bodies…"

"Well I'm not hanging around to find out--," Smitty turned and shoving Blake ahead of him, said, "Me and Blake are done in this bug infested shit-hole."

"Something moved!" Gene suddenly stepped back slipping as almost falling, shone his light toward the far end of the room, and said, "Over there… and behind that tipped couch!"

There were a series of clicking sounds as the safety catches went off on every weapon in the room. A moment later and with guns poised, slipping and sliding, we reluctantly began making our way to the opposite side of the room.

All that we could see was the legs and bottom of the couch. Over-turned and resting close to the wall, it was large, and the stuffing was torn and spread all around. Covered in that horrendous ooze, it was slippery and reflected hideously in the beams of our lights

Those horrible and filthy things… God, I can still hear them. They're squishing around as they suck at the blood and slurp up the liquefying fat and flesh. No—wait a moment? We're all the way across the room. How could I have possibly still heard them?

That's when I suddenly realized that the sound was coming from above and all around us…With Steve close beside him, Harry halted us with a hand while slowly making his way around, and then behind the couch. The expression on both men's faces with what they had encountered there now caused us all to hurry to where they stood.

There was absolute silence as we all stared down at the crumpled body. No older than sixteen, he lay on his left side with his face pressed tightly into the wet, and slime covered cushions. At first glance, it was apparent by the condition of the corpse that he hadn't been there for very long. Behind him and shoved against the wall were his knap-sack and bed-roll. A red winter coat and single brown leather boot had been pulled from the bag. It seemed apparent that having stopped there while hiking, something had surprised the young man.

Blake coughed up, turning and spewing vomit from between the fingers that had previously been clamped over his mouth.

Ignoring his brother's plight, Smitty leaned closer and scowling as he spoke, quietly asked. "How the hell did the poor little bastard manage to end up all the way out here?"

"The highway is about two miles North-west of here." Harry raised a hand in gesture, and said, "From the looks of things he likely hiked in and tried to take shelter here."

In the pale and trembling glow of Gene's flashlight I could see smaller grubs. Bloated, glistening and bloodied, they eagerly burrowed into the flesh of the boys back and exposed lower ribs. Their mucus mixing with his blood and coagulating seeped down, forming a grisly crust beneath the body.

Was it just some trick of the light and feeding worms, or had I seen the breath being drawn into that body? Several moments past as I watched and nothing happened...

"Over there on the bureau--," Blake directed our attention with the beam of his flashlight, and said, "It's a big old Coleman oil lamp. The kid must've brought it with him."

"Well go fetch the damn thing—just be careful." Smitty nudged at his brother and appearing concerned said, "If there's anything left—we can use the oil to light this dump up."

A sudden movement in the shadows caused us to turn back toward the boy. I thought that I had been prepared for the worst, but staring into his wide and tearful blue eyes, my heart stopped.

"Help me. Someone—please. Help—me..." He whispered as choking through a mouth-full of frothing blood, coughed up something dark and vile.

"Alive --," Steve gasped, his eyes torn with emotion as he said, "Suffering Christ, the kid's still alive..."

"There must be some way to get those fucking things off of him?" Gene drew his hunting knife, and cautiously approaching the boy, said, "Hang on there, partner, I'm going to see what I can do for you."

Following closely as Gene moved around the couch, we all leaned down to closer observe the young man.

From what I could see between the poor light and frothing blood there were over a dozen of the tiny creatures. About the size of a light bulb they had managed to bury their heads deep into the soft tissue of his lower ribs. What remained visible were only the short and twitching, clawed limbs, and pale slug-like bodies.

"It's no use—I'll kill him just trying." Gene cursed as while carefully prying at the squirming and struggling things, he said, "They're in too deep… and the more that we pull at them, the further in they go."

Blake wiped at his chin, his eyes red and still glistening, he said, "Did you try using a lighter? That always works with ticks and leaches!"

"Good point." Pulling a lighter from out of his pocket and igniting the flame, he lowly waved the open flame against one of the larva. There was a blackening of the tissue as struggling, the thing frantically burrowed inward! A jet-stream of blood spurting as the boy cried out and twisted in agony!

"They're killing me!" Blood exploded from the youth's mouth as he desperately fought for breath, pleading and weeping as he wailed, praying as he screamed, "Oh—God, help me!"

God was there on that bitter-cold and dark day, but he had come in the form of vengeance and not reprieve…

Tears welled in Gene's eyes with the realization, as trembling he stared up in disbelief, and said, "There's nothing, nothing that we can do for him. Oh Jesus Christ, have mercy. Not a single damn thing…"

Shrieking hysterically, the boy swatted at the bloated things hanging from all over him and kicked violently. Spasms of shock and pain rocking his entire frame as blood spewed from multiple and ever deepening wounds! Staring into my wide and horrified eyes he began begging for mercy, and saying, "They're eating me! Oh god! Make them stop! They're eating me alive! Please help me!"

In a moment of merciful release, shock caused him to fall backward, stunned and staring into oblivion. Watching as he lay there in a growing pool of blood, my heart raced as my soul desperately sought answers. Suddenly rolling onto his side and shrieking, the horrid things struggled while burrowing ever deeper into his back. There was no more choice. I just couldn't watch this poor boy suffer any longer… My hand moved to the revolver as without a second thought I pointed the weapon. Then looking into those wide and pleading eyes, whispered in silent prayer

"Mike? Jesus, what the hell are you doing?" Gene moved toward me but Harry caught him by the wrist. There was a brief exchange of glances and Gene fell silent... Not a sound or movement came from anyone, the tension and horror of the moment gripping all us in a state of suspended disbelief. Suffocating in the stench of ammonia and death the world swam in a nauseating and fevered haze. My soul struggled with moral and religious obligations, but my heart spoke the only truth that mattered in that moment.

"I'm sorry..." I squeezed the trigger. There was an eruption of hot lead, an explosion of blood, and the bullet shattered his skull while passing through his forehead! Those wide blue eyes rolling back as the jaw dropped open, and his skull and brains sprayed the couch behind him. A smoking cloud of Sulphur drifting between the revolver and the stiffening form, I stared down into his charred and bloodied face.

Gently taking the gun from my hand, Harry supported me while leading me away, and saying, "Mike, there was nothing else that anyone could've done for him. Nothing, do you hear me?"

"We should find his identification before we go." Steve pointed toward the boy's belongings which were still heaped in the corner, and shoved against the wall.

Intending to help with the search, Harry pulled me back, saying, "Just wait here for a second." He nodded at Gene who realizing his intention and moving close, rested a reassuring hand on my shoulder, and said, "Hang in there, brother. They'll handle this part of it."

There was an eerie look in Gene's wide stare. They were the eyes of a predator with conscience. I clearly saw that he understood and supported that final decision. There was no comfort in the thought, but I needed the support in that moment more than ever before...

"Are you going to be alright, friend?" It was unexpected but Smitty now attended at my side

"I should be--..." Glancing down at the torn and still smoking remains of the boy's face, I stepped back while almost fainting.

Smitty grabbed at my arm while assisting Gene within supporting me, and said, "No-one's going to be alright until we're gone and far out of this fucking place..." He looked to Harry and Steve, and asked, "How much longer?"

Frustrated and still fumbling through the pockets and pouches of the knap-sack while searching for identification, Steve growled, saying, "I'm moving as fast as I can, but this slime is all over everything." He wiped his fingers off on some clothing his pulled from the bag, and said, "I'll tell you to wait outside—but we don't know what might be waiting out there…"

"It couldn't be any worse than what's in here--," Blake slowly made his way across the room while going after the lantern on the counter, and peering fearfully about, said, "This place is crawling with those creepy fucking, maggot things."

"We'll be out of here in just a moment." Kicking the knap-sack aside, Harry pointed toward the corpse on the couch, and cursing, said, "His wallet must be in one of his pockets?"

The scene had already been horrific enough without the fact that the body had to be moved to reach his pockets. Harry had achieved this by using a boot to gently shove at the corpse, and roll it onto its face. With brains spilling from out of the shattered skull, and among the squirming and blood soaked things that still feasted upon the flesh, we all stood aghast. Ever so cautiously, Steve reached down and began wriggling the wallet loose from the back pocket of the boy's blue jeans. In the few moments it took to pull it free and step aside, he suddenly shrieked. Falling backwards against the wall and desperately swatting at his lower left calf, he cried out, "Something bit me!"

His movements greatly hindered while working his way back from the counter through that horrendous slime, Blake pointed, shouting "He's got one of those God-damn things on his leg!"

"Hang on!" Clambering around the couch and sliding across the floor, Harry grabbed at Steve while attempting to restrain the hysterical man.

"Hold still dammit! I can't help you if you fight me!" Leaning down and drawing up the cuff of Steve's pants, he gasped. To our utter horror, clinging and chewing into the soft tissue of his lower shin was a maggot the size of a fist.

"I'll need your knife!" Harry waved at Gene who immediately brought the weapon to where they struggled to stand in the far corner of the room. Working swiftly, he used his lighter to heat the tip of the blade, and then pressed it to the flesh of Steve leg, above and slightly ahead of the burrowing grub. The hideous thing began struggling, as frantically working its way back out, dropped onto the floor. Retrieving a large Mason jar from a nearby shelf and using my boot, I kicked the maggot inside and tightly sealed the metal ringed lid. All the noise and commotion must have caused a reaction as the entire place came alive from all around us. The stairs were absolutely full of the horrendous grubs. Streaming downward, they seethed through rivers of that vile mucus while coming toward us from all sides.

Noticing where his brother still stood across the room from us with the lantern, Smitty panicked, wailing, "Blake! Get the hell out! Get out here, now!"

There wasn't even time to react. The boards above suddenly groaned beneath an immense weight. Bending from years of decay due to exposure to the elements, the structure finally succumbed and failed. There was a thunderous crack, and as we all desperately scrambled toward the door as the ceiling suddenly gave way. Blake shrieked as the boards splintered, and the mass brought the entire nightmare crashing down upon us. In the chaos, he threw the lantern, which sailing across the room, crashed and shattered against the far wall. The oil soaked the wall and floor and resulting flames flashed as the room ignited.

"Get out!" Gene wailed, as frantically waving toward the ensuing inferno that flowed like a river from all about us, said, 'The ammonia in this stuff is feeding the flames!"

The building shook again, and spinning to look upward, I stared aghast. From out of the gaping darkness above Blake poured an endless stream of squirming maggots. Varying in sizes from a finger's length to something as large as a fist, it was an oozing and hellish river of death and seething decay.

"Smitty, get out of here! Run! Run for your God-damn life!" Harry ignited his lighter and tossing it against the oil soaked wall, leapt back in the resulting explosion of flames. I felt myself ripped to one side and then pulled forward as Steve physically dragged Gene and myself toward the door. Shocked by what had happened and still stunned, I realized that we had just been standing and staring. There was an eruption of flames, gun-fire, and screams filled the cabin.

Helpless, Smitty watched in horror as his brother, kicking and screaming, was drawn down and eaten alive by the ravenous mass.

"Blake—Blake—no--," Smitty wailed as reaching out in passing, I managed to take a firm hold upon the bereaved man's right sleeve! Attempting to pull him along through the ensuing chaos, he fought back and tore free of my grasp.

"Fuckers—you dirty little Fuckers!" He fired blindly into the swiftly approaching and seething masses, shrieking, "Blake! Blake—I'm coming, hold on!"

Dragged free of the fire and madness, my foot broke through the boards of the porch and I fell forward. Harry and Gene had unknowingly gone on ahead, but Steve came back for me.

"I've got you, buddy! Hold on!" Ripping at the broken and jagged boards with his bare hands, he pulled me free. Hauling me upward and down the steps, we stumbled and were launched forward into the deep snow. Clambering to our feet, we joined Harry and Gene who now turned back to look at the cabin. The flames had taken to the ammonia in that foul slime, and the resulting chemical reaction had turned the cabin into a literal inferno. To our horror, Smitty suddenly stumbled out through the open doorway. Absolutely covered in those horrendous and clinging grubs, he extended his arms in a desperate plea for help. Horrified beyond thought or the capacity to take action of any kind, we stood speechless. With their bloated and slippery bodies writhing from all about him, they burrowed into his flesh from all sides. Biting, tearing, they ripped and crawled beneath the skin of his face while he blindly thrashed at them. The nightmare lasting only brief moments seemed an eternity. Screaming at the top of his lungs, he was overcome by the sheer mass of the horde and dropped to his knees. There was a sudden roar and the sound of splintering wood and beams. It was an act of mercy when the blazing roof had collapsed, crushing, and finally killing him...

"Oh dear God, Smitty and Blake... they're both gone..." Harry stumbled back, staring into the flames as the winds howled through the growing inferno.

"There wasn't anything that any of us could've done for either one of them." Steve placed a supportive hand upon his friend's shoulder, and watching the flames grow higher, said, "It all just happened too damn fast..."

A shot rang out and spinning toward the source of the sound, I looked to Gene who still held the smoking revolver. His eyes were huge, wild and staring, as directing the barrel of the weapon to where he had killed an enormous grub, he said, "The damn things are trying to escape."

"Jesus, we can't allow a single one of those monsters to survive." Harry motioned toward Steve, and said, "Gene can go with Michael, you come with me. We need to do a perimeter check and kill anything that's still moving." He stared as the flames licked at the branches of the high pines and then peering over at me, said, "Watch out for the trees—those things could be anywhere."

Without a word we parted and began the search on either sides of the blazing cabin. I followed closely from behind Gene as we slowly made our way around the inferno. Retrieving long and sturdy sticks from the deep snow, we began using them to spear and shove anything we saw back into the flames. Among the slithering and charred survivors we didn't find anything larger than a squirrel. Watching the melting edges of the snow and low hanging branches, we searched thoroughly and within ten feet of the roaring flames. Meeting Steve and Harry at the rear of what remained of the cabin we passed each other, and continued searching where our friends had previously been. We did this in the hopes that the opposing team might notice and discover anything that the preceding group might have missed. This had proven pertinent, as we had soon discovered several grubs that our friends had failed to notice within passing the first time. Using our branches to impale and kill them, we swept the hideous things back into the blazing coals. Coughing and choking on the stench of burning death, we didn't stop until we were sure of having gotten every last one of them.

It was beginning to get dark by the time that we had all gathered before what remained of the old cabin. Reduced to little more than smoldering timbers and smoking ash, we bowed our heads in a final farewell to our friends, Smitty and Blake…

CHAPTER TWENTY TWO

"Oh Christ… What the hell is this?" Stepping back and pointing his revolver into the deep snow before us, Gene gasped, "Oh, now this just isn't right…"

Disgusted and horrified, Harry jabbed at the thing with a long and pointed stick, and said, "It's not an insect or an animal…"

Partially burned, the grotesque thing squirmed and struggled while attempting to make its way toward where we stood. Approximately the size of a small cat, it resembled something similar to a human fetus while still baring the larval aspects of an insect. With a large and eyeless head, it had short and useless forearms, and a bloated and segmented body.

"Oh, sweet mother of Christ…" Drawing his forty-four Magnum and blowing the horror into a smoldering and unrecognizable bloody mass, Gene choked on the words, saying, "I don't give a damn what it was…. its dead now…" Using a stick and impaling the thing, he tossed the monster and branch onto the blazing coals.

Drawing the mason-jar from my coat pocket I closely examined the grub. It was still alive, but seemed to have become dormant due to the cold. Rattling the jar ever so slightly and noticing that it moved, I quickly slipped it back into the coat pocket.

"Oh shit… There's another one." Steve led us back toward the cabin and near the forest's edge, and pointing, said, "But it doesn't look anything like the last one…"

It was even larger than the last and although having burned to death, its features were clearly visible.

"It looks like?" Gene squinted as while trying to make sense of the form, and looking back at us, said, "Is there a rabbit mixed into that thing?"

The nausea was growing as gazing down upon the burned corpse I could see the resemblance to a rodent. Once again, it was another grub, but had all the characteristics of something that might evolve into a ghastly mutation…

"I think that we got all those rotten little suckers…" Gene poked at the pine brush with a branch, and looking back, said, "But where the hell are their parents?"

"Doing what all good providers do..." Steve checked his revolver and looking into the growing darkness, said, "They're out hunting for food..."

"Oh—no," The thought arrived as I turned to look back down the path from where we had come, and said, "Tim's alone out there..."

"It'll be dark soon and the temperature is already dropping. There's no way that we'll have time to backtrack now, we'll freeze to death out there." Reloading his Winchester Harry looked between us, and said, "We'll just have to hope and pray that he made it—and stick with our original plan to meet him out on the mine road."

"What if he didn't?" Gene asked the obvious.

"The mine road is close to the highway, and we have a better chance of survival than we would if we tried going back from here." I spoke where Harry's grief had left him without words in explanation, and said, "There are old shacks up there as well, wood, and a chance to take shelter... We could light a fire and wait out the night if we have to..."

"What're you planning on doing with that?" Gene motioned toward the Mason jar that bulged from within my coat pocket, and said, "I mean, you're not seriously thinking about keeping it, are you?"

Drawing it back out, I watched as it wriggled around in a trail of blood and mucus, and said, "Only long enough to have it analyzed."

"I've got a feeling that you might not like the answer--," Steve rubbed his hands together for warmth and slipping back into his gloves, said, "You should just toss it into the flames with the others where it belongs..."

"You may be right--," I looked to the big man in all sincerity, and shoving the jar back into my pocket, said, "But I'm going to go on my gut-instinct here."

"We'd better get a move on--," Harry urged while peering high into the pine branches and observing the clouding heavens, said, "It looks like we might be in for some bad weather..."

Following Gene and his dogs ever upward we traveled through the deep snow and into the back-country. The hills rose steeply from before us, and in the distance I could see the frozen peaks of the Hedley mines. If it wasn't for Tim, and the desperate hope of finding shelter, it would have been the last place on earth I would have gone.

The memories of what lurked within those old caverns frightened me even more than the horrors that might be pursuing us now. During the day and while passing it might have been different, but not now and in the darkness…. Deep within my psyche, I knew that we would be lost if we should encounter the horror that haunted those dismal, old shafts. At least when fighting against a living thing there was a slight chance…

"What are you expecting the scientists to tell you about that thing?" Panting, Steve limped along on his injured leg from beside me, and said, "We already know they suckle like pigs at the bodies of their victims, grow enormous, and seem to change according to whatever they're eating at the time."

"I'm more interested in finding out whether they're a naturally occurring species, or something foreign."

"So, you figure that they're either someone science experiment or aliens--," Harry used the end of his rifle to shove a branch from out of our path, and said, "If I had to guess? I'd go with the alien theory…"

"I wouldn't be so sure of that." Gene called back while contemplating the possibilities, and said, "Towards the end of summer, I've seen squirrels with warbles. I've even seen a few dead ones that were totally infested with the damn things…"

"Warbles, what the hell is a damn, warble?" Instinctively scratching at his neck with the mere mention of biting insects, Steve stared aghast.

"They're flesh-fly maggots that infest squirrels, coyotes, and other wood-land critters." Gene called back, saying, "The flies lay their eggs on leaves. The animals rub against the leaves, and the eggs stick to their fur. When the maggot hatches, they burrow under the animals skin. Then they stretch the skin into these disgusting sacks, and rip a hole in the end so that they can breathe. They feed on the animal's blood until they're ready to pupate and become adult flies. Then they just drop out. I've seen it a few times when I used to help my Uncle with his taxidermy. But they aren't nearly as big or near as nasty as what we saw. The biggest one's that you'll ever see are in Asia, Costa Rica, and Africa. About two or three inches long, but nothing like these things…"

"You sure seem to know a hell of a lot about the damn things?"

Suspicion reflected within Harry's eyes, as he said, "You don't strike me as the type to have an interest in entomology."

Pausing on the path with his dogs and pulling up his right pant leg, Gene cursed, and said, "Well I sure as hell should! Because--," He nodded and holding the flash-light to his lower calf, said, "I was unlucky enough to get a few of the little flesh-suckers on my leg in Nam."

"Maggots did that?" I gasped while moving closer to examine the hideous and trailing scars.

"Some of it—my friends did the rest while trying to dig the dirty little worms out." He rolled down his pant cuff and trembling in the icy wind, said, "After that, I learned everything that I could about those rotten little bastards. I'll tell you this. You'll never catch me traipsing through any tropical rain forests, ever again."

"So, according to what you know about these things--," Steve followed closely along from behind Gene, and asked, "It's possible to survive them, right?"

"Oh sure, you can survive the regular kind as long as you don't get too many. But these things that we're up against, well, they're something very different…"

"How different are they, really?" Pulling the jar from my coat pocket and approaching the man, I held it before him, and said, "What makes them so different from our natural species?"

"They act similar but sure as hell don't look anything alike." Gene grumbled, as closely observing the grub through the mucus and blood covered glass, he said, "Real Screw worms burrow under the skin and hang out. What we saw was acting more like some kind of a tick or beetle grub."

Returning the jar, he continued along with his dogs, saying, "I'm not an expert—but I'd guess that it would have to be something pretty damn exotic. I've never heard of any bug that could survive the cold…"

"Whatever you do—don't fall or break that jar…" Tapping a finger into my breast, Steve warned, saying, "If that thing gets loose in your coat… Well, you saw what happened to that poor kid…"

"I know… but it doesn't look as though it's going to survive the journey home…" I had just finished replying when pressed against the warmth of my body, the creature suddenly become active. Its weight shifting in the jar against my chest, I could feel its claws and mandibles clicking against the surface of the glass. It was aware of my warm flesh and already reacting…

Gene tugged back on the leads as whimpering, the dogs faltered in mid-step and began nervously looking into the deep shadows from all about us.

"Stay sharp, gentlemen--," Drawing his revolver and peering into the dense pines, he glanced back, and said, "Our scouts just got a whiff of something they don't like…"

"Once those things discover what we did to their nest they'll be sure to follow our tracks." Harry urged everyone onward, saying, "But we can't fight them out here and in the open. Gene, get those hounds moving, we need to find cover."

There was a slight hesitation, but Gene followed orders like the good soldier that he had always been. We traveled a little faster at that point, and adrenaline fueled the desperation and fear that grew with every step. It was no longer a question of whether they might come after us, but how soon they would arrive…

The weather had changed quite quickly as we followed the most direct route along a steep ascent. Caught in a sudden and heavy snow-fall while navigating the precipice of a ravine, our efforts were hindered considerably. The path along the gorge was treacherous, as each step among the jagged rocks and ice might possibly lead to a sudden and unexpected fall. Trusting within Gene and his faithful hounds, we followed closely while navigating the almost impassable route. Powerful winds threatened to force us from over the edge as clinging desperately to the icy boulders, struggled through the ever deepening snow. With the beams of our flashlights reaching out and into the growing darkness, the whimpering of the dogs filled our hearts with dread. If we were caught by surprise upon that frozen ledge, the only escape would be a fall of several hundred feet…

Ascending ever upward and along rocky crags, we passed from out of the dense forest and higher into the frozen storm. Although I knew that the mine grew ever closer, it was lost from sight within the shadows and steady flurries. Bitterly cold and tired, and with so many terrifying ways of dying in that place, I found myself contemplating the least painful…

"It shouldn't be too much further now--," Gene shouted through the muffling effects of the wind and snow and pointing ahead, said, "This path crosses with the old mine-road just up ahead!"

The wind was growing steadily and glancing back, I saw that the snow was already filling our tracks within passing. The blizzard was becoming worse by the moment and I had been praying for well over an hour. The beams of our lights had already begun to fade, and with the cold killing the batteries, would soon be lost to utter darkness.

"It must be close--," Harry shouted, as drawing the frozen and fur collared hood of his parka about his face, said, "We'll be just fine as long as we keep moving!"

For the first time, I felt doubt within the words of my friend. It wasn't a question of his sincerity, but even through the blizzard I could see that the hounds became increasingly more nervous... They whimpered while moving erratically and as though confused as to what direction to follow. I knew that they sensed something in the night air, something that followed.... I could see the unbridled fear in my friend's blank stare. The expression was not empty, his eyes revealing unspoken knowledge, a mystery that he dared not explore. The chance of our deaths on that frozen cliff became all too real as time was quickly running out...

"Warn Gene!" Harry suddenly shouted, his eyes filled with panic as he said, "I just remembered! The path dead-ends just up ahead! He needs to make a sharp right or he'll go right off the edge!"

Realizing that Gene would never hear or see us in time, I swiftly drew my revolver. Then risking an avalanche so near the snow covered mines, fired a single round into the frozen night. The shot rang out and echoing through the darkness, halted Gene exactly where he had stood. Approaching and directing him toward the right, we began the final climb toward the old service road. With my heart pounding furiously and having trouble drawing breath in the icy winds, I stumbled blindly after my friends.

The final stretch was a steep ascent from between enormous and jagged rocks. The mountain offered little shelter from the blizzard as we travelled close against its side, and the forest loomed ahead in the blackness. It wasn't the shadows ahead that now troubled me, but the blackness and what might be following from behind... Clambering over a cement barrier along the road's edge, we hurried out and into a wide clearing. I knew this place… It was the main entrance to the upper mine shaft…

"Let's go, buddy!" Steve pulled me along as limping upon his injured leg, forced everyone ahead of him. His courage and consideration was an admirable quality, but for reasons beyond explanation, I now feared more for him than the others…

In passing the old mine entrance I felt something even colder than the night take hold of my heart. My father's life had been taken there and my own nearly lost. Pursued by an unspeakable horror I now found myself staring into the blackened mouth of the devils lair… The world and all sound seemed to vanish in that moment, and as all reality became focused entirely upon that single thing.

"Keep moving--," Steve barked while drawing me along, and saying, "We're almost there!"

In the deep snow and wind, fatigued and terrified beyond my wits, it was almost impossible to force one foot in front of the other. Yet, a desperate need forced me onward and somehow I managed. When we reached the bottom of the service road we took shelter beneath some immense, pine branches. It was a natural canopy and blocking the wind, offered momentary reprieve from the storm.

"You look like death warmed over--," Harry patted my shoulder and leaning closer while inspecting the pupils of my eyes, said, "How are you holding out?"

"All things considered, not so bad for a city-slicker that hasn't walked further than a corner market in years…"

"What if those things somehow change and become like whatever they've been eating." Gene tightly gripped the reigns of his dogs while looking between us, and said, "That would explain why some look so different and are like animals."

"It's not possible--," Harry brushed the snow from off the hood of his parka, and said, "There's nothing in this world that does that."

"Nothing known…" I stared among my friends.

"Gentlemen, need I remind you that we might be getting some unwelcome, and very pissed off visitors soon?" Steve gestured down the road with a sudden urgency, and said, "We should get our asses down to the road… as fast as possible…"

The discussion having ended quite abruptly, we returned to the night and blizzard while hurrying down the old service road. The storm had slowed to some degree, and the descent through the deep snow was easier than the previous climb. Still, I felt utterly worn, sick, and my entire body was numb due to the cold. There was a burning in my fingers and toes and I feared frost-bite....

By the time that we reached the bottom of the service road the wind and snow had seemingly just vanished. There was no sign of Tim or Harry's Chrysler, and we took shelter in an empty tool shed near the highway.

"Tim should've been here by now." The fear and doubt in Harry's eyes caused us to look toward the dark highway. Even without the blizzard winds, there was still a six mile trek through deep snow and wilderness between us and civilization.

"He'll be here." Gene offered a glimmer of hope in a moment of desperation, saying, "He wasn't in any condition to make that hike. So it likely took him a lot longer to get back."

Locating some old boards and wooden crates once used for mining supplies, Harry began breaking them down. We had all just sat around and watched as building a pyre in the middle of the open shed, he set flame to it.

"Who cares if the place burns down--," He scoffed, as holding his hands over the warming fire, said, "It beats freezing to death out here... Besides, if Tim does show up, he'll see us from a mile away now."

"You never mentioned how you managed to pick up those bugs over-seas." Kneeling before the fire and warming my hands, I looked curiously toward Gene, and asked, "Are they common?"

"My Platoon was out on a routine Recon mission." He began explaining, his glasses eerily reflecting the flames as he said, "That's where you get sent deep into enemy territory to observe, and take out possible North Vietnamese Army or Viet Cong operations. When we found anything, we'd just call in for air-support and bomb the living shit out of them."

"I wish that we had that option right now..." Steve stared into the flames.

"I hear you, brother, loud and clear...." Gene sighed, and adding more wood to the fire, said, "For private reasons I can't disclose my unit number or the location." He swallowed back a lump in his throat, and looking around nervously, said, "On one particular mission, we got sent into this little village out in the middle of nowhere. It bordered a river, was deep in the jungle and we had a bitch of a time getting in. It was surrounded in swamp, full of snakes, mosquitoes, leeches and other ungodly, biting things. Hell, we were just grateful to get back on dry land by the time we got there." Picking at a splinter of wood, he played in the flames, saying, "What we didn't know—was that we weren't just sent in for the usual reasons. You see, military intelligence was working on something new…"

"Was it a disease or virus?" Steve just stared.

Shaking his head and without reply, Gene drew a deep breath before finally saying, "The place looked abandoned—so we started looking through the huts. That's when I saw him… He came out of one of the huts—an old guy, maybe in his late seventies. He was nothing but skin and bones--," Gene's face twisted with pity and unspoken revulsion, as struggling with the memory, said, "He was absolutely covered, infested, and every inch of his body was sagging with those horrible, fucking things. His hands, face, belly, legs, they were hanging from everywhere!"

"How does something like that happen?" Harry stared aghast.

"In Laos the flies lay eggs on mosquitoes and then let them go. The damn things land on people and the fly eggs are transferred to another host. That's how I picked them up…." Gene shuddered, suddenly and violently scratched at his legs.

"What about the old man in that village?" Harry coughed while trying to light a cigar from out of the fire, and asked, "Did he make it?"

"No--," Glancing over at me in a rather sympathetic fashion, Gene swallowed hard and looking away, said, "I shot the poor son of a bitch. You see, although he was full of those things, they weren't your average, run of the mill, flesh fly. They were something special cooked up by military intelligence. That old man never had a chance…"

"Why would the military do something like that?" Steve appeared unconvinced, and frowning, said, "It wouldn't make sense to attack civilians."

"That's what a lot of folks thought. But we were told that President Nixon endorsed the idea of using these flesh eating flies. It was a way to covertly eradicate opium poppy in areas of Burma, Laos, and Thailand. It killed a lot of cattle and people, but war is war, right?"

"Sometimes, I'm ashamed to be human." Disgusted, Steve shook his head, saying, "What kind of a monster could condemn anyone to a death like that?"

"Could you explain the difference between the Warblers from here and the species in Costa Rica, again?" I thought for a moment, and added, "Also, that part about their reproductive habits."

"Warblers lay eggs on branches and leaves." Gene explained while leaning to avoid sparks from the fire, and said, "The flies in South America lay eggs on mosquitoes and let them go. The mosquitoes infect people by landing on them. The one's we saw in Laos, well they were a little bigger and different. They would lay eggs around wounds, your eyes, nose, ears, or any orifice if you're following me?"

My hand suddenly slipped to the jar in my coat, as gently feeling and finding the lid secure, sighed deeply.

"Those ones, they hatched right away and the maggots would dig into the wound and crawl around under your skin." Raising his beret and scratching at his head, he said, "After a few days they'd find a good spot, dig themselves right in and then hang on with tiny spines. They just look like boils until they poke their heads out and start eating you alive."

"Jesus Christ." Harry spat, saying, "I never knew that anything like that existed outside of horror films."

"I have a few friends that live in Vietnam." Steve shot a suspicious glance at Gene, and said, "Why don't they have problems with those Botflies or screw flies of yours now?"

"Simple--," Gene gazed straight into Steve eyes and said quite honestly, "Apparently, Nixon had some scientists create infertile males. So the next generations of flies were born dead. That way you could hit a place, take everyone out, and maintain population control with your insects…"

"What if they bred out of their own species?" My thoughts began racing.

"From what I read, that wouldn't work with most bugs. Oh, they could poke around alright, but nothing would ever come of it." Thinking briefly, Gene suddenly pointed to the jar in my pocket, and said, "Oh, that reminds me. Our critters eat the living and the dead. Botflies need a living host to gestate."

"So, what difference does that make?" Steve was visibly sickened with the thought.

"I'm just pointing out that their dietary requirements broaden their options on the evolutionary scale. Think about it—they'll survive longer than most things because they can eat almost anything..."

"That doesn't say much for the survival of the human race if these things ever get out of this town." Puffing at his cigar, Harry peered about in the dancing shadows of the firelight, and said, "Jesus, this just keeps getting worse... When we get back, I'll have to lie to the parents of that boy we found—because the truth would give them nightmares for the rest of their lives..."

"Which won't be too much longer the way this is going?" Gene scowled, and said, "Let's face it, chief. Those things have managed to eat their way through our little town in just a few months. Can you imagine what they could do if they ever reached the big cities?"

The dogs suddenly growled, barked, and then began baying out of control. Leaping up and drawing our weapons we poised while preparing for the absolute worst.

"It's the car—I see the headlights!" Gene waved the revolver toward the open doorway, and said, "Tim made it!"

Abandoning the old shed and fire, we waved our lights frantically before attempting the fifty yard stretch down the steep service road. Flashing the headlights in return, Tim remained parked in the plowed area to avoid becoming trapped in the deep snow of the service road. The wind howled, the darkness seemed to close in from all about us, and the forest stood ominously in the night. The journey had been terrifying enough, but not nearly as bad as those final and desperate moments before reaching the car. The tension was incredible as while remaining in a tight group, and with weapons drawn, we fought our way through the deep snow.

"Come on—hurry up!" Steve opened the passenger side door and shoving me into the front seat, dropped down beside me.

"Let's go!" Harry loaded all three hounds into the back seat with Gene, and then running to the driver's side, shoved Tim over.

"Where are Smitty and Blake?" Tim squeezed over as crushed

between us in the front seat, looked to Harry for an answer.

"They didn't make it..." Harry slowly pulled away while following through Tim's previous tracks in the snow.

"The dogs found an old cabin not far from the mine." Steve explained while rubbing at his lower calf, and saying, "Connie's body was there—..."

"The long and short of the story--," Harry interrupted, saying, "The place was some kind of nest filled with giant maggots. There was a fire, and Smitty and Blake were killed in the confusion. The rest of us were even lucky just to get out of there."

Tim's eyes widened as producing the jar and creature, I held it before him, and said, "I managed to capture one of them. It seems safe enough when contained behind glass..."

"It certainly resembles a maggot--," Leaning closer to further examine the creature, he shook his head, saying, "But not even the Atlas Chalcosoma, third stage, is anywhere near that big."

"Did you say, Atlas Beetle? No, this thing isn't nearly that large—it's--?" Surprised at his statement, I looked to the jar and almost dropped it while discovering the larva to have almost filled the container.

"Damn—it's almost four times its original size..." Harry sped dangerously through the deep tracks leading back toward the highway.

"The lousy thing sure chewed me up pretty good." Struggling with his pant leg in the front seat, Steve examined the bite.

"That wound looks like it might be getting infected..." Tim's eyes narrowed suspiciously as he glanced over at me, and said, "We better hope there isn't any kind of toxin in that things bite..."

"It's a little red and sensitive but I've survived far worse." Rubbing at the injury Steve winced, and said, "That maggot didn't cause anywhere near the damage that the big one did on the highway that night..."

"I wonder if the effects of the bites vary according to the maturity and gender of the insect." The concept terrified me even as the words had escaped me in thought.

"You know, that's something else that we never took into consideration when examining the bodies..." Tim's features paled as he looked to me, and said, "I don't know why it didn't occur to me at the time? We could have lost things, possibly even substantial evidence that was already missing when we examined the bodies…"

"You found that piece of shell or whatever it was?" Harry pointed out, saying "So what could we have missed?"

"I don't mean among the bodies at the parlor--," Tim appeared anxious as swallowing back his own fear, said, "What if the coroner had already removed all the foreign matter from the corpses, and anything that he considered, insignificant to the case. Although its winter, water is always full of leaves, mud, and insects. What if she was infected or--…"

"Infested--," Gene stared and thinking briefly, said, "Sure, it might have been using those bodies in the same way that the flies used the mosquitoes. If she was floating in the water of that ditch, most of it might have been washed away in the stream."

"And considering it to have been a hit and run--," Steve agreed, and said, "He would've cleaned away and disposed of anything that wasn't conclusive to the evidence."

"I'm starting to get the feeling that this is going to get a whole lot uglier, real fast…" Harry spat his cigar out the partially open window and glancing back at Gene, asked, "Where does that stream flow?"

"It comes straight down the highway and through the ditches past town…"

"Alright, that explains a few things…" Harry coughed and clearing his throat, said, "Gene, did you want to stay in town with us tonight?"

"No, I'll be fine at the farm." Petting Rosie on the head, he said, "Most animals won't come near dogs." He thought briefly before saying, "Well, not a whole pack of them, anyway."

It was hard for me to be in such close proximity of those large animals. After the near fatal incident with the mongrel pack I had never managed to regain my appreciation or trust for dogs. I could only hope and pray that fate would deal Gene a better card…

Slowing and pulling off to the side of the highway, Harry nodded toward a brightly lit farmhouse, and said, "I can't make it down your driveway. Did you want us to walk out there with you?"

"No—I've got my forty-four and the dogs." Gene began unloading his hounds and gripping his shot-gun, looked to me, and said, "If I were you, friend, I'd kill that thing in the jar before something else goes wrong." Patting the roof of the car, he bade us all a good night, and with his dogs in the lead, made his way down the steep driveway.

Watching as he plodded down past a shed containing skidoos and a small tractor, my hand slipped down to the jar. For reasons beyond explanation the creature now held some kind of significance in my mind. Having already destroyed the nest and preparing to kill the adults, I realized that it might be the last of its kind…

"How muddy is it back there?" Steve squirmed to look into the back seat.

Twisting and reaching in between the two larger men, Tim wiped a hand across the seat, and said, "It's just a little wet from the melting snow--," He sniffed at his fingers and frowning, said, "And smells of dogs…"

Without a word, Steve clambered up into the back seat, and grunting as he stretched out, said, "That's much better."

Noticing the lights flash on the front porch, Harry sighed and looking to me, quietly said, "Alright, he's covered and safe for the night. Let's get our half-frozen carcasses home too."

"I just realized something--," Tim stretched out while settling in the seat between us, and said, "If those creatures were tracking you, and possess any intelligence, whatsoever---."

"They might have discovered that our prints and scent vanished at the tire tracks…. And they might possibly follow the car back into town--," Steve finished the thought from out of the back seat.

"Right to Gene's farm…" Harry nervously tapped his fingers upon the steering wheel, and then contemplating briefly, said, "But in that case, wouldn't they just stay on the scent of the car until they found us?"

"Assuming that they even have the intelligence to figure that out?" Steve scoffed at the thought, and said, "Let's try to keep in mind that whatever they are, they're still just bugs."

"They were smart enough to locate the corpses of the women at my parlor--," Tim reminded them, saying, "And considering what you described about their assimilation of genetic material, they might be even further advanced than we might imagine…"

"I think that your slimy little friend is dead…" Harry curiously eyed the jar clasped tightly within my hands.

"What?" Gently shaking it and watching as the grub barely reacted, I panicked, and looking to Steve, asked, "Do you have a knife or anything that I could use to poke holes in the top?"

Pulling a pocket knife from his hunting vest, Harry handed it to me with a scowl, and asked, "Are you sure that you want to do that? We don't know if that things poisonous. Look what it did to Steve's leg."

"That's all the more reason to keep it alive--," I began poking holes into the metal lid, and returning his knife, said, "This animal might be important to the development of an anti-toxin or anti-viral agent."

"As much as I hate to agree--," Tim peered down while curiously eyeing the grub, and said, "He's right. If the animal proves to be poisonous, then it's also the only source we have for creating anti-venom…."

"Oh, I almost forgot about this--,"Reaching over the seat and dropping a wallet into Harry's lap, Steve said, "The name of the kid that we found at the cabin was, Brian David Anderson. He was sixteen years old."

Until that moment, the boy's death had begun to feel like it was just part of some foul and fevered delusion. Adding a name to the face, regardless of intent, my heart suffered with the guilt of his murder.

"He was from Penticton." Harry examined the driver's license and passing the wallet back, said, "Now why doesn't that surprise me?"

"With all the transients and runaways these days--," Steve stared from the back seat while saying, "Who can keep track of them all? In the end, we'll never know the names of all the victims, or know how many bodies were actually hidden in that old cabin…"

"Or for how long this has really been going on?" Looking into the jar I felt a mixed sense of horror and relief as the creature began moving around. It was sluggish but still alive…

"If this thing is really some kind of an insect--," Steve asked, "Then how long could it possibly live? Don't they usually have short life spans? I know that most of the little ones, like dragonflies and mosquitoes, only last a few days after reaching adulthood."

"The fact is--," Correcting Steve as we pulled in before the diner, I said, "It may have started as some type of larval or pupal stage, but we really don't know what the final version of this animal looks like."

"From what I can see--," Tim examined the grub as it slowed and seemed to look back at him, he said, "It's growing at an alarming rate, and anything with an accelerated metabolism, especially one that matures at this rate, never lives long." Looking between us as we parked, he said, "This creature goes against all laws of physics. According to the book that had the information about the blue and green bottle-fly--," He reminded us, saying, "Insects have become smaller over the millennia due to higher oxygen levels. To be any bigger, well, they'd need to have lungs."

"From what see saw at that old cabin--," Harry pulled into the lot and parking before the diner, said, "It looks like they all start out like bugs, and like Tim pointed out earlier, become like whatever they're eating. Need I remind you gentlemen—they're eating people now…"

"Which would explain why they might develop lungs--," Horrified with the thought, I gazed into the lights of the empty diner before us, and said, "And would account for their size and growing intelligence…"

"Okay then—hypothetical scenario," Steve turned toward Harry and pointing a finger, said, "Three months ago—and for whatever reason, these things appear. They take the people from that accident scene, eat the dead or less desirable one's, and lay eggs into the others. Obviously, they take their food back to a well sheltered area and to where they build a nest. That would explain why there weren't any victims found at the scene, and why your partner's body vanished." The twitch in Steve's left eye revealed his fears in revelation, and he said, "What if Harry actually managed to fatally wound whatever attacked me that night, and it crawled off and died."

"Assuming that there were two of them?" I followed the pattern, saying, "The second may have remained with the nest?"

"No—it would have likely moved the young into safer territory. Most animals do that when threatened." Tim interrupted and then said, "Which is how they came into Hedley…"

"Alright, so let's assume that being similar to other insects for the most part, that the adult dies of natural causes. It's established a nest in that old cabin, and leaves the young to fend for them-selves." Steve began tapping the back of the seat with a finger in thought, and saying, "The young one's aren't mobile as grubs or big enough to hunt large prey."

"So, as they develop they become cannibalistic to survive, and once big enough, start taking mice and squirrels--," Harry continued with the thought, his eyes growing large with the sudden realization, as he said, "Then the local cats and dogs start to go missing…"

"And when one of them got big enough--," Steve slapped the back of his hand against the seat, and said, "Pow, it takes out that boar at Barry's farm. By now, it would be a big son of a bitch, and that's when it takes Connie, and runs into poor old Shirley at the cemetery."

"If we're right about this, and they evolve according to what they eat?" Harry choked on the thought as fumbling for another cigar and lighting it, said, "They get smarter, bigger, and more dangerous with each kill."

"Eventually, they'll rise to the top of the food chain—," Tim stared down at the thing in the jar and almost whispering, said, "And we become their primary food source."

"Jesus—I hope to God that we're wrong about this whole thing." Harry grumbled as glancing at his watch, said, "It's just after eight and the diner's still open, anyone feel like eating?"

Disgusted and horrified, Tim looked down at the maggot, its tiny black pincers snapping, tapping against the glass as it struggled to escape.

"Well someone does…" He appeared as though he may be sick.

"Our boots are covered in crap and we smell like we've been rolling around in a pig pen full of roadkill." I looked to Harry in question while raising an eyebrow, and said, "Do you think that's such a good idea?"

He thought for a moment and then looking back at me, said, "If you saw some of the hog farmers and trucker's that roll through here— you wouldn't so worried about it."

"Oh no… Are you guy's hearing this?" Turning up the volume as the weather report came over the radio, Tim frowned and said, "There's a winter storm coming out of the North and they're closing all the roads. No one will be getting in or out of here for days…"

"Listen--," Steve leaned into the front seat while looking between us, and said, "We've already wiped out their nest, and just have to find and kill the adults now. This might just be a blessing in disguise. Most of the locals are out of town—and without traffic, the risks are far lower. This might just be an opportunity to clean things up around here before things get completely out of hand..."

"I admire your optimism but wish that I had half of your courage of conviction." Swallowing hard while sinking down into the seat, I struggled for the words, saying, "We have no idea of what might still be out there. Remember, what we destroyed were only babies, and if they grow at this rate--," I held the jar before my friends wide eyes, and said, "Who knows how many or how big they've become over the past three months..."

"Bottom line, friend..." Steve leaned into the front seat, his dark eyes focusing upon me as grinning cruelly, he quietly said, "It's quite likely that none of us are getting out of this alive. You just need to decide whether you're going to take that lying down or fighting..."

There hadn't been any need for a response in that moment, as nodding. Steve slowly sank into the shadows of the back seat.

"Well I don't know about you boys?" Harry turned off the car and glancing between us, said, "But I could really go for a hot cup of coffee right about now..."

CHAPTER TWENTY THREE

8:35 p.m.

The little bell above the door jingled as announcing our arrival, we paused to stomp the snow from our boots. Surprised while looking down, I took suddenly noticed that our boots were barren of the foul sludge. It appeared to have been frozen and then brushed off during our journey through the snow. The sounds of 'Patsy Cline' singing "Walking after Midnight" echoed from a plastic Philco radio behind the counter. Lost through a field of static, it only served to make the empty place seem even lonelier.

"I can't believe that stuff came off our boots?" Harry was astonished, but sniffing at his jacket, winced and quietly said, "But we'll likely have to burn all of our clothes later…"

It was becoming a routine. Feeling miserable, I squirmed about in the fouled military fatigues and dearly missed my own clothes…

As though reading my expression as we passed the front counter, Harry leaned close, and quietly said, "Once we're done here we'll run over to my place, shower, and find some clean clothes. I'm sure that I've got something that'll fit you."

I welcomed the thought with a friendly nod in thanks. We all took turns in the little diner bathroom. I spent the longest time in there, and vigorously washing my hands and face with soap, simply couldn't walk away from the source of that hot water. The warmth had also soothed the thing in the jar, as making an eerie and barely audible, humming sound, became dormant.

Pondering the noise briefly, it seemed more like a slight vibration against my body rather than being an intentional sound. In a nervous moment, I feared that it might be calling for help by means of some 'ultrasonic' frequency… Stop it Michael… Do not start attributing higher intellect and abilities to the creature, it's just an animal. An animal of unknown origin and a threat to all human life… Even if it was summoning the adults it would only serve to hasten the inevitable…

"What's bothering you?" Harry looked up as I slipped into the booth beside Tim, and he said, 'You've got that look on your face again. Like you stepped in something and you're worried that someone will notice."

"It's the grub--," I said, and speaking in all honesty, looked fearfully between my friends while saying, "It's making some kind of low frequency sound or vibration. I'm not sure if it's just a reaction to climate change, whether it senses food here, or if it's a method of communication between these things?"

From their expressions I was already afraid that Harry might insist that we destroy it immediately. Gathering his thoughts, he said quite plainly, "We need to end this thing as soon as possible. So, if it's calling for help--then it'll just bring them to us that much faster..."

I could see that Steve agreed while Tim peered down at the jar in my coat pocket.

"Maybe we should've brought the weapons inside with us?" Harry thought aloud.

Almost dropping his glasses, Tim eyed me fearfully before turning his attention toward the window, and saying, "This diner is all windows—and we're surrounded in glass..."

The thought had never really occurred to me until that moment but he was absolutely right. We could be seen from almost any angle and direction with exception to the area of the kitchen and front counter. We were sitting ducks in that place...

"I'll be right there boys!" Linda peeked out while calling from somewhere in the back. Her apology was accompanied by the busy clatter of dishes, as she called again, saying, "Sorry gent's, I'll just be a second!"

"It's hard to believe how she can stay so busy in a place that's so empty." Harry looked around and scoffing at the thought, said, "I just realized that we're the only ones in here."

"Well hello there, gents!" Linda hurried out from behind the counter, as wiping her hands on an apron, retrieved the coffee urn, and asked, "What can I get for you boys this evening?"

She hadn't commented on the odor, but her surprised reaction and slight hesitation was evidence enough. The reek of death hung like a vile cloud from all around our table...

"Coffee would be a great start." Searching his pockets for another cigar, Harry looked up at her and asked, "Would you have a few moments? I know that you're busy back there, but I could sure use your help with something. It's important..."

Immediately noticing the tension around the table the smile faded from her face. Wiping her hands upon her apron, she seemed reluctant, but politely said, "Sure, Harry… Just let me tell Bert. I'll turn off the water and be right with you."

Lighting a cigarette and watching as she hurried away, I turned my attention back to Harry, and quietly asked, "You're not thinking about telling her about what's been happening around here, are you?"

"As much as I'd like to warn everyone in town… Give me some credit—we don't need a panic on our hands as well." An obvious dread and growing paranoia filled his eyes. He moved slowly in the seat, turning and leaning as while searching the darkness beyond the surrounding windows. I knew what he was looking for and prayed that he didn't find it…

"At least there haven't been any more encounters or other incidents yet." Tapping his fingers nervously at the table, Steve said, "There must have been over sixty hunters out there and combing that forest today. I'm sure that if they'd seen anything we would've heard about it by now."

"No news isn't always good news--," Harry's expression was blank as sipping at his coffee, he said, "We'll have no way of knowing what really happened out there until someone comes back to tell us…"

Returning with a large platter of assorted muffins and donuts, Linda placed them down before us. Pulling a chair from a near-bye table and seating hers-self at the end of the booth, she pointed, and said, "I really wouldn't want those nice muffins and donuts to go to waste. There hasn't been anyone around to enjoy them, so Bert said that they're on the house."

"That's mighty fine of him--," Harry motioned for all of us to indulge, and looking back to Linda, said, "I'll make sure to thank him on the way out."

Lighting a cigarette, she took a long pull and leaning back into the seat, looked to him, asking, "So, what's on your mind tonight, honey?"

"Linda--," Harry fumbled for the words and appearing increasingly uncomfortable, said, "I realize that this is a tender subject, and especially right now. But I really need to ask you a few questions about, Connie? It's no secret around town that you two were pretty close. So you might be our only hope of getting some straight answers here?"

She became immediately defensive. Crossing her arms over her breast, her cheeks flushed, and eyes became glassy as jeering, she said, "She was the sweetest, most honest, and reliable little gal that I've ever known. God—I miss her so much." Sniffling, she fought back the tears, and said, "She was like a ray of sunshine around here, and always had a smile for everyone."

"I know—I remember her, she was a real doll." It was apparent that Harry was just as uncomfortable asking the questions as Linda was answering them.

Sipping at his coffee, he looked to her, and said, "Listen, I know that what I'm about to ask may sound of the wall, but I can assure you that it's of the utmost important. Linda, did she ever mention anything to you about a skin irritation, rash, infection, or strange swelling of any kind?" By now Harry's features had paled and become blank while fueled by fear and desperation.

Linda fell absolutely silent in that moment. It was apparent that she was hiding something as avoiding all eye-contact, quickly shook her head, saying, "Nothing that I can remember? I mean—if you're thinking anything illegal—she wasn't on the marijuana or anything like that."

"No—I wasn't thinking anything like that." He fumbled for a cigar and lighting it, looked to her as speaking through a cloud of smoke, he said, "To be honest, I'm more concerned that she might've come into contact with some foreign bacteria, virus, corrosive acid or chemical? Are you absolutely sure, without a single doubt in your mind, that she never said anything about any of these things?"

The tension was so deep in that moment that I almost expected her to collapse from the sheer intensity.

Chewing at a long and red finger-nail, she looked away, and thinking for a moment, said, "Well, now that you mention it? There was—something…"

"Please—I need to know…"

Apprehensive, she looked into the faces of all in our little group before turning back to Harry, and saying with great reserve, "Well, it's not the type of thing that one generally speaks about—and especially in the company of men."

"Don't concern yourself about that right now." He tapped his cigar into the astray and shoving it back into his mouth, said, "All that matters right now, is that you think very hard, and tell me everything that you know about this…"

It was quite obvious that she had either known or failed so say something, and feared saying anything now.

Until that moment Steve had worn a 'poker face' and been silent. Observing her every movement without reaction, followed each word, and scrutinized every reaction. Then, his thoughts caught somewhere between disappointment and frustration, he looked to Linda and muttering, said, "Is it possible that the young lady might have encountered a stranger or met with a friend from out of town?"

His words had fallen like a hammer in the stillness and she suddenly turned, wide-eyed and looking to Harry.

"No one is in any trouble here--," Harry reassured her as reaching over and petting her wrist, spoke calmly and quietly, and said, "I just need your help to figure some things out…"

"I thought--," She stuttered as she began fidgeting with her apron strings, and suddenly staring wildly at Harry, choked while saying, "I thought that the police had already solved the circumstances surrounding her death? It was an accident out on the highway—a snowplow or something, right?"

She desperately looked to all of us for answers, her eyes pleading as fear and doubt now caused her to tremble.

"Yes, they did establish a cause of death—but the investigation as to the person responsible is still pending--," Harry appealed to her sense and sensibilities, saying, "If you know anything—please, help us bring her killer to justice…"

'Why are you asking about bacteria and acid--," Visibly confused and terrified, she said, "Is there something that the police are hiding from us about what really happened to her?"

"Anything that could be revealed was already released to the public." Steve quietly explained, saying, "Anything else is information that only her killer would know… And it's the only way that we can catch and convict him now."

No sooner had he finished speaking, than did she suddenly throw her hands before her face and burst into tears. Hysterical and staring, the mascara ran like dark rivers from between her fingers. Our suspicions confirmed we knew that a mystery was soon to be revealed.

"It was a girl thing—it happens, you know?" Her words were hardly comprehensible as she wept bitterly, and said, "She had the usual cramping—but it got worse, and she said that something wasn't right. She told me that she hadn't stopped bleeding—and that it had almost been three weeks."

We all watched as she looked around the diner as though praying for release. Maybe she hoped that a late customer might arrive or that the telephone might possibly ring? It was hopeless and there was no reprieve for her that night.

"My wife used to experience severe cramping, and heavy flows that often lasted for quite some time." Breaking off a piece of muffin and dipping it into his coffee, he looked up at her, and said, "As a mature woman you must've known that can happen?"

"Of course, and I explained all of it to her... But she had another reason for being concerned about her time of the month..." She sniffled as her features twisted into a mascara smeared highway of tears. Biting down upon her lower lip she looked up, and suddenly said. "She met a boy here one night about three weeks ago. And well, did something that she would never have done before..."

There was nothing that anyone could have said in that moment to bring comfort to the situation. The entire hideous affair was slowly coming together.

Remorseful, she pleaded, "Please—you can't ever breathe a word about this! It would break her parent's hearts—and it's already been hard enough on them losing their baby-girl."

"I know that you all grew up and went to school here, together--," Harry rubbed at his eyes, saying, "We all did..."

"Connie's Grandfather, bless his heart, used to bring my family wild meat." Linda ran a hand through her dyed golden curls and sniffling, said, "He's long gone now, but her father still shares when they manage to get a decent sized buck. This whole town is just like one big and happy, family."

"Please—," Harry's demeanor now took on a sense of urgency, and intently focused upon the woman, he said, "From the beginning—tell me everything that you remember about Connie and this boy?"

"Well—it all started three weeks ago, it was a Friday and a bitter cold night." She sniffled and accepting another napkin from Steve, blew her nose before, saying, "The boy had come into the diner—it was somewhere near closing time… It was snowing really heavy that night and he was hitch-hiking. He said something about seeing his father in Vancouver. He was a sweet boy, and I could see that Connie liked him right away. Anyway, I was in a bit of a hurry, and she promised to close for me that night. So, just after nine, I packed my things and said good-night, and hurried off home."

"You left her alone--," Steve picked at the muffin, his eyes dark and assuming as he frowned at her, and said, "Without even knowing this boy?"

Tightly clasping her hands together on the table before her, she looked up quite thoughtfully, and said, "His name is Brian David Anderson, he's sixteen, and his parents are divorced. He lives with his mother in Penticton, and was hitch-hiking to Vancouver to visit with his dad. He left his parents numbers, and I've spoken to them both since. Apparently, he never arrived at his father's and he's been missing since that night…"

Harry grabbed my wrist without even turning to look at me. This had drawn Linda's attention but not her curiosity. She was far too caught up in the current conversation.

"I knew that Brian had stayed with Connie in the diner over-night. Because she told her folks that she'd stayed to help me do a cleaning. Bert was expecting the health inspector that week, so it wasn't a complete lie…" Bursting into tears ago, she coughed out the words, saying, "Her family never even asked any questions— they trusted me…"

"Can I inquire as to why you had been in such a hurry to go home that night?" Steve was polite but direct.

"I was meeting a truck driver friend of mine--," She explained while drying her eyes, and said, "He'd offered to give Brian a lift into Keremeos the next morning. But, by the time morning had come and I'd looked for him, the boy had already gone off. Connie said that he'd left some time during the early morning."

There was a moment of silence within reflection, as wiping the mascara from her face, hung her head in despair.

"Back to Connie now--," Harry spoke quietly while obviously

sympathetic of the woman, and said, "You said that she had excessive bleeding?"

Nodding and keeping her head down like some harshly scolded child, she spoked through the tears, saying, "It was less than a week later when Connie said that she wasn't feeling too well. I just assumed that it was the monthly curse coming back with a vengeance? But she was so scared when the bleeding wouldn't stop."

"There's no blame here—just a lot of questions to answers that get harder each time." Harry climbed from the booth and gesturing for Steve to follow, looked at me and asked, "Do you two mind sticking around here for about an hour?"

"No–not at all--," Confused as to where they might be going so late and alone, I raised an eyebrow, asking, "Are you sure that you won't need us?"

"No—not for this--," He scowled and moving from the booth, glanced at Tim, and said, "Are you sure that you'll be alright for a little while?"

"Of course--," Tim nodded in agreement while waving at the platter of donuts, and saying, "I'm sure that we'll manage to stay occupied, somehow."

Moving from the table with Steve, Harry paused while looking back at Linda. She peered up at him through wet and blackened eyes and in that moment, he did what any decent human being would have. Leaning down and embracing her tightly, he said, "I'm sorry for putting you through this. You've been an enormous help. More than you might ever know. And you have my word--," Stepping back and pressing a finger before his lips he solemnly swore, saying, "This stays off the record and just between us…

Wiping at her nose with the napkin, she watched them depart before looking to me, and asking, "You don't think that sweet boy had anything to do with what happened to Connie?"

"No, I can honestly say that I don't believe he did..." Having forgotten about the thing in the jar, I was startled by its movement and gently patted at the pocket. The motion seeming to have a soothing affect, the creature became absolutely still again.

She slowly moved from the chair and reaching a hand to her lower back, winced. It was obvious that her day had been strenuous and that she needed a very, very long holiday from everything.

Clearing Steve and Harry's cups from the table, she paused in thought while asking, "Are you sure that I couldn't interest either one of you in a nice, venison steak? Gene stopped by the other day and dropped off a prime rib. I could get old Bert to fix you up with a couple of real fine, medium-rare cuts."

The thought of wild meat had never enticed me but the concept of rare flesh brought my appetite to a grinding halt. Pretending to have to have missed out on something wonderful, I smiled kindly while thanking her, and said, "That's very sweet of you but its past my supper time, and I never eat anything heavy this late at night. It tends to keep me awake…"

"Same here, coffee is fine." Tim's attention kept traveling through the window and into the empty parking lot. Stirring far too much sugar into his coffee, he appeared strangely shocked when looking back and finally realizing it.

Placing her hands on her hips, Linda looked between us and appearing surprised, asked again, "Are you boys absolutely sure? It won't be any trouble at all. Old Bert's back there right now carving up some really nice pieces. I'm telling you—you're really missing out on a good thing. Bert and I had the first two steaks cut from that piece, for lunch. I like mine so rare that it's still kicking when it comes off the fork."

She laughed but Tim looked 'green around the gills'. I was surprised that she wasn't already wearing his coffee, and anything else that he'd previously managed to keep down.

"Um, no, but thanks—all the same." I flinched as the thing in the jar wriggled about in my pocket.

Motioning toward the platter of donuts and muffins and inquiring in his usual, polite manner, Tim asked, "If you wouldn't mind bagging those for us—I'd love to have them for later. My stomach's been acting up a little—and I'd sure enjoy them for breakfast."

"Of course I can--," Hurrying to the counter and returning with a large brown bag, she tilted the platter into it while saying, "There's a weird flu going around town right now." She leaned closer and whispering, said, "I might've had a touch of it myself? I've had to stay near the bathroom most of the afternoon." She prodded a finger into her stomach, saying, "It's been a little rough—but I think that I'm past the worst of it now?"

"Do a lot of people have this flu?" Tim eyed me suspiciously, his attention focusing intently upon the bewildered woman.

"No, just a few people… Bert and me mainly--," She appeared to suffer an odd delirium accompanied by an unnerving stillness, as placing her hand upon the table for support, shivered and said, "And… and…"

"Are you alright?" Tim grabbed at her hand as she dropped the bag and platter and it was sent crashing to the floor. A moment later and she fainted, her legs giving way as I leapt up and she slipped to the floor.

"Linda, look at me!" Kneeling beside the booth where Tim cradled the woman in his arms, I stared into her eyes. Noticing her pupils dilating, I waved a hand before them as she blindly stared.

"Linda, what's wrong? Can you tell me where it hurts and what you're feeling?"

"I don't know?" She gasped as groaning in pain, said, "I just got a sharp pain—in my stomach."

"Try to relax, just rest here for a minute." Gently allowing her to slip from his arms, we attempted to lean her against the booth. The movement causing further injury, she shrieked, and flailing blindly, doubled-over and collapsed to the floor!

"We need to call for an ambulance!" I moved to where sprawled on her side, she lay semi-conscious on the floor, and at the foot of the booth.

"The nearest ambulance is in Penticton and the roads are already closed due to the blizzard, remember?" Tim panicked, as looking around, said, "Get old Bert from out of the back. He served as a medic in the military in Korea."

"You go—I'll stay with Linda!"

Without hesitation he swiftly made his way behind the counter, and vanished through the kitchen doorway into the back. Her breath was coming in short and gasping bursts, and her chest heaved with every desperate attempt. She whimpered and began weeping as she trembled and shook. The spasms grew more violent with every breath that she took, and she flailed wildly.

"Linda, please listen to me—look into my eyes! Help is on the way! Hold on!" Firmly gripping her shoulders, I desperately fought to restrain her as she began wildly thrashing!

She fought to speak, the veins bulging in her neck and forehead due to the pressure and strain! Yet no sound issued forth from upon those violently quivering lips.

Gently clasping her face between my hands; I leaned close and pleading, said, "Linda, please! Talk to me! We can't help you— unless you tell me what's wrong!"

"Help–Oh God—it hurts!" She suddenly lurched forward as shrieking, began hyperventilating and kicking hysterically. Throwing her hands to her stomach and clawing, she screamed while tearing at her clothing! The apron flew off, buttons burst from her shirt, and I heard the material tearing.

Fear-fueled adrenaline drove her into purely mindless terror and I was helpless to stop her! Screaming, she flung her arms wildly, knocking me down in the sudden fury of the assault.

Even through that chaos, the sudden horror and realization of falling had caused me to stop dead! Rolling onto my side, I felt for the coat pocket while fearing to have broken the jar…

My fingers touched the material, there was dampness, and I noticed that our coffee had been spilled during the struggle. Panicking, I looked down at the coat pocket as my hand felt the secure lid of the intact jar within… Safe, thank merciful heaven the thing was still contained…

Crawling to where she now thrashed and convulsed upon the floor, I gazed down while utterly helpless. Staring blindly and frothing at the mouth she appeared caught within some wide-eyed nightmare.

With eyes bulging in shock she had extended both arms, as within a moment of sanity, pleadingly begged with clutching fingers.

Offering her my hand she had reached out and then began screaming hysterically! There was an explosion of gory froth from her mouth as she dropped, and seemingly life-less, slid through her own blood upon the floor.

"Stay away from her! Don't touch her! Mike—stay back!" Tim wailed as rushing from out of the kitchen, skidded across the floor! Panicking and shouting, he waved while pointing back at the kitchen door, and saying, "There's nothing that we can do for her! Bert's dead too! Oh my God—it's a nightmare in there! Run! We have to get out of here! Get to the door, now!"

Linda cried out from behind us. It was a mind-shattering sound that echoing of certain damnation, forced us both to falter before the counter and look back.

"Something–we have to do something!" I stared back at the blood-soaked and dying woman, my mind in a dizzying haze.

"No Mike—she's already dead. And if you go anywhere near her now--," He shouted in terror, saying, "You'll die too!"

Horrified, I spun toward where propped with her back against the booth, tore with bloody nails at her own flesh! Mindlessly shrieking while her belly began distending to hideous proportions, she suddenly split, bursting like an over-ripe melon! A river of bloodied intestines unraveling, and spilling out across the floor!

We watched in horror as dying she blindly clawed through her own heaving and steaming entrails. It was a futile struggle as within death she now gave birth to another horde of worms.

With her head lolling to one side she stared for the last time. Those wide and blue eyes becoming vacant as a feint quiver trembled upon her blood smeared lips. A moment later, she slid down and slumping over, the seething masses began ravenously devouring her flesh. There were hundreds, thousands of the horrendous, pale, slithering and oozing things… Swelling, growing as the frenzied sounds of their feeding became absolutely deafening. Hissing, clicking, snapping, I heard the noise of thousands of tiny mandibles chewing as they worked their way through the hapless woman's body.

"It's impossible—we can't fight these things! They're everywhere!" The sight of the nightmarish feeding frenzy now stole what little strength I had left. With legs turning to jelly, I helplessly slid down to my knees and upon the floor.

"Get up damn you!" Tim bellowed as tightly grasping me beneath the arms, heaved while lifting me from the floor, and shouting, said, "Get up–God damn you! Mike—I can't get through this alone—please—I need you!"

The desperate plea awakened a terrifying moment from the House of McCreary from deep within my mind. I saw Caitlin's pleading eyes, as suspended by a single hand she hung seconds away from certain death. The moment being part of this living nightmare now drew me back from the edge of madness. Coming to my senses, I stared around in disbelief and with only one thought in mind.

"We can't let those things get out of here! The whole town is asleep! They won't even know what's happening until it's much too late!"

"If we're going to do something we'd better do it real fast!" He gestured to where Linda's skeletal remains collapsed, and clattered to the floor. Moving as the hordes began spreading outward in a gore imbued pool from beneath the bones.

"Stay here—I'll be right back!" Without thought I spun and racing into the kitchen, faltered while encountering what remained of poor old Bert! Crumpled where he'd fallen between the counter and the grill, he was little more than a gruesome and bloodied heap of maggot infested bones.

"On the counter—the cooking oil and grease, dump it on the grill!" Tim waved frantically, and pulling a fire extinguisher from under the counter, began spraying the grubs that were gathering on the floor from all around us.

Grabbing the large plastic jug I ripped off the cap, hurriedly splashing the floor, corpse and counter. Twisting and leaning backward to avoid the fire, I cast the half full canister across the grill and the open flames. There was an immediate explosion as flames erupted from off the grill and the oil became a lake of fire.

Still fighting off the seething masses that now poured in from the open doorway behind us, Tim cried out, saying, "Get on top of the counter! I can't hold them back anymore!"

With the entire kitchen in flames and choking in the blinding, black smoke, we struggled onto the counter.

"Hurry—climb through the service window and onto the front counter!" Desperately shoving, he forced me through first before hurriedly following out from behind.

"They're everywhere!" The floor was absolutely covered in the hideous things, and as we searched for a way out, were utterly lost.

Choking on the smoke and half-blinded, Tim raised an arm before his face while looking toward the windows.

"The only way out is through one of those windows!" He waved, saying, "We have to jump from the counter to that booth--," He pointed, and said, "Smash the glass, and jump through! They aren't tempered—so it should take much to do it!"

Grabbing Linda's coat from where it still hung upon a rack near the counter, I wrapped it around my right arm, saying, "I'll go first and use a chair to break the window"

"No—use this!" Grabbing Bert's old mug from behind the counter, he shoved it into my hand, saying, "It's porcelain and will shatter the glass! Just give it a few good and hard whacks, and then kick it out, I'll be right behind you!"

With the coat wrapped tightly around my forearm, I leapt into the nearby booth and without hesitation, battered the mug against the glass! It shattered into shimmering webbing, and drawing back with all my strength, kicked it out.

During the ensuing chaos I failed to notice the grubs, which clambering up from all around me and into the booth, surged forward. There wasn't even time to scream! Tim leapt from the counter and as we collided, carried me out and through the exploding glass. We sailed out and into the night and dropping into the parking, crashed into a tangled heap in the deep snow. Scrambling back and away from the building as the flames erupted through the roof, we took cover behind a cement barrier in the parking lot.

Once more the panic sent me searching for the Mason jar, and to my relief found it resting safely in the snow beside us. Slipping it back into my coat pocket, I stared in shock at the blazing diner. It was hard to believe but the grease-fire had swiftly overcome the entire place.

Shielding my eyes with a hand while squinting through the brilliant flames, I slowly shook my head, saying, "Dear God—they were in the deer meat… The damn things were smart enough to infest other animals. Just like the flies did to the mosquitoes that Gene told us about. Tim, they're using our own food against us…"

"So, anyone eating that deer meat--," The thought terrified him beyond words, as stuttering, he said, "Oh no… How many people have eaten it? They'll all be infested… and spreading the larvae…"

The gas line suddenly ignited and the explosion caused the roof to rise before the entire building collapsed into itself.

Deafened and taking cover as flaming debris landed from all around us, I looked to my friend, and said, "I doubt that anything got out of there alive. But we need to track down where Gene got that deer meat. Then find out if he delivered any to anyone else, and whether he ate any of it him-self…"

"Let's get back to the motel." Clambering to his feet and pulling me along by a sleeve, he said, "We can call the others from there, and shouldn't be out here alone—and unarmed…"

Another explosion sent us sprawling and to where struggling in the snow, we looked back again.

Steve's 1971 Ford LTD was ablaze and resting on its side Caught in the flames and chaos of the diner, it was another victim of the horror that I knew was still to follow…

The snow had already begun as we fought the bitter winds back toward the little motel. It was only a short distance, but in the darkness and with the unknown close at our heels, every step was terrifying. Departing the safety of the street lights, we crossed the road onto the motel property, and into the blackness of the looming forest. Startled, I caught a movement in the shadows between the dumpster and building, swiftly and silently halting Tim. Having just crossed the road we now stood in open and plain view. The little lamp-post cast a pale glow through the flurries, while creeping shadows surrounded the empty parking lot.

"What is it? What did you see?" He stood close and whispered, and wiping the snow from his glasses with a finger, squinted to look around.

"I'm not sure?" Nodding in gesture and leaning close, I said very quietly, "But I thought that I saw something over there, in the shadows between the dumpster and the motel wall…"

Before we even had the opportunity to react something came out at us from the darkness, and we leapt back in fright!

It was the shape of a man holding a rifle, as waving he hurried to where we stood and stared aghast.

"What the hell is wrong with you fella's?" Gordon Farrell adjusted his woolen cap, and looking between us, said, "You gave me one hell of a fright, sneaking around like that! A man could give him-self a heart attack, especially after what happened to your room the night before."

Utterly relieved and with a certain sense of urgency, I took him by the shoulder while leading both men toward the motel, and said, "I'm terribly sorry—but you caught us by surprise too. We weren't expecting anyone, out here and in the dark…"

"Well I heard a damn explosion--," He spun back into the direction that we had come, and waving the rifle said, "I can still see the flames from here. What the hell happened?"

"There's been a terrible accident--," Tim improvised, and hurrying Gordon along again, said, "I think that it might've been a gas line? There was a fire, an explosion, and we managed to get out. But don't know what happened to Linda and Bert."

"Sweet suffering shit--," Gordon turned to look back as we arrived before the office door, and he said, "I just saw Harry go past like a bat out of hell a few minutes ago. There's no one else around—and the storm has the roads blocked." Stunned and peered over at me, he asked, "What the hell are we going to do?"

"Please—," I took him firmly by the shoulder and guiding him back toward the door, said, "Let's get inside and we can figure it out from there."

Without any further hesitation we moved inside and to where closing and locking the door tightly behind us, I followed the old man to the counter.

"Harry has you all settled into the new room already--," Gordon took down a set of keys from a board behind him, and dropping them on the counter before us, said, "Paid out of pocket for all the damages to the old ones as well."

"I would have settled that with you tonight." The guilt was terrible, but I was only too glad that he wasn't expecting any explanations.

"Is this room anywhere near his old one?" Tim pointed to the key in my hand, and concerned, he said, "No offence—but we wouldn't want any re-occurrences."

"Nope, I figured you'd like to be close to that meat-wagon of yours." He grinned through a mouth-full of black and decaying teeth, and said, "So I put you in 115 out back of the building. It's clean, quiet, has a couch, and kitchenette. From what Harry said, I figured you'd be more comfortable--," He gestured at Tim with a wave, and said, "Being as you're having company and all."

"I appreciate this more than you know--," Grabbing the keys from the counter I paused as leaning over, he sniffed at us, and I said, "We hauled some roadkill away for Harry today…"

"I figured that it must've been something like that--," His deep brown and aged eyes passed between us before nodding knowingly, he said, "You might want to take them things off before you stink up my nice room? Harry left clean things for both of you earlier."

Sniffing at the furred collar of my coat and groaning, I quickly agreed, reassuring the old man, and saying, "We'll strip on the mat inside and then leave these things in bags outside the door."

Reaching under the counter and producing several large, green garbage bags, he handed them to me, and pointing to the phone, said, "Make sure to call me once you've put them out. We don't need any more incidents like the other night, happening again."

Having been unaware of my little confrontation with Gordon and the raccoons, I nudged Tim before he said anything, and said, "No we don't—and thank you, again." Waving the key with the intention to leave, I halted as the old man spoke again.

"That was a strange thing—what happened to your room. It's usually quiet as a grave around here. Well—except maybe for when those asshole mine surveyors were in town?"

"What, mine surveyors?" Tim wandered back to the counter.

"You know, those punk, snot-nosed, uppity, little shits." The old man cursed as rolling his eyes, he said, "They had about six guys mucking around up there at the old mine. Stayed here for three weeks, never saw much of them. But the buggers were up all hours of the night. Driving in and out, banging doors, and bumping around with all sorts of odd equipment." He spat into the corner and glaring at us, grumbled as he said, "I would've tossed their sorry asses out, if I hadn't needed the money so much..."

"What were they doing up there?" I had my suspicions...
"How the hell should I know? But the one fella said that they had to clear out until spring. It was something about—gas pockets and other such, bull-shit. In my day, we panned for gold. That's how I earned the small fortune that eventually bought me this place... but those were better times."

"Do you mind if I make a quick call?" Tim gestured toward the telephone on the counter.

"Sure thing, help yourself, son." Watching Tim retrieve the receiver before speaking again, he scowled and said, "But it won't do you a pinch of good. The damn lines went down with the storm over two hours ago."

Curiously sniffing at the air, Tim's eyes grew wide with dark suspicion, and looking to old Gordon, curiously asked, "Hey Gordon—what's cooking?"

"Well now, that's my dinner—smarty-pants." The old man sighed as smacking his lips, he said, "I was just cooking me up some mushrooms, peppers, and onions—to go with a nice venison steak." Rubbing his hands together as while excited and looking between us, he said, "That sweet little gal from the diner, Linda, brought it by earlier today."

Almost losing his glasses Tim took off like a shot! Running around the counter and from behind the old man, he scrambled off and into the adjoining apartment with Gordon in close pursuit!

"Jesus boy—what's gotten into you?" Gordon grabbed a golf-club from behind the door and brandishing it above his head, chased after Tim, shouting as he said, "Don't you know what you're doing is against the law? You don't mess with another man's home and privacy!"

By the time that I had reached the kitchen Tim had already grabbed the plate from off the counter. With Gordon struggling all the way, he had plugged the drain and hurriedly tossing the raw meat into the sink, began filling it with scalding hot water.

"Hey, cut it out you crazy, son-of-a-bitch! This isn't funny, boy!" The old man shouted and cursed as swinging the club and narrowly missing Tim's head, he said, "That's my damn supper! Knock it off!"

"Gordon, please listen to me!" Pulling the club from his hands and throwing it down, I grabbed his wrists and staring into his face, pleaded, saying, "Look–look into the sink!"

Bewildered and angered to the point of shaking, the old man glared. There was defiance in his eyes, but doubt still caused him to turn and look down into the sink. The raw and bloody steak simply drifted while floating in the half-filled sink of steaming hot water.

"Okay, so you managed to ruin a perfectly good steak and my dinner?" He suddenly tore free of my grasp, and spinning around, swatted Tim in the back of the head, shouting as he said, "Now what in the hell would make you go and do a thing like that for? Are you out of your cotton-picking, mind?"

Stunned and with his ears still ringing, Tim grabbed and physically forced Gordon's head down and into the sink! As inches from the water, he shouted, saying, "Take a closer look you stupid old bastard! And you tell me?"

In that moment and as the two men struggled before the sink, they both suddenly became still and fell absolutely silent.

Moving closer to where the stood I gazed down amidst the clouded and steaming waters. Ever so slowly the steak began convulsing, and tiny, bloody orifices began appearing from through-out the meat... As we stared the vile worms wriggled out and squirming, died while struggling to escape the scalding water.

Gordon's grew bigger than they had ever been, as horrified he now desperately fought Tim to escape the edge of the sink.

"What on God's green earth just happened here?"

"All that we know is that these parasites are an invasive species and deadly--," Tim discovered a tea kettle full of water, and setting it to boil, kept a close eye on the sink, saying, "If they're ingested, within hours they'll grow, and then eat their way back out of their host..."

Cautiously leaning toward the sink, Gordon reluctantly peered into the still and steaming waters. Still partially trapped within the deer flesh, the ghastly things drifted while eerily swaying, their pulpy flesh becoming pink in the blistering water.

"Was that the only steak she brought?" The kettle whistled, and wandering over, Tim emptied the boiling contents into the sink. The grubs were dead but he wasn't taking any chances.

"Sure was." Gordon stabbed the maggot riddled steak with a long barbecue fork, and drawing it from out of the water, held it before his wide eyes. A slight movement as one of the larger grubs slipped out of where it clung in the meat, and he dropped the fork and steak onto the kitchen floor.

Leaping backward, he could only stare at us with the sudden realization, and then quietly said, "You boy's saved my life... I owe you both an apology and my sincerest gratitude."

"Dammit!" Tim shoved the old man back and away from where the steak had fallen.

Looking to the floor and where the partially blanched and bloody steak lay in a gelatinous puddle, I gasped.

With the dead grubs dropping away from the meat, others now wriggled free from where they had safely hidden while buried deeply in the flesh.

Grabbing the cast-iron frying pan from off the stove, Tim flung the sizzling contents over the writhing larvae. There was a hiss as the boiling oil smothered the steak, and the worms shriveled, blackened, and became still. The stench turning us away as the steaming grease pooled around the remains on the floor.

Quickly retrieving a dust pan and broom from a kitchen closet, Gordon cautiously cleaned the mess, asking, "It's safe to get rid of this now—isn't it?"

Our expressions must have been enough to raise doubts. Placing the pan upon the stove, he dropped the steak into it and turning up the heat, stood back to watch.

"Did Linda mention giving anyone else any of those steaks?" I asked as we all stood and observed as the deer steak started sizzling in the remaining oil of the pan.

"Truth is I don't rightly know?" Gordon shrugged, saying, "But the only folks that I know who really liked a nice deer steak, were Connie's family, Bert, Linda, and me. A lot of folks prefer regular meat these days… Damn." He choked, gasping and shaking his head while pointing into the pan, and saying, "They're still something alive in that damn thing…"

"Not for long…" Tim grabbed at it.

CHAPTER TWENTY FOUR

10:15 p.m.

With the kitchen fan blowing and the windows wide open we silently watched as the steak became nothing more than a charred mass. Even after having turned off the heat and allowing it to cool, Gordon wasn't satisfied until he'd battered the remains into ashes with a shovel in the snow.

"So, what's going to happen now?" The fear shone brightly in the old man's eyes as we all stood around the counter in the little office.

"Harry and Steve should have been back by now." It was my first thought, and turning to Tim, I said, "If the phone lines are down and the blizzard's blocking the roads, we have no way of even contacting them."

The lights suddenly flickered and reaching onto a shelf behind the counter, Gordon produced a small wooden box. Sliding it across the counter, he said, "It looks as though things are really going to go for a shit soon. Candles–I'm sure that you'll need them before this night's over."

"I wouldn't suggest driving the Hearse over to Harry house--," Tim shrugged, and said quite hopelessly, "Even if it starts, the tires aren't good enough to make it through the snow…"

"Well, you boys are in luck." Pulling a set of keys from his pocket and slamming them down, he winked, and said, "I've got Lenny's plow tonight. He wasn't well after what happened to Marlene, and I told him that I'd plow the route for him tonight."

"It may not be safe out there—," Tim swallowed hard as nervously glancing toward the door, said, "Aside from those grubs—Harry suspects that there might be a bigger creature. It might even be responsible for the deaths around here, and possibly giving birth to those worms…"

Shocked but willing to accept any explanation after seeing the previous horror, Gordon silently looked to me in question.

With little purpose in concealing the facts anymore, I felt obligated to inform the old man, and said, "Tim's right—there might be something else in that storm out there—hunting us now."

The lights flashed and flickered and it was apparent that the power might soon fail. With the storm howling beyond the window the old man has just bowed his head for a moment, and then slowly nodding, looked back at us.

"We may all be in a heap of trouble? But, there're a lot of women and young children in this town--," Gordon's expression hardened with courage of conviction, and he said, "We can't help anyone if we can't get to them. One way or the other—those roads have to be cleared. So, I'm going out there—come hell or high water. Knowing Harry, in this storm, he's likely stuck down at the station. I'll take the plow and run over there first... I'll let him know you that you boys are here."

Tapping a finger against the jar that bulged in my pocket, I looked to old Gordon, and asked, "You wouldn't happen to have any weapons around here, would you?"

11:10 p.m.

Even the huge diesel plow moved slowly as the snow, having made passage almost impossible, was still coming down with a vengeance. With the telephone lines having been brought down in the storm and the high-ways blocked we were utterly alone...

"How long have you been doing this?" Tim blew into his fingers as rubbing his hands together for warmth, said, "I knew that you owned the motel, but didn't know that you helped Lenny with the plow?"

"None of us are getting any younger—and we old folks need to stick together." The old man gripped the wheel tightly with both hands, and glancing over, said, "You get to living somewhere long enough—folks tend to take things for granted. I've been at this for about six years now. I don't mind pulling my weight, and it gives me something to do in the winter, and when things get slow at the motel."

Cramped tightly together in the little cab, I curiously looked over at Gordon, and said, "I lived here as a boy—and don't remember seeing you around?"

A sad smile shadowed Gordon's face as he shook his grizzled head, and said, "Fact is, I owned the place since it was first built, and just had other folks running it for me. I had me some delusions of grandeur when I was younger. I only moved here about nine years ago now, and should've done it a lot sooner."

"It's a nice old place." Tim shivered as the heat in the old truck left much to be desired, and he thoughtfully said, "I'd rather have a motel than run the parlor."

"It's for sale--," Gordon rubbed at a stiff neck and cracking his knuckles, said, "I'm getting to old for this shit anyway. I'll give you a good deal on the place—if you're serious?"

All things considered, there was no guarantee we would survive the night much less have the luxury of considering anything beyond that. Tim's expression had said it all and the old man turned his attention back to the road.

"I'm planning on retiring in May." Gordon navigated through an icy patch, saying, "Figuring on moving to Florida. Soak up a little sunshine before they drop my tired old bones in a pine box."

"I've always despised the winter months and hated the cold." It came more out of thought than intending to say it, but shuddering in the chill, I said, "I never think about mortality... it just seems to close all the time."

"Well son, when you live through a war--," He sighed while reminiscing, and said, "You lose a lot and realize that the things really worth having—can't be bought. After that you tend to enjoy every day for what it's worth. Live, love, and laugh as much as you can. Of course, some things still bother me." His eyes dampened in the deep shadows of the cab as shrugging, he said, "Losing loved ones, moving away from the old homestead, and never cared for much for good-byes."

"Me neither." Fumbling through my numerous pockets in search of a forgotten package of cigarettes I was sadly disappointed.

"My father never believed in saying good-bye." Tim muttered as adjusting his glasses, said in reflection, "It seems like bad luck in our business."

His eyes dreaming and distant, Gordon spoke to the ghosts of his past while saying, "During the war we never said good-bye." Raising a hand and waving in parting, he called out in a haunting voice, saying, "It was usually, God-speed or—till then, friend! That was it—Till then and until we meet again."

"Till then—I like that." Patting the old fellows shoulder I leaned back while entertaining the thought. After all, it was more like an inviting promise of safe return than a fare-well.

"Those mine surveyors that you mentioned earlier?" Tim squirmed uncomfortably on the seat beside me, and leaning to peer over at Gordon, asked, "When they signed the registry what company name did they use?"

"Now that you mentioned it, I don't recall them ever using any company name." He thought for a moment, and then looking back, said, "They rented three rooms. It was some big fellow, older man named—John, Yeah—that was it, called him-self, John Smith."

"John Smith..." The expression on Tim's face spoke volumes and only served to fuel my previous suspicions.

Everyone knew that mine was closed down permanently. Having been declared a hazard after the cave–in that killed my father and seventy others. It was highly unlikely that anyone would ever work there again.

"We're almost there." Gordon motioned as we slowly approached the little police station, and he said, "But there aren't any lights on— and I don't see Harry's car?"

Slowing to a stop Gordon parked before the station, and peering inside the dark building, he said, "Maybe they're over at the house?"

"No—he wouldn't have gone off like that without checking back with us first?" It made no sense and I was quickly becoming worried.

The driver's side door suddenly flew open, the storm blew, and shrieking in terror, Gordon frantically kicked at something that tried to get inside. In a moment of sheer terror a sound suddenly stopped us dead, as leaning forward we all looked out.

"Son-of-a-bitch--," Harry struggled to avoid the smoldering ashes as Gordon kicked the cigar from out of his mouth. Cursing, he dusted the smoldering embers from off his coat.

"Shit! Harry, sorry!" The old man placed a hand before his mouth, saying, "You scared the devil out of us!"

"The diner's been burned!" Steve panicked as appearing from behind Harry, he said, "We went back there looking for you guys. It's nothing but a ruin—gone! The car got stuck. So we had to leave it there and hike back here."

"Linda and old Bert are dead." Tim leaned out over Gordon and explaining, said, "The deer meat was contaminated with the damn larvae. That's how these things have been getting into people. The meat was infested."

"Oh dear Christ--," Harry spun toward me, his expression livid with inexplicable horror as he asked, "How many people ate that deer meat?"

"I don't think that it would've affected everyone?" Tim raised a finger in thought, and said, "Anyone that cooked the meat through, and ate it well-done, would have killed the parasites."

"Connie's father took down a good-sized buck a last week. Not a lot of people care for wild meat around here anymore. But according to Linda, Gene delivered one half of that buck to the diner this morning." Harry remembered, gesturing with a finger as he organized his thoughts, and said "There wasn't anyone else in the diner all day—according to what she said."

"These boys caught me just when I was fixing to have dinner--," Gordon pointed between us as wide-eyed, he said, "Saved my ass they did. Damn meat was just crawling with them worms. Finally had to burn it to a cinder to kill them all—but we did."

The storm raged beyond the cab as our friends leaned close while fighting against the gale force winds. The flurries were blinding as unable to see beyond only a few feet, the world became a blur in the headlights.

The street lamps flashed, we all looked, and the little town fell into complete blackness as the power failed.

"The other half of that deer should still be in Connie's dad's freezer." Steve shouted, saying, "We need to get to them right away!"

"Get on the boards and hold on--," Gordon called out to them, saying, "I'll get you over there right away!"

With Steve standing on one side and Harry on the other, they clung to the mirrors as we traveled down the main street. The wind and snow creating a blinding veil in the blackness, we traveled slowly while cautiously navigating the storm. Had it not been for the winter clothing and supplies gathered by Steve and Harry earlier, they might certainly have frozen to death along that stretch of highway.

When we came to the Shephard farm, and due to the black-out, we had no idea if the absence of light had meant an ending for the family. They were either asleep and without oil lamps or candles, or something had already gone terribly wrong…

"So what do you figure we should do?" Gordon called out his open window to Harry as switching on the over-head flood-lamps, pulled off to the side of the highway.

"Well, first of all--," He thought for a moment before calling back, and saying, "I think that we should send two people for help. The story might not sound quite as crazy with more than one witness?"

"Who should go?" Steve shouted from through our open window, and across at Harry.

"Gordon and Tim--," He spoke without a thought, and shouting, said, "They could make it into Penticton with the plow—and bring help!"

"What about us? Without the plow we're stranded?" Steve made a valid point, as brushing the snow from his face with heavy gloves, he said, "We'll freeze to death out here! It must be minus twenty five already!"

"Connie's father own skidoos—he's a hunter--," Harry motioned toward the snowbound and dark farm, and saying, "We can take them over to Gene's farm from here!"

"It's a long-shot at best!" Steve was right bit we were running out of options fast.

"What other choice do we have?" Harry became desperate as brushing the flying snow from his eyes and face, he said, "We can't just sit and wait while those things eat their way through town! Guys—we're all out of ideas and almost out of time!"

"Alright—let's go!" Steve waved, and drawing open the passenger side door motioned for me to follow.

"Tim, you stay here with Gordon while we check this out!" Harry passed me a pump shotgun, and looking back at Gordon, said, "Stay sharp—this shouldn't take long!"

The unrelenting, blinding and heavy flurries had made our efforts even more difficult than before. Fighting our way up the steep drive and through the deep snow in the darkness, the flood-lamps were our only source of comfort. The plow vanished in the flurries behind us, the darkness closing in as with rifles and flashlights in hand, finally managed to reach the house. Gasping and heaving for breath, half-frozen, we fell against the front door while taking shelter from beneath the awning.

"What's this?" Harry leaned closer and shone the beam of his light through the screen door. His eyes growing huge as while seeing a small hand-written note that had been taped to the door he read it aloud, "Gone to Summerland. Please leave mail under door, thanks."

"They're not home." Steve shoved his way past Harry, and cursing under his breath, said, "Jesus—if they ate any of that deer or took any with them we're screwed! We need to know for sure! We'll have to break down the door!"

"Hang on a minute." Harry grumbled as shielding his eyes and leaning down to retrieve a key from under the mat, waved it at Steve, and said, "We're all family around here, remember?"

In moments he had the door open, we were all inside, and closing it quietly behind him, whispered as he said, "And be careful... The family may have left—but we don't know if we're alone here..."

"Check the kitchen first." Steve insisted.

Slowly walking through the entrance and into the hallway, we passed a large living room, dining area, and silently made our way into the adjoining kitchen. With the beams of our lights held low, we moved around the sink, an island with hanging cookery, and finally came to the fridge. Peering around nervously, Harry slowly reached for the fridge handle, and hesitating only briefly, quickly pulled open the door. My heart almost stopped in that moment as our lights flashed into the pale shelves, and we stood silent.

"Just some ice cream, television dinners, frozen veggies, and fruit." Harry's voice was harsh from the cold, fatigue, and his battered nerves. There was a moment when it appeared as though he contemplated indulging the contents of the fridge, but closing the door he stepped away. At that point who could have blamed him? Our world was on the brink of catastrophe...

"What about this?" Steve motioned toward a large floor-model freezer that stood in the kitchen hall.

"Don't open it--," Grabbing at Steve's wrist, he looked up at the larger man, and said, "Let's check first..."

Leaning down and gently pressing an ear against the freezer lid, Harry's eyes flashed in the deep shadows. Listening for several moments, he kept returning to listen again even while having seemed satisfied. It was this doubt that now had us all on edge of sheer panic… I could hear my own heartbeat in that moment, and Steve's raspy and heaving breath was almost deafening.

Obviously in pain due to his injured leg, oblivious, Steve had thoughtlessly placed a hip against the freezer. In the process of shifting his weight from off the bad leg, he moved, accidentally bumping against it. With a sudden and great violence, something crashed heavily against the sides from within. It sent both men tumbling backwards, and the lid bent upward under the pressure.

"Oh Christ—there's something really big in there." Harry pressed his full weight down upon the lid, and desperately looking around the room, said, "Quick, find something to tie this thing closed."

Rushing down the hallway, Steve vanished into the blackness of a back room. I heard his movements on the steps, and assumed that he'd gone down into a basement. Moments seemed to last forever, as fearing to even breathe, we remained completely silent. Although we had startled it, the thing in the freezer seemed unaware of our presence. Waiting for Steve to return, I prayed that there would be time…

"Well we know one thing for sure now--," Harry whispered, saying, "If that grub of yours was calling for help—this thing would've heard it come running by now."

He was right, as even through the thick material of the parka I could feel the slight vibration of the larva. Still, I had my doubts…

Peering back at my friend through the cold shadows of the dimly lit hall, I said, "What if they're methods of communication are more animal than insect? What if instead of a general call answered by a hive, they have a distinctive sound. A signal that once identified was only responded to by the parents."

I might have been completely wrong but it was enough reason to cause doubt in my friend. It sounded ludicrous, but I had my reasons for suspecting the possibility… Judging by his reaction I felt inclined to explain further, and whispering, said, "The theory is based on the call of seal pups, which even among massive crowds, can be distinguished above all others by their parents…."

"Please—let's just focus on killing these things and getting this nightmare under control…"

It was apparent that I wasn't reaching him and in some cases it might have been for the best. He was right; these things weren't a subject for study as much as a direct threat to all life on earth…

"I found something that we can use--," Steve returned with a length of chain and padlock, and looking between us, said, "This will have to happen fast and smooth. I'll lift the back end of the freezer, and you guys slip the chain around and fasten the lock."

"All that movement is bound to drive this thing crazy." Harry looked to where the tiny latch had just barely held the lid closed, and said, "Any noise from the top or sides and it'll try getting out again."

"Then maybe it might be best if you run the chain down from the top—and Mike padlocks it from the bottom. That way, it'll go for the floor of the freezer when it hears you—and not break out through the lid."

"What if you drop it while I'm under there?" I could hardly hear my own voice, but the answer never came anyway. Instead, Steve just glared and nodded for me to move. Accepting the padlock and quietly kneeling beside the freezer, I looked to Harry with a nod.

Moving with a grace that I had never assumed him capable, he quietly draped the chain across the lid while allowing it to dangle upon either side. Now, it was just a matter of catching both ends and fastening the padlock before anything went wrong…

The moment had come. Bracing him-self, Steve took a firm hold upon the end of the freezer and stared down at me. Even in the pale glow of our lights I could see the fear in his eyes. I knew that we only had one chance and that failure was not an option. Swallowing hard, I took hold of one end of the chain and gritting my teeth, nodded at him. In a burst of speed and immense strength he heaved up the end of the freezer while I slipped beneath. There was blackness and an utter panic as I desperately searched for the opposite end of the chain. Sensing the weight shifting inside the freezer, I gasped as something monstrous slammed against the walls from within. Steve fought to maintain his grip, swaying dangerous while struggling in motion with the thing. In blind fear I fumbled around in the darkness. Feeling around, I suddenly discovered the chain to have slipped back due to the angle, and grabbed out for it. Taking hold, I quickly pulled the ends together and secured the lock in place. There was a sudden and severe sloping of the freezer as it swung dangerously from above. The weight and angle being too much, Steve cried out as it slipped from his grasp. Sliding out from beneath, my coat was almost caught as the freezer came crashing down.

Having been pulled free in the last moment by Harry, I stared as he ran a hand through his hair while attempting to appear calm, and said, "Well, that could've gone a lot worse. Now let's get this damned thing out of here…"

"Are you okay?" I looked to where Steve now leaned against the wall while favoring his previously injured leg. There was sweat on his brow, and it was apparent by his expression that he was suffering from the wound.

"I'll be okay—the damn leg just didn't want to hold…"

"That bite must be getting infected--," Harry leapt back as the freezer thundered with a brutal assault from within, and gasping, he said, "We've really pissed it off this time."

I watched in utter astonishment as the heavy unit bounced as the sides were brutally battered, and it began bending with each and every effort.

"That freezer isn't going to take too much more of that." Steve hurried back, and looking to Harry with a sudden urgency, asked, "What the hell are we going to do now?"

"Let's drag this damn thing out of here before it gets loose--," Harry slipped the revolver back into its holster, and said, "We'll get it out into the open and then burn the damn thing…"

Without any proper means of safely moving the freezer we simply took a firm hold, and struggling, hurriedly made our way out of the house. We had barely escaped the front door when the pounding and struggling thing had forced us to place it down. Terrified that it might escape at any given moment and unable to lift it again, Steve shoved it through the snow.

"We'll need some gas." Harry motioned toward the garage, and said, "Connie's dad always keeps a can for the lawnmower in there."

Without another word I rushed off to find it. There were only moments between, but as I returned with the gas, I found my friends struggling to keep the freezer closed.

"Hurry—the bastard's almost got this lid torn free of its hinges!" Steve fought against the monsters furious attempt to escape.

"What happened?" Tim startled us while approaching from out of the blinding glare of the flood-lights.

"Get back to the truck!" Harry frantically waved his revolver at the freezer, his voice barely audible in the howl of the icy wind as he said, "You do not want to be here right now!"

"There's a pile of dry timber in that shed—," Steve shouted through the storm, as throwing his full weight down upon the freezer lid, said, "Let's build a pyre, drag this bastard on top, and light the whole damn thing!"

It was as though the thing in the freezer had heard and knew…. The lid and sides began pounding so furiously that the welded seams started giving way. Without concern for wind, weather, or darkness we all rushed for the shed and began dragging out and heaping all that we could carry. Although standing in the deep snow, the freezer shifted each time the thing lashed outward. The lid had broken from its lock, the hinges would soon give way, and all that now held it was that length of chain and the padlock.

"Move—move—move!" Steve howled as dropping the last arm-load of wood onto the pile, he took up the gas can and doused the huge pyre.

"It's almost broken free!" Harry assisted Steve in weighting down the lid as they slid it toward the heaped wood. Struggling as the horror fought us every step of the way, we managed to climb the wood-pile, and drop the freezer atop the pyre.

"Burn it—burn it!" Harry bellowed, his eyes wide as the freezer violently shook and rocked while threatening to slip down.

Drawing and lighting my Zippo, I flung it toward the wood-pile, the world passing into slow-motion as I watched breathlessly. When it came down I thought to have seen the lid snap closed and the flame extinguished. A moment later and it exploded, as beneath gale winds and blinding flurries, the flames engulfed the freezer. There was an inhuman shriek that wailing into the winds mournful cries sent us all backward. In that same moment the chain broke and the lid erupted from off the freezer. Flung aside, it traveled with such force that it was sent spinning off and vanished into the blizzard. Gun-fire rocketed through the blinding and bitter cold night. There was a high-pitched squealing that became a deafening and unearthly screaming. Splitting the night, it echoed before booming into an ear shattering, and deep base tone that vibrated painfully within my ears and mind. I fell to my knees, and covering my ears with both hands, stared upward as the nightmare was revealed.

Rising from out of the battered freezer and among the flames, it stood well over the height of an average man. Six-legged and moving up-right, the creature had a bloated, segmented, and serpentine body. Hunched over, the upper torso was guarded by a thick shell and was covered in a coarse black hair and spines. Armed with what appeared to be large and scythe-like appendages, it shrieked while it swung them like twin blades. From just beneath those vicious scythes also rested a secondary pair of arms. Far shorter but equally as deadly, the spiny, heavy, and crab-like claws snapped. Cruelly curved, powerful, and shining black against the flames, I knew they could effortlessly snap through bones... Its head being larger than a man, it had huge and oval eyes upon the sides. The mouth was round and from all about were a series of sharp and beak-like mandibles. It was this exact radius and type of bite that might produce a wound similar to the one upon Steve's abdomen...

Thrashing out with blinding speed, it tore at the sides of the freezer while attempting to avoid the billowing smoke and flames. The wind howled, the flames grew, and showers of embers exploded into the night.

"Shoot for Christ sake!" Harry emptied his revolver into the monstrosity, and cried out, "Shoot the bastard! Shoot!"

Stunned by the horror we had just stood while staring in disbelief. Awakened in that moment, I drew the revolver and emptied the chamber into the thing! The shots had found their mark each time, but the monster unhindered by bullets continued to fight. Like an immense spider, the legs began emerging from within. Its huge claws clamping down and gripping the sides, it prepared to leap from out of the inferno. All efforts failing and our bullets spent, we floundered before the monster and storm.

"Die—you rotten son-of-a-bitch!" Steve swung an axe, burying the weapon deep into the back of the squealing creature's head. There was a geyser of yellow filth as he twisted the blade ever deeper, and buried it into its brain. Caught within the flames, the horror lashed out, casting him backward and into the blizzard. It happened with such force and ferocity that I feared he might not have survived...

The answer came quickly, as appearing from around the blazing pyre, Steve dropped to his knees. Unable to fight any longer, I went to his side through the deep snow, and taking hold of the man, assisted him back to his feet.

From behind us came another barrage of hot lead. Unyielding, Harry took up his rifle and wailing, emptied the Winchester into the thing. Unlike Steve, his aim had targeted the soft tissue from just beneath the front of the head. Assuming they had lungs in order to achieve such enormous size, it only stood to reason that they must somehow breathe. Barren of the usual ports extruding from the sides of their bodies to draw oxygen, the creature was more animal than insect. The brain may have been small and recessed, but Harry's guess and aim were both true.

Flailing out of control, the monstrosity suddenly vomited a vile and green filth. The flames, smoke and mortal wounds becoming all too much, it finally succumbed. Collapsing back into the freezer, it struggles became weaker until all movements finally ceased. Its skin began blistering, hair and spines burned away, and flesh blackened. Smoke poured from out of the cracks and seams of its shell, and from somewhere between the heat and extreme cold it suddenly shattered. The charring stench of its death filling the night as it slowly and finally sank from out of sight. With the freezer ablaze and belching foul smoke, it now appeared as a furnace in a frozen Hell. In my eyes that was exactly what it had taken to bring down a devil…

"That wasn't an adult creature." Tim fought the wind with a hand before his face, as through the billowing smoke, looked back, and said, "It wasn't fully formed and still had soft parts where the shell hadn't hardened!"

"Well we know how to kill the bigger ones now…" Reloading his Winchester with rounds drawn from a coat pocket, Harry waved toward the road, and said, "At least we have a fighting chance."

"We should split from here." Regaining his composure, Steve patted my back in thanks while looking to Harry, and said, "Tim and Gordon should take off while they still have the chance. We have no idea of what might happen next, or what we're really up against yet. Someone has to survive to warn people…"

There were a lot of mixed emotions but none quite as devastating as the horror and frozen storm. The decision had been made whether anyone liked it or not.

CHAPTER TWENTY FIVE

1:18 a.m.

After sadly going our separate ways, we had taken two skidoos from the garage and set off down the highway toward town. Riding with Harry and almost completely blinded by the blizzard, I kept looking back to make certain that Steve still followed. I could see the dull glow of his single head-lamp, but nothing more in the presiding darkness. Still haunted by thoughts of Tim's lost stare as he pulled away in the plow with old Gordon, the bitter cold and horror of it all was finally taking its toll. I wondered whether any of us would survive to see the dawn, much less share another day together.

Through everything I had ever experienced in my life I had never been colder or more terrified. Adjusting my goggles and placing a hand securely over the jar in my pocket, I forced all thoughts from my mind. If there would be any chance of survival I would have to maintain my composure, and focus without panicking.

Passing through town we had seen oil-lamps and candles burning in the windows of several homes. These were few and far between, and there hadn't been signs of any other signs of life. I wondered if like moths, these nightmares were drawn to light. In which case, anyone placing lanterns in windows would have only been ringing the proverbial, dinner bell...

There was a quick stop at the police station and where gathering ammunition and using the facilities, we prepared for the worst. Even with the power outage there had still been enough water for quick showers. We had done this in a desperate attempt to warm ourselves, and then slipping into fresh clothing, got into snow-suits. Carrying a pack rather than taking my coat, I slipped the jar into one pocket, and loaded the other with supplies. This contained additional flashlights, batteries, and ammunition for my revolver and police issue, pump-shotgun.

"How you holding out, buddy?" Harry handed out candy bars and sitting beside Steve, looked to his friend and asked, "How's that leg doing?"

"I've been a whole lot better--," Steve gobbled down the candy bar as we took a few moments to gather ourselves, and he said, "But I'm sure as hell glad to get out of that weather and into this suit."

"Enjoy it while you can because it isn't going to last…" Harry looked apologetically between us, and frowning said, "We need to get over to Gene's right away, and warn him, "

Loading his shotgun and revolver, Steve shoved the weapons into his pack, and nodding, said, "Okay, let's show these killer cockroaches what we're really made of…."

With the deepening drifts and white-out conditions the short journey to Gene's farm-house had taken far longer than anticipated. It had become so cold that even while wearing snowsuits, boots, and heavy gloves, we could hardly feel our fingers or toes. The lenses of our goggles kept freezing, and I was sure that if it became any colder that we would most assuredly freeze to death. Shaking violently while holding on for dear life, I feared the storm might take me before anything else did…

When we came upon Gene's property we could barely see the lights of the house through the blizzard. The wind cast huge drifts across the highway, and the storm blocked all view beyond several feet in any direction. Parking closely together, we halted near the top of the drive nearest the highway.

"His lights are still burning," Harry pointed while shouting back at me, and said, "Let's go down and have a look!"

"Mike, draw your revolver and be ready!" Steve shouted, his voice seeming distant through the storm, as waving toward the farmhouse, he said, "Lights or not—we have no idea of what we're walking into down there!"

"Leave the skidoos." Steve insisted, saying, "We can't risk taking them down there and getting buried in the soft snow."

"It'll be fine--," Harry argued, saying, "Either way, if we need a fast way out of there, we won't be doing it on foot in this storm."

Dismounting, Steve left his skidoo at the top of the drive and went on ahead.

"He's always been a stubborn son of a gun." Cursing, Harry guided the skidoo down the steep drive past Steve, and then parked before the front door.

"Shouldn't he have seen or heard us?" Climbing from the skidoo I turned to look as Steve approached.

"You wouldn't hear an oncoming locomotive in this damn, blizzard." Harry looked toward the house, and waving his Winchester, motioned for us to follow.

Moving closely from behind as we moved up the steps, I slipped off to one side as we entered the covered porch. It wasn't fear that had caused me to do this, but respect for professionals in the field. I knew that our lives depended on their expertise and experience, and wasn't willing to risk any more than necessary.

From somewhere out of the storm I thought to have heard the droning hum of a generator. There was a hesitation, and at the same time the lights flickered from all around us. Alerted by Steve who halted suddenly at the front door, we watched as he pointed toward the large living-room window. Even through the storm, I could now clearly see the fear that was reflected within his dark eyes. The curtains had been pulled tightly closed, but as we looked, an enormous shadow crossed from before our eyes. The awkwardly moving shape appeared to be dragging something, and we knew that it wasn't a human…

Motioning toward the window with his Winchester, Harry gestured that he would enter first, and wanted Steve to follow from right behind. He signaled without a sound, and then nodded between us to confirm that we understood. Poised with weapons in preparation, we looked to each other as the moment for action came. It all happened so fast that I hardly even saw anything. Leaning back, Harry kicked at the door handle. It failed to open on the first attempt as throwing all his weight into a shoulder, cast himself forward in an immense effort. There was a sound like thunder as the door lock broke, and splintering from the frame, sent the door flying inward against the wall. Rushing into the room behind Harry and Steve, I pointed the weapon into the deep and surrounding shadows. With my heart pounding and every nerve burning with terror-fueled adrenaline, my eyes desperately searched the room.

Harry stood to my left and Steve was close upon my immediate right. It was a large living-room with two couches, lamps on tables in between, and an easy-chair before the hearth. There was a scent of cooked meat in the air and the distinct odor of ammonia… There was a sudden flash, the generator died, and the house fell into utter blackness from all around us. Moving closer together and taking defensive positions, we stood back to back.

"Don't move a muscle..." Steve growled in warning, his flashlight beam falling to where one of Gene's hounds lay sprawled in a slowly pooling, lake of blood.

With the wind and snow blowing in through the open door-way from behind us, we stood motionless. In the frozen darkness the moments seemed to pass like hours and then we heard it... It was faint at first, and then I became aware of a distinct, shuffling sound. It was coming from out of the darkness of the nearby kitchen, and seemed to be moving toward us, ever so slowly.... Something that moving from just beyond reach of the flash-light beams, lingered in the blackness of the doorway...

Raising a finger before his lips, Steve looked between us while lowering his light. Cautiously, he slowly began making his way across the room, wincing as the boards creaked beneath his weight. The sound came again, only closer this time. It was almost as though whatever we now pursued was aware of us, and doing exactly the same thing... Shooting us a nervous glance, he pointed into the blackness beyond the kitchen doorway, and motioned with his shotgun. It was time. Bracing for the battle to come, I looked to Harry. His eyes narrowing in the pale glow of our lights, the fear had been replaced by blind determination. In a moment that blurred all reality we suddenly moved. Racing across the room and charging into the blackness, there was a shriek and we faltered.

Paralyzed with fear, I stared down the deadly double-barrel of the twelve gauge shot-gun within Gene's shaking hands.

"It's here, man..." Lowering the weapon, he climbed to his feet from where he'd fallen back against the counter. Whispering while staring in absolute horror, he said, "It's here and in the house with us..."

"Never mind that--," Harry was desperate and whispering while grabbing at Gene's shirt collar, asked, "Did you eat any of that venison?"

"No, I hate wild meat--," He seemed shocked, and shaking his head, said, "Besides, after what we saw today, I might never eat meat of any kind, ever again."

"That's good--," Steve growled while scanning the shadows for even the slightest sign of movement, and said, "Because anyone that did is already as good as dead…"

"Linda and Bert…" Gene's eyes revealed the terror and guilt that he felt when Harry silently and sadly shook his head in response.

"Where is it—and what is it?" Steve whispered while peering back out through the door and into the living room.

"It's a praying mantis, centipede, and snake all at the same time." Shaking his head in suspense of disbelief, he gazed over in a barely audible voice, and said, "It's super-fast, deadly, and can change form and color at will, like an octopus or squid… One moment, I thought it had spines on its back. But they just shrank away when it needed to get through a smaller space…"

Steve and Harry were speechless, and all that I could do was look between the men in utter dismay.

"This isn't an animal or insect--," Gene's words were almost lost in the gusts that howled in through the open doorway, as he said, "I'm telling you, it's some kind of god-damned, government experiment gone very wrong…"

The sound of shots being fired off in the distance suddenly drew our attention to the open doorway.

"Oh, Christ no… I hope Tim and Gordon didn't come back…" Harry took the words right out of my mouth.

"If that thing is out there—you don't stand a chance--," Gene grabbed fearfully at Steve who moved toward the door, and gasping, said, "It took all three of my dogs out before I could even grab a gun…"

Gunshots rocketed through the storm from even close than before, and puling free of Gene, Steve cursed, saying, "We can't just leave them out there to die."

Without another thought we moved swiftly from out of the kitchen, across the room and back out and into the storm. With the shots booming ominously close, we turned and struggling through the deep snow, began making our way up the drive and toward the highway. We all knew that being caught in the open could mean the end of all of us, but no one cared. Driven through the blizzard by fear fueled adrenaline, we desperately scrambled up the steep drive. Blinded and stepping back, the flood-lights of the plow suddenly appeared on the highway through the blizzard before us. The truck suddenly veered, and slamming into a huge snow-drift, the flood-lamps cast a crimson glow through the storm. Caught within winters bright and bloody eyes, we desperately raced toward the old truck. It was still running and as I approached, could clearly see that the driver's door had been torn away. Drawn outward, it swung in the bitter gusts while hanging from a single and twisted hinge.

"Oh no, someone get over here and help me!" Steve plowed like a bull through the deep snow. Leaping up and crawling onto the passenger side seat, he desperately grabbed and held the bloodied form of Tim, crying out, "Talk to me, buddy—I've got you, you're going to be okay!"

"I'm not gone yet...." Spitting blood, he struggled to speak, saying, "We got as far as the old cemetery..."

"Why the hell did you come back?" Harry climbed onto the running board while assisting Steve.

"I couldn't just go..." Tim choked out the words as we carried him down and looking up at me, he said, "Friends don't do that... Not true friends..."

Resting him upon the running board with his back against the truck, I supported him while asking, "What happened out there?"

"Old Gordon, he managed to crush and kill one with the blade of the plow." He coughed while looking up at me, and said in a proud moment, "We got one of the bastards, Mike... we got one..." The glasses slipped from off his face as his head slowly slumped to one side.

"No—you're not slipping away from us that easy!" Grabbing and holding him tightly, I shouted into the storm, "Come back damn you!"

There was coughing, a splattering of blood that smeared my snowsuit, and he looked up at me. He struggled for consciousness in the cold and through loss of blood, but was still very much alive.

Retrieving his glasses from where they had fallen in the snow at my feet, I slipped them back onto his face, and said, "Hang in there—we'll get you out of here."

"The only reason we're still alive--," Harry cursed while looking in the direction of the farmhouse, and said, "Is because whatever the hell killed Gene's dogs, must've buggered off just before we went in there."

"At this point we should just count our blessings. Let's get him over to the skidoo--;" Steve lifted Tim from the running board like a child, and carrying him away, said, "I'm sure that I can make it back to the station with him. I'll be back once I get him somewhere safe."

Unable to be of any assistance, I hurried around the truck and to where Gene stood on the running board. With a hand over his mouth and back against the open door, he turned away from the open cab. Already expecting the worst, I climbed onto the running board and peered inside. What met my eyes in the dim glow of the interior lights was beyond description. All that remained of poor old Gordon was now spread throughout the gore-soaked cab. He was little more than a heap of hideously mutilated flesh, steaming organs, and shattered bones. Almost unrecognizable, the pulverized face stared upward as the rest of the twisted corpse was tightly wedged between the seat, steering wheel, and dash. Crushed into the floor, it was hard to believe that this had once been a human being... Spinning from the sight, I fell to my knees in the deep snow and was violently ill.

The skidoo with Steve and Tim suddenly roared past, and I felt Gene's supportive hand upon my brow.

"I've got you, man--," He turned with the wind as the steaming bile blew against us, and he said, "Finish what you have to do—but hurry. We need to get the hell out of here before that thing comes back!"

"We need to torch the truck—we don't know if Gordon's remains are infested!" Harry returned with a rag that he'd found in the back of the truck, and unscrewing the cap from the fuel tank, said, "I'd say that our only choice is going back to the house--," Shoving the rag into the tank and pulling out his lighter, he said, "And if I were you? I would be running right about now!"

Turning and swiftly making our way back through our own tracks, I saw the flash of his lighter and ignition of the material. Moments later, he was wildly running after us as the flames brightened from above the fuel tank. In the few moments that it had taken for us to scramble down the steep drive, an explosion sent us all tumbling forward and into the deep snow. With the brilliant flames erupting high into the night and a second explosion sending fragments of the truck in all directions, we cowered in the darkness. Surrounded in the flaming ruins of the old plow, we struggled to our feet and made a mad dash toward the house.

Almost blinded in the raging winds and snow we stumbled up the porch, and without concern for anything else, literally fell in through the open doorway. Following Harry and Gene back into the kitchen and from where we quietly waited, I whispered, saying, "We should block that doorway and see if we can get the generator started again."

"There isn't any generator anymore--," Wild-eyed and staring in disbelief, Gene cursed, and said, "I saw what was left of it lying in the trees by the highway... That thing tore it out and tossed it in the ditch..."

"There's no point blocking that door--," Harry thought aloud, and glancing back at me, said, "It'll just kick it aside when it comes back. Besides, Steve needs a way back inside and we need a fast way out."

"Comes back? What makes you so sure that it will?" Gene stared out and toward the dark opening of the doorway.

"Two things--," Checking the chamber of his revolver, he reloaded while glancing back at me, and said, "I noticed that dog missing from the floor when we came back in." He raised his eyebrows in question, and then asked, "And you smell it don't you? That strong odor of Ammonia, just like back at the cabin..."

"Oh Christ—it's building its new nest here..." Gene slapped a hand to his brow and panicking, said, "We can't stay here. We'll end up becoming food for the new horde..."

"Boys—there's a good chance that none of us are getting out of this alive." Slipping the revolver back into its holster, he pulled the Winchester from the pouch he carried on his back, and said, "But if we're going? We're taking that crawling nightmare and its brood with us..."

Images of young Brian's death at the end of my revolver flashed through my thoughts. If I didn't make it out I would just consider it poetic justice. If I did survive, I was sure that it would only be by the redeeming hand of God...

With the scent of cooked meat still hanging heavy in the kitchen, I spun toward Harry, and said, "Tim and Gordon should've gone after Connie's parents. If they ate any of that venison—or took it with them to Summerland..."

"No—they're alright--," Gene interrupted, pointing to his fridge in thought, and saying, "They never even touched that deer meat. They put the whole side into that deep freeze and the other half went to the diner. I know, because I'm the one who helped them load it in there, and then delivered the rest to poor old Bert and Linda."

There was guilt and shame in Gene's eyes with the realization of having un-knowingly signed both their death warrants…

"So, between the diner and the freezer at the Shephard farm, and old Gordon's infested steak--," Accounting for all the venison I thought aloud, and said, "And burning down the nest in that cabin."

"This is the last nest--," Harry lit a cigar, his eyes flashing in the blackness as puffing at it, peered back through a cloud of smoke, and said, "All that we have to do now is wait until they come home…"

"There isn't going to be any, we, in this one, old buddy." Steve suddenly appeared from out of the darkness, as startling us and stepping into the kitchen, he said, "Tim's in critical condition. I managed to get a message through on Lenny's old CB radio and their sending medics with a Sno-Cat. But, someone has to meet them part way."

Harry was left utterly speechless.

"Lenny still has his old snow-plow--," Steve explained, saying, "The two of you can take Tim and make it out of here. You said it yourself--," Steve's eyes were dark and brooding as peering over at me, he said, "Someone has to survive this to take a warning to the outside world…"

'That thing will be coming back at any time now…" Attempting to dissuade Steve, Harry faltered as he was bluntly cut off.

"If you don't do this--," Steve growled with certain determination, and said, "Tim will die—and only God knows how many others…"

There was a strange stillness between them as it was apparent that neither expected to see the other alive again…

"Steve, take this--," Harry insisted, as shoving his revolver into his friend's hand, said, "For good luck."

Embracing Steve, he turned to me while unable to express his feelings. It didn't matter, here really wasn't anything left to say at that point.

"Go and save Tim--," I hugged my old friend, and patting his shoulder said, "Maybe, we'll all see each other again… Till then…"

"Till then…" Swallowing hard, Harry turned away.

"Let's get you out to that skidoo--," Steve slapped his friend on the back, and peering over to where I stood with Gene, said, "Hang back, if anything goes wrong, there's no reason for all of us to be caught in the open."

Without another word they vanished into the blackness. With all the commotion and time that had passed since the last incident, I now wondered how much longer our luck would last...

CHAPTER TWENTY SIX

There was a span of what seemed fifteen or twenty minutes, as standing in the frozen silence, we kept looking at one another. It was a nervous glance, and the type that rabbits might exchange while accidentally encountering the den of a fox…

"I've been through and done many things in my life--," Gene's eyes flashed with unspeakable fear, as shaking his head apologetically, he swallowed, and quietly said, "But I don't think that I can do this…"

A large shadow suddenly moved through the living room, the floor creaking beneath its weight as it swiftly entered into the kitchen! Our weapons had been drawn and preparing to fire, we halted, not a moment too soon.

"Listen to me--," Having overheard Gene, Steve now gripped the terror-stricken man by the shoulders, and almost face-to-face, said, "This might be our last chance to stop these things before they eat their way through this town. That includes women, children, and even babies… Now, I don't know about you? But, I couldn't live with myself if I just left them all here to die, and especially like that… could you, soldier?"

Gene stiffened to attention and shaking his head, stared Steve right in the eyes, and said, "No sir, I certainly could not, sir."

Scowling, Steve quietly said, "Then let's teach this bastard what hell is really all about…"

Saturday January 6, 1973.
12:16 a.m.

It was so cold that I had to fight to avoid from allowing my teeth to chatter. Terrified of making even the slightest sound we stood in the frozen and absolute blackness.

"How do you want to do this?" Whispering as while still concealed in the kitchen and waiting, I turned to where Steve stood beside me.

He had the desperate and hungry look of a predator. His eyes glinting in the blackness, he wiped at the frost forming upon his brows and mustache, and said, "All that we need to do is seriously wound the damn thing. Then torch the whole fucking place."

Gene's reaction was nothing short of numb as agreeing, he leaned closer, and quietly said, "I have a gas stove." He motioned in gesture to the oven behind us, and whispering, said, "All we have to do is put out the pilot-light, and then one match will send this whole place straight to the fucking moon."

"And who's staying to light the match?" Pulling my lighter from the pocket of the snowsuit, I looked between them.

"Quiet..." Steve threw a hand before my mouth, and leaning ever so slightly, peeked into the darkness of the living room. There was an immediate tension. I felt it in every muscle and nerve as sensing that we were no longer alone, the breath almost froze in my lungs.

Drawing his revolver with lightning speed Steve leapt out and into the living room! There was the flash and eruption of gun-fire before I could even react,

Launching forward, I followed from behind him, blinded, desperate and staring into oblivion. Nothing, not a single movement or sound... Whatever had happened was over as fast as it had begun.

My heart thundered as staring blindly into the pitch-black I whispered Steve's name, "Steve, where are you? What's happening—are you here?"

Receiving no reply, I reached for the flash-light in my coat pocket, and slowly directing it before me, switched it on.

No sooner had the light parted the shadows than did Steve suddenly slide down from beside me. Staring wildly and with his back pressed against the wall, he slid down to the floor.

Realizing to have been abandoned by Gene, I dropped down beside Steve, terrified and whispering, I said, "What happened—are you alright?"

"I pumped five rounds into the thing." Steve swallowed hard, his bottom lip quivering as he desperately gripped at the ghastly wound on his upper shoulder, and shuddering, said, "But it just—swatted me aside like some little kid. Bullets–twelve gauge solid slugs." His eyes bulged as sweat formed on his brow, and he said, "Had no effect. I might as well been throwing stones. This one doesn't have the same weakness as that thing at the Shepherd place..."

Turning the light toward where I had last seen the dog, I slowly followed the bloody smear. It trailed across the floor, up the stairs, and then disappeared into the darkness of the attic.

Gene suddenly appeared from out of the shadows of the kitchen.

Creeping over and leaning close, he grimaced while noticing Steve's wounds, and whispering, said, "Get him out of here. This thing is too strong for any of us… I'm going to knock out the pilot-lights—and take this fucker down…"

"The hell you will--," Steve shivered, the floor glistening with his blood as he looked between us, and groaning, said, "I'll take it from here."

The house suddenly echoed with the thunderous sounds of pounding, scraping, and thumping from the attic. The creature was preparing a nest and soon it would need to feed its young…

"If we're going to move we need to go now…" Climbing to my feet and offering Steve a supporting hand, I said, "Hurry…"

"We'll go into the kitchen altogether." Gene choked, his attention focusing in the deep shadows of the open hatch-way, as he said "At the back of the kitchen is a door leading onto a rear porch. We can get out of here that way."

"It's going to come back down here when it's finished with those hounds." Steve grimaced, the blood running from between his fingers as he looked up at me, and said, "It dragged a body in here when it came back—but it wasn't Tim or Harry… I'm sure of it…"

Gene helped me haul the big man to his feet, as gasping in pain he struggled to refrain from making any sound. Fearful of having drawn the creature's attention, we hesitated before moving.

The room became deathly silent, and then all eyes were cast above as something heavy moved across the floor. Several loud crashes sent tremors through the old structure, as causing the floor to shake beneath our feet, suddenly all became still…

"We'll stay here for a moment—and just until you're ready." Gesturing toward Gene while fearing to make even the slightest sound, I said, "If it comes down those stairs we'll keep it occupied. Get into the kitchen and when you're ready—wave and we'll all make for the door."

"I can jerry-rig something--," Gene thought for an instant, and then appearing suddenly confident, whispered, saying, "I've got candles—I can light a few and put them inside the cupboards so they don't get blown out. If I crank up the gas, it might take a few minutes, but that should do the trick." He became hopeful, and looking between us, said, "Then we can all get out of here together."

"Gene--," Steve looked up at the man and grimacing, said, "You're a good soldier and an even better man... I'm sorry about what I said and did before..."

"Thank you, sir. It's been an honor." Gene saluted.

Bracing him-self against the door frame, Steve reached down for his revolver, cursing in pain and whispering, he said, "Tim said Gordon killed one of those things out on the highway... I wonder what will happen to the body during the spring thaw."

"I wouldn't worry about that. I think the insect part of them makes the males harmless in that respect, because they can't produce eggs--," Whispering while watching as Gene cautiously slipped away and into the kitchen, I said, "No eggs, no parasites, and no infestation."

"What makes you so sure that they killed a male?"

"Because female insects are always far larger--," Nodding toward the stairs and hatchway, I whispered, saying, "And that one turned the snowplow inside out... The animal that Tim told us they killed was smaller. He said that Gordon crushed it with the plow blade."

An unearthly howl suddenly echoed through the house as Gene stopped cold. Clenching his fists and grinding his teeth, he gazed upward at the pitiful whining.

"Oh, God--," He whispered, his eyes traveling across the ceiling as he said, "Oh my God, they weren't dead..."

"It must have stunned them—or stung them?" Steve shuddered as his features paled with the loss of blood.

"I've heard of wasps that stun their prey by stinging them, and then lay eggs into the living host." I spoke without thought, and looking into Genes wide and horrified gaze, apologized and looked away.

"I'm sorry, brother, but there's nothing that we can do for them now..." Steve trembled as he fought the pain.

"That thing is laying eggs on my babies." Gene winced, as tightly clasping his hands over his ears, fought to block out the cries of his dogs. They yelped, crying out desperately as they endured a nightmare of hellish pain and living death. The sounds were enough to cause me to cover my ears as well while imagining the horror of what was happening from just above.

"Don't let their deaths be a complete loss--," Steve pointed at Gene and gasping in pain, said, "Get going while it's busy and you still can. Let's put an end to this, God damned, nightmare..."

One of the hounds suddenly uttered a mind-shattering cry that sent us all back against the wall. Enraged and horrified, Gene looked between us before finally agreeing. Staying close to the wall, he began cautiously inching his way along. The floor creaked beneath him with every step, as creeping across the room, his eyes never moved from the ceiling. There was a pounding from above, the sound of a large dog's legs flailing in a futile struggle. I could imagine the poor beast restrained, as being fastened to the floor with thick mucus, eggs were laid upon its flesh. They would hatch shortly upon contact, and the young would begin burrowing into the dogs warm flesh... Forcing the images from my mind I looked into the darkness across the room. Having reached the hall, I saw Gene .slipping through the door-way and disappear into the darkness of the kitchen.

"He's made it..." Attempting to comfort my friend, I whispered saying, "We're going to get out of here..."

"Not if he doesn't hurry..." Steve gestured with a glance at the ceiling, and said, "Things are getting quiet up there. It's almost done with the dogs..."

Steve was becoming worse by the moment. I could see his life literally flowing away from the gaping wound. It required stitches and he was slowly losing consciousness. Leaning close and whispering, I asked, "How bad is that arm?"

"It's the least of our worries right now--," Directing my attention toward the kitchen, he cursed, and said. "It looks like we're on our own..."

I could only stare in disbelief a passing the open door-way behind us, Gene vanished into the blizzard. Anger and disappointment became blind fear as the sounds of creaking boards now drew our attention upward. Something heavy scraped over the ceiling and now moved across the floor from just above us. The whimpering of the dogs became little more than a whine, and we both knew that the thing was almost done up there...

At the end of my nerves, I jolted with every creaking of the old attic boards. Obviously well aware of our presence, the sounds of its movements brought our attention to where it paused before that blackened portal, and from just above the stairs.

"I refuse to believe that Gene just abandoned us." Whispering while removing the safety from my pump shotgun, I slowly aimed for the top of the stairs, and said, "He's up to something. I just know it... He must have come up with a better plan..."

"You better hope so—because in about ten seconds, that thing is going to come through that hatchway up there... And when it does, it'll be looking for something else to feed to those maggots..."

I knew that he was right, and though terrified was unwilling to accept that Gene would have just left us to die. It just wasn't something that a man of his general character would do... Especially after what the thing had done to his dogs...

"If he doesn't come back... What do you suggest that we do?"

"When I tell you to? Make for the kitchen and crank that gas on full... Once it's been going for a few minutes--," He raised the shotgun, and said, "All that it'll take is one shot to send the whole place to the fucking moon..."

"Steve, we aren't going to have time for that." Motioning with a finger toward the ceiling as the sounds of something heavy moved over the boards, I whispered, saying, "At best, we've only got a few moments..."

"It doesn't matter. For me, it's not about time or even getting out of here, anymore." His dark eyes drifted back into the blinding shadows of the attic, and he said, "Get into that kitchen, crank the gas, get out that door, and run as fast and far as you can..."

A sudden and suffocating stench forced me to throw a hand before my face. I could feel the hot bile surging from the back of my throat and fought desperately to hold it back. That sound? What was that? It almost sounded—wet? Oh my God...

Steve tapped at my wrist, and gaining my attention, gestured with a nod toward the stairway. The beam of his fallen flashlight cast a feint glow on the bottom of the stair. In the pale light my heart skipped a beat as watching in horror, the steps suddenly oozed with thick and steaming mucus. Glistening, the foul substance purged like vomit, and spilling down the steps, accumulated in thick pools at the bottom of the stairs.

"Look familiar? Okay—enough bullshit--," Poking at my shoulder and staring in defiance, he said, "Get into that kitchen and get that fucking gas cranked, now."

Before I could even react a loud crash halted me within mid-step.

Pressing my back against the wall, I stared in utter and complete horror... From out of that portal above the stairs two claws now gripped the opening, as ever so slowly, the monster slipped down. Revealing only its head, two large and pale blue, luminescent eyes stared coldly from out of the shadows. Undoubtedly, these were the horrible and glowing eyes that Steve and Harry had seen that night on the highway. Every nerve screamed, every thought pleaded for escape. Somehow I managed to elude the instinct to just panic and run, and stood absolutely silent.

From out of that amassed and leaking filth now appeared two, crab-like and clawed appendages. Tightly clamping to the edge of the opening, the boards split and splintered beneath an immense pressure. I heard the creaking sounds of something heavy, as slipping from out of the blackness above, knew that it was coming... The boards bending and cracking as turning, it had slowly maneuvered into the blackness from behind the stairs. From there it simply hung suspended as while silently observing our every movement. Much like a bat, its long and powerful hind legs held it tightly fastened to the ledge. Slowly and by the slightest of degrees, it began lowering its massive bulk until hanging only mere inches from off the floor. The long and centipede-like body was covered with armored plating, and the scales glistened with that foul slime. I saw no distinctive markings, but knew that this was the Queen that we all feared.

Like the previous nightmare, it held two large and scythe-shaped appendages before its tiny and triangular head. Numerous and hideously clawed limbs twitched, clicking ever so slightly in the darkness. They were like the fangs of a spider anticipating the fly. Protectively concealed within a scaly and spine covered shroud, the head moved ever so slightly. Those pale eyes, unblinking, shining, suddenly focused upon me.

Horrified, I leaned closer to my injured companion and whispering, asked, "Steve—what's it doing?"

"Waiting, it has all the time in the world... and we don't..."

Reacting to our sounds, it parted those immense scythes from before its head in order to closer examine us. The flash-light beam catching its mandibles, they twitched as uttering an unnerving squeal, parted to reveal several rows of razor sharp teeth.

Gently forcing me backward and against the wall, Steve used his body to shield me while slowly raising his gun.

It seemed undisturbed by our presence and much like a cat that was observing mice. The head moved ever so slowly and from side to side, the pale eyes flashing with a strange and frightening curiosity. This wasn't simply the instinctive behavior of an animal, but the patient observations of an intelligent, predator...

Moving painfully slow, I turned while looking between the doorway and entrance to the kitchen. It was the same distance to travel from either end of the room. Aware of how futile an escape attempt would have been, I now considered a final and desperate attempt.

"Do you think?" I swallowed hard and whispering while watching the thing, said, "That there's any possibility—that we might make it to the kitchen?"

"Not even the slightest, fucking chance..." His breath came in short and rasping, gasps, and I knew that his life was fading. In the same moment I caught a moment from the direction of the creature. The bright blue orbs faded into the shadows from behind the stairs, and the once twitching claws became absolutely still. We were trapped...

"I know what the sneaky bitch is doing..." Steve spoke without removing his eyes from the thing, and whispering, said, "She's waiting for the male..."

"Oh, she isn't aware that Gordon killed it..." The thought suddenly occurred to me as sinking into deeper despair, I said, "What's going to happen when she figures it out?"

"She'll just raise a new male from the eggs in the nest that she's making up there. Either way, we're toast no matter how you look at it..."

"What do we do now?"

"The way I see it—there's a chance for you to still make it out of here.... I'll keep her busy..."

"Steve—I'm not just leaving you here to die with that thing..."

"Guys--," Gene whispered, as peeking in through the front door, looked around, and said, "I'm back—hang on." Creeping toward us he suddenly became rigid while noticing the monster. It had moved ever so slightly, but made no motion toward us. With a moment of silence passing, the monstrosity once more drifted into that strange and trance-like state. The little head slipped down behind the spiny shield of its neck, and it folded the inter-locking and massive claws before its face.

"The gas is cranked--," Gene's voice was carried off in the howling winds as he pointed toward the kitchen, and whispering, said, "I remembered something while I was back there." He stared wild-eyed and opening his vest, revealed almost a dozen sticks of dynamite which were strapped to the inner lining of his military vest.

When Steve saw that he looked at me with a sudden urgency. His intentions were clear, and although I disagreed there was little choice in the matter. With motions so painfully slow that they seemed to take an eternity, Gene slipped out of the vest and offered it from out of the open doorway. The exchange had been terrifying as we dared not even breathe. The wind and storm raged from beyond while concealing most sounds, but we feared the one that might awaken the devil.

Finally taking a firm hold upon the vest and explosives, Steve looked over at me, and speaking without uttering a sound, mouthed the words, "Get out of here, partner. Go while you still can..."

I fought against the foundations of everything that I had ever believed, and still couldn't leave him there like that.

His face twisted with grief while fighting the pain, and he said, "The night that you left the diner with Tim... I ate one of those God-damned, venison steaks... Medium, fucking rare..." Reaching into his coat and producing his badge and wallet, he shoved them into my hand, waving me off as he looked away.

Trembling with the knowledge that his life was truly forfeit in that moment, I struggled to maintain my composure. Attempting to slide badge and wallet into a pocket, the shotgun slipped out of my grip and clattered to the floor. Spinning toward the monster I saw that it was awake. With eyes blazing, it hissed while swinging its massive body down from the hatchway.

"Run! Run damn you!" Steve wailed as stepping forward, opened fire upon the hideous thing. In an explosion of screaming lead and smoke the creature screeched in fury.

"Go—go-go-go!" Gene shouted as we hysterically ran out of the house and into the frozen storm. An unearthly shriek ripped through the night as the gun-fire ceased, and we were left to the howling call of the blizzard. Desperately pulling me along, Gene shouted as we fought our way back and toward the remaining skidoo.

"We can still make it! Come on, Mike! Don't let me down now!"

A sudden and deafening roar sent us flying through a dizzying barrage of splintering boards, billowing smoke, and raging flames. The entire world went black as something heavy suddenly crushed me downward, and I fell forward into the deep snow. Blinded and gasping while fighting for breath, I tried to call out as the pressure forced the air from my lungs. There was a blinding and brilliant light, searing pain, and then a hand came out of nowhere. Thrashing and fighting for breath, I was dragged back out and back into the frozen night. Realizing to have been struck and pinned by a portion of the old roof during the explosion, I gasped in horror. It was fortunate that Gene had been strong enough to lift the splintered and smoldering wreckage, or I would have certainly died there.

"Hang in there, buddy!" Wiping the blood from my brow with a sleeve and supporting me, he said, "It's going to be okay--," Pointing toward the blazing ruins of his house, he shouted, "Steve did it—he took that bad bitch out, it's over, man!"

"Oh God, Steve..." Looking back, I was immediately blinded and casting a hand before my eyes, realized that he was truly gone...

The light of the inferno was so intense that it spanned clear across the property. It shone in the peaks of the frozen pines and its glare brightened the highway before us. There was a sudden movement in the rubble, and we both turned back to gaze into the blazing nightmare. Caught in the powerful gusts and flurries, the flaming debris was tossed from all around. Through the blizzard the world swam in a blinding haze, but I kept looking, watching for movement from out of the chaos. With blackened ash and flaming fragments still raining hell from the heavens, I felt my knees buckle from beneath me.

"It's nothing, man—just nerves. Its dead—come on! Let's get out of here before we freeze to death!" Supporting me, Gene carried me along and toward the lone skidoo at the top of the driveway.

Even with the soaring and brilliant flames it was hard to make anything out in the blizzard. Though half-frozen and being unable to feel our hands or feet, we supported one another while stumbling up the steep drive.

"Oh shit!" He stopped suddenly.

Resting on its side beneath one of the deep and trailing drifts, the skidoo was literally torn to pieces.

"I've got one in the shed across the highway!" Directing my attention across the road and to an old wooden shed, he said, "I tuned it up last week and it's full of gas."

It was as while turning from that scene that I glanced back, and almost pulled Gene down with the sudden panic of what I saw. The thing crawled out from beneath the smoking debris, as faltering briefly, suddenly reared-up on its hind-legs. Those pale blue eyes widening, and suddenly burning with a cold and unspeakable hate. That's what the Queen had been waiting for… Steve had been right, there were two males…

"Run!" He pulled me along as we raced madly through the deep snow and across the highway. Scrambling over a drift on the other side, we almost fell while running the last few steps to the shed doors. Panicking, he threw them wide open and shoved me inside! We had barely entered and slammed the doors closed, when we heard the screeching from outside!

Intending to bar and block the door-way, I fell back as Gene shouted, "Don't—if you do that we'll never get out of here!"

The walls shook, things fell from the rafters, and I wailed as the monstrous thing crawled up from the side. Thrashing wildly, it reached the roof, and began tearing its way in from above.

"Wait a second!" He leapt onto the skidoo, as pulling the keys from his jacket and fumbling through the ring, said, "Okay I got it! Come on—get on!"

Leaping on behind him, boards and ice crashed from above, the ceiling exploding inward as the engine roared to life.

"Hang on!" Switching on the head-light and quickly applying the gas, the cold engine sputtered and threatened to stall. Revving it up and forcing it onward, we burst forward in a roaring cloud of smoke. As we raced upward and onto the highway, the monster crashed through the roof of the shed from behind us. Gripping him tightly from beneath the arms, I spoke the words to the 23rd Psalm. The engine howled, snow exploded from all about us, and we raced madly into the blizzard. Through the confusion and blinding flames fear had caused me to glance back and onto the highway behind us.

From out of the flurries and cast against the brilliant glow I saw a shadow emerge.

"It's coming after us!" Leaning closer and shouting into my friend's ear, I said, "Faster—we need to go faster!"

Without reply, Gene forced the snow-mobile into full-throttle, and we raced against the devil through the ever deepening snow. Ever onward and ever faster, we fled before the horror that even now grew closer by the moment. Unable to see four feet in front of us through the flurries, every twist and turn became utterly terrifying. From out of the darkness behind us I could no longer see the approaching threat, but felt it. Then it happened, in one mind-blowing and completely devastating shock. There was a sudden eruption, a blinding sheet of ice and snow, as having encountered an un-even drift, we bounced and slid out of control.

"Hang on!" Gene wailed while fighting to maintain his grip upon the handles. Skidding from off the road and soaring over a steep embankment, we came down in a frozen ditch. The deep snow buffering the impact, I almost lost my hold as we bounced. Either by skill or sheer, blind-luck, Gene managed to correct our course. Speeding past tall pines and narrowly missing several smaller ones, we raced upward and out from the ditch. Exploding through the ice and snow, we breached the tall embankment as sliding, raced down the highway once more. With the violent impact we had bounced back and lost both of the shot-guns. Without the weapons we were now at the mercy of speed and the storm. Nearing that familiar and final stretch of highway that led into town, a sudden and brilliant light appeared beside us.

Crying out in despair, Gene cursed while shouting, "Oh no! It the fucking, South-bound three a.m. train! But it's never been on time!"

With the terror of that hideous thing behind us and unable to remember exactly where the tracks crossed the high-way, I leaned closer, asking, "Can we beat the train?"

Abruptly shaking his head he shouted back, and said, "Not a chance! We'll never make it—the tracks are much too close!"

Glancing over my shoulder, I saw the radiant eyes of the monstrous insect in swift approach. It was less than a cars length away and gaining speed.

"Just do it!" Desperate, I shouted into his ear, saying, "The make is right behind us!"

The light was getting brighter by the second and the illumination turned the insect into a horrendous an enormous shadow.

"We're never going to make it!"

"Don't stop! Punch it, Gene! Punch it!"

Suddenly, we struck something on the highway. Gene shrieked as losing control and drifting side-ways, we suddenly collided with an embankment and the machine whipped out from beneath us. Violently thrown to the high-way and tumbling, I spun out of control. Darkness and ice, my body was tossed like a rag doll until finally coming to a sudden stop in the deep snow. Battered, bruised, but seemingly un-broken, I tried climbing to my feet. Blinded in the blizzard and by the approaching light, I turned away and looked straight into the glowing and hateful eyes. Raising those immense claws and poising for the strike that would end my life, it suddenly hesitated. It's small and triangular head tilting curiously as though mesmerized.

"Mike—look out!" Gene launched forward, grabbing me about the waist and pulling me aside. There was a roar and sudden rush of wind as the earth rumbled and everything became black. Falling, I tumbled down an embankment and to where crashing through thin ice, sank into the frozen waters. There was a sudden silence, and helpless, I was caught in winter's deathly embrace. There was a sharp pain at the back of my head, as slipping ever downward. I could feel the heated flow of my own blood. Weighted by the wet snowsuit and unable to resist the bitter cold any longer, I closed my eyes. With all thoughts fading into shadow, the world as I had known it suddenly ceased to exist…

EPILOGUE

Friday January 19, 1973.

There had been a brief stay at the Penticton hospital, and where heavily sedated, I was treated for abrasions and a minor head injury. I remember that there were some strange questions asked by men in black suits. I told them everything that I knew, which at that time was absolutely nothing. In the end it didn't really matter anyway. It all just became part of an elaborate cover-up.

Harry's final report was bleak to say the least. Then again, who would have ever believed the truth? The deaths had all been reported as due to 'freak accidents' that occurred during one of the worst 'winter-storms' in years. A gas-line explosion in a local diner was held responsible for the deaths of, Bert Wilkins, Linda Evans, Sergeant Steve Harris, Smitty and Blake Blanchard, and an elderly hotel manager by the name of, Gordon Farrell. Added to this was the strange disappearance of a boy named, Brian David Anderson. His name was recorded along with several other lost souls, whose remains have never been found...

Tim recovered nicely, and we ended up sharing a room in the same hospital for several weeks. He's still the local funeral director, and the insurance money paid for all the damages. Gene Doherty never did recover emotionally from the loss of his dogs and home. He never spoke of the incident, and from what Harry told me, now raises Huskies in the Yukon.

Hopefully, whatever nightmare crawled out of the bowels of that old mine is finally and truly extinct. Harry had seen personally to my belongings, and as far as the evidence goes? I still have a Mason jar containing a monster, which although very much alive, now sleeps in a very cold, deep freeze... In parting, may I suggest that the next time you order a steak, that you insist that it be well done? It would be a real shame to discover, alone and late one night, that stomach pain was actually your dinner eating its way back out... With the recent publication of my book I plan to keep a promise to a very special lady. I really hope that it doesn't give her bad dreams. The adventure continues...

www.ingramcontent.com/pod-product-compliance
Lightning Source LLC
Chambersburg PA
CBHW030359180626
46812CB00005B/1841